Tell Me What You Like

by Kate Allen

New Victoria Publishers Inc.

Published by New Victoria Publishers, Inc., A feminist literary and cultural
organization, PO Box 27 Norwich, Vermont 05055

Printed on recycled paper
Cover photo by Judy M. Sanchez

Library of Congress Cataloging-in-Publication Data
Allen, Kate, 1957-
    Tell me what you like / by Kate Allen.
        p.   cm.
    ISBN 0-934678-48-0 : $ 9.95
    1. Policwomen--Fiction.   2. Lesbian--Fiction.   I. Title.
PS3551. L3956T4 1993
813 ' . 54--dc20   92-47054
                                                        CIP

With special thanks for the support of Jean Bendick, and the support and editing of the lovely and luscious Karen Henry.

One

The foyer of the bar was plastered with fliers explaining how dykes could take square dance lessons (poster hand drawn and photocopied), see a Motherlode concert at the old Ogden theater, or come watch an all female strip review right here at Denver's Blue Ryder in two weeks. (This poster was the slickest.) Officer Alison Kaine paused as she entered the double doors, still amazed that such shows happened. An event like that would have been picketed when she was nineteen, and she would have been right on the front lines protesting it as degrading to women. She didn't know if it was a sign of more diversity and tolerance or if they were all just going straight down the tubes. There had even been drag queens lip-synching *I Am Woman* (talk about a blast from the past!) on the main stage of Gay Pride this year, and women who would have rioted twelve years ago just lay on the grass with their artificially inseminated babies and clapped.

Alison had lost herself in musing for a moment too long, so Officer Robert Ellis, her partner of two years, was giving her just the smallest of nudges in the back. Just a friendly little 'We have things to do' nudge, not a 'let's get the hell in and out' nudge, which is what she suspected that he really felt during these routine walk-throughs of the bar. Not because he ever said anything, but because even she felt uncomfortable, for god's sake, and she belonged, at least in the generic sense.

It would only take ten minutes to make sure that none of the cowboys from the Mile High Rodeo next door had spilled over looking for trouble or, worse to most of the dykes' thinking, to propose a sexual adventure. Both things had happened several times in the three months since the Rodeo had opened, which was why this swing-through had been added to begin with. The sergeant in charge of the shift had not come right out and said, "Let's assign Alison because she's queer," (it was always a bit unclear who at the station knew and who didn't,) but she suspected something like that had gone on and Robert had just been stuck on because he was her partner.

In response to Robert's nudge she finally swung into her Barbara Stanwyck walk. She could handle most of the Blue Ryder's weekday theme nights. She could handle Old Dykes' night. (There was another, more official

1

name, but that was what everyone called it, including women who attended and yet complained bitterly about anyone else using the term.) She could handle and even crack an occasional smile at Country/Western night. It was only Leather Night that made her freeze at the door, and she hadn't found anyone—not her best friend, Michelle, and certainly not Robert—to talk about why yet.

Well, Rob might feel out of place, but at least he didn't have any of his own hissing at him under their breath as he walked by. Why did so many dykes feel compelled to make comments about woman cops? Was it because they assumed she was straight, or had somehow sold out, or was it just that general fuck-the-cops-till-I-need-them attitude held so dear by middle America?

She sucked in a huge breath to fortify herself. It was a bad move. The air was heavy with smoke and the cough she couldn't choke back sent her gum flying onto the floor. Hastily she wrapped it in her shopping list, trying to look as if it had been planned. Smooth move there, Alison. No wonder you can't find a date. Robert was already half way through his tour of the bar and dance floor area, and she was still having an obsession scene in the doorway.

She Barbara-Stanwycked her way back towards the bathrooms, keeping her face blank as if she were not hearing the comments following in her wake. The girls in leather were the worst of all her lesbian sisters about using sexuality as a weapon. She scanned the crowd as if they were any old bar crew and not one that tugged at her with conflicting emotions; she never got propositioned anymore anywhere but here, and here it didn't count because it was meant only to embarrass her.

"Love a girl in uniform, babe," mock-whispered a tall blonde, seated not more than a foot from her path, and Alison almost stopped to tell her to get a new line. Three out of four women who tossed comments her way beat that old uniform theme to death. It didn't make her feel angry or turned on; it made her feel lonely, and like a scarecrow, a figure stuck up on a pole whose total essence was a suit of clothes.

She cut her eyes to the side without moving her head, wondering how smart it would be to break out of her role as bland and impartial guardian of the law, fantasizing about a brisk exchange that would make her look good, but what she really found herself doing, was looking at the blonde's outfit. Specifically looking for any sign that said what the woman did, or what she liked, or if maybe the comment wasn't just an ugly little bit of cop-baiting, but something that contained some real passion....

Sucker! Worse, the woman saw her looking before Alison even realized what she was doing, and was delighted to have caught her. "Hey, baby," the

2

blond said in that throaty whisper that she managed to project like a shout through the bar noise, "you're a lucky girl. I'll go either way." She clasped her hands together over her head like a prizefighter, showing that both wrists sported several studded leather bracelets.

Alison's face burned with a blush that spread down on her chest. She could hear laughter behind her as she moved stiffly away. She was going to start wearing sunglasses in the bar, dammit; she was going to get neutered; she was going to go straight; she was just going to fucking shoot herself so that she didn't have to go through this crap once a week.

She stiff-armed the door of the women's bathroom, hoping that the dopers had all gotten the word and she wasn't going to have to bust someone for toking in the can. That would be the icing on the cake—to have to write up a ticket for something that was not only barely worth her time in court, but that she didn't think should be against the law. If there were any smokers she was just going to shoot them down and then turn the gun on herself.

The door, which she knew from a hundred walk-throughs should just swing wide, was sticking, so she hit it again grumpily. It gave suddenly and she went flying through, barely saving herself from landing on her hands and knees.

She didn't understand, at first, what she had fallen into. Sure, she'd read *Coming to Power* and all the back issues of *On Our Backs* and *Bad Attitude*, but they hadn't prepared her for two women doing a quick scene in the bathroom of the Blue Ryder.

She was really slow tonight—it wasn't the outfit of the top woman (very butch, all in black, slicked back hair, leather vest and studs up the ass) or her attitude (a fuck-you-and-everything-you-represent look) or even her position (one hand wrapped in the medium length hair of a woman in a purple sweater and the other down the front of her jeans) that finally clued her in. It was the look that crossed the face of the woman in the purple sweater when her eyes fluttered open—that 'dammit-I-was-going-to-come-and-now-I-can't' look that Alison had become familiar with on the face of her last lover, Lydia. That was what made her realize that the two had been standing against the door going for it and she had knocked them down to the ground and was about as welcome as your mother walking in on you in high school.

"So do you like to watch, or what?" hissed Leather Vest in a nasty voice.

That was all it took. Alison went straight from a feeling that could be described as apologetic to full force rage. Fuck these women and their shitty attitude and their judging! She wasn't the one who couldn't wait till she got home, and she was damned if she was going to be made to feel in the wrong. Normally, consensual sex in public was handled, by all but the most zealous officers, by asking the participants (who were usually a straight couple with a few too many, getting carried away in a parking lot) to pull themselves together and then giving them a little lecture. It was like the one-joint bust; unless one of the parties was really determined to be an asshole it wasn't worth wasting anybody's time.

But this woman obviously was going the asshole route. "So what are you going to do," she sneered, "arrest us?"

The woman in the purple sweater, who after that one little flicker had kept her eyes firmly shut, made a distressed sound.

"Oh, my," another voice said.

Great, thought Alison, just what we need—more dykes in the bathroom. Nobody in the world was more willing to butt in than dykes. They had opinions and convictions on everything. (A woman in the food line at Michigan last year had, with no encouragement at all from Alison, gone on for ten minutes about renaming dildos.) If she was really pissed enough to make an arrest she'd better do it quick before the whole thing turned into another Stonewall.

But when she turned to give the woman coming out of the stalls a quick look (no sense getting shot in the back by a crazy) she felt her anger dissipating as quickly as it had come, to be replaced by a kind of rush-of-pleasure, thank-you-goddess-for-not-letting-me-miss-this-one feeling.

The woman was a sight to behold. She didn't have that unfortunate air of having raided her big brother's closet that trailed so many leather girls. Everything she wore was new. Everything she wore was hers. Her black leather jacket and matching mid-calf skirt had come from an expensive women's shop. Separately they could have made it at any office party— possibly even with the spike heeled boots, black suede with a tiny touch of gold on the toe and strap—but not with the mass of gold chains she wore around her neck, beneath a red silk blouse that was unbuttoned just one notch too far for the office. Not with the black beaded gloves she carried in one hand. She had enough accessories to blow herself right out of the mainstream and into a walking fantasy.

"Oh, my," she said again, looking at the three of them. "This is kinky." She maneuvered herself delicately around them as if they were a dog mess. She had one hand on the handle of the door before she paused to lean down and pat Purple Sweater on the shoulder. "If I were you," she said in a tone of motherly advice, "I wouldn't pay full price on this one." Straightening from the pat she looked Alison full in the face for the first time and added, "Nice props, though."

That did it for Leather Vest. She jerked both hands back. Anger rose off her like steam as she glared at the door.

Alison was quick to jump in. "How about if we zip our pants up and discuss this?"

"Butt out!" Leather Vest was not so pissed at the woman in red that she was willing to give up being a last-worder. Robert's theory on last-worders was to run them in every damn time, see if they still felt so smart-assed after a couple of hours of paper work. Alison was not a total convert, but maybe it was warranted in this case.

"Well, then," Alison drawled, "we have option number two, which is going downtown to talk about lewd and lascivious behavior."

"We choose door one." Purple Sweater leapt up with a suddenness and agility that surprised both of them. "Come on, Dominique." She tugged on Dominique's hand, but was obviously not surprised when the other woman set her heels belligerently. Oh, well, she motioned to Alison with one raised eyebrow and a shrug, I tried, time to cut my losses, she's not my girlfriend, can I go now, Officer, please? She was out the door before Alison had time to finish her nod.

"I hope you got off," sneered Dominique, obviously determined to top the scene to the very end. Alison considered telling her that the stage name was over used by every other woman who considered herself a dom. Maybe that would take the wind out of her sails.

It was a power play now, and Alison didn't see how she could afford to lose. She said, "Well, that remark just added tricking on the side."

"You can't prove that!"

The door swung open again. Alison felt as if she were in a gay Neil Simon play. This time, however, the new cast member, whom she recognized as the owner, was someone she could use to gain the upper hand.

"No," she answered, "I can't. But I can make sure that everyone pays real close attention to you just in case. How do you think the nice woman who owns the bar is going to feel about you if she knows that every time you're here, and lots of times that you're not, there are going to be cops swinging through three times a night just to make sure you're not turning a quick one in the can?" Fat chance, she thought, but enough to shake up the owner. No bar could hold out under that kind of surveillance. You could always find something if you wanted to get ugly.

"You're out—eighty-sixed!" The owner played to Alison as if to a script.

"Oh, come on, Jenny." Dominique was trying not to whine, but she couldn't quite keep the edge out. For a moment Alison felt sorry for her. Perhaps this bar was her only social outlet. But it was too late to back out.

"Out. Period." Jenny had a frantic look in her eye, and Alison knew that she was trying to figure out how to call her off. I'm just a poor working woman trying to make it, don't screw me!

The door again. This time it was Robert, holding himself in that tense but determined way Alison had noticed on all male cops in women's bathrooms. He fixed his eyes firmly on her in an effort to avoid everything else. Sometimes Alison thought that her partner would rather get shot than see a woman peeing.

"Alison?" said Robert.

"Out!" said Jenny.

"Fuck you!" said Dominique.

"Let's go," said Alison. Time to let the girls handle it themselves. She gave Jenny another nod and a thumbs-up, good-job sign. Dominique tore out the door as if she were going to go right through Robert, who was so busy not seeing the women's bathroom that he danced out of the way only at the last minute.

Alison followed, and he followed her without comment, pausing a moment to touch his hat to the owner, in one of his curious, older generation gestures.

He gave her one tiny little nudge when they were halfway across the floor. True to fashion, half the dykes in the bar were rallying to one side of the cause or the other. Dominique, being herded to the door by the bouncer, was surrounded by cajolers and supporters. Satellite groups had broken off and were heading determinedly to the bar to either confront Jenny on her internalized homophobia or congratulate her for weeding out women who promoted violence against women. So do we mix into this? Robert was asking. He didn't push it when she shook her head no; they both had their field of expertise and this was hers. Jenny had responded hard and fast. Alison had faith that she would keep her word for her own sake. Which was just as well—there were cops down at the station who would love a chance to drag a butch dyke in to see if they couldn't rewrite the sodomy laws. But she tried not to talk bad about cops to dykes the same way that she tried not to talk bad about dykes to cops.

"Vacation all set up?" was the first thing Robert said once she had settled behind the wheel of the cruiser.

"Oh, fucking in the bathroom," she answered before she took in what he had said. In two years she had never gotten used to the way his mind darted off onto restful little by-ways while hers always plodded (obsessively, her ex-lover, Lydia, had said) ahead in a straight line. Something about Dominique had unnerved her, and she didn't like the way she had handled the situation. Why, she had fallen right into the power play, as though the woman had

6

seduced her into it knowingly. Something about the whole situation did not set well, but she couldn't move beyond the simple feeling.

"Must be a hell of a vacation," he observed dryly, and she had to backtrack before knowing why she was laughing and blushing. He took advantage of her confusion to hit another weak spot. "Talked to your dad yet?" He thought, sometimes, that he was her conscience as well as her big brother.

"No! Give it a rest! Let's talk cop talk! Don't you want to know what was happening?"

"Alison, I don't need you to tell me what was happening. I can tell you what was happening. Fucking in the bathroom. Maybe tricking. She didn't want to cooperate. You should have brought her in, but you didn't because people should solve things themselves if they can and you want to be extra careful because you have power issues. Same song, different verse. You should work on a playground, Alison. 'Did you talk to Johnny about how it made you feel when he threw sand in your face? Let's try that.'" She gave him as much of a withering look as she could spare from Colfax Avenue on a Friday night. "Yeah," she replied, "well, you smoke."

As she hoped this retort reminded him that it had been a while since he'd lit up. Which distracted him from the next part of the 'You-should-have-been-a-playground-teacher lecture.' Which was 'What ever made you decide to be a cop anyway?' Which lead right back to 'Have you told your dad you're thinking about quitting?' Better second-hand cancer than that. She was glad her vacation started the next day.

* * *

The upstairs apartment, though it had its own outside exit, also had a door on the landing that came directly into Alison's kitchen. Through her gloom Alison could hear someone pounding on it, but she did not bother to get up and answer. It would be Michelle, and to Michelle, knocking was merely a polite ritual that was not to be taken too seriously. Her lover, Janka, who was a bit more socially skilled, gently tried from time to time to persuade her to see the error of her ways, but Michelle's consistent answer was, "If she's fucking she should lock the door!"

Sure enough, after five impatient knocks Michelle was across the kitchen and into the front room, still making knocking motions with her fist. "What's wrong?" she asked.

"How do you know anything's wrong?"

"Hank Williams. Whenever I hear 'Your Cheatin' Heart' I know there's been a crisis."

Alison could feel herself getting more and more depressed and did not

7

answer. No problem, because conversation with Michelle was similar to the door routine. It would go on whether one participated or not.

Sure enough, Michelle, surveying the room, continued just as if she had answered. "Nails, shingles, cat carrier but no cat, boots—you should be packed and half way up to the mountains by now. The mountain dykes are planning on you giving them a hand on the new bunkhouse. Oh, shit. They cancelled on you, didn't they?" Michelle's face became as fully dejected as Alison's. She sat down heavily on the couch beside her.

"Herpes outbreak," said Alison briefly. "And a storm put a branch through the chicken house. They're stressed. They're processing."

"Oh, wow," said Michelle in a voice that was fraught with disappointment. At thirty-three Michelle was a tiny woman who had not grown appreciably in stature since she and Alison had become best friends in fifth grade. Her size, combined with her perfect little baby-dyke face and short, short hair, tended to inspire the reaction, 'Oh, how cute'— in the same tone in which one comments on puppies—from most of the dykes she met. Her response to this stereotyping had been to become super capable, a kind of miniature Wonderdyke who rarely needed to ask for help with anything. (Janka had confided that she had fallen in love with Michelle immediately after listening to her discuss the ailments of her chainsaw, which was half as big as she was, with one of the mountain dykes.)

She was perfectly suited for this role of Renaissance woman, for she naturally tended towards the hyperactive. The part of this 'overawareness'—as Janka politely referred to it—that was not worked out in gardening, roofing the house, fixing bicycles, her Sunday paper route and all the other odd jobs she used to support her real interest, stained glass, often expressed itself in little dramas—heightened exchanges with clerks, friends, people at the bus stop. She did not really even have to be involved in an exchange, but was fully capable of benefiting vicariously from another's woes or joys. So Alison knew that even though she was genuinely sympathetic about the crimp in her plans, she was also getting a little endorphine rush.

"Hey, is that 'Walking the Floor?'" Janka stuck her head in the door. "Is something wrong?"

"Alison's vacation got shot." Michelle answered in a despairing tone, though slightly distracted by a ball-and-slot puzzle she had picked up from the coffee table. Anyone with whom Michelle spent time quickly learned that readily accessible games and unfinished knitting were a good defense against having one's silverware drawers rearranged during conversation.

"Really? What a drag." Janka came in, Alison suspected, not so much to commiserate as to make sure that Michelle didn't merge so far into her dopplegänger role that she got depressed, too. Being Michelle's lover took vigilance. Michelle seemed within reason, so Janka turned to Alison. "So what are you going to do instead?" she asked, dismissing the whole tragedy in one sentence. A lot of Janka's life philosophy revolved around 'over and done with', something that Alison, who tended to hoard slights and disappointments, had a little trouble with. She would have liked to have gone over exactly how disappointed she was and how much she had been looking forward to her break, and she knew that Michelle alone would have let her do it.

"Oh, I guess I'll unload the car," she said grudgingly, wondering where she was going to put the bulk food she had been asked to bring. "Then I guess I'll do some work around here."

"Going to make sure you stay depressed, huh?" Janka ran her hand back through her shoulder-length strawberry blonde hair. "Well, that ought to do it. Maybe you could do your taxes or balance your checkbook, too."

Alison fantasized briefly about smacking her. She decided not to, not because Michelle, 110 pounds or not, would take her head off, or even because it was against her own personal politics to hit other women, but because it just seemed unfair to punish someone because she was right. "So what do you suggest?" she asked, still sullen at not being allowed to feel sorry for herself.

"Go do something fun," advised Janka. Michelle's ears perked up like a dog about to be taken on a walk, or in this case, about to hear about a walk. "Look, I just picked up *Westword* and *Outfront* at the laundromat—they both have entertainment sections...."

Just in time Alison realized that if she didn't come up with something herself she was going to be sent off to a glass blowing demonstration or an exhibit on women archaeologists. "Cheeseman," she said hastily, naming the neighborhood park which had a large gay section. Janka appeared unsatisfied so she added, "I'll watch the dykes and work on my quilt."

"And come have dinner with us," Michelle added.

"And come have dinner with you," she agreed, and because they were her dear friends, she made every effort not to show that it could in no way come close to replacing a week in the mountains.

Two

The gay end of Cheeseman Park was usually good for a cheer-up, but Alison didn't feel her usual lift as she walked through the acres of gay boys tanning. Even the dykes splashing topless in the fountain with their dogs failed to elicit a smile. Damn the mountain dykes! Colleen had been apologetic when she called, suggesting another week, but this was the week Alison had her vacation. What was she going to do now, spend the week visiting the Mint, the Capitol and the Coors brewery, as if she were someone's out-of-town grandparents?

A soccer field had recently been added to the far end of the park, and as far as Alison could tell, at any time of day or night and in any weather, there were twenty-two dykes on it. Occasionally when she drove through, Alison would see a forlorn group of men standing on the sidelines with a ball, looking longingly, as if they were the uncoordinated kids who hadn't been picked at recess, but the dykes weren't going to give it up, uh uh, no way. In a country where women earned seventy cents to a man's dollar and there were only two women in the Senate, there was at least one place where dykes ruled.

Alison plopped herself down by the field and opened her bag. It was as good a place to feel sorry for herself as any and, should she decide to switch modes, it was a better place than most for cruising. Of course, she reminded herself, with a pessimism that was so fierce as to almost be enjoyable, everyone on the field was probably married or dysfunctional.

Alison's mother had taught her to sew when she was twelve and it had not been the horror story that all of her friends had experienced in forced Home Ec. classes. Alison, who could put on a butch facade that could stop women in their tracks, actually liked to sew. It had taken years to come to terms with this, as she had come out in a lesbian climate where fixing your own TV or car was highly honorable, but a traditionally female skill such as sewing was seen as only one step up from consenting to have ten babies while chained to the stove. But she was getting older, and everyone was getting mellower, and one day about two years ago, she had finally decided to hell with them all and taken her quilting with her to a meeting. (It was also the day she had announced that she hated softball, had always hated softball and

10

was never ever going near a right field again no matter who had to forfeit.) She was currently working, with much referral to books, on a variation of a Bear's Paw quilt. She pulled a square out of her bag and jabbed at it angrily a few times with her needle, then laid it in her lap.

She popped one of the Diet Pepsis she had stuck in her bag (caffeine was, in Alison's mind, as much of a miracle healer as penicillin) and looked up at the game. She had only played soccer during one dismal semester of freshman gym, but it wasn't hard to sort out. There were a few idiosyncratic things going on that baffled her at first—the main one being that some of the players seemed to be playing for both teams, appearing first in a red shirt and moments later in a blue. The color of the shirts was the only common factor, otherwise advertising everything from Margie Adams tours to the local dyke garage. After a few moments of careful study she realized that somehow the two teams, obviously involved in a pick-up rather than a league game, had arrived at some agreement in which any player on the side-line—and there were never more than two out for brief rests—would be called in for whom-ever signalled first, regardless of team or position. Alison wasn't the only one confused by this; she heard more than one groan of self reproach as a ball was sent to an opposing player who had been an ally only ten minutes before.

As always when she came across a group of dykes, Alison was amazed at how many women in town there were whom she didn't know. Where did they hide themselves, and what did they do when she was at the Gay Pride March or a Kate Clinton show? Actually there were a few who looked famil-iar, the red center half, for example, and the sweeper. Neither had called for a sub during the time she watched so they were possible to identify by position. She had seen them both at the Blue Ryder on Country Western night. They were good two-steppers, obviously lovers. In fact, now that she thought of it—of course, she had seen a whole table of these women at the bar more than once, sweaty, tired-looking, wearing black and purple uniforms that said 'Blue Ryders' across the front.

Slam! The ball was suddenly down by the end line, and though there was a terrific sprint by the red backfield it was obvious that the goalie, a tall woman with dark curly hair pulled back into a ponytail, was going to have to go one on one with the current blue center forward. As she ran to the top of the box, Alison thought that she looked familar too, but then dismissed the thought. She must have seen her at the bar with the other women, probably some night when she was in uniform and not at liberty to take second looks. She was a damn good goalie though, not only challenging the lone opposer, but making three saves immediately afterwards as everyone from both teams converged on the ten yard line.

11

Finally the box cleared. The goalie stood alone, wiping her face with the hem of her shirt, which had a red and purple labrys on the chest where most goalies had a diamond. Alison bent her head back once more to look at her work. Maybe, she thought as she picked up her needle, this week wouldn't be too bad. Maybe she could go camping for a couple of days by herself. Maybe Michelle could even be persuaded to take a day trip. Maybe…she stopped trying to fool herself and took a couple of resigned stitches. Maybe, in fact most certainly, she would just stay at home because she didn't like to camp out alone, and Michelle was always backlogged with work. She sighed, and looked back up towards the game just in time to catch an out-of-control ball smack in the face.

Both her vison and thoughts were blurred for a moment, and this might explain why she not only didn't recognize Stacy the dark-haired goalie who came over to retrieve the ball, but in fact dazedly agreed to go over to the Arvada Center with her to see a quilt show later that afternoon.

* * *

Life was good, thought Alison as she lay in bed the next morning. A quilt show was an odd date, but somehow Stacy's knowledgeable comments and tips had been more heady than an erotic movie. And she had asked Alison to come to the next soccer game. Yes

So buoyant was her mood that at first she could not comprehend the headline that blared at her when she unrolled her newspaper. WOMAN KILLED NEAR LESBIAN BAR it read. After the first moment of denial, her mind went into an acceptance that was all too real, wondering, "Oh god, was it someone I know?"

She pulled herself together enough to read the details which were few. The lesbian bar, the Rubyfruit, was not one that Alison visited often and never on duty. The body had not been discovered until after closing, had taken place in the parking lot until after closing. A stabbing. No witnesses. The name of a stranger.

Alison suddenly remembered the pain and anger of breaking up with Sandy four years before and wondered if this were a crime of passion. The police, of course, had "no comment at this time."

It made her remember the whole dreadful scene with the leather dyke in the bathroom at the Blue Ryder. She could still see the woman's hard, angry face. Busting women in the bathroom! How trivial. Would that she could have been preventing a murder instead. She threw down the paper on her way to the shower, cheered only by the fact that she would see Stacy at the game later in the afternoon.

"Why didn't they stop the game?" Alison was trying not to hover, but she was having a hard time being butch as she watched Stacy's nose bleed. Stacy, who was using her extra t-shirt to staunch the flow, tilted her head back. Alison stopped her and pinched her nostrils, holding her chin level.

"Not in this league," Stacy answered in a muffled voice. "They stop for nothing short of death, and then your team members have to eat the body. Actually, I could have come out, but I'm the only goalie since Andrea broke her finger, so…." She shrugged.

"Going to the bar?" A blonde forward whom Stacy had introduced before the game as Liz, slapped a zip-lock of ice on top of Stacy's hand. "You big sissy," she said. "You could have stopped that last goal if you'd let that eighteen-year-old kick you in the head."

Stacy groaned. "Next year we play in the over-thirty league or not at all. Death to the eighteen-year-olds!"

"And the cute dykes, too," added Liz. "They cause too damn much trouble." She gave Alison a look that said she considered her one of the cute dykes and wouldn't insist on immediate execution.

Stacy, catching the look, clipped her on the back of the head with the bag of ice. "Get your own damn dates. Quit cruising mine."

"This is a date? You've lost your touch, girl. Only adolescent boys ask their dates to sports events in which they are starring."

"Wrong," said Alison and Stacy in chorus, and then laughed.

"Perfectly acceptable lesbian date," said Stacy.

"It was actually our first date that was unacceptable," said Alison. "Straight event, pink collar art." She choked a little over the word 'date'. Oh, Sappho, don't let her be toying with me!

As if she'd read her mind Stacy added, "We didn't have sex or fall in love, either. We broke every convention. We expect to be confronted and publicly humiliated."

"Well, you might like that," said Liz. "Do you know what a lesbian second date is called?"

"A housewarming," chorused all three women. Stacy laughed, spraying blood.

"God, you're a catch," said Liz. "Come and talk to me when you get tired of the macho approach," she told Alison.

"Do you want to go to the Blue Ryder?" Stacy asked. She tentatively moved her head into an upright position. "Sunday night is kind of soccer nerd night."

"It's open even after what happened at the Rubyfruit last night?" Alison was incredulous.

"Yeah, as far as I know. Besides, the murder didn't happen in the bar itself. And the Women Against Violence to Woman are patrolling the parking lot. It's a matter of principle—we can't let something like that shut us down, right? So, will you come?"

"Sure." Alison thought that even though she was a cop on vacation, maybe it wouldn't be such a bad idea to patrol the bar. Then she laughed at herself. She was making excuses when what she really wanted was a date that felt like a date with this woman, not a tour of a quilting show.

"Great. Meet me there, okay? I've got to run by my place for a quick shower."

"Sure, but don't run," nodded Alison, though she regretted the answer when she got to the bar. Arriving without Stacy, she was too shy to join the soccer players who were pushing tables together by the dance floor. She considered calling Michelle. They had not connected since the previous afternoon, and she knew her friend would be upset about the dyke who had been killed. She also knew, however, that Michelle would need to do immediate and intense processing, and that a pay phone in a bar was not the ideal place. She compromised by leaving a message on her own machine, to which Michelle was known to listen three or four times on a slow night. Then she picked up the local gay rag, intending to sit by herself and see if she could pick her friends out of the personals.

"Alison!" Oh, shit, it was Stacy's friend, Liz, waving while every other head at the soccer table perked up in interest. Flushing, Alison decided that joining them quickly was the least likely to cause commotion.

"So, what position do you play?" Liz asked without preamble. She rubbed her hands together as if she were about to choose from a pastry tray.

"No soccer," replied Alison, holding up two fingers to make a cross, as if she were warding off vampires.

"Liz thinks everyone is a soccer player just waiting for the right position," warned a stocky woman who had been playing backfield.

Liz cackled wickedly. "And you are proof positive."

"Yeah," the woman admitted. "I just came to watch this evil woman I had a crush on, and she dumped me the next week for a twenty-year-old and then sprained her ankle and never came back, and I've been on the team for three years."

"Death to the cute dykes!" intoned Liz, thumping her chest with a closed fist.

"Death to the cute dykes!" echoed the other woman, raising her mug of beer. In a whisper to Alison she warned, "Don't let her get you on the dance

14

floor for a fast number—she'll try to measure your endurance. She's a law-yer—can you imagine her in court?—she never lets up one second."

"Are you hitting on my date again?" Stacy slipped into the chair next to Alison. "Do you want a sandwich?" she asked. "They're good. I'll buy."

"Now, that's what I call a date," said Liz. The DJ, who had been having a problem deciding the theme of the evening's music, went directly from a Janet Jackson number into the *Cotton-Eyed Joe*. All the players around them rose en masse.

"I ordered a drink," Stacy told Alison. "Would you pay for it? I've got to pee bad." She put her wallet in Alison's hand. As Alison watched her walk away, she wondered why she hadn't used her own bathroom at home. In fact, she obviously hadn't showered, either, so what had taken her so long?

"Diet Coke?" Alison pulled two bills out of Stacy's wallet, figuring that she was the kind of girl who tipped generously. A small business card fluttered to the floor, and she bent to retrieve it.

Anastasia, it said in black gothic on cream, and below that, Tell me what you like.

There were bells going off here, but for a moment Alison could not make the connection. She knew she had seen Stacy before the soccer field, but she....

"So. Are you with Stacy?"

"Huh?" The only woman who had not joined the *Cotton-Eyed Joe* was the sweeper, a tall woman with a chestnut colored pony-tail. Alison remembered that she and Stacy had worked well together during both games, but also that they had exchanged sharp words several times.

"I mean, do you know what she does for a living?"

Click. Suddenly Alison knew where she had seen Stacy before. And maybe what she did do for a living.

"She makes quilts," she said, stalling for time. Go away, she thought, I need to get this into perspective. All too vividly, she remembered Stacy 'leather-femmed' in the bathroom when she was deciding whether to ticket Dominique; Stacy saying, "If I were you I wouldn't pay full price on this one."

"I don't mean that," the sweeper snapped. "She can't support herself with her quilts. I mean do you know what else she does for money?"

Regardless of her own jumbled feeling Alison resented her tone. "So what are you, a jilted lover? Is this a 'she done me wrong and I just want to warn you' routine?"

The woman made a face as if she'd bitten into something sour. "Please. I just don't believe in the kind of violence against women that is promoted by

15

lesbian s/m activity. Stacy talks a slick game—I just wanted to make sure that you knew what she was into."

"Hey," someone's voice intruded over the table, "has anyone seen Dominique?" Smoking and dressed from top to toe in tight leather, the woman asking looked breathless, impatient.

"Great. I know," Alison said to the sweeper. "Now I'm going to go get a sandwich, okay?"

"She was here a while ago," answered on of the players who had not succumbed to the charms of Cotton-Eyed Joe. "But Jenny asked her to leave. She was eighty-sixed Friday night, you know." The speaker was careful not to look at Alison.

"Damn," said the smoker who then threw down her cigarette and split out the front door.

"And we're not taking any more leather dykes onto the team," the sweeper warned Alison as if there had been no interruption. "I don't care what Liz says about needing players, I've got the votes behind me...."

Fuck you, thought Alison hotly, not knowing whether to protest her ambitions towards being a soccer player or her ambitions towards being a leather dyke. But she knew she was reacting toward attitude as though someone had just made a comment about her as a cop, and she resented the comments doubly.

"So, Trudy, saving another innocent from a fate worse than death?" Arriving, Stacy spoke without any emotion except resignation.

"Just talking." Trudy leaned back in her chair. "You know how it is—jobs just seem to come up."

"Especially mine, huh? Hey," she raised her voice and addressed the table at large, "is there anybody here who doesn't know what I do for a living? Did anybody miss that, somehow, or need an explanation?" The conversation died, and though there was only the tiniest movement, Alison saw all the players shift into the attitude of two camps. Oooh, old quarrel. "Look, she knows, okay? That was what you wanted, right? I'm not going to take her home and have my wicked way with an innocent."

"At least not nonconsensually," Alison heard murmured from Stacy's camp. A brief laugh rippled, but Stacy did not join it.

"As far as I'm concerned, it is none of your business, but you did it anyway and it's done. And you're still the team captain and I'm your only goalie. Let's talk about that if you want to talk about power issues! Or better yet, just go sit down and let us get some food."

"Why?" Trudy persisted, "Are you afraid you...."

"Trudy, what I am afraid of is that you are going to bore me to death with the same old shit. It's not a soccer problem, it's between you and me, and it's shitty of you to try and suck everybody else in. If you want to talk to me you call me." She reached down and plucked the card that Alison still held from between her fingers, slapping it down on the table in front of Trudy. "You have my card." Turning to Alison, she said, "Come on let's dance."

Alison shot up, grateful for the chance to escape. She had fantasized a first dance with Stacy slow and sensual, but she did a kind of automatic shuffle, her stomach churning too much for her to even notice the other woman's moves. Subconsciously, had she known all along that Stacy was a leather queen? Was that why she had said 'yes' so eagerly when Stacy had approached her, and, oh god, was she finally going to have to deal with this when so far she had managed very nicely not to—? She was never to finish the thought, because just at that moment she glanced over Stacy's shoulder, seeing the door to the women's room and beyond, the back door that she knew led to the alley. Just as she raised her head that alley door opened and a woman staggered in. The area was not dim like the rest of the bar, so Alison could clearly see the look on her face—a mixture of horror and disbelief, battling with a fear that she was going to get sick before she reached the bathroom. Just the look was enough to rivet Alison's attention, even if the woman hadn't screamed.

Alison didn't even register darting across the dance floor. She was just suddenly there, reaching out.

"Out there, I think she's dead," choked out the woman. She made a gesture with her hand towards the back door. "I was just opening the door to get some air—"

The bathroom door opened. Out stepped one of the soccer players, drying her hands on the bottom of her T-shirt.

"Call the police and an ambulance right now!" Alison told her brusquely, raising her voice over the music. She gave the woman a little push, hoping that she was the obedient type, and then cautiously opened the back door. Like fifty percent of all off-duty officers during the summer, she was disregarding regulations not carrying a gun. Where was she going to put it when she had on shorts and a T-shirt? She was often careless with her purse—when she had come out purses were practically spat on as symbols of oppression, and she had only started using one in the past several years. She still spaced it out too often, leaving it on the back of her chair or in her car, and she didn't trust herself to carry a piece in it. Her worst nightmare was that some crazy would lift it while she was on the dance floor and start shooting up the other dykes or the straight cowboys, and she'd have to explain the carnage.

17

Cautiously, Alison opened the door.

The alley was dimly lit by the night lights of the surrounding warehouses. A woman lay within the bright circle cast by the bulb above the door of the bar. Alison didn't hesitate. There was nowhere to hide, and she could see, even before she knelt beside the woman, feeling for her pulse, that she had not been attacked with a gun. Like the woman who had been found the night before, someone had stood right beside this woman and stabbed her. An initial quick calculation seemed to indicate that the victim had been strangled first, then slashed across the throat and stabbed in the chest.

She was a big woman, Alison noticed in a detached way. Whenever they had to deal with children beaten or women raped or strangers' heads shot off in Seven-Eleven stores, she automatically became this detached persona who could comfort, take notes, mediate and protect without ever having her own heart touched. Somewhere in the very, very back of her mind she was aware of her heart crying aloud (oh, god, another dyke, oh, if I'd only been five minutes sooner) but the cries were not allowed to affect her now. Months from now they might be still part of nightmare, but at this moment they did not exist. Instead she noticed that the dead woman was big. Big and tall, and probably strong, as if in life she worked out. A witness might comment on those things, and probably also on the bloodless pallor of her face. There was nothing else to distinguish her from a hundred other dykes with short brown hair and brown (lifeless) eyes. She wore jeans and a vest that might have been any color before it was stained crimson.

"Oh, god." The words were almost as bloodless as the face of the woman who lay on the dirty pavement.

"Oh, Alison," Stacy said in the same automaton's voice behind her, and then, began to retch.

Great. Puke on the crime scene. Everybody would appreciate that. Alison leapt to her feet and propelled Stacy backwards all in one motion. Of course, she would have followed when Alison abandoned her on the dance floor. It was a marvel that the whole gang was not out here already contaminating the area. Stacy was puking in earnest now. Alison, without compassion—compassion would contaminate her detachment just as surely as vomit would contaminate the scene—dragged Stacy backwards through the door and pushed her into the bathroom. It was as much as she could do for her. Her own job was to guard the door until someone else arrived to take over.

Liz, thank goodness, had taken on a professional air, and was keeping Stacy and everyone else inside, calming Jenny who was freaking out. And then the sirens came closer.

Alison was not among the curious women who ringed the police barricade whispering as the ambulance pulled up. She stood deliberately aside, shivering in her T-shirt, her detachment like a uniform, nor did she speak to the police officers who were asking people to move along. She hated that part of human nature that allowed onlookers to get their endorphine rush off the tragedy of others. This dislike was the only feeling she allowed herself to have as she waited to give a statement to the detectives. She knew, had Stacy been one of the women pressed against the barrier speculating, she wouldn't have been able to force herself to decently see her home, let alone date her again.

"You!" Uh oh, of all detectives to be put on the case, not Phil Jorgenson, the man whose prejudices were well-known at the station. Hadn't there even been a threat of a grievance against him last year because he insisted upon bringing in petitions—against regulations—calling for the repeal of Amendment 2 which protected the rights of gays in housing and work along with those of other minorities? She had a hunch by the way he addressed her, when he knew her name perfectly well, that he was going to put her down and comment on her lifestyle in front of all these women, and so she stared into space, determined not to respond like a stray dog.

And if Phil Jorgenson was on the case, then it meant none other than Ed Jones, his shadowy mimic of a partner, was surely close behind. She knew for a fact that Robert, whose trust she had gained in their very first week when she had saved his life with an instinctive reaction, had actually slugged Phil in her defence in the men's locker room (not that they spoke about it). Because of her father's career on the force, she had known many of the older men—his peers, before she had joined. They had all tolerated her with the same fond air of resignation that Dad so often had, an air that said, she may be queer, but by god, she's our queer. She was also used to turning around sexual remarks, using a loud voice meant to embarrass the initial speaker in front of his buddies.

But Jorgensen and Jones were a new breed, open about their gay bashing.

"You," Jorgensen said again as if to a loathsome stranger. He came closer so he was able to grab her elbow as he shouted in her ear. She jerked away, glaring at him, wondering who the hell had assigned them to this case, and if it was one of those silly scheduling coincidences, like the one that had put the Planned Parenthood and the Right-to-Life booth side by side at the People's Fair last year. Or was it something deliberate, a stroke from someone higher up who shared their bigotry?

"What are you doing down here?" He asked snidely, and then before she could answer, "Cruising?"

Later Alison had no idea what hot answer she might have come up with had she had a chance to reply then. But at that moment Jones drifted over,

19

and Jorgensen turned to address him brusquely, "We're not going to get a thing off of this scene. It's totally contaminated."

"What are you talking about?" Alison was stung out of the cool role she had decided to play, but the sound of panic in her own voice brought her back. "There was no contamination whatsoever. I made sure of that." She was pleased that she sounded assertive and sure of herself.

"I take it you saw this woman attacked, Officer Kaine?" He remembered her now that he wanted to use her title as a weapon. Never before had the word 'Officer' sounded so much like 'Idiot.'

"No, but I was there immediately afterwards, after the first witness to the body came in the bar. You will want to talk to her. I kept everyone clear until the police came."

He threw up his hands, as if unable to believe the word of anyone in shorts and a T-shirt who would choose this kind of environment. And then he walked away, barking orders to the police and ambulance personnel.

Three

"Alison," said Stacy in a hesitant voice, "do you want something to eat?"

Alison looked up with a start. She had almost forgotten where she was. Frankly, she wished that she was at her own place, where she could brood among friends, but Stacy had been in no shape to take herself home, and it would have seemed callous to drop her off without seeing that she was settled safely.

Lifting her head, she appraised the other woman. Earlier—when Stacy was being 'Ms. Save-the-Day-Goalie'—she had radiated enough sexuality to animate Alison's fantasies for nights. Now, she looked tired and waif-like. Her purple sweats, which had seemed so sexy in the bar, were too big, and she still had blood from her nose on the front of her shirt. She needed a shower, thought Alison in the same dispassionate way that she sometimes decided that KP had slept in the cat box one time too often and popped him into the sink.

"Alison?"

Alison shook herself mentally. Stacy was probably right to try and raise her blood-sugar; lunch seemed a life-time away, and she had never even ordered that sandwich at the Blue Ryder. It would also give Stacy something to focus on. She's as upset as you are, she told herself, and nodded at the offer. Trying to choke down that resentful little part that was saying, "Yeah, but she got to fall apart, she got to be comforted, she got to throw up." For Christ sake, she thought, disgusted with herself, are you jealous over somebody puking? Apparently the answer was yes, if it represented being able to fall apart and be cared for. She was ashamed. To distract herself she followed Stacy into the kitchen. She recognized it immediately as the kitchen of a non-cooking dyke, even before she saw the baffled look on Stacy's face as she peered hopefully into the refrigerator. The counters were covered with dirty dishes and empty Chinese take-out containers and nowhere was there a sign of any tool that could be used for chopping or grinding or grating or even stirring. Even in the midst of her depression Alison felt a small spark of anticipation. She was a good cook, and non-cooking dykes were easy to wow with a home-made meal. Successful date.

21

"Hm," said Stacy in a tone of wonderment that indicated that the fridge had been absolutely packed with groceries that morning and their disappearance was a mystery.

"Tea?" suggested Alison. Now that Stacy had mentioned food she realized that she was ravenous.

"Oh, yeah!" Stacy brightened. She opened one of the brightly painted cupboards. Sitting in the middle shelf was one mug, stylized to look like a black cat. Its tail was the handle. Stacy picked it up and stared at the empty shelf in the same befuddled way she had stared into the refrigerator, making it clear by her action that she was close to the nonfunctional level.

Rousing herself, Stacy said, "Umm, there might be another mug in my workroom. Would you look?" She pointed with her chin.

There was a fancy phone on the wall by the door she had indicated. On the list of preprogramed numbers, right after "Mom" and "Liz" was written "Wok-in Noodle". Alison punched number three and handed the receiver to Stacy before she went through the door.

"Wow!" she called back into the kitchen. "I didn't know...I mean I knew that you made quilts but...." I didn't know that you were a fucking artist, she thought, making a full turn to look at the walls, all four of which were covered corner to corner with bulletin boards which were in turn, covered with quilts in every stage of development. There were single blocks, and whole chunks and raw-edged squares and triangles arranged together like the same puzzle over and over and over, each varying from the one before only by the slightest bit. Wherever there was no cloth there were clippings— photographs and cards and bits from magazines. They had no common theme: animals, people, places and designs, but in all of them Alison could see something that caught the eye and could be translated into a quilt. "I didn't," she began again, and then stopped again, suddenly embarrassed by the conventional little Bear's Paw she had shown Stacy at the soccer game.

"What? I hope you like almond chicken," Stacy picked up a mug herself off one of the three long work tables. There were a number of them scattered throughout the room, and they all kept to the cat theme. On this one two black cats stalked each other warily around a fern. "Yeah, it's kind of my passion." She exited the workroom as if it were of no further interest, though Alison suspected that at any other time she might have happily given a tour.

It was only after ten minutes of focusing on almond chicken and moo goo guy pan that Stacy mentioned the workroom again.

"Actually, I have a show coming up," she said suddenly, with her mouth full.

It took Alison, who had been sucking down egg rolls as if there was no tomorrow, a moment to connect. "Where?"

"At the art museum. They're doing a series on Colorado artists that they're calling 'Maverick Quilters.'" Then, without any preamble at all, just as Alison was about to reply with congratulations, she burst out, "Oh, Alison, I knew that woman."

"At the bar?" It was something that had not occurred to Alison, and her first response, somewhat to her own annoyance, was that of a cop. "What was her name? How did you know her when nobody else in the whole bar had even seen her? I was beginning to wonder if she was in the right place."

"Melanie. Melanie Donahue." Stacy took a long draw on the tea she had made in the microwave. "I'm not surprised that nobody else knew her. She lived out in the suburbs—she had for years. She had this lover who was totally closeted. I guess the girlfriend had a little girl and she—the girl-friend—decided that the lesbian lifestyle might put a crimp in the kid's chances to go to the prom or something. Anyway, they did the real straight scene—had barbecues with their neighbors for socialization and pretended they were just housemates. I guess she just kicked the traces over...tonight?" She checked her watch. "Last night. God, what a thing to happen the first time you go out." The food, the drink, the shower she had taken while wait-ing for the delivery, had helped her to regain some composure. Now she was jittering nervously again, that same combination of despondence and hys-teria. She ran her hand back through her wet hair, curls already springing up again, and then began opening all the fortune cookies.

"I don't think any of these are for us," she said. "We must have gotten someone else's cookies." Then, without lifting her head she asked, "Do you want to spend the night? I could stand to be held."

Oh, shit. Alison hated these ambiguous dyke invitations. At least when she was dating guys she had been able to be sure of one thing: "Spend the night" had meant "Wanna fuck?" With dykes it could mean anything from that to comfort me like a sister, and any misinterpretation was going to end up making you look insensitive at the very best.

"Umm," she said, and then having started out stupidly, rushed to finish in the same vein. "I'm not into leather, Stacy...." She knew this was a bad opening and wanted to take the words back even before Stacy's reaction.

"What?" Stacy threw her hand out and the fortunes scattered across the kitchen floor. "Jesus, did you think that was an invitation for a scene? How insensitive do you fucking think I am? Could you play after a night like this?"

"Well, no, I mean I don't, I never...." Alison floundered heavily.

"What a minute," Stacy held up her hand. "Let me backtrack here. What do you mean that you're not into leather? Like, you're not in the scene, like you're a novice?"

"Uhh," said Alison stupidly, nodding her head in a circle that covered both yes and no.

"Oh, Jesus." Stacy covered her face with one hand. "I had no fucking idea. God save me from novices."

"Did you...?" choked Alison, somewhat horrified by the idea that was presenting itself.

"Of course I did," snapped Stacy. "Why the hell do you think I wanted to go out with you? I thought that it was a miracle from heaven—an intelligent leather girl who's interested in quilts! Please, god, let her be able to cook, too, and I'll never ask for anything else!"

Before Alison could answer there was a knock at the front door. Stacy barely glanced at it, and made no move to answer it. Liz, who apparently had Michelle privileges, threw it open. She was carrying two pints of Ben and Jerry's ice cream.

"I saw your light," she said, "and figured stress eating was in order. Oh, good," she said, looking at the table, "you've already started." She handed a pint to each of them and started eating the leftover kung pao chicken with Stacy's fork.

"She's a fucking novice!" said Stacy to Liz in a voice little below a shriek.

Liz, who was high-grading the almond chicken, stopped and looked at Alison with as much astonishment as if she had suddenly sprouted another head. "Bad call," she finally commented, and then filled her mouth so full that any follow-up was impossible.

"I...." Stacy threw her hands up, shouting, "Look—I'm too freaked out about everything. Everything! I'm going to go have a smoke!" She stormed out of the apartment.

"Wait!" Alison started to protest. Goddammit, there was a dyke killer out there. It was foolish to be out on the street in a bathrobe after midnight.

"Umm." Liz, her mouth full, shook her head and waved negative with her hand. Taking Alison by the elbow, she led her over to the front window. After a moment the front porch light went on. They could not see Stacy herself because of the porch roof, but they could see her shadow cast out onto the street. The shadow sat on the railing and began to smoke rapidly.

"I wish she'd stop smoking," said Liz between mouthfuls.

"I wish she'd stop screaming," said Alison, who was having the very non-butch urge to cry.

"Ahh," Liz waved her hand to dismiss it, "she's always like that when she's stressed. Goddamn queen of the scene. Give her a cigarette or food and she'll pull it together."

"Why the hell is she so upset?" Alison burst out.

"Well, I'd say it's because somebody she knew got killed tonight, wouldn't you?" Liz looked at her as if she were an idiot.

"Well, yeah, but...."

"Ahh...." Liz threw up her hand again. "That might not be what she's screaming about, but it's what she's freaked about. Take my word. She's dated too many vanilla girls to lose it over that." She gave Alison an apologetic half smile. Alison realized that she had come close to being insulted.

"Well, what...," she began indignantly.

"Look," interrupted Liz, "what if you met this woman at a gay place? A bar? Just your type. Hotter than a two-dollar pistol. And you asked her out and she said yes and it was great and you were thinking baby-oh-baby and at the last minute she said, 'Oh, by the way, I'm not a dyke, I just like to hang out there.'"

"I didn't tell her I was into the scene," Alison said in an offended voice. "I didn't even realize she was until tonight when Trudy started talking."

Liz started to give her an incredulous, 'Are-you-an-idiot-or-what?' look but then, as if she realized she were being a little too harsh, fairly successfully changed it into something that could have been read either as plain surprise or mild heartburn. "Well, we've seen you at the Blue Ryder every Thursday for the past six months."

"That's my job," Alison protested. "What do you think I do, rent a uniform and another cop once a week for a prop so I can do a walk-through scene?"

"No, but not every cop who walks through has this look." Liz rolled her eyes from side to side like a kid in a candy shop, not moving her head, as if that would ruin what little control she had.

Alison flushed to the roots of her hair. "I'm getting sunglasses," she mumbled.

"And," continued Liz, as if she'd asked, "novices—well, what do you do if someone who is just coming out wants to go out with you?"

"Begone, evil one." Alison held up crossed fingers and hissed. "Look me up in two years."

"Because...?"

"They fall in love with you if they sleep with you and have second thoughts about doing the right thing and go back to their boyfriends and husbands. Or at least they used to. I haven't actually been around someone who was just coming out in years."

"So." Liz threw her hands up, indicating that was that. Alison scowled out the window, wondering if it would be tactful to leave by the back way while Stacy was still outside. She was willing to bet that the overnight invitation had been withdrawn.

Something suddenly occurred to her. Liz had said...Trudy had mentioned...did that mean that Liz was also into the leather scene? She shot an inquiring look sideways. Unfortunately, Liz not only caught it but fully interpreted it. She bared her teeth into an evil smile and said, "Heh, heh, heh." Alison gave her a fuck-you look, hoping that it was as fully readable.

* * *

"Where have you been?" Michelle demanded.

Alison turned slowly. Stacy—and this was so far the largest strike against her—had not had any coffee—not even instant!—at her house and so Alison was not in the mood to take shit. "Out," she answered, holding her copy of the *Rocky Mountain News* in front of her face to reinforce the hostility in her voice.

It did not work. Michelle rode right over the top of her bad mood. Michelle's theory of moods and getting your way was always to be more so. She could be more crabby, more stressed, more angry and more hyper than anyone else when occasion demanded. She had out-crabbed Alison so often that it was hardly a challenge anymore.

"Yeah, well, do you know who that woman you were fucking is?"

Alison read a number of things in her voice, including the hope that she didn't know and could still be saved from evil. The hope was overlaid with a fear that she recognized and that drastic measures, like ostracism, would have to be taken. Well, just let Michelle try to shun her into changing her ways. She'd bring up that year when Michelle had decided she was bisexual and had brought home sensitive New Age guys from her stained-glass classes. She didn't even bother to ask how Michelle knew she had been out with Stacy. Michelle had friends everywhere who reported back to her with more reliability than the CIA.

"Yes, I do know what she is and what she does and what she wears while she does it. Incidently—we didn't fuck, I fell asleep on her couch while she obsessed over ice cream."

"Yeah, well." This was dismissed in a sneer as if it were even more kinky than sex surely would have been. "So you feel okay about going out with a woman who is a batterer? Are you going to start wearing a leather jacket and letting her slap you around?"

"Maybe, Michelle." Privately Alison thought that at this moment smacking her friend would be much more satisfying. When Michelle was in this berserker state she had to keep reminding herself why they were friends.

26

"And did I mention that she had a booth two doors down from us at Michigan last year? That was delightful, let me tell you. All these women—some of them trying to come out—feeling like they're in a safe place and here she is wearing a leather skirt at the festival, doing her little thing and making play dates on the side, and this fucking stream of leather women in and out of there like it's a bar on the Castro."

"She sure does nice work," Alison said.

Michelle stopped right in the middle of her tirade.

"What?"

"She does beautiful work. She's got such a sense of color."

Michelle regarded her blankly for a moment.

"You are nuts," she finally said. "You are fucking nuts. You have been alone too long, you have been a cop too long—I don't know what it is, but you are fucking nuts. There is some crazy out there who is murdering lesbians, you are dating a woman who beats up on other women—and not just as a hobby either, for money!—and you are standing here talking about her 'work' like you are some little old lady at a quilt show. You've flipped out. I can't even talk to you." She stormed out the front door, slamming the screen behind her. It was what Alison had hoped for, but still she felt as if she had been slapped in the face. Even adding a large grain of salt to account for Michelle's love of the dramatic, it had still been pretty harsh. She gulped the last of her coffee and poured herself another cup.

A knock at the back door, and Janka stuck her head in.

"Was all that screaming and slamming my honey?" She was wearing one of her hippie-weaver-at-the-craft-fair outfits instead of her usual sweatpants and t-shirt, which meant that they must be really backed up with their laundry.

"Yes," answered Alison shortly. "Are you planning on not speaking to me if I go out with Stacy, too?"

Janka picked up KP and spent some moments arranging him on her chest like a scarf. "She's upset, Alison," she finally answered.

"She's upset?! I'm fucking upset! How do you think it feels to have your best friend do a blackmail scene on you?"

"I don't think she sees it that way. But, anyway, she's freaking out because she knew that woman."

"Stacy—yeah, she told me."

"No, the woman who was killed last night."

"Oh." It brought her up short and jarred her out of her own rage.

"Not well. Or at least, not for a long time. They worked on the newspaper together." The women's newspaper had folded years before, but linear

27

time meant nothing to Michelle where dyke-bonding was concerned. A wedding was a weak ceremony compared to protesting together.

"Stacy knew her too," Alison said absently.

"Oh, shit." Janka started so violently that K.P leapt down in disgust. "She's not thinking about going to the funeral, is she?"

"I don't think so."

"Hmm." Janka obviously had not made up her mind on the s/m-dykes-are-evil issue, but wasn't about to say anything that could be construed as going against Michelle.

"Why?"

"Chelle is thinking about going. That shows you how upset she is." Michelle didn't do funerals—she planted trees or did vigils or made squares for the AIDS quilt. Alison knew that she would never go through with the plan, but it gave her an idea of her own.

"How'd she know about the funeral?" she asked. "Is that information in the paper?"

Four

Armed with what newspaper coverage she could find, as well as a begged, borrowed and not quite stolen police report from Robert, Alison set out for her first inquiry into the death of Melanie Donahue.

"Coffee, please," was the first thing that the drawn, blond woman said after Alison approached her. The woman had regained her composure a little since leaving the funeral home for the diner with Alison tailing her. No longer crying, her hands shook as she tapped out a cigarette. She was just at the right level of pliability—numb, with questions of her own.

Alison waited for her to take two swallows of coffee. "Krista," she said gently, "I'd like to ask you some questions about Melanie."

Krista jerked her head the slightest bit, but her voice was steady. "Who did you say you were?"

Here was where things might get sticky. "I'm a police officer...."

"I've had the police," Krista interrupted, in a voice that would have been petulant, had it not been so overlaiden with grief. "I've had the police and had the police, and they haven't done anything."

"I know you have." She decided to come right out with it in hopes of forming an alliance. "But I thought I might pick up something they hadn't. Because I'm a lesbian, and Melanie was a lesbian...."

"She wasn't a lesbian." Krista put out her cigarette almost angrily.

Oh. Had she missed something? Michelle never gave the time of day to straight women.

"She wasn't a lesbian," repeated Krista, and then paused. "She just loved me. Why do people have to put labels on that?"

Uh oh. Stacy had told her they were closeted, but she hadn't said that Krista couldn't say the L-word. How to handle this and still get the scoop?

The waitress, wanting to know if there was anything else, gave Alison a brief reprieve. As Krista wearily scanned the menu Alison considered what she knew. Despite the current set up, Melanie must have been out and about once upon a time if she had worked on *Big Mama Rag*, and bonded with Michelle. Michelle considered closeted dykes a waste of time.

"Why was Melanie at the Blue Ryder?" she asked carefully.

29

"She wasn't at the bar! She was killed in her car and dumped there. Her car was then parked two blocks away, no fingerprints anywhere, just blood."

Alison said nothing. There was nothing else by the Blue Ryder but warehouses. For a moment she was disgusted. Like Michelle, she had no patience with these women who couldn't even say who they were. Krista was probably the kind of woman who 'couldn't understand' why anyone would want to talk about their 'sexual preference.'

Then she looked up and saw that tears had reformed in Krista's eyes. For Christ's sake, Alison, the woman had just lost her lover, whatever she chose to call her. Show some compassion.

She reached out and recurled Krista's fingers around her coffee cup. Obediently Krista took another sip, and Alison thought, with a twinge of disgust, "This is the kind of thing that I am good at. Squeezing out information on cases that aren't even my own." But it did not occur to her to stop.

"Where was Melanie going, then?" she asked, catching herself only at the last moment to keep from saying, 'supposed to be going.' The road to the Blue Ryder was a dead end. She hoped that Krista would not protest again that she had already been over this with the police, for she no longer had any grounds on which to plead for support or solidarity. If Krista didn't call Melanie a dyke, then she sure as hell didn't call herself a dyke, and that made Alison no more than a busybody.

But Krista answered eagerly. "To her therapist's. She usually had a Wednesday appointment, but she'd made a special one. She'd been real stressed out. She must have been on her way home."

For a moment Alison could not understand her eagerness. Then it came to her. It had been clear from the report that Jorgenson did not believe that Melanie's destination was any place but the bar. Krista was anxious that her version be proven. But why was the name of the therapist not in the report Robert had given her?

"Where is her therapist's office?" she asked. "What's her...."

Krista shook her head. "I don't know. Melanie was very...private about her." She was flushing, and Alison thought, you fought about it. You didn't want her to talk to anyone else about queer problems, and by the time you came around she wouldn't tell you anything.

"How long had she been seeing this woman?"

"About a year." Krista hesitated slightly. That you know about, thought Alison. But she said nothing. It was time to stop, before Krista either broke down or became hostile.

As she pulled her wallet out of her bag she thought of one more question. "How did she pay? Did she have duplicate checks? Would the name be there?"

30

Krista's mouth tightened."We had a joint checkbook. But she always paid in cash."

Didn't want you to know how much it cost, thought Alison. She shook the woman's hand, offering condolences again and gave her a business card, knowing that it would probably go right into the trash the moment she had time to rethink.

"Do you know what the killer took?" Krista asked in a voice both bitter and heart-torn. "Her necklace. They left her wallet and her credit cards and took the necklace I gave her, and it didn't even cost twenty dollars."

* * *

Mulling over what Krista had said, especially that Melanie was seeing a therapist, Alison was almost late in meeting up for dinner with Stacy.

Alison hadn't been to this particular restaurant since she had broken up with Sandy five years before. It was a little disconcerting to find it exactly as it had been then, like some kind of personal time capsule. Alison looked over the hostess' shoulder, hoping to dispel the odd sensation with a glimpse of Stacy. "Mmm, I'm meeting someone. A woman."

"A couple?" the woman suggested, as if it were something negotiable.

"No, I...," Alison tried to protest, but the hostess swept away, beckoning her to follow. A couple or nothing, take it or leave it.

"Alison!" Stacy, wearing a blue dress, called from a booth, sounding delighted. The hostess smiled smugly, flicking her eyes over to the young man sitting next to Stacy, as if to say, "I told you so."

"Alison, this is Mark."

Alison stuck out her hand, trying to hide her irritation. Call her a pig, but she hadn't expected an extra man on her date. Mark's hand was rough, as though he had been handling brick, or lumber, and so big that it swallowed hers up. She felt an odd sense of disconnection, as if her fingers had actually vanished.

"We're doing a little business. It came up after I asked you to join me. It will only take a couple of minutes." Stacy gave Alison a little wink that said she recognized the flash of jealousy and hoped she could be a good sport for five minutes. She gestured towards the table. The silverware had all been pushed back and the cloth covered with a jumble of photographs.

"My portfolio," Stacy said. "Mark is my photographer."

Alison attempted to drop her hand, but the man did not loosen his grip in response. Disconcerted, she glanced into his face. He was good looking, blond hair cut short on the top and a blue stone in one ear. Maybe ten or twelve years younger than her. When she met his blue eyes he smiled and released his grip immediately as if, having bested her he could now afford to be a good winner. On the table beneath his other hand was a legal-size manila envelope.

"We're working on the display for my show," Stacy continued blithely, unaware of the exchange. "They want to put together this little 'at home with the artist' display." She waved a photo.

Alison took it by the corner. It was an excellent shot of a geometrical piece done all in blues.

"This is the best." The boy's youthful voice confirmed her age estimate, although he was beginning to get a touch of smoker's gravel. The photo he handed Alison was surprisingly good. Stacy, in an old pair of shorts and a loose tank top, stood staring at the bulletin board. Her left hand was folded across her chest—in it she clutched a forgotten pair of shears. Her right hand was up stroking her mouth, which was slightly open in contemplation. She was totally unaware of the camera.

"I hate that one," Stacy protested. "I look like a geek."

"It's the best one," Mark repeated. He met Alison's eyes and smiled, as if they shared a joke about how silly and vain Stacy was. She could not keep from smiling back. As they talked, choosing this photo and that, she sorted through the pile on the table. Unlike other portfolios she had seen, there were at least as many pictures of Stacy as there were art shots. There was Stacy with her headphones on, bent over a piece of red and white fabric. Stacy in a tatty bathrobe, her hair twisted back in a braid that had obviously been slept in, her forehead propped against the sewing machine as if she were about to fall back asleep. Alison wondered about the sense of intimacy inferred by the photos. If Stacy had just gotten up, where did that mean Mark had been?

A bit troubled—Stacy wasn't, please, god, no, not bi, was she?—Alison put the photo down. Stacy and Mark were arguing fiercely over another photo. Her two cents would probably not be appreciated, especially since once again she agreed with Mark's 'artistry over vanity' approach.

She went through the pile of photos again, picking out, in her mind, the ones she would put on the wall were Stacy her girlfriend. She noticed that Mark, in his agitation, had lifted his hand off the envelope. Without really thinking of it as snooping, but moving stealthily nonetheless, she eased it towards her and snaked two fingers into the envelope.

She was startled enough by the one picture that she let out a tiny little, "Oh!" which she immediately wished she could recall because it sounded so girlish. The photo was black and white, and it had the grainy look of being shot through a scarf. There was a quilt on the wall in the background (in

Stacy's apartment it was hard to get a picture that did not have a quilt in the background) and Stacy was turning away from it, still contemplative. Her hair, which had been pulled back for work in most of the others, swung across her cheek with the turning motion. A dangling earring reflected a tiny point of light in the dark mass. She was dressed in the same leather outfit Alison had seen her in at the bar. She was wearing the beaded gloves—one hand reached up to brush the hair back.

"I don't think we'll use that one." Mark's voice was without inflection, but his eyes were unsmiling. It was all Alison could do to keep from dropping the photo before his look.

Stacy craned to see. "Guess not," she said, and immediately went back to the quilt pictures. Obviously she had seen it before.

"The other one is better," said Alison in a voice that she fought to keep disinterested. She handed the envelope back as if it were nothing. Mark took it without thanks.

"I've got to go," he said abruptly, sweeping everything into his briefcase. To Alison's great relief Stacy did not urge him to stay.

"Nice to meet you, Alison. I'm sure we'll see one another again." He had turned the charm back on. His smile, as if they had shared a joke, was hard to resist. Alison allowed the corners of her mouth to lift in response.

"Are all the men you know weird?" she asked Stacy after he had gone.

"That's a little redundant, isn't it?" asked Stacy, lifting her head from the menu. "'Weird men?' Anyway, the vibes were because of that last photo, which, incidently, you were being a little nosy about." Alison smiled her most appealing 'that's-the-way-I-am-love-me-anyway' smile. Stacy returned a smile of forgiveness and continued. "He's been taking my quilt shots forever—he's really good. So last year I got asked to submit some photos for this leather woman calender, and I couldn't connect with any women whose work I really, really liked, so I thought, what the hey, Mark knows what I do, he can handle it."

Alison opened her mouth. Stacy, catching the look, said, "No, they weren't sex shots and no, I didn't get in it, probably for that reason. They were all kind of like that one—I decided to go the leather girl-with-real-life route. But the point of this long story that is keeping us from getting food, and I'm starved, is that he couldn't handle it, and we had kind of a confrontation about it and had to process, and it was a giant pain in the ass and I don't know why the hell he still carries that picture around. I think it's so he can remind me of how wicked I am now and then. Juevos rancheros," she said to the waitress.

"Actually," Alison said, trying to keep her voice matter-of-fact when it wanted to break like a thirteen-year-old boy's, "this kind of brings up some stuff that I wanted to talk about."

"Oh, dear." Stacy, who was wearing her glasses, pulled them way down on her nose and peered at her worriedly. "Do we have to do this?"

"Yes," answered Alison, much more firmly than she felt. "Because I have to get clear how I feel about this before we—"

"Make mad, passionate love?" Stacy interjected in a low, sexy voice, leaning over the table so that her breasts were dangerously near the candles. For a moment Alison almost forgot herself, and just put her hand across the table to be led away. Then she steeled her resolution.

"Go any further," she said as if Stacy had not spoken, though her heart was pounding. "I mean I—" She stopped abruptly, afraid of feeling like a fool with a schoolgirl crush.

"This is the dating thing, isn't it?" asked Stacy, fidgeting with her fork.

"Yeah! I mean, I have to decide how I feel about what you do. It would be like—well, if I made plutonium triggers up at Rocky Flats or worked as a furrier or something. You'd have to think about that, wouldn't you?"

"Let me ask you something, Alison. Don't you think that there's a certain similarity between what you do and what I do? That maybe I'm having little second thoughts about dealing with your line of work? I mean, at least what I do is consensual."

"No! What are you talking about?"

"You don't think that being a cop is all about power? You don't have any qualms about working in a system that is still incredibly oppressive to women, not just as criminals but as victims, and on the force as well?" Stacy leaned back and folded her arms across her chest, all traces of seduction gone.

"I think that this is just stonewalling. This is just attacking what I do as a way of keeping from being attacked yourself." The waitress had brought by a bowl of chips and salsa, and in her agitation, Alison tore into them. Stress eating was always good.

"If you believe that then you don't understand what I do and you don't think about what you do. S/m play for me is not about tying someone up and beating them bloody. It's about power and giving up power. Now, you tell me all about how nobody with the police department is in it for the power."

Hmm, definitely time for a new line of attack.

"Don't you think that it's oppressive to other women to play a dominating role? Don't you think it supports stereotypes that we really need to move away from rather than reinforcing?"

"Look," said Stacy "if you have a real objection, then go ahead and tell

34

me about it. But don't just give me something you've gleaned from reading back issues of *Lesbian Connection* because you think that it's the PC thing to do. Because if you're really concerned about perpetuating stereotypes, what the hell are we doing here, doing the butch/femme thing?"

Alison looked down at her jeans and T-shirt. "Well," she said in a voice that was just short of a whine.

"Alison," Stacy said, "correct me if I'm wrong, but am I getting a few mixed messages here? I mean, is it really fair to me to be asking me to defend this disgusting shit on the one hand, and to be hinting that you'd like to be seduced into it on the other? That feels a little weird. Actually," Stacy corrected herself with a sigh, "it feels a little familiar."

Alison blushed, embarrassed by both her transparency and her confusion. Did the word seduction have to be raised so soon?

"Let's just leave seduction out of it," she protested "and…."

"Oh, baby," Stacy purred, "leaving seduction in is your only chance. I don't do s/m 101 for free anymore. It gets pretty damn boring being a continual education display. It's like being the token dyke at work, you know? You're these people's only role model. If you get a bad haircut are they going to take it as a serious political statement? If you take a Twinkie in your lunch is every straight girl at the office going to go home and tell her family that dykes have no respect for their bodies? I feel like photocopying a basic stance-sheet and handing it out. This is what I do, this is what I don't do, this is why, incidently, these are my other hobbies if you give a shit and if it was a choice between kinky sex and reading, I wouldn't be turning in my library card. So now let's talk about something else."

"Well, how I am I supposed to find anything out?" Alison asked with the hint of a pout. It was a bad habit in which she had been encouraged because several of her past lovers had found it attractive.

Stacy, too, smiled at the way her full lips were drawn up.

"I'd love to slap that look off your face," she said conversationally, and then, before Alison could even think of an answer, "Have you tried reading?"

Alison's expression changed to one of horror. "Yes," she answered shortly.

Stacy looked at her. "Oh, dear," she said. "Alison, I need to tell you a basic truth right here. Have you ever heard the expression, 'It's dangerous to give a lesbian a guitar?'"

Alison burst out laughing. "No!"

"Well, that's because I made it up, and it hasn't yet gained popular acceptance. But I don't need to explain its meaning, do I?"

Alison shook her head. "Oh, I was at the music festival," she warbled tunelessly, her fingers picking out the same three cords over and over, "and it filled me with a great joy to see so many women-identified-women that I thought I'd write this song...."

Stacy held up her hand. "You got it. Well, unfortunately, a variation of this disease tends to affect s/m dykes who pick up pens. I mean, there is some well-written information out there that can be really helpful to a novice. I take it, however, from the look on your face, that you have attempted to delve into the land of fiction."

Alison nodded warily.

"Okay, let me just add a few disclaimers. Not all s/m dykes are racist. Most s/m dykes I know take to heart the motto 'Safe, sane, and consensual' and are just as horrified by rape/slash scenes are you are. We do not eat our dead. Someday—and I truly believe this—there is going to be a tremendous uprising of editors in the ranks of the s/m community and there will be an end to the dreadful practice of publishing rough drafts. But until that day...well, don't take it all to heart."

"In other words, I should talk to a good role model," Alison said, rather pleased with herself for having brought the conversation to this point.

"Okay, okay." Stacy threw up her hands in resignation. "Actually, I should quit fighting this and start seeing if I can't get points every time I'm a good role model. You know, the way you used to get extra stars on your sash for selling a record amount of Girl Scout cookies?"

"Aren't 'good role model' and 's/m' kind of oxymoronic?" asked Alison in a bid for humor that won a brief snort.

"So I hear day and night from a good portion of the lesbian community. Oh, well, I guess if we were the kind of girls who could be swayed by public opinion I'd still be a housewife for Jesus and you'd still be—what would you be?"

"Not still, but some nice policeman's wife waiting for the kids to get into junior high so that I could go back to a desk job that wouldn't endanger me as a mother."

"And they say we're sick," laughed Stacy. "Anyway, s/m 101...." She stopped and hit herself in the forehead. "What am I doing? I hate doing this by myself. I can take you to s/m 101." She looked at her watch and then waved for the check. "We've just got time to make this."

Five

"Where are we going?" asked Alison.

"Peony's." Stacy named the gay coffee house. "We usually meet at the Blue Ryder every other Monday, but they're closed tonight because of the killing. Jenny was shook."

A few blocks later they entered Peony's, famous for its carrot cake which was listed on the menu as 'Better-than-sex.' Alison following Stacy who wended her way past the crowded tables. It was the kind of atmosphere in which one could have the most intimate, private conversation, knowing that everyone else was so busy with theirs that no one else was paying attention.

"Alison, you remember Liz, right?"

Liz, waving a sandwich dangerously in one hand, scattering sprouts right and left, gave one short nod, continuing her heated discussion with the woman beside her. She jabbed her hand at a photocopied paper on the table to make a point, leaving a smear of mayo on it.

"And Diane." Stacy gestured towards the woman across the table who was a serious lipstick dyke, the kind that Alison didn't know how to relate to, so tended to put in a 'dumb blonde' category and dismiss.

"I hate this," said Diane without preliminary. "You guys always make me do outreach and novice groups and I hate it."

"It's because you're so nonthreatening," soothed Stacy. "You don't scare anybody."

"Like Liz does, right?" Diane lifted a skeptical eyebrow.

"It's because you're so pretty, Diane. Women want to come just to look at you," said yet another woman to whom Liz had been orating, and who was the only one at the table in serious leather. She had created the opening in the conversation to speak by taking Liz's elbow and directing her sandwich abruptly into her mouth.

"And Ruth," Stacy said with a nod of introduction.

"That's bullshit. It's all bullshit. You make me do it because you're too lazy. You're all liars, and the next time that I'm in top space I'm going to punish everyone severely. And you have to help me with my visual aids." Diane heaved a briefcase up onto the table, and ignoring indignant squeaks

37

from Liz who still had her mouth full, created a space to lay down an over-sized sheet of paper by rearranging everyone's dishes.

"I wanted to do a bell curve at first," Diane explained, "because I always end up talking about how we fit on a bell curve. You know? I was going to have women who do real intense near-death scenes here," she pointed to the right side of the paper, "and women who do really light fantasy over here. But then I decided that I couldn't because I didn't have the statistics to make it accurate, and if I put it on as a joke, even if I *told* everyone it was a joke someone would freak out and use it in an article, so..." she drew a long breath and gestured, "...it's just going to be a list."

Alison, who had been staring at Diane's fingernails with a mixture of horror and awe, responded to a sharp elbow from Stacy and looked at the paper.

S/M DYKES it was headed. Below was a list written in red magic marker:

Dykes whose only kink is a leather fetish
Dykes who do gender bending
Dykes who do piercing
Dykes who do power fantasies
Dykes who like to get spanked
Dykes who use a lot of sex toys and call what they do s/m even though no pain
  is exchanged
Dykes who have full-time slaves
Dykes who are full-time slaves
Dykes who connect with other leatherdykes and play only once or twice a year
Dykes whose only hobby is s/m
Dykes who play only with a monogamous partner
Dykes who do cutting
Dykes who only top
Dykes who only bottom
Dykes who switch
Dykes who switch but don't admit it
Dykes who like rough sex
Dykes who don't have sex while playing
Dykes who play with men, but only have sex with women
Dykes who do only bondage
Dykes who do heavy beating scenes
Dykes who practice s/m activities but don't label it s/m

"Well, that's a good start," commented Ruth. Having been distracted from the nails, Alison was now trying to read all of the buttons on her leather vest without appearing to be staring. Besides the jacket, she was wearing a pair of leather pants which were laced ornamentally up the side.

"Put down Soccer players who are going to the gay games" suggested Liz, "because nobody has bottomed the way Stacy and I have to that damn Trudy. It's just been one big humiliation scene spanning a year."

"Only consensual activities listed," said Diane. "That soccer shit is just plain abusive. If I want to count mental abuse I'd have to put down half of the vanilla relationships in town. That does explain why you've been so toppy lately, though. Don't ask me to dress up in a soccer uniform, okay?"

"So, you must have turned out to be kinky after all, huh?"

Alison, who had been trying to imagine Diane in Stacy's purple and black uniform, didn't realize for a moment that Liz's bright question was directed towards her. Another nudge from Stacy was required to refocus her.

"No! I mean, yeah, I mean…." She looked to Stacy for help.

"Just curious. You are all being used as visual aids. Try and provide a good role model." Stacy waved at the waitress.

Liz rubbed her hands together in a gloating way. "Another innocent sacrifice to the goddess of perversion. Another vanilla dyke to be lead along the primrose path. Another—"

"Oh, stop it," said Diane, reaching across the table to rap Liz on the knuckles. "You're going to scare her. You can be so obnoxious—If you don't eat, you're all freaked out because you're low blood sugar, and if you do eat you're hyper." She picked up her marker and wrote in 'Dykes with s/m fantasies who never act any of them out.'

"Liz treats the scene just like she does soccer," explained Stacy. "Everyone is a potential recruit."

"Except that being in the scene is probably a lot less painful," interjected Ruth. She gave an exaggerated shudder. "I don't know how you girls do it. I haven't even been able to watch since the last time I saw Stacy get kicked in the head."

Liz, nursing her offended knuckles, glared at Diane and said, "Fantasies don't count. Saying that you're an s/m dyke because you have fantasies you never act on is like saying that a dyke is bisexual because she has fantasies about men that she never acts on."

"Hmm." Diane crossed out the offending line and wrote instead, 'Women who call themselves s/m dykes because of their fantasies and feelings, even though they may never act these out sexually.'

"So, do you do uniform scenes?" Liz asked Alison brightly, her hands carefully out of Diane's reach.

"Liz! She's *just curious*! You're being a pig! That's like asking if you do courthouse scenes!"

"Well, but I *do* do courthouse scenes."

"And everybody knows it because you won't shut up about it. But that doesn't mean that everybody wants to talk about buttfucking within five minutes of meeting you."

"Lo," said Stacy to Alison, "and behold. Living representatives of the leather community. Look at them carefully before deciding if you want to be categorized with them."

"Ask me some questions," said Diane, still busy with her marker. "I haven't appeared before a group in a while. I could use the practice. You're my panel," she ordered the other three women.

"Why in the world do you wear high heels if you're not forced to?" The question seemed to leap out of Alison's mouth of its own volition. Liz howled with laughter. Alison blushed beet red. Good job, Alison. Stacy was going to want to take her along all the time.

"Because," said Diane, "there are women who are driven mad with lust by it."

"Me for one," said Ruth.

"And I like that kind of woman. And, to answer all your unanswered questions, no, it doesn't mean that I'm an idiot, no, it doesn't mean that I can't take care of myself and no, it doesn't mean that I'm afraid to get my hands dirty or that I automatically freak out when I see a mouse, although I certainly reserve the option, or that I necessarily fit any of the other stereotypes that I am sure, from having held them myself, that you have. I paid my dues as a flannel-shirt dyke and I now have gotten to the point where I feel that I have the right to create my own sexual image without sticking to dyke standard rules."

"This question," said Stacy from the side of her mouth, "appears to have been asked before."

"Ask a technique question," advised Ruth.

"Ask for dessert," said Stacy, who had finally corralled the waitress.

"Cheesecake," said Alison, who had sampled the charms of this particular coffeehouse before, without looking up. To Diane she said, "Do you do s/m for money?"

"No!" trilled Diane, going suddenly into a kind of Barbie at her dumbest mode. "But I have a friend who does!"

"How does she justify prostituting herself?" Alison asked. She could feel Stacy glaring at her, but she seemed to have gotten on a roll from which she could not recover. "How is she able to distinguish work from lovers?"

"Luckily, the little lady is on our panel tonight." Diane abruptly closed down Barbie. "Take it away, Stacy."

Stacy, apparently deciding to take the situation with good grace, half stood and gave a bob. "Hi," she said, "my name is Stacy, I top for a living, I work about twenty hours a week, I charge lots of money, I have my own dungeon and equipment, most of my clients are into heavy beating scenes, privately I switch and play much lighter with lots of fantasy and fucking, I don't have genital contact with my clients, so no, it's not illegal, I only do women, privately I tend to get into serial monogamy." She ran out of breath and sat down suddenly.

"Who are you talking to this time?" Liz asked Diane. "The Kiwanas?"

"Women's group at the Gay and Lesbian Community Center."

"Oh, then how about this one? How do you justify participating in violence against women?" said Liz.

"This is a hard one," said Diane, squinting at them thoughtfully. "And one of the reasons that it's hard is the huge split that we have created in the lesbian community over the s/m issue. Because we have become so polarized and so absolutely pro-con, right-wrong there is a tendency on one side to say, Well, those women are just neo-Nazi sickies who shouldn't be allowed to say they're dykes and who should be stopped at all costs, and on the other to say, Fuck you, you don't listen anyway. It's important to realize that, just as referring to the lesbian experience means referring to millions and millions of women, each with her own unique story, s/m dykes, just as you can see on my list here, have a huge array of feelings and experiences. I can tell you a little about my own experience and maybe get my friends to do the same."

She smiled persuasively at Liz, who slouched down in her seat mumbling, "I'm not going to do another 101 scene."

Diane threw up her hands. "My experience with the lesbian s/m community has been fairly positive. I had been out a long time before it entered my mind that this was something in which I might be interested. I had done a lot of your basic dyke stuff, but always had that feeling of not quite fitting in. I was always labeled as too sexual and too femme. When I finally met some leather dykes, the first feeling that I got was that they were prepared to really honor and enjoy these two qualities. Before that, the feeling I had gotten from the community was, 'Well, we'll like you in spite of that, but it's big of us.' I really enjoy feeling appreciated rather than just tolerated. There is a lot more room for and acknowledgement of butch/femme stuff in the leather community." She stopped and looked at Liz.

After a moment of silence Liz sat up and spoke, with some bad grace. "I'm in the scene because I like pain. I hate doing this display, because I know that most of you are thinking that makes me a bad or sick person, and it personally is an uphill job to try to feel good about yourself when you're faced with that kind of feedback all the time. Which is why a lot of leather-women tend to hang out together even if they don't have a lot of other common interests. But anyway, the right kind of pain with sex makes me very high. If you have trouble imagining that, think about going on a roller-coaster or running a marathon or doing a polar-bear swim. These are all things that give people the same kind of rush that I get from a beating. The thought of doing any of them fills me with horror, but I've learned to accept that people get their endorphines in different ways." She slouched down again and scowled.

"More coffee?" asked the dyke waitress in a barely civil tone. She gave them what Alison, by now, had learned to recognize as the 'goddamn leather-dykes' glare.

"I've played soccer with you, haven't I?" Liz went straight out of her sullen mood into one of a charmer. "You play with thirty-something, right? You play...." She snapped her fingers, trying to recall.

"You play right half," supplied Stacy. "You scored a goal against me in our last game. Went right off my face into the cage. You play indoor at the Sportarama, too, don't you? Coed on 'Fags and Dykes' in the Sunday over thirty league?"

The woman refused to be charmed. They were scum, and talking about soccer was as much a trick as monkeys typing Shakespeare. She slammed down the check with a jolt that sloshed everyone's coffee over and huffed off to take care of her legitimate customers. Liz and Stacy looked at each other and shrugged.

"Leather P.R." said Stacy. "A thankless job."

"Fuck 'em if they can't take a joke," said Diane. She stuffed her list back in her briefcase. "I gotta go." She rose without good-byes. Alison watched her walk away from the table, wondering if she could ever be driven mad with lust by a woman in high heels. It was a possibility.

Outside the temperature had dropped and the wind was blowing. The closest parking Alison had been able to find was several blocks away. She hunched down in her sweatshirt and put her hands in her armpits. Stacy was powerwalking down the street so that she had to hustle to keep up with her.

Halfway down the block was a tiny men's bar. In front of the door were four people handing out leaflets and hassling the customers. Stacy had her head down against the wind, but Alison looked at the two couples curiously. They were dressed as if for church, the women in long coats over dresses with heels. One of the men was trying to give a leaflet to two gay men on their way into the bar. He was about Alison's own age, dressed in a blue suit.

"God loves the sinner!" he called after the men when they pushed past him. He turned towards Alison, and she ducked her head too late to keep from catching his eye. He held a leaflet out to her. "God hates the sin, Sister," he sang out in a strong, pleasant voice. "Don't stand by idly while someone you love prepares to go to Hell, or your children are seduced into a path of abomination!" He held a leaflet out to her, smiling a smile that assumed they were conspirators in the fight for the righteous.

"Take that bullshit and peddle it someplace else," Alison snapped at him, forgetting her plan to pass like strangers. "It's oppressive and it's offensive!"

"No! It's the word of God, and with our help these people can be saved!" He reached out to take her elbow, and savagely she shook it off, wondering what conceit could make one person believe he could save another's soul. "Well, I'm one of 'these people'! A dyke, get it?"

She turned to follow Stacy, knowing from experience that shouting matches with religious maniacs were fruitless, but the man stepped in front of her. "Get out of my way!" she snapped.

"Just let us help you into the light, Little Sister," said Blue Suit in his fine speaker's voice. She put her elbow out to push past him, but before she was even aware of the danger, the second man who wore a red tie, had grabbed her wrist from behind and was holding it tight, not quite pinning it behind her back, but close enough so the pain was the same. Her cop training kicked in and she slammed her heel backwards, hitting him in the shin. He jerked her arm up so hard that she screamed, "Jesus!" and he clapped a hand over her mouth.

"Don't take the Lord's name in vain, Little Sister," he said gently, as if he were admonishing a much loved child.

Up until this point Alison had felt only anger, but now, looking into the eyes of this man who was so certain that he was doing the will of God, she was afraid. She had never known anyone personally who had been kidnapped for 'deprogramming' but she had read about it. She knew that the packet homophobic parents paid for sometimes included a taste of 'normal sex' in the form of rape.

She tried to jerk her head around, looking for Stacy, but she must have walked on, unaware. Or were the women distracting her? Was this a well-planned ruse? Surely not, not right in the open on the sidewalk. But, even as she thought about it, Alison realized that the street was virtually deserted except during those moments when someone was entering or leaving the bar. Did she hear a car idling by the curb? Again she tried to struggle, and again she was brought up short by a wrenching jolt of pain. Dammit, she'd taken self defense, but as long as he had her pinned this way she was helpless. She had been foolish to speak without assessing the situation better.

Out of the corner of her eye, she saw a group of gay men approaching the

43

bar. Her whole body sagged with relief. But, as if he had read her mind, the man holding her turned his back on them casually. She could tell he was thinking that if he just kept his cool they would probably not even look his way. So confidant was Red Tie, in fact, that he nodded to Blue Suit who stepped around them calling, "God loves the sinner!"

That was what did them in. The men might not have heard the single, strangled noise that Alison was able to squeeze past the beefy hand which shifted only slightly when she bit it. But Blue Suit had identified them as enemies, and the gays were wary. She didn't see what happened—all she knew was that the pain in her arm was, for a moment, worse than it had been before. Then she was free. The relief was so sudden that her eyes filled with tears. One of the gay men was leaning over to pick her up off the sidewalk.

"Are you okay?"

"Yeah, I…thanks…I.." She couldn't explain to him those moments of terror when she realized that she might really be in danger.

She glanced over at the curb. There was not actually any real fighting going on, but there was plenty of shouting and shoving between the two groups. A tremendous push from the smallest of the gay men sent Blue Suit reeling off the curb and into a puddle that covered a trash-clogged grate. That ended it. The evangelist couldn't possibly get his momentum back in a suit that was stained with oily water and gum wrappers sticking to the pants. The wind had blown his fliers up against the building and out onto the pavement. Alison grabbed one as it scuttled past, at the same time craning her head to try and spot Stacy. Surely the women couldn't have overpowered her, could they?

Then she caught a flash of red in the doorway of the leather shop that was next to the bar. At first she couldn't believe that after her fearful fantasies, Stacy was just standing there in the doorway, talking to the two evangelical women as if they were all old friends. Alison's fear suddenly turned into anger so intense that it was only with difficulty that she didn't grasp Stacy by the arm and shake her.

"What the fuck are you doing? What do you mean by just leaving me alone with those crazies while you have a little chat?!" She could feel herself working up into a frenzy, but there seemed no way to stop. All she could think of was the terror she had felt when Red Tie had clapped his hand over her mouth, and the whole time Stacy hadn't been twenty feet away, exchanging recipes with the Jesus girls.

"I thought you were talking, I didn't think…." That one phrase said it all; of course she hadn't thought that there would be any problem walking through a gay neighborhood she'd walked through a dozen times before.

Alison, however, was beyond reason. "You sure fucking didn't think! I'm about to have the shit beat out of me by the God boys, and you don't even look around to see where the hell I've gone!"

In turn, Stacy's face grew dark with anger at her tone, and then blossomed with concern as she got past the cursing, far enough to take in what Alison was saying. The delicately made-up mouths of the two other women formed almost identical O's of concern, and they rushed past Alison towards their men. Stacy reached out to put a hand on her shoulder.

With great effort Alison composed herself. She stood still against a wall, sucking in great gasps of the night air. The adrenaline that had raced through her like lightning was gone, and its void left her weak and shaking. She watched the scene playing out before her with the same detachment that she might watch a play.

Blue Suit had finally climbed out of the gutter. He shivered as the wind plastered the wet cloth up against his legs. He and his cohort were obviously fuming, spoiling for a chance to let God work through their fists. They were not, however, confident enough of a David and Goliath scene that they were willing to rush into a situation where they were outnumbered two to one. They were making do with shouting Biblical threats. The gays, of course, were shouting back, so that when the two women rushed into the scene it was impossible for Alison to hear what they said. Blue Suit grasped one by the arm and pulled her close, as if he could not believe what she was saying.

He turned with a look that was so full of malice that everyone on the sidewalk was suddenly silent. Alison found herself, like all the rest, turning her own head to see what could possibly have caused such a look.

"Hey, Brother Malcolm," Stacy said, and Alison wondered what effort it took to appear so nonchalant while having such a beam of hate focused on her. "Long time, no see." Silently, all heads turned back towards the man, and Alison was reminded of the theater when everyone in the audience waits for the climactic line. She found herself leaning forward anxiously, wondering if it would be the well formed tones of 'God hates the sin!' again, or if there was a special line for a sinner with whom one appeared to be acquainted.

"Bitch!" was what he finally sputtered, in a voice so small and mean that it robbed him of any shreds of dignity that had survived the dunking. His hand closed on the arm of the woman and he began to hustle her off. The grip looked harsh and painful.

* * *

Finally reaching Alison's parked car, they climbed in without a word. As Alison pulled into traffic, the silence became thick and obvious, almost as loud as the buzz of conversation at the coffeehouse.

45

"Well, you're sure a hell of a fun date." Alison took it upon herself to blast through.

"Oh? And tell me yourself, do you do the berserker thing often? I mean, can I look forward to that if I forget something at the store?" Well, obviously Stacy thought she was owed an apology.

"No. Only when I've had my arm ripped out of its socket by a Jesus yuppie and then think my date's been abducted. That does tend to send me into a frenzy. But I'm sorry I screamed at you."

Stacy waved the apology aside. "You mean that fucker put his hands on you? Oooh, I should have held a pillow over his face while I had the chance. I'll bet I'd be up for parole by now."

"Actually, it was his sidekick who tried to dislocate my shoulder."

"But he called the shot, right?"

"I take it you know this man?"

"Another skeleton in the closet. Boy, I should have just spilled it all at once, huh? Remember I said I was married? Well, that was him, the husband from the Twilight Zone. Two years of wondering, 'Am I crazy, or is he?'"

"Oh, Stacy, you've got to be kidding! How…?"

"How did I get with such a nut?" Stacy asked bitterly as they reached Alison's apartment. "Well, mainly because he wasn't such a nut then. He was a nice Christian boy, I was a nice Christian girl, we went to Sunday school and youth group together, so I figured why the hell not? It wasn't like there was some guy who I liked better, or that I even expected to ever like some guy better. I hadn't quite gotten the whole picture yet, but I had figured out that much—it was never going to be like it was in the movies for me. And if I was a little unhappy, hell, my mother was a little unhappy. His mother was a little unhappy. That was what life was all about. At least I'd be out of my parents' house. I suppose you're one of those dykes who never slept with men, right?"

"Well, yeah, but…."

"I knew it! I hate you, I hate you all! Oh, I always knew I was a dyke, I came out when I was fourteen, I was out at my high school, I've been going to Michigan for ten years, I never had to fuck men to find out who *I* was!' Fuck you all."

Alison could think of no reasonable reply until they arrived at her place when she said, "I'm going to make some tea."

There was a legal sized manila envelope on her kitchen table. On it, *Robert dropped this by* was written in Michelle's handwriting.

"So I suppose you've never had any fucked-up relationships, have you?" Stacy followed her into the kitchen, still upset.

"Look, Stacy. If you want fucked up, sit down because the whole list is

46

going to take a while, okay? I mean, isn't it true that dykes invented co-dependent relationships? In fact, if you've got the time, I'll just call Michelle and Janka down and get out the slide projector—I believe they have a whole show put together called, 'Assholes we couldn't keep Alison from dating and how right we were everytime.'" She slammed the kettle onto the stove.

Unwillingly Stacy gave a small guffaw. "I would like to see that," she said. "Am I in it?"

"Without a doubt. I'm sure you already have your own section. My parents do another version of the same show called, 'I don't know *what* Alison saw in *that* girl.'"

"So," Stacy flopped down into a kitchen chair and continued her story, "he wasn't nuts to begin with. Not any worse than any of the other Bible thumpers that I grew up with. And then we decided to...," she paused dramatically and hummed the theme from *Jaws*, "make Babies! Because that's what nice young Christian couples did, right? Only we couldn't. He could have dealt with it, I think, if it had been me. He could have been generous and forgiving. But he totally freaked out when we found out it was him. Total denial. It couldn't be him, God wouldn't do that to him, let's just do it two or three times a night to make sure, and for godsake, don't get up afterwards, the right one might leak out! Like increased effort is going to negate mumps at fourteen, right? And the more obsessed he's getting about having his *own child*, the more he's getting attracted to religious crazies. He starts doing the Right-To-Life thing, right? Carting around bottles with fetuses and blocking clinic doors because maybe that will convince God how sincere he is, and maybe then we'll find out the whole thing was just a matter of mixed up files."

"What were you doing?" asked Alison, taking down two of the hand-thrown mugs Janka had given her for Solstice. She was dying to open the envelope, but didn't want to seem disinterested in Stacy's story.

"I was making a lot of quilts," said Stacy. "And visiting the women's bookstore in disguise without ever bringing anything home. And falling in love with my best friend. And so..." She accepted the cup of Sleepytime Tea (Alison had put in two bags). "...we finally got in bed and—bad movie, right?—he busted in on us! It couldn't have happened any other way, we were all primed for drama and craziness."

"Then what?"

"Well, you know how you cure a lesbian, don't you?"

Alison made a face. "You show her how good sex with a real man is."

"Bingo. He decided that we'd do a little rape scene and I decided that I'd hit him in the head with an alarm clock instead and get the hell out of there."

She spoke lightly, but Alison could see her throat moving in a silent retch.

"So did you move in with your girlfriend, then?"

"No, I spent the next week at a Battered Women's shelter. I was lucky—my parents pretty much ostracized me—of course he told everybody all the gory details—wanted to make sure who the villain was—but my sister had some money and she helped me get an apartment and get by till my next paycheck. I had some money in savings, but they were joint accounts...." She let the sentence trail off, and rolled her eyes back in her head to indicate that the money was good and gone.

"Wow." Alison did not quite know if comfort was in order. Perhaps Stacy was like Michelle, who told her most awful experiences to be laughed at, and froze at a sympathetic word. Experimentally, she stroked Stacy's hair.

"Oh," said Stacy, "one more twist. Just to make us eligible for the O. Henry award. The woman I was talking to at the store while you were getting hassled—that's Nina. My old girlfriend. The one he caught me in bed with. They're married now."

Alison froze. Catching her look of horror and disbelief, Stacy threw up her hands to indicate her own incomprehension. "Hey, she was raised in the church of the nuts. She really *believed* she had sinned. There was nothing that I could say to make a difference. She wouldn't talk to me, anyway—I was the Great Satan at that point."

"So he transferred from Right-to-Life to Death-to-Dykes?" Alison picked up the envelope and began struggling to open it. Robert had taped it as if it were going overseas.

"Like that." Stacy snapped her fingers. "*Everybody* does Right-to-Life—it's hard to be a big frog there anymore. But Kill-the-Queers is a wide open field! Check this out—he *makes his living* doing this shit—he does counseling and 'support' groups and there's been some talk about 'reprogramming.' It's also the perfect way to carry out a personal vendetta without seeming ugly."

Alison had gone back to stroking her long curls. "You think?"

"All I know is that he shows up at a hell of a lot of events I'm attending. Maybe I'm just being paranoid—I guess there aren't that many dyke happenings in town—we might just read the same calenders. But tonight was obviously unplanned. I don't think he brings Nina with him if he thinks he'll see me."

"What was she telling you?"

"You're never going to believe this one. She's pregnant. Guess we had a miracle after all."

Alison gave one last jerk on the envelope and the contents fell out on the floor.

48

"What is this?" Stacy bent to help her gather the contents.

"Robert left it. Copies of the homicide report, I guess. He knows I'm playing Nancy Drew."

"Alison." Stacy's voice was a hoarse whisper. "Who is this?" Her hand was shaking as she extended a photocopy.

Alison turned it over. "It says it's Tamara Garrity, the first victim." What in the world was the matter? Her name had been in the papers now; it couldn't be a surprise. Perhaps Stacy was upset because the woman in the xeroxed photograph was so plainly dead. Or was that only obvious to some-one like herself, who had been in the morgue more than once?

Stacy made a little choking noise. She wrapped her arms around herself and began rocking, murmuring something over and over.

"What?" Alison had to lean forward to hear.

"It wasn't the name she gave me." Only after she repeated it twice and then waved the the photo did Alison understand.

"You mean you knew her, too? But why didn't you ever...."

"It wasn't the name she gave me," said Stacy again. "It says her name is Tamara, here, but the only name she ever gave me was Laura." She shivered and wrapped her arms back around herself. Alison shivered in imitation, somehow unable to ask the only question that was in her mind. When Stacy said she knew these women, did she mean they were clients?

* * *

Alison was still puzzling over this the next day when she left the Blue Ryder. She had thought that Jenny, the owner, would recognize the photo of Melanie right away. She had expected Jenny to say that Melanie had come in every Thursday regular as clockwork. But Jenny didn't remember ever seeing her in the bar. In fact, she had reminded Alison, she had seen the body and thought it was strange that Melanie had been left by a bar of which she was not a patron.

Alison had scored in one way though. On impulse she had described the encounter with Malcolm to Jenny, and the answer had been a prompt, "Yes." The Crusaders had been to the bar a number of times, and on at least one occasion a woman had been grabbed." Jenny didn't know if the goal had been snatching or roughing-up—either way, other dykes had intervened.

So, she had to think of a new line to follow. What about Tamara Garrity? Did she have a lover or neighbor or roommate who could give her some answers?

Six

Tamara's address was not far from Alison's own, but there all similarity ended. Alison had pictured a divided Victorian, like the one she and Michelle lived in, and had imagined it in the middle of the gay ghetto. But Tamara had lived in what was, for Denver, practically a high rise. Alison's hopes of an intimate neighbor went down. Still, she was here and might as well try.

No one answered the door of number 445 though Alison knocked much longer than was polite. She stood for a minute, chewing her lower lip and try-ing to decide on her next move. The elevator clanged open and she glanced over her shoulder. A small, round woman dressed in a mail carrier's uniform exited the car. The woman gave her a quick once over, followed by an 'I-know-you-know' look. Maybe this was going to be her break. Alison knocked on Tamara's door again.

Bingo. The woman approached her, a look of concern on her face. "Um, excuse me, um, I don't know if you know…um, are you a friend of Tamara's?" She was having trouble blurting on the news. Alison didn't blame her—for all she knew, she could be an unsuspecting out-of-town lover who might go into hysterics.

"I know Tamara is dead. I was hoping that she lived with someone. I'm investigating the murder." Alison hadn't known that she was going to say this until it came out, but she was pleased. It was much neater than the 'I'm a police officer, but I'm on vacation and this isn't official' line, and it shouldn't get her in trouble at work because, after all, anyone could ask questions. Now all she had to do was hope that the woman was a fan of dyke-detective novels and would recognize one great chance to help a sleuth and be forthcoming. She pulled in her stomach and tried to look cool without actually changing position, wishing she had put on a black turtleneck and shades, instead of her paint-stained Holly Near T-shirt. Dyke detectives were always quite attractive on the page, and had at least one affair per story with a witness, victim, or suspect. Oh, well, at least her notebook looked official.

"I probably knew Tamara better than anyone else in the building. Do you want to come in and talk to me? My name is Becky, by the way."

"How well did you know her?" Alison asked as the woman led her into a pleasant, cluttered apartment.

Becky shook her head and dropped into an armchair. "Not well. I mean, I think it's awful that she was killed—I was really freaked out. But, in kind of a generic way—you know, more freaked out that another dyke was killed than that a friend was killed. I didn't cry. We had a chit-chat dyke-talk in the hall kind of thing. We never went out or asked each other in. It's scary—two dykes killed at two different bars now—makes you wonder."

"Did she go out to the bars a lot?"

"Well, she talked about it a lot. Whenever we were in the elevator together she always mentioned The Rubyfruit. You ever been there?"

Alison shook her head. "Not for a long time."

"Lot of leather dykes there. Lot of ultra-femme leather types. She liked pretty femme women—I saw her bring a couple home and they were all the leather skirt and high heels type."

Like Stacy, Alison thought with a flash of jealousy. "Do you know where she worked?" she asked, not so much because she wanted to know—it was probably in the report—but just to keep Becky flowing.

"In some bank downtown. It was a real kick to see her come home in her bank drag, you know, suit and pumps, and then to see her go out later in her butch stuff. Total transformation."

"Did she have any special friends? People who came over regularly?"

Becky shook her head. "She hadn't lived here that long. She was just transferred a couple of months ago. I think that was partly why she didn't seem to really know many people. But she was also a really private person— almost paranoid. You know, you'd ask her something casual like, 'Where are you from?' and she'd turn it."

That explained the fake name to Stacy. "Did you see her the night she was killed?"

"Nah. I'd gone out with a friend to catch the early show of *I Heard the Mermaids Singing.*"

Alison was momentarily distracted. "I've been meaning to see that. What did you think?"

Becky made an awful face. "Boring. It was the kind of film that was so arty that it should have had subtitles even though it was in English. Slow plot. But my friend loved it and said I had the attention span of a five-year-old."

Alison laughed, and now that she found Becky relaxed, she switched tactics, asking abruptly, "Did you ever see her with her clothes off?"

Becky laughed. "You don't understand. She liked leather women, and she liked femmes. Body-builder types. She did not go for fat mail dykes with

51

frizzy hair. It was not that kind of relationship."

"No, I didn't mean that. But there's a pool and a sauna in the building, right? I wondered if you had ever seen her changing clothes, anything like that."

Becky took a moment to answer. "Yeah," she said slowly, "I did run into her once in the locker room. I had forgotten that."

"Did you notice any scars? On her back? A sunburst?" asked Alison, mentally referring to the police report.

"Yeah...when she was bending over...before she knew I was there. But I didn't say anything—like I say, she was pretty private. To tell the truth, she really hurt my feelings that day. As soon as I said 'hello' she jumped a foot and scuttled off into one of the cubicles, like I was going to drool on her or jump her bones or something. I mean, I may not be as hot-looking as she was, but I'm not desperate. Then I decided later that she might have been paranoid about the scars. It was obviously deliberate scarification—it couldn't have been from an accident or an operation. Maybe she'd been hassled about it before."

Becky walked her to the door. "Say," she said suddenly, "did you ever see those scars yourself?"

"No, I didn't know her. I've never seen anything but the morgue photo."

"Oh, yeah, I guess that's right." Becky looked a little queasy. "Anyway, there was one thing about them. They made a starburst, like you said. But the last ray," she made a downstroking motion, "it wasn't like the others. They were all very neat, like they'd been made with a ruler. But the last one was more jagged, more like a hack than anything else."

The elevator arrived, and Alison stepped in. Just before the doors clanged shut Becky called, "The last scar I was telling you about? It was much pinker than the rest. That one was new."

* * *

"Um, hi." Stacy stared through the cracked door blankly. Oh, dear, thought Alison, this was a bad move. Not everyone liked being dropped in on without warning. She should have called first. She was losing her social skills. Well, she'd just have to go into Approach Number Two, the 'Do-you-have-a-few-minutes-so-I-can-ask-some-questions' mode.

She cleared her throat, but before she could launch herself Stacy's face cleared and she smiled.

"Oh, *hi*." She pulled the door open wide. "Come on in—I guess it is quitting time, isn't it? I'm sorry—I get so engrossed in my stuff that I lose contact." She zipped back into the workroom for a moment to turn down the stereo. The room looked as if a fabric bomb had exploded inside it, but Alison was less interested in that than the philosophical question posed by Stacy's music—could a Dead Head ever find happiness with a Patsy Cline fan?

"Did you bring me a present?" Stacy asked like a three-year-old, looking at Alison's canvas King Sooper's bag.

Alison ceased her musing, which had gone beyond the music question and onto that age old question of why dykes thought about everyone in terms of Long Term Relationships instead of dating.

"What I actually was thinking of doing was making dinner, if you're not busy?"

"Great! Real cooking! But I do have a gig at nine, so that time frame would have to be okay with you."

A gig. Oh. Alison opened her mouth with a hundred questions, and then snapped it shut again, not sure if she wanted to hear any of the answers. She contented herself with nodding.

Stacy was not the kind of woman who could be pressed into even the simplest prep-cooking. Alison didn't even try to hand her the potato peeler she'd brought from her own house. That was fine—what she really wanted while she was cooking was to be entertained, and Stacy was perfect at this job. While Alison scrubbed and grated, she talked about soccer and quilts and the fact that Lynda J. Barry was having a play produced. She did not talk about the murders.

It was not until the food was on the table that Alison had the chance to ask her own question. "Were both those women who were killed your clients? Is that why you knew them?" Dead silence. Touchy subject, obviously, and made worse by the fact that Alison had never before tried to get information from someone who was not only reluctant to give it, but also a potential girlfriend. She let the question lie between them and pretended great interest in her cheese sauce.

It took Stacy several minutes to answer. Or, rather, to explain why she couldn't answer. "I can't tell you that, Alison. I promise women total confidentiality, and I wouldn't have a clientele if I wasn't known for keeping it. Telling you would be like breaking a trust."

Alison was not ready to give up this easily.

"The women are dead, Stace," she said bluntly. "They don't care about their reputations anymore."

"Right, and as soon as you're dead you want your private stuff in the newspapers, is that it? Doesn't matter to you anymore, so who cares about your family or your girlfriend? Sorry, but that one just doesn't cut it."

This one was hard to argue with, as Alison actually sympathized. Yet, it was important that she find as many links as possible between the two women, for if they could discover why the murderer was choosing these specific women they would be that much closer to reeling him—or her—in. She tried a different approach.

"Stacy," she said, "I'm the police. This isn't like spilling something to your friends over coffee. We're the good guys and there have been two murders, remember?" For a moment Alison thought that she had persuaded her, but only for a moment.

"That doesn't matter. It's like being a journalist or a priest—it's not suddenly okay to spill a confidence just because the cops get called in. Particularly," she hesitated a moment, "when you're not even official."

"All the more reason to tell me before someone 'official' shows up at your door! You know why I'm even taking an interest in this case—culturally I have an advantage over the men assigned. They don't know anything about dykes or the way they live. I do. I can also be a buffer, as protective of *all of us* as possible. I believe I can be the one to find out what's going on a lot better than the on-duty detectives who are going to come around eventually."

Stacy looked off into space and played with her earring. Alison knew that further pressuring was not going to make her talk. Nothing made a witness hostile more quickly than feeling that her ethics were not respected. And to be truthful, it wasn't as if Alison really needed this bit of information any more. Of course they had both been clients. Why else had Tamara given a false name? Where else would Stacy have met Melanie, who had been weaned away from the lesbian community and socialized only with straight people?

But she wanted to hear Stacy say the words. She wanted Stacy to confide in her, because she knew from experience that once Stacy made that first confidence the next would come easier. And somehow she was sure that she would eventually need more information from this source.

So how could she get her to tell freely? She had snooped just a little that night she had come home with her, glancing at the books and magazines and the clothes hanging in the open closet. What had these things told her about the woman?

She got up to scrape her plate and glanced around the kitchen. It was in worse shape than it had been the day before. She wondered if Stacy just waited until there was mountain of dishes and then did a marathon washing, or if she just continued to do one fork, one plate, one mug at a time. On the kitchen table, next to Stacy's elbow, was the plate off of which she had obviously eaten her last meal, and beside it was a paperback mystery, face down.

Mysteries. Maybe that was it. Could she be lured into giving information by the promise of a real live mystery?

Alison started to run some water into the sink. "I talked to Krista Jenkins today," she said casually.

"Who's that?" Stacy asked in a voice which might have been convincing had Alison not seen her stiffen. She knew the name, all right. She and Melanie must have chatted a little before getting down to business.

"And I talked to a woman named Becky over at the Regency Arms." Stacy said nothing, but Alison could tell that she recognized either the name of the woman or the building. She said nothing more for a moment. This was where she would find out if Stacy was going to play.

Stacy licked her lips. "So, what did they have to say?"

"Actually, they both had a lot—" Alison started eagerly, then stopped abruptly. She laughed at herself. "I forgot you weren't Rob there for minute. I'm going to have to call him."

"So tell me, instead."

She turned and faced Stacy, her face earnest. "Well, I would like to. But, you know, I can't act on this by myself. The best I can do is collect information and give it to the detective, and hopefully explain the particularly lesbian nuances. But lots of times we withhold as much information about details from the public as possible. Knowledge of details that haven't been in the media are one way to sort out who knows something and who's nuts."

"Well, I'm not planning on phoning in a confession," said Stacy impatiently, "and I won't tell anyone else. My lips are sealed."

Alison looked at her considering. "I sure missed Robert today," she said again. "He is such a good sounding board." She paused a moment. "I guess I better not, though." Come on, Stacy, you show me yours and I'll show you mine.

"Well—" Stacy stood abruptly and looked at a Nature Company poster as if she had never noticed it before. "I suppose you're right. The important thing is catching the killer. I would *never* say anything about a live client, but maybe you are our best bet. But I'm not talking to the real police—get that straight!"

"Okay," said Alison solemnly, thinking that she had been watching too many police shows, "just between you and me."

"They were both clients," said Stacy shortly. "Now tell me what these other women said."

Now the point had changed. It was no longer Alison's goal to force information out of Stacy, or even to get her to confide. Now what Alison wanted to know was what it was that Stacy wanted so badly to find out.

"Becky was Tamara's neighbor. She lived next door. She's a mail carrier. I caught her on her break." She dropped each sentence separately, with a little

55

pause between. Stacy would soon be chafing with impatience and might prompt her.

"She didn't know Tamara very well. She saw some of the women she brought home. She liked femme women, and Becky thought that she met them at the Rubyfruit. Her latest scar wasn't like the others—it had been done badly. Incidently, what do you know about scarification?"

"I didn't do that hack job on her, if that's what you're asking. I don't do blood sports."

"Hmm. She worked at a bank." Alison was surprised that, listed, the information gleaned from Becky was so short. She had the feeling, however, that it was not Tamara in whom Stacy was interested.

"Krista Jenkins says that Melanie was not a lesbian."

She expected some surprise or indignation, but Stacy said rather smugly, "I knew that."

"Oh, I didn't realize that you talked."

"Fuck you."

"Well, I suppose that Krista also denied that Melanie was into kink? I didn't ask."

"Yeah, I think that was quite a little secret between them."

"My friend Michelle was a friend of Melanie's." She startled herself by inserting this dated tidbit and was gratified to notice Stacy's face change for a moment. For just a few seconds she looked startled, or possibly anxious. Alison had been right. There *was* something about Melanie that was worrying Stacy. "Melanie supposedly was—"

"I've got to change clothes," Stacy interrupted. "I don't want to have to rush." She raised her arms over her head and stretched slowly, sensuously. Alison's eyes were riveted on her as she crossed over to the playroom.

"Keep talking," she said, as she pulled back the bolt on the door. "I can still hear you.

Alison's mouth went completely dry and for the life of her she could not remember one other thing that the woman had told her in the restaurant. Like a string of firecrackers the fantasies exploded inside, each overlapping the one before. Stacy, in her chic leather jacket, parting Alison's shirt and pulling on her nipples...her own mouth upon Stacy's, one hand wrapped in her hair...herself pressed against the wall while Stacy held her wrists above her head...

"Where did Krista think Melanie was that night?" Stacy prompted. She stood in the doorway now, wearing a royal-purple silk tuxedo shirt that came down and covered her thighs. And nothing else. "What did Krista say?" she asked again, slipping in onyx cufflinks. Her voice was innocent, but there was a gleam in her eye that told Alison she had known all along she was being played.

Alison tried to regain some composure by turning away, as if the stove were suddenly very interesting.

"Krista said Melanie went to a therapist," she said to the right front burner. "But I don't think that's true." Rattled, she had blurted out more than she meant to. But it didn't really matter. Doubtless the therapist line had probably covered some sessions with Stacy. But on the day of Melanie's death, Stacy had been first at soccer and then at the bar. Melanie must have been using it as an all-purpose excuse. Alison cut her eyes sideways and watched without comment as Stacy slipped on a pair of tight leather pants and then tossed her curls back. God, she wanted to hold this woman!

"Well," Stacy said, "Look, come over and work here tomorrow morning, if you want, please?—I've got company coming now. Hate to hustle you, but...."

And that was how Alison found herself outside, having told everything that she knew and having gotten nothing in return.

* * *

"Knock-knock!" A male voice trilled from beyond the front door of Stacy's apartment at precisely ten am. The sleigh bells that she had hanging on the back of the door jingled.

Alison looked up from Stacey's worktable vaguely. Oh, dammit, Stacy *had* mentioned someone was coming by, but Alison had been too engrossed in experimenting with Stacy's rotary cutter.

"Honey!" called the man who pushed the door open and then, "Oh!" He brought his hand up daintily to a mouth that had formed a perfect moue of embarrassment. "You're not the big girl." He startled Alison by suddenly swooping away and gathering an arm load of dirty mugs and plates. He gave a little shriek as he took them into the kitchen. "Oh! She's been cooking! She's sick, isn't she? Tell me the truth—she's in the hospital—that's why she's not here, isn't it?"

"She's at the—" tried Alison.

But the man stuck his head back out of the kitchen interrupting. "Actually," he said contemplatively, "there might be one other explanation for the state of this kitchen." He walked back towards Alison with his chin in his hand. "Yes. Liz said that she was dating again." He walked around Alison, looking her up and down. "I must have been out of my mind to think for a minute that Stacy created that mess herself. Why, there are three bowls and a frying pan in there. I didn't even know that Stacy *owned* a frying pan."

57

"Neither did she. It was in the bathroom. I'm Alison." She stuck out a hand.

"And I'm Lawrence. I'm the cleaning lady." Suddenly brisk, he dropped her hand. "Well, I must get busy. Otherwise I'll be here all day, and even if I don't have better things to do yet, I certainly hope to by this afternoon." He winked at her and flew back into the kitchen.

Alison followed, pushing back Stacy's chair with her foot because twice already this morning she had tried to pick it up by the back, and both times it had come apart. Perhaps this man was a gift from the goddess—a treasure trove of information dropped out of the blue with only the instructions: Chat me up.

"Let me give you a hand," she said. In the name of getting information she had helped fold newspapers, held fussing babies and pushed stuck cars. Dishes looked almost pleasant.

Lawrence had bundled himself into a bright pink apron that had *Kiss the Cook* printed on the front. Someone had taken a marker, crossed out *Kiss* and written in *Blow*. He was busy scrubbing the sink.

"Well, I won't say no to that. I have a special to fit in this afternoon— one of my regulars is having the girls over for bridge tonight and she wants me to give the place a once over."

Alison began scraping dishes. "How many regulars do you have?"

"Oh, it varies. Between five and seven a week. That way I don't spend my whole life picking up after dirty dykes, but it gives me a little pin money."

"Are all your customers dykes?"

"Oh, yes. I would not have it any other way. Faggots are too damn fussy—they always think that they could have done the job better themselves if they hadn't been out getting rimmed. And straights are so damn boring— they can sit and talk to you the whole time you're working, and you don't find out a thing about anyone you know. And children!" He shuddered. "I would rather clean up after an orgy where there were twenty people and whipped cream than two kids. At least after an orgy you *know* what *they've* had in *their* mouths! And you know how it is—if you work for one dyke, you work for them all. Especially if you're operating underground like Anastasia and me. Then it's all word of mouth. She refers for me, and I refer for her." He whisked the pile of dishes away from Alison and plunged them into the hot water. She felt as if she were moving in slow motion.

"Did you work for either Tamara Garrity or Melanie Donahue?"

He raised an eyebrow. "Oooh, cop stuff…Stacy mentioned you were a cop, so listen, I've been forewarned.Well, I can't help you. I didn't know either of them well. From what I hear—and this is just gossip, understand—

Melanie's girlfriend kept a pretty darn tight hold on the purse strings, and they were respectable roommates, anyway. A faggot cleaning their nice Aurora house just *wouldn't* have done."

"But you did know her?"

"Well, I'd met her, of course. I'm the one who recommended both of them."

"Huh?"

"Recommended! I mean, she has to get her business from *somewhere,* and she always sends *her* friends to the store. Now, understand, I usually wouldn't pass this on—I am the *soul* of discretion—but after all, the women *are* dead, aren't they? And it's not as if I know they ever did anything with her or even called her. I just recommended her and gave them her card."

Alison was totally lost. "Recommend to who for what?"

He gave her a somewhat pitying look. "You are an innocent, aren't you, girl? Recommend to Anastasia, of course. It happens all the time when I'm at work. You see, my boyfriend manages the Leatherworks, and I work there three nights a week. I would work more, but I get better money doing this, and this way he doesn't know about every single nickle and dime I'm making. I think it's so important to keep finances separate, don't you? But the store is a good place to meet interesting people—not that I ever do anything anymore—you know, safe sex and all...." He glanced over at Alison and mercifully got to the point. "Anyway, to make a long story... Every once in a while some woman will come in and ask if I know anyone who does sexual counseling—and of course I always give them Anastasia's card. I mean, people figure that you can ask the clerk in a sex shop anything, because he's paid not to laugh."

"They ask for some one who does what?"

"Sexual counseling. How else do you think she's going to advertise? But it's like I said, most of your customers are word of mouth through people you know. I just happened to remember those two women because I saw their pictures in the paper and thought, How awful! And they had always gone together in my mind before anyway, because they were both Dominique's old girls."

Dominique. Full circle back again to the night she had first met Stacy. She remembered the look of loathing that had passed from the one to the other in the bathroom of the Blue Ryder. Was this the reason?

"So these women used to be customers of Dominique, but they switched?"

Lawrence shrugged. "Dominique's been known to fuck up before—be slow with a safe word or something like that, and that just *isn't* done. I cer-

59

tainly don't recommend her. But she gets some business because she'll do some things that Anastasia won't—you know, blood sports and semi-public fucks and stuff like that."

"I know," said Alison, thinking back to the unpleasantness in the Blue Ryder. "I walked in on her."

"That was you?" Lawrence hooted, but Alison did not comment. Lawrence had hit on something that she needed to think about. She had never, even for one moment, considered that the killer might be a dyke. She had assumed that it was a dyke-hater on the loose—one of 'them' rather than one of 'us'. But what if the motive was not generic at all? What if it was as specific as paying back two women who had rejected you? Dominique probably had a lot of pride tied up in her work and it would have hurt more ways than financially to have lost two customers. And, if in paying them back, Dominique had seen the chance to hurt the woman who had stolen their business, that wouldn't have been a bad thing either, would it? Anastasia's clientele might abandon her completely if it got out that both victims had been clients of hers.

But *could* one dyke do that to another? Like Michelle she had come out to feminism at the same time she had come out to lesbianism, and because of that, her first impulse was a firm 'No!' They were all sisters suffering from the same oppression. They had gotten beyond that physical shit and could settle it with words and see it through with love.

It was a beautiful concept. Except that she had known lesbians who hated other lesbians, both specifically and collectively. She had seen love affairs that had gone bad and business relationships that had soured. She had witnessed fist fights at bars and softball games and had watched close friends become embittered. Hell, she had been in some of those very places herself. She couldn't ignore evidence just because she didn't want it to be a dyke.

The sleigh bells on the door jangled and Alison jumped guiltily. She didn't want Stacy to catch her pumping the help.

It was not Stacy, however, in the front workroom, but another man, bent over her worktable.

"Can I help you?"

"I don't know. Is this yours?" He gestured to the pieces she had laid out on the table. She hadn't recognized his back but his gravely voice clued her in before Mark turned his head.

"Yes," she said, fighting not to sound defensive and to keep from going into the whole spiel about how she was just an amateur and her work shouldn't be judged against Stacy's.

"Do you mind if I take a couple of pictures of it?"

"Why?" She could not keep the amazement out of her voice. "Stacy's stuff...."

"Yeah, she's good. But this is nice, too. The colors, the shapes...." He made an expansive gesture as he pulled the camera up to his face and Alison suddenly saw what he meant about the way that the blue triangles lay against the print.

"Can you pick up the scissors?" Mark asked, snapping. "Yeah, just sit down and cut out a piece. Oh, your hands are great. Quilter's hands—just like Stacy's." Abruptly he was done, and he wandered away from her and over to Stacy's work in process. Alison clipped one more corner, feeling a bit foolish.

"This is going well," said Mark. "I love almost everything she does. You know, I got my first break off a photo of her work."

"Really?" Why the hell was he here? She was puzzled by his at-home attitude.

"Oh, yeah. It was for a competition, a calender of contemporary quilters. She didn't get in, but one of the winners was local and she saw the photos and wanted me to do hers."

"Stacy must not have much luck with calenders," said Alison. Mark looked at her blankly. "You know...she didn't get in the leather calender, either." She had spoken without really thinking and regretted in immediately.

He stiffened visibly. "Well, I've got to go." His tone had turned from friendly to surly.

"Was that the nasty Mark?" Lawrence gauged his appearance directly to the slamming door.

"Yeah. Is he here a lot?" Alison tried to convey bland interest instead of the raging jealousy she felt.

Not successfully, for Lawrence, when he answered, sounded amused. "His mom lives upstairs," he said, "but in case you're concerned, Stacy doesn't do ac/dc. I think she knew him when he was a kid."

Well, that was interesting. But before Alison could ask a single question the bells jangled again.

This time it was Stacy. "Well, finally!" she said. "Everybody and their sister was at the fabric store. Don't leave the cutter unsheathed, Alison, I've seen some bad slices off them. And you—don't try to leave without cleaning out the refrigerator," she said to Lawrence. She bustled him into the other room. For now, at least, there was nothing more that Alison could learn from him.

Seven

'Homeless Cat Center' read the sign on the brick house. This was the place Jenny had said Dominique worked during the day. Twenty cats lounged in the outside run, watching Alison approach the front door.

"Hi." The staffer was a pleasant looking woman, maybe ten or fifteen years older than Alison. She was wearing a blue smock with black cats dancing across it over her gingham blouse. Her short, dark hair was fluffed up in a soft perm.

"Does—" began Alison, and then stopped herself short. Okay, Alison, you almost fell into the stereotype trap again, didn't you? Take away the smock and put on a leather vest and heavy chain, slick back the hair and there was the woman she had almost busted the other night. So what had she thought she was going to wear to work—full leather drag?

"Can I help you? Do you want to adopt a cat?" Friendly words were laced with frost.

Oh, shit, thought Alison, she recognizes me too. Well, just because she was a cop didn't mean she couldn't be a cat lover.

"Do you have any special requirements?" asked Dominique grimly. "Officer."

"What do you mean?"

"Well, you are a cop, aren't you? Like the same cop who was harassing me the other night, who got me eighty-sixed from the bar?" Dominique's voice was bitter.

"I meant, what do you mean, 'requirements'?" Alison was damned if she was going to argue with the woman. She would force her into some kind of civility by pretending she was a legitimate customer.

"Oh. Male or female, color, sex, age, breed, declawed?" Dominique answered grudgingly, shooing a black cat off a pile of paperwork.

"Why don't you show me around and give me some ideas?" suggested Alison. After a moment of hesitation Dominique stepped reluctantly out from behind the counter and beckoned Alison to follow. Tersely, she pointed and gave out information about the free roaming animals.

"She's very gentle. They're all neutered. He needs a single cat household.

Kitten room." She pointed to a screened-off enclosure. As if on cue, a trio of grey kittens appeared on the other side and, putting their front feet on the screen, began to cry in unison.

All detecting was momentarily forgotten. "Oh," said Alison, "can I go in?"

Dominique noded shortly, but as Alison knelt to pick up a kitten she said in an accusing voice, "I thought you wanted a cat. Kittens are easy to place—everybody wants a kitten."

"Really?"

"If they're socialized. Speaking of which...." Dominique crouched beside the one piece of furniture in the enclosure, a battered, overstuffed chair, and reached up underneath it. She pulled out a ginger colored, tabby kitten just a little older than the others. Frightened, he struggled, but she soothed him gently.

"There you are, sweet one," she murmured, "nobody is going to hurt you." The kitten gave one small purr. Then Alison took half a step close, and like a shot he was out of Dominique's arms, scrambling up over her face and head and to get back to his hiding place.

"Oh, I'm so sorry!" Well, that probably fucked any chance she'd had of cooperation.

Surprisingly, though, Dominique took the injuries in stride. "It happens all the time," she told Alison brusquely, after they left the enclosure and as she swabbed her face with peroxide. "Now, did you see anybody you were interested in?"

Oh, to hell with it, thought Alison. She was tired of bullshitting, and there was no sign that Dominique was going to let down her guard.

"I didn't come to look for a cat," she said. "I came to ask you some questions about the two women who were killed."

"Why ask me?" Dominique spoke stiffly, her fists clenched.

"You tell me. They were both clients of yours, weren't they?" Was Dominique really going to help her out? Or did she, like so many people, have something that she hoped to hide by seeming to cooperate?

"They both did some...counseling with me," Dominique said tersely. Alison wondered for a moment if this were a euphemism used by the s/m community world-wide or if it were just a flash word in town. "But that was a long time ago."

"How long?"

Dominique shrugged.

"A month? A year? Six months?"

"A couple of months." Dominique busied herself with the first-aid kit and did not look at Alison.

"Why did they leave you?"

"We decided—mutually—to terminate our professional relationship." Dominique's voice was in careful control, and the phrase slid out as if it had been used many times before.

"Yeah, well, that's not what I heard," said Alison rudely. Her instincts told her that Dominique might be the kind who would tell her the most if she could be goaded into a rage.

"Well, f...." Visibly, Dominique controlled herself. "Well, that's what happened. Why do you care about this, anyway?"

"It just seems interesting that both of the women were customers of yours. Dissatisfied customers. Very interesting." This offensive role was one of Alison's least favorite. For a moment she considered abandoning it and just trying to appeal to the woman's better nature. Or would she be appealing to the conscience of a woman who had killed twice?

"What's that supposed to mean?" Dominique's voice was losing its thin coating of civility.

Alison shrugged. "Just that when we look for suspects we look for something that might link the victims. We look for someone who might have had a problem with both of them."

"And this is supposed to be it?" Dominique's voice was shaking, but still controlled. "Boy, you guys must really be pulling at straws if this is all you've come up with. I suppose you've never changed your doctor or lawyer or cleaning lady, have you? Do you think any one of them would come after you with a knife? Do you think they'd even miss any sleep? Get real! A business relationship isn't a love affair! Find their ex-lovers if you're looking for someone who's that pissed off!"

Her outrage seemed genuine, or was she just a good actress? Was she just remembering how angry she had been when the women had terminated her?

"Why did they dump you?"

"Who the fuck knows? Maybe they didn't like my outfit, maybe they were the kind that needs to have somebody new once in a while. Maybe their 'problems' had all been worked out." She was still angry, but the rage was no longer building.

Alison changed tack abruptly. "Do you know if they went to anyone else when they left you?" She was curious to see if Dominique knew or would admit to this information.

Something like a smile crept over Dominique's angry face. "Yes. Anastasia, Stacy Ross, picked them up. Both of them. So there's your link. Why don't you go question her? Maybe she's gotten into something really

64

kinky…maybe she's doing death scenes now. Go talk to her!"

"We've been in contact," said Alison in a voice that she hoped was matter-of-fact and nothing more. "Where were you Friday night?"

"What?"

"The night Tamara Garrity was killed."

"None of your—" Dominique stopped abruptly and considered. Aha, thought Alison, someplace that we can check easily. Come on, give it to me.

"I was at the Rubyfruit."

"The bar where Tamara was killed?"

"Right. And so was every other leather dyke in town." She laughed a rather pleased laugh.

"Why?"

"Because they were hosting the Ms. Colorado Leather contest. The prelims. You know, the girl from our state goes to the nationals." Dominique seemed prepared to be scornful of her ignorance.

Hmm, she didn't know, but she could ask Stacy or Liz, and save herself from being laughed at. She started to ask about the bad cutting on Tamara's back that Becky had described, but the door bell rang, and from the front room someone called, "Is anyone here?" With an air of relief Dominique moved to go. Alison caught her sleeve.

"Look," she said quickly, "I know you're not being totally straight with me. I know you don't like me, either. But think about it this way. I'm a dyke. You're a dyke. I'm not going to protect a murderer but I don't think that you're the one." She lied without a qualm. "I'll bend over backwards to make sure you don't get harassed for things that have nothing to do with the case, or for just plain being a dyke. Maybe the next cop who comes by won't feel that way. There's a lot of guys in uniform who don't like queers." She felt a little guilty about trying to shake up the woman this way. Even if it were true, she hated to build onto that crooked and ignorant cop image, ready to arrest and punish the person of whom one did not approve. Maybe she was just messing up the chances of the legitimate detectives, good old Jorgenson and Jones, who would surely be visiting within the next couple of days. No, Dominique was not the type who would open up to a straight man. If she told anyone, it would be Alison.

She opened her wallet and took out another of the business cards her father had given her the Christmas before. Briefly, she thought that he would be pleased if he knew that one was really being given for business, instead of just to someone met at a party. Then she thought it was probably the second that would be thrown away in as many days. Dominique did not reach for it, so she laid it on the counter.

"Just remember," she said. "Call me if you change your mind."

* * *

When Alison returned home she found Michelle sitting on her front steps reading the local gay rag. She lifted her head and smiled as Alison approached. Alison could see that she had progressed from the 'I'm-pissed-because-you're-a-p.i.-idiot' stage to the 'Let's-talk-this-over-stage,' though the process was by no means irreversible. Fine, talking to Michelle had always been a good way to put her thoughts in order.

"Where have you been?"

Alison dropped down beside her. "Out pretending that I'm a detective."

"Have you found out anything at all?"

"One thing. But it seems kind of thin by itself. They both went to the same counselor. They both dropped her and started seeing another woman. But it could be coincidence. You know, the community is small, a lot of us tend to see the same people and go to the same events without being connected in any other way." Now that she was home, what Dominique had said seemed to make sense. She herself had changed dentists last year, and she wasn't always looking over her shoulder expecting him to leap out in revenge.

"Well, did either counselor keep any kind of notes? Anything that told what they talked about? Could it have been something they both knew or had seen?"

Oh, shit, she'd backed herself into a corner by trying to be discrete. "Um, I don't think so. I mean, they weren't that kind...."

Michelle looked at her with pursed lips. "Yeah, that's what I thought about 'counselors'. Don't try to bullshit me. I knew Melanie, remember?"

"I wasn't trying to bullshit you. I was just trying...." What she had been trying to do was avoid a lecture. She changed the subject. "I thought Melanie was really closeted."

"She didn't used to be. I mean, she was always discreet about her specific sex life. But other than that she was just like the rest of us: 'Hi, I'm a young dyke, fuck you if you don't like it, stranger.' And it wasn't hard to figure out what she liked, in hindsight, anyway. The women she was seeing might have been low-key themselves back then, but a couple of them have become rather infamous around town since. In fact, here's a photo of one."

She picked up the paper and pointed to a photograph on the front page of a lesbian newspaper which showed several women in leather standing in front of a row of motorcycles.

"What's this a picture of?"

Michelle scanned the article. "Blah-blah-blah, blah-blah-blah, at the

Rubyfruit...blah...."

"Hey," Alison snatched the paper away from her. "This is the local Ms. Leather Colorado contest, isn't it?"

"So?"

"This was the night and the place of the first murder."

"And the murderer is going to be in the picture. Right, Delafield."

Alison lowered the paper. "Thank you for your support. No, you're right. Too much to hope for." She jerked the paper back up to her face. "But wait a minute—what's this in the background?"

Michelle, who had been resisting glasses, squinted. "Someone with a sign?"

"Yeah. A picketer. And look, by this woman's foot, a leaflet. I've seen one of those fuckers before." She put the paper down. "Are you busy?" she asked, "or would you like to play detective with me?"

* * *

In the end it was Janka whom they sent in to see the Crusaders. Not just because, as even Michelle herself admitted, she was less likely to get excited and blow her cover. There was also her 'begging for money' outfit in her favor, a grey suit she wore only to the bank and to see her father. She pointed out the finer points of the ensemble to them before they got into the car.

"Grey pumps," she said, lifting one foot. "Matching purse."

"Take off your labrys and your earcuff," advised Michelle. Hastily Janka stored them in the purse which was empty except for the pamphlet Alison had picked up at the bar.

"What's your name?" Alison asked nervously as she pulled away from the curb. "Are you sure they're open?"

"They said they were open when I called," said Michelle. "Jesus, how many times do I have to tell you? They're not going to close in the middle of the day when they have a customer coming."

"My name is Norma White." Janka spoke nasally. In her own voice she asked, "Are you sure they'd be clued in to my real name? Surely there are straight girls named Janka Weaversong? Okay, okay, Norma it is, and I live in Wheatridge. I just found out the awful and ugly truth about my baby sister. She left her husband—such a good man!—and it's even worse because there are two children involved. I'm sure it's just a phase, in fact I'm absolutely sure that she would snap right out of it if I could just get her away from the wicked slut she's been seeing."

"Don't say slut," Alison said. "In fact, if you can avoid it, don't say lesbian or gay. Stick to homosexual, and hem and haw a lot. Be horrified and

67

totally embarrassed that you've been driven to this."

"Isn't this a little far-fetched?" asked Michelle. "I mean, do you really think that they're going to say, 'Hey, don't worry, we can knock that dyke right off, no problem?'"

"No, I don't think that, Michelle. But it would be real interesting to find out what those people are doing. Like, are they involved in kidnapping or harassing or reprogramming? And exactly how devoted are their followers? Remember when Anita Bryant went on the rampage, and every so often a faggot would turn up beaten up with a sign on him that said, 'This is for you, Anita?' That's pretty damn close to killing. You know we've been murdered in the name of religion before. Don't say dyke."

"Yeah, yeah," muttered Michelle, "cops and robbers."

"Oh, you're just pissed because the pumps wouldn't fit you," said Janka.

The Crusaders' organization was located in a little store front that was across the street from both a bakery and a laundromat, so after parking around the corner and giving Janka a five minute head start, they slipped first into one and then the other.

"The perfect stake-out," said Michelle, cramming a maple bar into her mouth. "I just wish I'd brought a load of towels." Alison, sitting on an orange plastic chair that was bolted to the floor, glanced nervously over her shoulder. "So, Alison, what are we looking for, anyway? You think that they're going to expose old Norma, conk her on the head and carry her out feet first in a rolled up carpet?"

"I just think we should keep an eye out," said Alison vaguely. She didn't really feel as if Stacy's story were hers to share. "Get away from the window."

"Hey, they don't know me," answered Michelle, sucking cream filling from her fingers. "For all they know I'm just another dyke spinning a load of khaki pants and flannel shirts. Grab a paper. It'll calm you down."

Alison began to comply, but suddenly Michelle grabbed her by the shoulder. "Oh, I can't believe this…this is just too fucking weird!" She pressed her face up against the window and then jerked back. "Jesus, I'm glad she didn't look! This is so bizarre!"

"What?"

"No, no, don't look. For all I know you may know her, too. Okay, face me like you're talking to me and look over my shoulder. See the woman who's standing in front of the building talking to the guy in the suit?"

"That's one of the guys who grabbed me the other night!" She gaped, recognizing Red Tie.

"Okay, don't get freaked. Even if he sees you that doesn't mean he's going to clue into anything other than the fact that you don't have a washer and dryer. Look at the woman. I know that woman. That woman used to be a dyke. A big time stomping dyke! That woman published poetry that contained phrases like 'Castrate now'."

"Well, maybe she's just dressed up to scam them, too."

"Right, and she grew her hair out for the occasion and had a professional put on her makeup. No, I'm talking stomping and screaming with a mohawk and tattoos." Michelle looked momentarily startled. "Boy, I wonder what she did about those tattoos. No, I heard that this happened, at least the going straight part. I heard she got into this self-help seminar and fell in love with the mediator and got fucking married! She left a friend of mine! And she was calling her lesbianism an unfortunate phase!"

"Does she know Janka?"

"Oh, I don't think so. This was quite a while back." Michelle pressed her face back up to the window. "This is too good to be true. Alison, I can't pass this up. Who knows when I'm going to get another chance like this? Don't worry, she'll never connect." Before Alison was quite able to understand what she was talking about Michelle had slipped out the door. Alison heard her call, "Hi, Sharon!" in a loud voice as she strode across the street.

There was nothing Alison could do to call her back without blowing her own cover. A woman carrying a huge basket of dirty laundry and trailing two small children came in. When the door swung open Alison strained to hear the women across the street, but all that came through was an occasional high shriek from Michelle. Michelle was playing Michelle, and in very high form; words were not really needed to understand the scene. Michelle greeted Sharon and tried to give her a hug that was stiff-armed. Feigning ignorance, Michelle asked how she was doing and why she hadn't seen her in ages. Sharon informed her of her new state of enlightenment and introduced the man. Michelle expressed astonishment and then laughed so hard and long that she had to hold her sides. She ignored Red Tie totally. Sharon looked sour. Michelle, pulling herself together, mimed a mohawk haircut and something else. What was it? Oh, she was asking about the tattoos. Sharon, deciding that there had been enough of this nonsense, attempted to take charge and tried to urge a pamphlet onto Michelle. Michelle glanced through it and laughed again. Red Tie attempted to enter in. Michelle ignored him and continued to address Sharon. Sharon deferred to Red Tie. Michelle was getting angry and starting to shout. Uh-oh, here came Janka out the front door, talking to a man who looked familiar. Oh, it was the infamous Malcolm! Janka did a double-take when she saw Michelle on the sidewalk screaming at two of the brethren, but she covered it by clutching Malcolm's arm for support. Oh, no, there was one of them right in front of the den of the righteous! Janka was a good actress, thought Alison. She should start taking her around as a mouthpiece. For a moment she forgot all about the current drama and imagined the perfect detective squad. She would have Lawrence for extracting confidences, Robert for intimidating people and Janka for undercover work. Michelle could come along to help intimidate, jump-start cars and pick locks.

Oops, while she had been distracted the two men had moved in on Michelle, doing a squeeze play on her just as they had done on Alison in front of the bar. Malcolm, although he appeared to still be talking in a calm, persuasive voice, had reached out and put a hand on Michelle's arm. Possibly he intended this to be more calming than intimidating, but of course it was having the opposite effect on Michelle, who began whipping her arm up and down in an attempt to make him let go. So, great, what should she do now? Janka was looking slightly apprehensive, but made no move to intervene. She stood next to Sharon, shaking her head.

"Hey! Hey, you fuckhead! I'm going to call the police! I'm calling the cops right now if you don't stop harassing that woman!" The woman with the children had rushed to the door and flung it open. Her shout brought a small crowd from the bakery. "You self-righteous bastards! Did you ever hear about everybody having the same rights in this country? They'd persecute you in Russia, did you know that? I'm calling the cops!"

Malcolm decided that retreat was strategic. He dropped Michelle's arm and gestured to the other man. Between them they swept up the women and disappeared into the building.

The laundromat woman pulled her head in the door and glared at Alison, daring her to say anything.

"Um, would they really persecute them in Russia now?"

The woman laughed. "Well, it sounded good."

"Do they have that kind of scene often?"

"Not exactly that same one, but someone's always dragging in some poor, browbeaten man or some teenager who's crying. It makes me sick."

Oh, there was Janka coming out again, escorted by both men. All three looked up and down the street, checking to see if the wicked homo was gone. Oh dear, problem, they wanted to walk Janka to her car. Okay, she had it covered. She pointed to the cafe on the corner and her watch; her husband was going to meet her. Thank you very much. You've been helpful, I'll be calling back soon. She clicked off in her pumps and after a moment the men went back inside.

* * *

"I can't believe the nerve of that woman!" raved Michelle, throwing herself down into one of Alison's kitchen chairs.

70

"Time out," Alison said. Michelle had dominated the ride home, and she was sick of it. "Janka's turn. She was supposed to be the one doing undercover."

"Yes, honey," Janka inserted, "what were you doing out there?"

"She was pretending she was Kate-fucking-Delafield," crabbed Alison. It had been too long since she had eaten.

"And you're the only one who gets to play that part, right?" Michelle was in high spirits, so rarely did she get to satisfy her need for drama in such a satisfactory manner. She slipped out of her chair and went to the refrigerator, knowing from years of experience when Alison was about to hit the blood sugar bottom.

"I found out that they're willing to grab people," she yelled over her shoulder.

"We knew that. Let Janka talk."

"Oh, god, it's good not to be Norma anymore. Well, they were very sympathetic. I whined and cried and moaned about how awful the whole thing was and they said, 'Yes-yes, there-there, they were sure she was a nice girl who had just been lead astray and they were sure they could help, particularly since the relationship had just started, and was I sure it was the first one?' And I said 'Of course!' and that it was just because she had been so stressed out over these problems with her husband, and he was a very good man, but possibly not as sensitive as he could be....'"

"Ha!" Michelle laughed. She set a plate of crackers and fruit on the table, picked up a slice of apple and stuck it into Alison's mouth. "You said he was a lousy fuck, right?"

"Hey, I had those people convinced that I had never said the word 'fuck' in my life. I only hinted—they brought up the marital bed. But they said yes, it sounded like I was right, and that it would help if my sister could be separated from the influence of this other woman, and they were sure it would help if she would come to one of their support groups."

"More about the 'support groups' later," said Alison. "Even I got a little dirt from one of the neighbors, that woman who yelled at them from the laundromat."

"So I said that I was sure she wouldn't come and I certainly couldn't force her by myself, she's being very hostile to me...."

"What about the imaginary husbands?" asked Alison.

"They're imaginary faggots," piped Michelle cheerfully, pouring everyone a glass of milk.

"Hers is too stressed out to deal with anything at all. In fact, he can't even take care of their kids, so they're with her and that other woman, which is

71

another thing worrying me. My husband is older than me and has arthritis. No help there."

"Oh, you're good," said Alison admiringly, biting into a cracker. "Where'd you learn to lie like that?"

Michelle leaned forward anxiously to hear the answer, as if afraid that it would involve deception over past lovers.

"This isn't lying, this is theater," Janka said. "I became Norma White. When I got out of there I started looking for my station wagon. But, to get back to the story, they said I should just ask her to go, and if that didn't work, perhaps they could get someone to help persuade her. That was the word they used, although I got the feeling it might have been synonymous for strong-arm. Or if I could get her to come to my house they could arrange to have a meeting there. You know, like I could lock all the doors and they could shout at her and pray for her and show her flip charts. Or so I assume. Then I fussed around some more and said oh, if I could only take her somewhere for a little vacation, I could pay for it and it would do her so much good, after all, we had the same upbringing and all she needed was to clear her mind and remember the values we had been taught, but I knew that she'd never come with me. Now, they didn't bite on that one...."

"Well, I hardly expected them to pull out a gunny sack and chloroform the first time you talked to them," said Alison, more mellow now that she had eaten.

"...but there were some looks. They have definitely done some dirty work."

"Did anybody seem to be nuts?"

"Oh, hell, they were all nuts. Why the fuck else would you devote your life—and they were all volunteers—to making sure that other people were miserable?"

"Oh, god, people do that all the time. I mean more than Moral Majority nutty. Like crazy—fervent enough to kill a queer for Christ."

"Sharon told me that I was going to burn in Hell if I didn't change my evil ways," Michelle volunteered, finishing off the last of the crackers. "She also told me I should pluck out my eye or cut off my hand before allowing it to offend the Lord."

"What did you say?"

"I asked if she'd had a clitorectomy. That's when the shouting started. Apparently we no longer use those words in front of a woman whose main verb and adjective used to be variations of 'fuck.'"

"Speaking of which, I can't wait to get out of these fucking heels." Janka tipped back her chair and stretched. She had put her labrys necklace back on.

"Yeah, and I've got to get to work," said Michelle, "I've got a commission that's due on Saturday. Say," she said, as she and Janka got up, "isn't that your phone ringing?"

* * *

Finding the address that the woman had given her over the phone was not hard. Unlike Tamara's highrise, this house was like Alison's, a Victorian, but had not been cut up into apartments. The yard was small and beautifully kept, the kind that stable married people keep. And as far as Alison could tell, a most married couple lived here.

"Oh, yes, come in...you're the policewoman. My name is Beth Caldwell." The woman who answered the door was somewhat older than her absent partner, Dominique, and her voice had a breathless, uncertain quality to it, as if she were not quite sure she were saying the right thing. She was dressed in a tan skirt and a cream-colored blouse. Her grey hair was brushed back from her face in soft wings.

"Please sit down." Beth indicated a comfortable couch and a pair of rattan chairs. Before sitting down Alison glanced around the room. It was lined with old-fashioned display cabinets, the kind her grandmother kept china and silver in. These housed a collection of shells, feathers, bones and fetishes. Alison put out a hand to finger a clay pot that looked like a tiny horse lying on its side, then jerked it back guiltily.

Beth laughed. "Oh, go ahead and touch it. I have everything fragile locked up. This is the hands-on exhibit. We got that in Bolivia a couple of years ago. Of course, it's only a copy." She sat down across from Alison. Coffee and cookies were laid out between them, but she made no effort to touch anything. "Two detectives came to see Denise yesterday," she said abruptly.

"Denise? Ah...did they say why?"

"They found her business card on one of the...," Beth gulped, "...dead women. But why did they come? She told me that you already talked to her."

Alison hesitated a moment before answering. "We're going to have to keep on coming back," she said finally, a true though somewhat evasive answer. "Until Dominique...Denise...tells us the truth."

"She did tell you the truth!" The woman was becoming more agitated. Alison looked away. The trick with this kind was to handle her gently, not excite her to the point where she wouldn't speak. Playing it right was crucial; this woman would tell her everything she knew if she thought it would protect her girlfriend. Carefully, not pressuring, Alison looked down at the coffee table. It, too, was rattan, with a piece of glass over the top. Under the glass were a number of photographs, mostly of Dominique, who photographed well.

73

"We're going to have to keep coming back," she repeated, without looking up, "and eventually we'll find out what it is that she's keeping from us. And then, even if it's the most innocent thing in the world, even if she was just keeping quiet because she was embarrassed or because she didn't think it was important, we'll have to look into it as thoroughly as if it were a motive, because we'll wonder why she didn't tell us to begin with."

"Oh." Beth looked across the room. Alison looked at the photos. There were several of Dominique holding a fishing pole and wearing a squashed, cloth cap. Her face was sunburnt.

"She didn't do anything wrong!" Beth burst out. "She didn't kill anyone! She couldn't have! She couldn't harm anyone like that! Oh, I know that you think differently because of her job, but it isn't like that. That's like saying...like saying that if you shot someone in the line of duty—have you shot anyone?" Alison nodded. "Well, it's just as foolish to come after Denise thinking that she hurt someone as it would be for the police to come after you every time there was a shooting. Do you see the difference?"

Alison nodded. "Well, everything is reported and reviewed, but yeah, I understand...what consensual is. I don't know if these other guys are going to understand, though."

"Then you have to explain it to them! That she is very gentle, that she would never harm anyone. Pain on a job, something a customer requests, that's playing. It's not like sneaking up behind someone with a knife."

"I see the difference," Alison repeated, "I have a friend in the same line of business." She said it in part to create confidence, but also because she was dying to toss this questioning to one side and ask instead: how do you stay with her and does it bother you, and are you into the scene yourself? For this was obviously the household of two people who had been together a long time.

Beth relaxed visibly. "Then you know." She sat smiling across at Alison as if everything were solved.

Alison hated to delude her. "But she still has to tell us everything. Even if she couldn't have done it. The detectives didn't say she was a suspect, did they? But she might know something, she might know something without even knowing she knows it, and if she would just tell us everything then we could sift through it. If she doesn't, we can't help but be suspicious she had something to hide."

"It's not that she has anything to hide...it's been a hard couple of months for Denise. For me too. If we hadn't been together for so long...if it hadn't been such a long time. But it has been hard for her. Her dad died, and there was a fire at the cat center. There were alarms...she and the other woman

74

saved everyone they could, but they couldn't get them all. She was burned, too, she was in pain. In a way I don't blame her...but it really only makes it worse and she knows it...."

Alison knew better than to cut her short, but she tried gently to guide her. "Why did the two women terminate her services?"

Beth looked at her in a helpless way. "She's been sober for ten years," she said, almost whispering. "This was her very first slip."

Oh. Click. Like a line of dominoes it started falling in place. Stacy's voice in her head saying, She started doing things like ignoring safewords and, honey, that just isn't done. And how Becky said that the last cut was more like a hack. Alison flashed back on the workshop she had furtively attended at the music festival. A woman, wearing nothing but a squash-blossom necklace and a pair of blue gym shorts, had lectured them about s/m safety, saying, "No drugs or alcohol during a scene. Never."

"She's dry now," Beth said hurriedly. "She's been going to AA two or three times a day even." Her voice was anxious, saying without words, 'please don't think she's bad, please don't think she's weak.' Alison tried to smile reassuringly, but she knew that 'dry' could only cover a few days at the very most, for she remembered smelling liquor on Dominique's breath in the Blue Ryder bathroom.

"So she started working drunk," she said slowly, "and it made her care-less—maybe even mean?" She glanced at Beth who gave a small nod. "And clients left her. The night of the leather contest—did she come home drunk?"

"I don't know. I was asleep."

"Did...."

The front door flew open.

"Beth, I'm home!" cried Dominique. No, thought Alison, Denise. She'd never thought of her by anything but her working name, but it didn't fit into this tidy, comforting house. Her head was bent over a bundle in her arms. "Did you—" She looked up and stopped suddenly. Alison, who did not know whether a smile or a severe scowl was more likely to keep from getting the stuffing beaten out of her, braced herself for being yelled at. But, "Ah, honey," said the butch dom, exactly like Ricky Ricardo, "I told you I would take care of this!"

"But you weren't," said Beth firmly.

"We were talking about the murders," said Alison cautiously.

"No shit! I thought you were over here selling Tupperware!"

"Denise," Beth warned as Dominique dropped down on the couch.

Alison decided that jumping in with quick questions was the best strat-egy. "The night of the contest. You said you were there. Was Tamara there?

75

Did you see her?"

"Oh, yeah, she was there." The top of the bundle, now on Denise's lap, had come undone. A small black head popped out. The kitten did not attempt to struggle free, but lay listless as Denise stroked him. "Everybody saw her. She was in the contest. Came really close to winning, too. She was a beautiful woman and loved being the center of attention. She was great on stage, and funny. She could handle remarks from the audience." Now that Denise had decided to speak she was full of information. Alison tried to sort it quickly. How did this description of Tamara Garrity fit in with the one her neighbor had given of the woman who was so private? Really, it wasn't such a hard picture to put together. It was no different from Stacy, who was all flash and glitter at the bar but who worked at home in a ratty old T-shirt, or Liz the lawyer/soccer player.

"There were demonstrators there, the Crusaders. Did you see them?" Alison had long learned from Robert that bouncing from one topic to another was a good ploy, startling people from their predictable line. Sure enough, Denise blinked and snapped her mouth shut over already formed words.

"Yeah, they were there when I came in, and when I went out."

"Did you talk to them?"

"Not talk, really. Yelled at them when we came in. They've been around a whole lot lately—it seems everywhere I've been. One guy got all fired up and preached a little."

"Did you talk to Tamara?"

"No." She hesitated and then said, "Look, I'm sure Beth has told you about the problems I've been having. Tamara and I didn't exactly part on the best of terms. I was pissed off. I called her at home once to have it out. I was very uncool." Which would explain why Tamara had given a false name to Stacy who couldn't track her if things went bad again. "Anyway, she avoided me like the plague. I saw her across the room. I was with friends, working a little on the side."

Lawrence had said that quick, sometimes semi-public tricks were Dominique's specialty. Alison bet that she'd done a hot trade that night, that is, with women who were wet from watching the show and couldn't wait.

"So you were in and out of the parking lot quite a bit?"

"Some," said Denise, glancing sideways at her. Alison thought of her using the bathroom at the Blue Ryder. She seemed to remember, from the one time she had been to the Rubyfruit, that the bathrooms were more private there, just one room which could be locked. That would be exciting, having Dominique in her leathers holding you with one hand against the door, thrusting up hard and deep, while on the other side someone shouted

76

for you to hurry. The fantasy changed, becoming not Dominique and some faceless woman, but Alison herself and Stacy. Alison crossed her legs, glad she had been questioning randomly, for she could not for the life of her remember where she had stopped.

"Uh, the man who preached. Did you hear what he said?"

"The regular stuff. 'Get thee behind me Satan,' and 'God loves the sinner but hates the sin' and did 'we want to burn in Hell just for a little pussy'...."

"Denise!"

"Sorry, baby, just condensing. I think he really said 'pleasures of the flesh.'"

"But you never talked to Tamara that night?"

"No," Denise answered, far too quickly.

"Never went outside with her?"

"No!" She was almost shouting now.

"Honey," Beth began, but Denise interrupted.

"I said no. How many times do I have to say it?" The kitten in her lap mewed weakly, and she picked him up. "Look at this little guy," she said to Beth. "He's so afraid of the other cats that I had to bring him home just to give him a break."

"Willy's not going to like that," warned Beth.

"I know. I'll try to keep him upstairs." She was being deliberately distracting. Obviously she had not yet told everything, otherwise why all the fuss about admitting that she was drunk and on bad terms with Tamara?

"Was Tamara there when you left?"

For the first time Denise hesitated. "Yeah, I think so. Yeah."

"When was that?"

"Well, I don't really know. It was late."

"Like how late? Was it closing? Was it before midnight?"

"I just said I didn't know! What, do you think that if you ask it again I'm going to remember all of a sudden?"

"Were the Crusaders still there when you left?"

"I didn't notice." She was sullen again.

So you were drunk, thought Alison, and the end of the evening isn't quite so clear as the beginning.

The kitten had gotten up the courage to do some tentative exploring. Cautiously, he climbed down onto the floor and sniffed Alison's foot.

There was a rustling sound. "Oh, no," said Denise. "It's Wild Willy." She grabbed for the kitten and missed. There was a terrible snarl followed by an earsplitting wail. The kitten shot under the couch. A huge grey cat, his ears flattened to his head, was advancing towards them, pulling himself by his front feet. His paralyzed back legs dragged behind him. He gave Beth a look that, more clearly than words, asked what she had been thinking of to allow a vile intruder into his house.

"Oh, Willy," Beth said, picking him up and cradling him against her chest, "you know that I'm always going to love you best. You're always going to be my boy." She scratched him under the chin and his threatening expression changed to one of pure, silly, kitty bliss.

"Put him in the kitchen," suggested Denise, down on her knees in front of the couch. Beth walked out murmuring kitty endearments. A moment later the sound of an electric can opener was heard.

"How did you get home from the bar?" Alison asked Denise.

"A friend dropped me off."

"And how did you get to the bar?"

Dominique laughed humorlessly. "Boy, you just don't miss a trick, do you? I drove my van. I had to go back and get it the next day. There, there, baby." Dominique had stroked the trembling kitten and was cradling him gently.

"I don't know if this is going to work." Beth returned from the kitchen without Willy. She looked anxiously at the kitten, who had hidden his head beneath Denise's arm.

"He's so afraid," said Denise. "He really needs to be in a one cat home where he'll get lots of attention." There was a moment of silence, and then, as one, both women turned towards Alison with smiles on their faces.

"I have a cat," she said, holding up her hands. "He is vile tempered and jealous. He would eat this one right up."

"But didn't you say you were looking for a friend?" pressed Denise.

"That was just...." Alison hated to say 'a ploy'—it sounded so sneaky. The kitten moved a forepaw feebly and she looked at him closely for the first time. He was all black, except for one tiny, tiny spot of white just to the side of his mouth. His eyes were round and blue. He looked absolutely exhausted and forlorn.

"I have a cat," she said again, and then she remembered the black cats that had stalked across Stacy's mugs and the half-empty bag of cat food beneath her sink.

"Well," she said, and Denise, who had doubtlessly done this type of thing many times before, took swift advantage. Without knowing quite how it happened Alison found herself holding the kitten in her arms. Tentatively she stroked the little forehead with one finger and was rewarded with a tiny purr. She looked up at Beth and Denise and they smiled sure, satisfied smiles. Alison sighed, knowing that she had been beaten.

Eight

"Oh, hi!" Stacy seemed happy to see her, but anxious as well. "You can only come in for a second. I've got someone coming soon." She was holding a Swiss army knife with the scissors extended. As she let Alison in, she clipped a cuticle and then put the knife away in the pocket of her blouse. Stacy was partially dressed for work, wearing the black skirt Alison had seen her in that first night, the night she had flashed back to so many times in her fantasies. This time her top was black, too, a funky denim blouse that fit tight at the waist and wrists, and was ornamented with silver zippers and studs. The top three snaps were undone and she appeared to be wearing nothing underneath.

"That's okay. I should have called first. I just wanted to bring you a present." Alison licked her lips, not entirely because she was nervous about the cat reception.

"Oh, I love presents!" Stacy squealed like a little girl. "Come in while I finish getting dressed." Alison followed her into the living room and sat with the swaddled kitten on her lap. Two black stockings and a pair of black spike heels were lying on the couch. Alison felt herself flush, but kept a carefully blank expression on her face as if she were just watching Michelle change out of her sweats. Stacy carefully rolled one of the sheer stockings and pulled it over her foot, her ankle, her thigh. Her skirt was too tailored to reach beneath. She had to push it up, bunch it around her waist, to reach for her garter. Black garters, attached to a black and red lace belt spanned Stacy's waist above black satin panties that were cut almost as high as a g-string. It was all Alison could do to keep her mouth still. She could not keep from staring. And she wasn't meant to. Stacy was teasing her, putting on a show for her, suggesting that she was just as wet beneath her satin panties as Alison was beneath her jeans. Every move right down to the way she strapped on her shoes was beautifully planned. Captivated, Alison sat to watch the other woman dress.

Stacy picked up a pair of earrings and sat down next to Alison. She handed them to her. They were heavy.

"Put these in for me," she said, looking into Alison's eyes, and Alison obeyed without thinking that the request was ridiculous. She brushed back the curls that clustered around Stacy's ears, trailing her fingers over her neck and even down her shoulders. Stacy turned her head for the second earring, sitting sideways, but Alison did not comply. Instead she reached across to clasp Stacy's arm above the elbow, and then to slowly run her hand up to her shoulder. She pushed away the open shirt and touched flesh. She pulled her towards her, one hand on the shoulder, the other on her jaw. As she brought Stacy's face close and began to brush her mouth with her lips she thought again of the fantasy she'd had at Dominique's, the thrill of the quick, illicit encounter. Only this time she imagined that it was she in control, that her thrusts were making Stacy moan aloud, were making Stacy's earring jingle as her head was pushed. She wanted to tease Stacy the way she had been teased, to run her hands and lips over her body with a thousand promises until she was begging for more, and then to push her away with a smile, saying I have to go now, didn't you say you had a client coming? And then she would go home and lie in bed with her hand between her legs, imagining Stacy with a soft whip, crooning, 'Tell me what you like,' and all the time wet and swollen herself, wanting.

The kitten that Alison had all but forgotten gave a small mew and Stacy jumped as if she had been shot. She leapt to the other end of the couch.

"What the fuck was that?"

Before Alison could answer the kitten struggled out of the blanket. He gave another teeny mew and took one step towards Stacy.

"Um, I said I had a present for you." Alison was anxious. Maybe she had overstepped. Perhaps the toys and cat food were being kept as a kind of shrine or were a sign of a wound not yet healed.

"My cat was black," whispered Stacy. "Did you know that?" Alison shook her head, though it had not been hard to guess. "He got cancer. I had him for eight years, ever since he was a tiny baby, littler than this one. I had to feed him with a bottle." Tears were running down her face, dripping off her chin and making dark spots on her shirt. Alison sat still, unsure of how to comfort her.

The kitten was watching Stacy with concern. He took a few steps forward and then retreated to Alison who was at least a known. Two steps forward, and this time he completed the length of the couch, going up onto Stacy's lap. He put his paws onto her chest, and then climbed high enough so that he could first sniff and then lick her face.

Stacy put one hand over him, just holding, not petting. She gave a watery smile, wiped her nose on the back of her expensive sleeve, and then looked horrified when she realized what she had done. Alison opened her mouth to speak, but was cut short by the doorbell.

"Oh, shit!" Stacy stood, placing the kitten gently on the couch. "Come on, I'll have to let you out the back way, gotta be cool about privacy." She grabbed Alison's hand and pulled her up. "Just a minute," she called.

"Wait, wait!" Alison spoke in a whisper, but dug her heels in. "I want to ask you something first."

"There isn't time for this, Alison!"

"It's quick, it's quick!" Stacy was hustling her through the string of rooms. "It's just something I want to know about Tamara Garrity."

"I'm not going to tell you anything else about her. It's confidential!" Stacy unbolted the door of the playroom.

"It's not that, it's just an opinion, a guess about what you think she would do in a certain situation." Alison was trying to eyeball as much of the room as she could without actually doing a 360. It was warmer than the rest of the house and lit by candles so that it was hard to take in details quickly.

"I have somebody waiting!"

"Let her wait. You're topping the scene." I know you have somebody waiting, Alison thought. That's why I'm asking, because right now you would tell me anything to get me out of here.

"All right, all right, but hurry." Stacy had not let go of Alison's arm and she was very aware of the firm way she held it. "What is it?"

"What kind of person was Tamara?" Alison asked. "She broke off with Dominique because she was drinking on the job." Stacy raised her eyebrows but said nothing. "After that, do you think that it would have been likely that she would have changed her mind and hired Dominique for a quick job at the bar the night of the contest?"

Stacy furrowed her brow. "Laura—Tamara—liked to be center of attention," she said slowly, echoing Dominique without knowing it. "She told me once that she even liked going to the dentist, and getting her hair cut because of that. And she liked things a certain way. She liked certain things done and said at just the right time. One-night stands frustrated her. She didn't get off unless she was with someone who knew just exactly what to do. And she liked sex with a scene. She had basically told me from day one that I was just a fill-in until she found someone who would fuck her, too. She was really excited by being in the contest, I could see that, and she wasn't there with anyone. Yeah, maybe if she'd wanted a quickie that night she would have gone to Dominique in spite of their history."

"Even if Dominique was drunk?"

"You haven't seen Dominique drunk. She's not a fall-down-and-puker. She holds a lot of liquor, and sometimes you can't even tell. And a car fuck's not like a private cutting scene—people all around if anything went wrong. Look, I really have to go now." She thrust Alison towards the door. It was set with a deadbolt, and there was no key in the lock.

"Dammit!" Stacy held up one finger and hustled back through the apartment. Alison seized the moment to stare at the exotic straps and harnesses.

"Got 'em!" Stacy clicked back in all too soon, waving her key chain. Alison turned to go. At the last minute, just before they opened the door, Stacy seized Alison's hand and pressed it up beneath her skirt. Alison caught her breath. The satin under her fingers was soaked. Before she could so much as run her fingers over the hot mound Stacy slipped away.

"Why don't you come over tomorrow?" she invited before pushing Alison out the door.

Alison stood for a moment on the landing. Had she just received another quilting invitation or...something else?

But as she made her way down the back stairs she was not wondering about this, but whether being with Dominique had been as safe for Tamara Garrity as Stacy had assumed it was.

* * *

When Alison got home there was a message from Robert on her answering machine, just saying 'hi' and asking if she had found out anything new on the case from her...here he hesitated, not quite sure of the appropriate phrase to use and settled finally for 'inside sources.' Returning the call while she heated a chunk of bean soup she had made the week before, she asked about the baby and they exchanged shop gossip, but hedged around her progress. She had nothing that she wanted to share, yet. Robert advised her to get out of town for at least the weekend, and she knew that it was not entirely because of the reason he gave—that he did not want her to return to work crabby and tired. He was frightened for her, and that meant the word around the station was that they still thought it was a slasher striking dykes at random.

As she finished her dinner Alison went through her mail, such as it was. The only thing of interest, unless she wanted to get her carpets cleaned, was a flier headlined Women Against Violence Against Women. It had been hand delivered. The graphic was a line of women walking arm in arm silhouetted against a street light. Alison had just started in on the text when there was a knock on the kitchen door.

"Hi." Tammyfaye, Janka's cat, shot past Janka and began sniffing around the bookshelves, which were one of KP's favorite hiding places. "We heard you come in, then we didn't hear you moving around...well?"

Alison waved the flier at her. "Yeah, I got one of these, too." That Janka had come alone could only mean that Michelle was stewing again about Alison entering the leather kingdom.

"Makes you feel kind of paranoid, doesn't it?" Janka said.

"I'll say."

"We were here when they delivered the fliers, so we got one of these, as well." She showed Alison a larger poster printed on yellow paper. The women marched across it in black.

"What is it?"

"They're trying to put together a safe house/safe ride program. If you've got a car you can get a sticker for it. The poster goes in a lighted window—it makes you kind of a block parent for dykes on the street."

"Did you get one for me?"

"No, they wanted to talk to the women they gave them to, in person. They're trying to be really careful about giving them out. It's not like a mass mailing or anything. They want to be sure they're going to dyke houses. You can call, though." She indicated the two numbers that were listed for rides and information, "And they'll deliver one."

"This is a pretty big job they're taking on."

"Yeah. Well, you're probably busy, but we wanted to be sure you were okay. Oh, and don't forget your whistle." Janka tugged at a piece of yarn tied around her neck and brought up a ceramic whistle.

"Yeah, I've got one on my key chain."

Janka turned to go and then swung back. "If you go out," she said, "take your gun, okay?" She paused, and then laughed humorlessly. "Wow, I never thought I'd hear myself say that. Just be really careful, okay?"

"Yeah."

* * *

The Rubyfruit was not crowded, but there were enough women so Alison did not feel as if she stood out. She saw Liz with a group of women but did not go over. Janka's last comment had put the idea of visiting the bar into her head. She had showered and put on a bulky red cotton cardigan that disguised the outline of her holster.

She asked for a Coke at the bar. As the very young bartender turned away she studied her hair, short and dark like her own but without touches of grey. Alison wondered if she could get away with spiking hers up in the front like that. The bartender turned back to her. Alison said casually, "I couldn't get away for the contest last week. How did it go?"

The bartender leaned on the bar with both arms, not at all averse to a little chit-chat. "Too bad. Were you going to be a contestant?"

83

Alison stammered, startled by the very idea. "Uh…um…no, I just wanted to watch, I…um…."

"Oh, you should consider it next year. You'd look hot in a leather jacket, you know, instead of a sweater, one of those really tailored chic-chic ones. Asymmetrical." The woman leaned across the bar, pushing the cardigan open to trace the lines of the imagined jacket a quarter of an inch above Alison's chest. The nights were getting chilly, but she was wearing only a green tank top, and the move pushed her breasts together so that the double women's symbol she wore on a chain around her neck was totally lost in her cleavage. "Black would look so good with your hair."

Though she had not touched her, Alison felt as if the lines had been not unpleasantly burned on her chest, bisecting each nipple. It took her a moment to realize that the woman was flirting with her. She was flustered by the image that she suggested—herself on a makeshift stage, all eyes on her approvingly, applause, encouraging calls. (Get real, girl, insisted the voice of reality, Michelle would be picketing.) For a moment she knew what Tamara Garrity had meant when she had confided that she liked to be the center of attention, knew the hot flash of excitement that had sent her, if Alison's theory was right, to arrange a tryst with Dominique.

"And some nice big earrings. Silver, to bring this out." The bartender made a motion above Alison's head, and again it was as if she actually felt it, as if a warm wind had ruffled the strands of grey. The bartender formed a big loop on each side of Alison's head, and at the end of the second her fingers brushed her skin for the first time. Just a whisper on the neck that made Alison shiver.

"Hey, Carla!" The other bartender was motioning towards a small crowd that had built up at the other end of the bar.

Carla straightened slowly, obviously more interested in describing the rest of Alison's outfit than mixing drinks. "The contest went fine," she said as she turned. "Take a look at the pictures over there."

The photographs were nothing professional, just a bunch of snapshots mounted on a big piece of butcher paper and stuck to the bulletin board that usually advertised dance lessons and free kittens. There was a small crowd around them, laughing and pointing, and passing a pen from hand to hand to write comments on the paper. *Vickie bribes the judge,* one printed beneath a picture of a woman with long blonde hair kissing another. Someone else snatched the pen to write, *Dommie takes a little time off.* Dominique hadn't mentioned being in the contest, but the photo showed her standing on a table and posing. The photographer had cut off the top of her head.

"Hey, who is this?" asked one of the women, leaning forward and sloshing a little beer. "Give me the pen—I want to write down my phone number. She's hot!" There was an instant of uncomfortable silence. The woman was not so drunk that she couldn't tell she had said something wrong. "What? Who is she?" She tried to make a joke. "One of your exes?"

"Shut up, Roxanne," said someone in a soft voice.

Another woman said, "They shouldn't have put that up." They drifted back to their table, whispering.

Alison looked at the photograph of Tamara Garrity. She looked very different than she did in the one which the morgue had provided. She was, as everyone had told Alison, very handsome. The photographer had used a zoom lens to capture her head and shoulders. She was parodying the pose of a fashion model, one hand up to brush back her thick black hair, hair long enough so that she could pass easily at the straight bank job. She had turned her head towards that bare arm so she had been caught in profile, pouting, her eyelids lowered seductively. Alison was not sure what all the contest entailed, but if it was looks alone, Tamara should have walked away with first place.

Alison reached up and pulled the photograph off the wall. Who would care?

"Excuse me. Have you heard the scoop on these?" The stranger speaking to her was holding a stack of leaflets. Alison took one, thinking it was just an ad for another dance or concert, then realized that it was the same flier that had been left in her mailbox.

"I got one at home."

"Well, then you know about the two dykes who were murdered last week?"

"Yeah."

"Well, the police aren't really making much of an effort to do anything about them. Dykes getting killed are a low priority." Here Alison had to shut her own mouth, insulted, but not sure how to argue since she knew the police hadn't made much progress. "We need to be sure we're taking care of ourselves and of one another. We need to make sure we're not alone at night, especially at the bars, since that's where we're being stalked. There're women here who will walk you to your car and make sure it's safe before you get in, or who will give you a ride home if you need it. We're urging women not to go home alone." She smiled. "That has been popular, at least. We're also handing out these." She pulled out a handful of referee's whistles, each with a shoelace threaded through the ring. "It would help us out a lot if you could give us a dollar, but it's fine if you can't. We want everyone to have one. Keep it in your hand or your mouth when you're out on the street."

Alison took her keys out of her pocket and showed her the whistle already on the chain. "What are we supposed to do if we hear one of these things?" she asked, curious to hear their strategy.

"Whatever makes sense. Nobody expects you to run out in the street and stop a slasher by yourself. Unless you're in a large group the best thing to do is make lots of noise, try to scare him away. Scream, blow your own whistle." Alison thought of the loaded gun beneath her sweater.

They talked a moment longer, and before moving on, the woman gave her one of the larger posters for her window.

It was getting late. The young bartender to whom Alison had first spoken was slipping out from behind the bar. Alison hurried to catch up with her.

"Hi again." Her voice came out sultry to her surprise.

"Hi." The woman smiled a slow smile that took several seconds to reach her eyes.

"Could I talk to you a minute?"

"You bet. I need to go downstairs, and I'm not supposed to go alone anyway. Why don't you escort me?" She made it sound suggestive.

There were no direct stairs to the basement storeroom. They had to go out the back and around the side of the building. Two women were lounging by the door, and another three, one carrying a baseball bat, were returning from patroling the lot.

"We got it," Carla told them. "We're just going to get some napkins."

It was cold out and Alison was glad for her sweater. Carla had pulled a bulky leather jacket out from behind the bar. She zipped it up and snapped the collar shut. "We're only going over there." She nodded towards the steps that led to the basement door. They could have walked straight along the wall to the stairwell if the last two cars in the row hadn't been parked so close to the building that there was no room to squeeze between. They detoured around them.

Carla unlocked the door at the bottom of the stairs.

"Why don't you lock it behind you?" Alison suggested.

"I was planning to," said Carla as she turned on the dim overhead light. Again that slow smile. Alison realized that her safety suggestion had been taken differently.

"You'd look so hot in a leather jacket," Carla said, picking up the conversation as if there had been no pause. For a moment Alison thought that she would draw the hot lines above her breasts again. But instead, she slowly unsnapped and took off her own jacket. She reached over and began to pull Alison's sweater off. Alison took a step back, but Carla firmly pulled her closer. They both knew that the protest was token. Carla ran her hands around Alison's back.

"Oh!" She started. "You have a gun."

"I'm a cop," said Alison. "I have to wear it, even when I'm off duty." She wondered if it would repel or attract the other woman.

"So are you going to have to arrest me?"

"Not unless money changes hands. No." Not even then, because now Alison wanted to finish what she had started. She wanted to find out what kind of thrill women were experiencing when they left the dance floor for half an hour with a stranger.

"Okay." That was it for Carla; the gun was unimportant history. "Put this on," she said, holding out the jacket in one hand. "I want to see how hot you'd look."

"You'll be cold." It was the only protest Alison could force through her dry lips.

Carla laughed. "Don't worry." She slipped Alison's cardigan on and then stood watching. Slowly Alison pulled the jacket on, the zipper up. She snapped the snaps at the neck and wrist, trying to make each movement as sexy and deliberate as she could. The dim light and the faraway sound of music from the dance floor made everything surreal and a part of her just watched, unable to believe that she was playing leather games in a basement with a woman she had just met.

"Oh, yeah." Carla indicated a turn without touching her, moving her hand in a slow circle above her shoulder. Slowly Alison turned away. Carla stood behind her, put her hands around Alison's waist and pulled her back to front in their first real touch. Alison shivered and for a moment thought of breaking free. But she had gone too far and spun too many fantasies. Carla brought both hands up to her hair and for a moment Alison stood passive. Then suddenly she was rubbing her ass against Carla's front, grabbing her hands and pulling them down over her breasts. Hot, wanting, she was as hot as she had been at Stacy's when she had held her face in her hands and she flashed back on the wet satin feel of Stacy's panties beneath her fingers. Then Carla was fumbling with her belt and she was not objecting. Even though Alison had never done anything like this before, she was reaching down to help her, pushing her pants down around her ankles and stroking herself because she couldn't wait. Carla's hands were parting her thighs, entering her, playing with her ass and Alison closed her eyes, letting her take control. Let her worry about being missed or walked in on. Carla was speaking in her ear, words she thought about before while making love but had never said. Hearing them aloud sent a shock through her body that went straight to her clit.

"I want to fuck you," Carla was saying. "I really want to fuck you hard. Please."

Alison was saying yes, yes, urgently. She experimented with saying it herself aloud, "Yes, I want you to fuck me," and felt another hot rush. Carla thrust her fingers deeper insider her. She was hot enough to come immediately but deliberately she took a deep breath, wanting it to last more than a few seconds. She heard Carla unzipping her own jeans and she tried to turn, eager to thrust her fingers inside her, to stroke her as she was being stroked. But Carla gave her a push forward, a hard push that made her put her hands on a table to balance herself. She entered Alison from behind so that she gasped.

Then Carla pulled her fingers out and Alison could not bite back a moan of disappointment. She gasped again as she was entered by something much bigger, much smoother. At first, even as Carla began pumping her slowly, Alison did not quite get what was happening. Then, like a flash she thought, "Packing!" She had read about it in *On Our Backs*, but had thought that it was something that stomping butch women did in San-fucking-Francisco, for Christ's sake. She never would have suspected it of the sweet young thing who worked behind a Denver bar. A multitude of technical questions flashed through her, gone before they could even be put to words. She no longer cared how it worked, just that it was inside her and pulling out. Carla must have been thinking of this when she had first spoken to her; even while she was tracing the earring by her cheek, she must have been imagining pulling down her pants. Alison moaned as Carla grasped her by the hips and pulled her back so that her ass slapped against Carla's pelvis, taking the dildo deeper inside than she would have thought possible. Alison's mind was so open now that images seemed to be pouring in and out. Like a runaway soundtrack, she heard her own and Michelle's voices arguing on and on in her mind. Dozens of conversations over the years melted together: it's okay to use your fingers, she wants me to try something else, well maybe if it's natural, maybe if it doesn't look like a prick or smell like rubber but boy, these sure are nice to clean and I really like the way it feels, do you think it's okay Chelle? She felt herself lying on her back in Sandy's bed and Sandy, who had a very politically correct lavender dildo without a head, sliding it in just a little, teasing her until suddenly she was out of control, pumping as hard as she could and Alison was rising her hips up off the bed to meet her. Then she was back again in the dingy basement, rubbing her own clit frantically while Carla thrust from behind and told her take it, take it, come on, let me fuck you. Then she was coming, screaming silently, her knees buckling, saved from falling forward on her face only by Carla's arm around her waist.

She had no idea how long she had crouched on the floor on her hands and knees before she felt it was safe to stir again, and no idea if Carla had joined her in orgasm or if hers were enough to satisfy. There were a multitude of questions which she wanted to ask, none about Tamara Garrity, but she could not form them with her mouth as she scrambled to her feet and pulled up her pants. Carla stroked her face gently. She had thought she would be embarrassed but she was not. She was glowing.

"We probably ought to get upstairs," said Carla with a grin, "before the boss sends someone to look for me."

Then it did occur to Alison to wonder if this was something that Carla did all the time. Would the music on the dance floor shut down when they reappeared and the regulars, greeting them with cheers and applause, check Alison's walk for shakiness? Oh, well, there was nothing she could do about it now.

Now that the good time was over Carla was impatient. She was unlocking the door, a box of napkins under her arm, while Alison was still buckling her belt. She still had on Alison's sweater, a bit of advertising that Alison felt they could do without. She sprinted across the floor and caught the door just as it was closing. She also caught the heel of her boot in a crack where the concrete had settled unevenly. Her ankle twisted painfully, bringing her to her knees. It was an old injury, and for the first moment it was impossible to tell if it was just going to be that one shriekingly painful twinge or if she was going to end up on crutches again. She pushed the door open with her hands to call Carla.

Carla was already at the top of the stairs, wrestling with the awkward box. She stepped over the edge of the stairwell and between the closely parked cars.

"Hey!" Alison shouted, but there was a great surge of music from the bar that covered her call. Carla did not turn. Alison started to shout again, but at that moment the woman disappeared. She did not turn left to go back into the bar, she simply disappeared, first there, and then not, the box of napkins hitting the asphalt with a dull thud. It took only a few seconds for Alison's mind to play back what her eyes had seen, but it felt like forever, as if she were a slow child putting together information that everyone else had figured out long, long before. Again she saw Carla stumble and fall hard to the right as if she had been jerked. As if, in fact, she were being pulled in behind the VW van. Only a few seconds, but Alison was already up the stairs, fumbling for her gun beneath the unfamiliar jacket, cursing the goddamn snaps that had seemed so sexy not ten minutes before. Her ankle was pulsing with pain—she was going to pay for this!—but she ignored it. She had no doubt

89

at all it was the killer who had grabbed Carla, and the only thing on her mind was getting to her in time. The short tape of memory played again, and this time she saw a glove-covered hand slap over the woman's surprised mouth as she was pulled sideways, the glint of moonlight off something upraised like a knife. She could not tell if these were things she had really seen, or touches provided by her adrenalin-fueled imagination. She was only a few seconds from them—she could actually hear the wordless scuffling on the other side of the car—but a few seconds was all that it would take for Carla to be turned into a drained corpse like the others. Bent over, Alison sprinted forward to round the tail of the car. Then she felt one giant stab of pain in her ankle, and it simply collapsed beneath her.

As she lay on her side in the parking lot litter it seemed as if everything had slowed down. She was part of some horror flick being shot in slow motion in order for the audience to get the full effect of suspense and bloodshed. She jerked her head to the side, scraping her face painfully on the rough surface. She could now see beneath the car that separated her from Carla. The light was very, very poor; she could locate their feet only by their desperate, dancing movements. Her eyes could not divide them into murderer and victim. Even as she was bringing her gun up she was thinking about screaming, about the whistle around her neck, about the warning time either might give the murderer, about how the scene would be confused by a gang of civilians, about the very little time it would take to plunge home the knife. Then, still in slow motion, she squeezed the trigger, aiming beneath the car, praying she would hit the murderer and not Carla, but knowing, even if her bullet did not strike at all, that this, more than any other, was the sound that would cause him or her drop Carla and flee. As the sparks flew from the barrel and the sound, magnified in the tunnel of cars, came back to her, a little part of her was aware, with some annoyance, that she was lying in a little puddle of oil and her good pants would be completely ruined.

Then, with a snap, as if the sound of the shot were the signal, everything seemed to go back into its own time. She saw a dark bundle drop to the ground on the other side of the car. Even as she was shouting futilely, "Stop, police!" at the top of her lungs, she could hear someone pounding away on the blacktop behind the building. Overlaying that was the sound of a whole crowd of women coming from the other direction—screaming, shouting, whistles blowing. Hands too excited to be gentle lifted her up. She jerked away, ignoring questions. Using the car as a handhold, she pulled herself to a position where she could scan the lot, though she already knew that the killer had escaped again.

* * *

The ice-pack which Alison had strapped to her ankle with an ace bandage had leaked during the night. The whole bottom of the bed was soaked with cold water. When the phone rang Alison woke from a dream about the North Pole, about how she and Perry had finally reached the top in triumph, but somehow without their shoes.

"Hello?" She let the receiver fall down onto her chest.

"Alison?" She could just barely hear the voice, tiny and faraway as if a house pet or stuffed animal were on the other end. "Alison, I read in the paper that there was another attempt. It said that there was a policewoman on the scene of the crime. Was that you? Alison, are you okay?"

She managed to lift the receiver again with great effort and spoke into what she hoped was the right end. "I'll call you back," she said, although she had no idea who the person on the other end was. The phone fell onto the floor beside the bed, and after a moment the buzzing stopped. She drifted back into the dream, only now Perry had disappeared, taking her pack with him, and she had been left alone in the frozen waste to face a killer, someone so cloaked in furs and skins as to be totally unidentifiable. She could tell nothing about the person wielding a knife the size of a machete which for all her efforts, she could not manage to turn aside. She could feel it slicing through her clothing, cutting through another layer of fur each time it came down. Then she remembered she had her gun and she reached beneath her coat to get it. But it was lost beneath the bundle of furs and when she finally did get it out, it was frozen and wouldn't fire. The knife had come close now; the last swoop had laid a delicate scratch down her chest. The next would cut her open as if she were being dissected. The blood would run out and freeze on her clothes. It would never be known that a dyke had been on the first polar expedition; Perry would feed her body to the dogs because they were short on supplies and he would know that was the way she would have wanted it.

But then the murderer stopped, looking at the gun that was not only frozen, but now frozen to her hand, and began to laugh. And the laughing went on and on and on....

This time Alison woke totally and shot out of bed as if she had been catapulted. The bread sack on her ankle slipped beneath the bandages and fell to the floor with a smack, breaking open and spilling water all over the carpet. She didn't notice.

"Jesus, what a dream," she said aloud, though not even KP was there to hear her. "Jesus, what a night." She caught sight of herself in the mirror over the dresser. No wonder Jorgenson and Jones had treated her as if she were a madwoman. Her hair was spiked up with little streaks of oil, and there was still dirt and gravel embedded in the open wound on her cheek. Why hadn't anyone cleaned her up? She supposed it was because all energy had been focused on Carla, whose head had been bleeding as if it would never stop from a gash that went almost ear to ear across the back. Alison had told the bar's owner, who was one of the people freaking out the most, that scalp wounds always bled a lot—Carla would get some stitches and be almost as good as new. But then she'd made the mistake of saying that Carla had been lucky that she'd ducked her head, receiving the slash to her scalp when it was obviously meant for her throat, and that had set the woman off again. She had invented a reality where Alison was an armed guard sent especially to the bar to guard her staff and wanted her to know that she had fucked up royally. At the height of her tirade she had even threatened to withhold her paycheck. It might have been funny in other circumstances.

The detectives didn't think so—and they showed it. Or rather, Jorgenson showed it, and Jones mimicked his air. Groaning, she flashed back to their arrival the night before:

"Oh. Officer Kaine." Again that inflection meant to remind her that officers were not detectives, should not make the mistake of thinking they were detectives, or even believe that detectives might be interested in what they had to say. Again that slow sweep of the crowd, the look of undisguised distaste on his face. "Here you are again. Do you need a hobby, Officer Kaine, or do you just need...." He didn't finish the sentence. He didn't need to, because like every out dyke in the world, she had heard it whispered behind her back, yelled on the streets, even offered up politely at parties as if it were a feasible piece of advice she didn't know about. Do you need a hobby, Officer Kaine, or do you just need a good hard fuck?

"This scene," she said, ignoring their comments, "is contaminated. There was a rush of people after I fired. But I took a statement from the woman who was attacked while she was fairly lucid, before she went to the hospital, and there were a number of women patroling the lot—I thought...."

She stopped. Jorgenson was shaking his finger very slowly in front of her face, the way her second grade teacher used to do. She had hated that teacher.

"You thought?" he said, "You thought? You suggest?"

"Well..." began Alison, but he cut her off again.

"Don't think, Officer Kaine. Don't try to tell me how to do my job. You seem to think you're some kind of expert consultant here. Of course it would be wonderful if we could have homosexual officers on homosexual cases..." He put a broad look of disgust on his face which Jones was miming, just in case she was too stupid to get the sarcasm, "...but it just wasn't in the budget this year. Maybe you can have it put on the ballot next year. But for now,

Alison, I'd think of myself more as...oh, Typhoid Mary. You know, she showed up and people died?"

"Fuck you, Phil," she said without heat, as though it were as standard as 10-4.

"I'm writing that down, Officer Kaine."

"Actually, I'm writing it down." Suddenly Liz appeared at Jorgenson's elbow, and damned if she didn't have a notebook out.

Jorgenson considered ignoring her, but there was a courtroom presence about her that was hard to dismiss. He settled for being rude. "Who are you?"

"Well, that kind of depends on what starts happening within the next minute and a half. Right now I'm a very concerned tax-payer, wondering why the hell you've spent ten minutes queer-baiting a police officer who undoubtedly saved someone's life here tonight, instead of getting down to procedure. That's good for a letter to the mayor, with a copy to your boss. I'm not, as yet, Ms. Kaine's attorney, but that can change rapidly." She tilted her head to look at him as though she were wearing bifocals. She said, "You choose."

Thank god for Liz.

Shaking her head, Alison staggered into the bathroom and turned on the shower as hot as it would go. She added the tiniest possible stream of cold and forced herself under the spray. She made no move to wash herself, but just stood and let the hot water beat down on her. She picked up the bottle of shampoo and set it down, picked it up and set it down, and picked it up again. The fourth time she poured some out into her hand. Black suds ran down over her shoulders as she soaped up her hair. She wondered if the people at the hospital had just gone ahead and shaved Carla's entire head. It wasn't just the major wound they needed to get at. Carla, who was so calm about the whole thing that Alison had suspected she was on the verge of shock, had told the detectives that she had smashed the back of her head into the face of her assailant. Because of the copious bleeding, they didn't know if she was possibly oozing blood from several places that might be teeth marks.

The police were impatient to see if there was a distinguishing pattern. They had to grab onto something, for it was the only information Carla had been able to give about the person. Carla had not seen anything but gloved hands and what might have been mechanic's overalls. Other than that, she had not even been able to say, big or little, black or white, male or female, young or old.

The door to the upstairs apartment was open, and the smell of fresh coffee floated down the stairs. Tammyfaye and KP were nestled together asleep in the center of the kitchen table, where neither one was ever allowed for any reason. Alison, who could not yet face kitty aerobics, let it slide. Instead, dressed in her robe with a towel wrapped around her head, she followed the smell upstairs. She took her newspaper with her.

"Hi!" Michelle was dishing up grilled cheese and dolphin-free, packed-in-water, tuna sandwiches. "Did you have a hot date last..." She turned and stopped in dismay. "Oh, goddess, you look like death warmed over! Oh, Alison, if you want to play out some little bondage scenes go ahead, but please don't get into shit where you're letting people beat up on you! I can't deal with that at all, it's not erotic, it's just plain sick...."

"I didn't let anybody beat up on me, you asshole," Alison snapped. She held up a hand to forestall the indignant reply. "Okay, I'm sorry. I *feel* like death warmed over."

"What happened?"

In answer Alison unfolded her paper and sifted through the front section. There it was, buried on the tenth page. She tapped the article with the opal and silver ring that she wore on her left hand and got up to pour herself a cup of coffee.

"Oh, no, again?" Michelle bent over the table, moving her lips as she read. "This is you, the officer at the scene?"

"That's me."

"Oh, I didn't see your eye before. You've really got a shiner." Alison remembered hitting her face against the handle of the Volkswagen as she went down. "Boy, the cops sure were lucky you were right there, weren't they?"

Alison took a sip of the hot coffee before answering. "They didn't think so," she finally said bitterly.

Michelle's phone began to ring. After answering, Michelle handed it to her with a look of warning which could only mean one thing.

"Hello?"

"Alison Jean? This is Dad."

Oh, shit. She loved her father dearly, but he was one of the last people from whom she wanted to hear at the moment. She knew what was coming, and it would make her feel like a little kid being called on the carpet.

"Honey, what's going on? Your mom and I thought you were in the mountains staying with your friends, and then we hear a rumor," he said the word as if it hurt his mouth, "that you're not, and before I can get anything but your machine" (another source of contention) "I go into the station this morning and find out that you've been involved in a shooting!"

"Oh, Daddy." Oops, there she went into the little-girl-in-trouble role immediately. Gotta try to fight that. "You're making it sound worse than it was. All I shot was somebody's tire. I'm sure you read that in the report."

"Well, yes, but I don't understand why you changed your plans and didn't tell your mother or me."

Because I met a hot new woman, Dad, and I know that you and Mom won't approve of her. You haven't liked anybody I've dated since Sandy, and that was five years ago. Because I've been digging around on a case that doesn't belong to me, where they do not want my help, and I knew I'd get a lecture for that. Aloud she said, "Colleen got sick right before I was going to leave. It was too late to reschedule, so I just decided to stay home."

There was a long silence on the other end. He was deciding whether to pursue the hurt feeling, or whether to just accept the explanation so that he could continue questioning her about the incident last night.

"Well," he said finally, "it's a good idea to let your mother and me know where you are, just in case anything happens." Unsaid was, "Because it's not like there's anybody else to take care of you, honey." She wondered if he would have time to throw in the rest of the lecture. No, that was unfair. It was too caring to be called a lecture. It was more like concern that had settled into a few routine phrases. Why don't you settle down with some nice woman who will take care of you so we don't have to worry that you've had an accident and can't call? After all, you're over thirty. Look at how much happier Michelle is since she's settled down. And whatever happened to that nice Sandy woman you used to go out with?

"Sorry, Dad, it's just that this is the first vacation I've had since Lydia moved out, and being alone really appealed to me." Bringing up Lydia, who had amused her father, but of whom neither of her parents had approved, was a response to the unvoiced criticism. Better nobody than a flaky dope-smoker, Dad.

"Hmm." He took the point and dropped the subject. "Honey, what exactly went down last night? How did you get involved?"

This could only be handled bluntly. "It was a dyke bar, Dad. I was just there to dance. That's exactly what I told those asshole detectives when they asked me."

"Honey, please." She could hear the wince in his voice. "That attitude is not going to help your career any."

"Dad, they were being totally unreasonable." Now she was back in grade school, explaining why she had smacked one of her classmates. "They were acting as if this woman had deserved to have her head sliced open just because she was hanging out at a gay bar. You know that's not right."

"Well..." Her father, as often happened when the subject of her lesbianism came up, was caught between a rock and a hard place. Secretly, she thought that he might have liked to express an opinion similar to that of the two detectives, though she knew, no matter what his personal feelings about anyone, he never would have allowed it to affect his work as they had. However, the only creed in his life that came before 'The Police Department, Right or Wrong' was 'My Family, Right or Wrong.' If his beloved only daughter, who had honored him by following in his footsteps, insisted that she really was homosexual and it was not just a phase she'd been in for fifteen years, then, by god, gay was good, not matter how he personally felt about faggots in public. She felt a rush of warmth towards him and hoped that somebody would have the nerve to make a remark about dyke officers to his face.

"Are you sure about that, honey? You weren't just upset? You know how you get when it's late and you haven't eaten...."

"Dad! Get serious! Are you really suggesting that I've gone from throwing temper tantrums at bedtime to shooting at people?"

"No, but maybe if you were upset you took some of the things the detectives said wrong...."

"Dad, I've been around homophobia enough times to recognize it. Have you met these men? I don't even think they're admitting the deaths might be linked—it's just coincidental that three lesbians have been attacked in one week outside of bars."

"Well, why don't I ask around about it? I'm sure it's all a misunderstanding, but if not I'll find out what's going on."

Now Alison felt like the precious child whose daddy had come to school to straighten things out while all the other kids snickered. She opened her mouth to protest, then shut it. If he could put a bug in the right ear, then let him. She didn't want more women to die because she was being proud.

"Your mother says hi." Oh, the official part of the conversation was over. "We got a letter from Eugene yesterday and he had some bad news. It turned out that Mary Lou did miscarry, but the doctor says it's really common with a first baby, and it doesn't mean there's anything wrong...." He was starting to settle into a nice chat but she just wasn't ready to deal with it.

"Dad, I've got to go. I've got the tub running downstairs. I'll call you later to hear everything."

"Oh." His good-bye was rather cold, and she knew that it was going to take more than a phone call before he forgave her for trying to live her own life. She'd be over there for dinner within a week.

"So, are you going to get hassled at work for being at a dyke bar?" Alison felt a little annoyed that Michelle didn't at least pretend that she hadn't been

96

listening to her conversation, but then, subtlety had never been one of her strong points.

"I don't know. My opinion for a long time has been that everybody at the station knows. They'd have to be dense not to. 'Hi, my name is Alison Kaine. Notice the way I dress and look and the fact that I'm thirty-three and live with another woman, without any kind of husband or kids anywhere at all in the background. Does that give you any kind of clue, folks?'"

"Yeah, but a lot of people don't know because they don't want to know. Look at Janka's mom. We lived together for two years, we slept in the same bed in the woman's house, we made wills out in each other's favor; the woman knows all this and when Janka just happens to refer to me as her lover, she goes right over the top as if she didn't have a clue. People get very weird if you get in their face about something they're ignoring."

"Well, the offical policy is no gay discrimination, but you're right, all the queers are very low-key. But I'll tell you what. The highlight of the whole evening was when Jones asks me, 'And can I ask what you were doing here in the first place, Officer Kaine?' and I say, 'I'm a dyke, Detective. I'm on a god-damn date, and I'll bet she doesn't ask me out again!' It was very freeing. Oh, and it goes without saying that they don't approve of women who swear, either. I believe there's a little note attached to the report about unprofessional behavior."

Michelle laughed, then said primly, "You always did like to make things hard for yourself."

"Look who's talking! Ms Confrontation herself! Ms Why-can't-I-make-out-at-the-Linda-Ronstadt-concert-in-front-of-the-drunk-cowboys-and-show-them-we-really-are-everywhere? Oh, I don't care right now. I am just so pissed off at the way these guys treated me—the way they treated everybody there! It was like, 'Well, you're the dregs of the earth, but this is America, where even queers have rights. We'll have to write our congressmen and see if that can't be changed.'"

"Well, did you tell them anything you've found out?"

"I tried. It didn't work. It was fucking embarassing. Here I go around all the time saying, 'Oh, cops aren't really pigs, that's a stereotype, we don't really get into the profession because we want power,' and these guys come along and say, 'Actually, we're just exactly like every bad TV show you've ever seen. We have rubber hoses in the car, we'll be bringing them out later.' I hate it that all these women went away with that impression."

"You know," Michelle slipped in, "That's just how I feel about leather dykes representing the lesbian community."

Alison looked at her sourly. "Well, you can just give me the leather dykes any time at all over Jones and Jorgenson because they were right there in the parking lot when I needed them and they would have kicked ass if we could have caught the guy. But we can go into that later when I feel better. Right now I've got work to do."

"What?"

"I'm going to go see the woman who was jumped last night. I want to ask her some questions."

"Why are you bothering with this if you can't tell the guys who are on the case? What good is it going to do?"

Alison sighed and ran her fingers through her hair. "You know, Chelle, I can't tell you. But this can't keep on happening! It's got to stop before somebody else's lover gets it!"

"Do you know where this woman lives?"

"Yeah. She was pretty much in shock last night, blood all over and she knew she had just been lucky, so I went through her wallet. I knew I would want to talk to her today." She laughed. "Actually, there is one part that's kind of funny. She was being really passive and letting people take care of her. So the ambulance pulls in with its lights flashing and the siren going, and all of a sudden she sits straight up and starts saying she doesn't have insurance, she can't pay for the ambulance, she wants somebody to take her to a Med Express place because they charge less and she just needs stitches. So the other bartender starts going around with a hat, and women are chucking in five and ten dollars, and since there's a pretty big crowd she's got a big wad of money. So Carla is still fussing, and her friend bends over and says, 'Hey, don't worry about it, we've got it covered financially,' and she says, 'What if they undress me? I'm packing!'"

Michelle looked somewhat disapproving, but laughed. "Kind of the equivalent of getting in a car wreck with dirty underwear, huh?"

Nine

The weather was still holding, extrordinary for a town where it was not unknown to snow on Halloween. Alison untangled her bike from the junk on the back porch. She thought, as she coasted down Thirteenth, how curious that her father, of all people, had not warned her to be careful. Everyone else had. Even Detective Jorgensen last night had said grudgingly, "Well, you know what you can expect if you continue to hang out in places like this." Perhaps it was because somehow her father had never really associated her and Michelle and their friends (they were such nice girls) with gay bars which, she suspected, he pictured as sleezy and underworld. She sighed—educating was difficult.

Carla lived not far away in the gay ghetto. In fact, Alison thought that she recognized the house as one occupied by a former lover of Michelle's ages ago. Once an apartment fell into lesbian hands in Capitol Hill it tended to pass from one dyke to another for years and years until someone was evicted or died.

"Who is it?"

She recognized Carla's voice, cross and a little bit frightened. She wondered if yesterday Carla would have bothered to check before opening the door in broad daylight.

"Alison Kaine." Had she ever bothered to tell the other woman her name? Should she say, The woman from last night? The cop? She hoped that Carla would connect. Though she felt a little thrill when she thought of their encounter in the storage room, she didn't want to have to yell: "The woman you fucked in the basement!" It would be a particular blow to the ego if Carla asked, "Which one?"

"I brought back your jacket," Alison said, and those seemed to be the magic words that unlocked the door.

Alison had thought, looking in the mirror that morning, that she looked like death warmed over, but compared to Carla she looked like a beauty queen. Carla's head had not been shaved entirely, but there was a crooked bald path running from ear to ear across the top, crisscrossed with too many stitches to count. Alison stared and then tried to look away.

"I brought your jacket," she repeated foolishly, trying not to allow anything that was flashing through her mind to show on her face. Like, Jesus, if Carla's head was carved up like a jack-o-lantern, what would have happened if her neck had been hit instead? She wouldn't have lasted the time it would have taken the ambulance to arrive. "Uh, I brought you a book, too. I thought you might be taking it easy a few days." She had dug out an old copy of *Motherlines*, which she read every year when she went to Michigan.

"I'm going to be taking it easy for a couple of months," Carla said sourly, closing the door behind her. "I can't go to work like this. Have you ever seen anything so ugly in your whole life? The only reason I even let you in is because you're a cop and you've seen worse, right?"

Not much, thought Alison.

Because it was obvious that they were not just going to pretend that everything was okay, she walked around Carla to get the full effect, handing her the jacket as she circled. The back was, if anything, worse than the front. A wide, vaguely oval-shaped space had been shaved, and the bruised and puffy scalp was covered with small cuts. It looked as if Carla must have hit her assailant more than one time.

"Did they get anything off this?" Alison touched it gingerly. Her mother had spent a great deal of her childhood impressing upon her that human bites were much more dangerous that those of a dog or cat and she rather expected gangrene to already be forming.

"Of course not, I'm not made out of Silly Putty. I tried to tell them that, but nobody was listening to me. It was like the Barber Shop in Hell."

Alison seated herself without asking, looking around the living room. Why, what a treat! This was obviously a young cooperative type household like the ones she and Michelle had lived in when they first came out. The furniture was battered and mismatched, and the posters on the walls reflected at least three different tastes. There was a chart dividing chores in the hallway, though it looked as if 'vacuuming the living room' had been skipped several times. Someone had left a woodworking project on a low table made of orange crates and a door with its hinges removed. The table, sans door, matched the bookshelves, which were crammed with every modern dyke novel ever written. Most of them had been written after Alison came out. She still remembered her initial excitement over that first purple, black and orange-covered copy of *Rubyfruit Jungle*.

She was glad to see that houses like this still existed, having lost track of them since she and her friends had gotten older and become more upwardly mobile. She herself had not lived with anyone (except Lydia, who had not ever been invited or officially announced that she had moved in, but had brought things over one at a time and then been conveniently evicted from her own place) since she had started getting a salary, but she treasured the memory of the years that she had roomed with two to four other women.

Carla pushed a grey tabby off the beat-up couch and sat beside her. During Alison's own communal period, most of the furniture had been secondhand from her parents, who could do little to hide their horror whenever they visited.

"So, you think it was a man?"

"Oh, come on. I can't believe a woman would do this. But, if you mean, do I have any reason to think it was a man by the way the body felt or anything I saw, no, I don't. We've been through that, believe me. I was up most of the night at the police station, after forking over more than a month's rent in the emergency room to get this number done on my head. I can't believe that anybody would attack me. I can't believe that I look like this and all they did was pat me on the shoulder and say, 'It will grow back.'"

Hmm, depressed. Alison tried to cheer her up before rushing right in with her questions.

"Hey, it's not that bad," she said. "Why don't you just...."

"Dye it pink and pretend I did it on purpose, right? That's what everybody has said. If I wanted to look punk I'd have a safety pin in my nose already. And I've heard the hat ideas, too," said Carla, sulking.

"You could shave your head completely. I'm sure there is a certain element who would be attracted to that."

"And I'm sure I want them to come on to me. As far as I'm concerned, anybody who is attracted to stitches is somebody to stay away from." She crossed her arms, an 'I-dare-you-to-make-it-better look on her face.' "And I don't want to hear about how lucky I was, either. Why did it have to happen at all?"

In the daylight, and acting like a spoiled child, her age showed as it hadn't the night before. Oh, Alison had known she was young, but now she couldn't believe that she was old enough to have landed the bartending job, let alone that she had left her sobbing for breath on the floor of the storeroom. She had been chicken-hawking without even realizing it. She shook her head mentally, a little disgusted with herself, and then stopped. She had nothing to feel bad about. If nothing else, the experience had confirmed that she did not want any more of Michelle's match-ups, nice but vanilla, for her next lover. She wanted someone like Stacy, like Carla ten years older. She really was one of 'those kind of girls.'

She gave up on trying to be cheerful, saying in a serious voice, "You're right, Carla, it shouldn't have happened, not to you, not to anyone. That's why I want to talk to you. I want to find out if you know anything that could help us keep it from happening again." She excused the plural by telling herself that it was classist to allow only royalty to use the royal 'we.' Then she forestalled the standard objection. "We have to go over it again and again, because you might not know what you know, or you might not have remembered something because it seemed insignificant." She hoped the implication that she was allied with Jones & Jorgenson would not come back to haunt her later. Carla nodded sullenly.

"Do you know this woman?" Alison showed her the photo that she had purloined from the wall of the bar.

"I didn't know her name until the cops told me it last night. But I've seen her lots at the bar."

"Did you see her the night of the Ms. Colorado Leather contest?"

"Sure. She was one of the contestants, right?" Carla was pouting just the tiniest bit. Obviously she thought they should be talking about her, not something that had happened almost a week before.

"And do you know this woman?" Alison showed the photo of Dominique that she had lifted from their coffee table when Beth and Denise had left the room to find a box for the black kitten.

"Yeah. I know Dominique to talk to. She's in a lot, too."

"Have you noticed anything strange, anything different about her lately?"

Carla pulled her knees up beneath her chin and considered her bare toes.

"Well," she said slowly, "she's been in a lot of fights. Usually she gets along pretty well with everyone, but lately it seems like every time she comes in she's shouting at somebody."

"But you haven't had her eighty-sixed."

Carla shrugged. "She hasn't hurt anyone. She's a good tipper. And women come in looking for her. Customers of hers."

This was the opening for which Alison had been waiting. "You ever been a customer of hers?"

Carla looked at her as if she was crazy. "Are you kidding? I don't have—" She stopped in the middle of what she was saying as if she had changed her mind.

"You don't have what?"

"I don't have to pay for sex." She seemed slightly embarrassed, and Alison could see why, for the line that logically followed was, "I did it with you in less than an hour, didn't I?" She was embarrassed herself. Well, that was what happened when you were a cop and had casual sex with strangers. Sometimes you found yourself questioning them the next day.

"You've never been in any kind of scene with her?"

102

"No."

"Nothing?" Alison pressed. "Not a group thing? Not something where money wasn't involved? Not a quickie like we did?"

Carl looked a bit startled by this last question, as if the incident were something that should not be mentioned, or at least not outside a brag session. But she still answered, "No, nothing."

"Are you sure?" It didn't make sense if Carla were not an ex of Dominique's. Then Alison's whole neat theory went right down the drain. If the connection was not Dominique, then what was it? "No. For one thing, she plays a whole lot rougher than I do. I don't pretend I'm in the big girls' league."

Carla didn't seem to be lying. She didn't really even seem to be very interested. So where did Alison go from here?

Reluctantly she took out a photo she had taken of Stacy at a soccer game. "What about this woman?"

Because of the mud and the unfamiliar surroundings this one took a little longer.

"I think so," Carla finally said uncertainly. "Isn't this that tall woman with the curly hair? The one with the funny name?" She waited, looking to Alison to supply it, but she was silent. "Kind of old-fashioned, like a flower? And she does the same thing as Dominique, only not as rough and not at the bar?"

"Have you ever been a customer of hers?" Alison asked the question quietly, almost holding her breath. Because if the answer was yes, she would have to consider something she had been keeping herself from thinking. That perhaps the connection was not Dominique, but Stacy.

"No, I told you, I don't buy it. But, I know that remark of mine was kind of piggy—that I don't have to. I'm sorry I said that. I have a friend who goes to see a dom regularly, and she says it doesn't have anything to do with being able to find a lover. It has to do with getting exactly what you want with no strings attached. Sorry about that."

"But you've never been with her, even not as a customer?" Alison had let out a breath of relief when she'd answered, but she felt duty bound to pursue the question as far as she possibly could.

"No," Carla shook her head again, impatient to get off talking about other people and back to talking about what had happened to her. To mollify her Alison walked quickly through the attack. Jones and Jorgenson had prepped her beautifully. She automatically went into all the details about what she had seen, heard, felt, smelled. Unfortunately it was precious little. The bare bones of the story were just what Alison had surmised. Carla had not realized that she was not right behind her. She had turned to speak to her and had felt herself grabbed from behind. Because of the van no one at the door had seen it happen. The attacker had clamped a gloved hand over her mouth and pulled her behind the Volkswagen. She had struggled, had ducked her head down instinctively to protect her throat. She had smashed it back to hit him—which was how she insisted on referring to the assailant— several times, she thought. She had heard the one shot, then the assailant had dropped her and run. It could have been the Pope, the President, or her own father. She just didn't know.

"Hmm. Let's get back to the night of the contest. Did you by any chance see this one leave?" Alison tapped the picture of Tamara. She was not expecting much but Carla was surprisingly positive.

"Yeah, I did. You see, there was a cover charge that night, and it was my turn to work the door. I had just come on—I remember that, because she was like the first woman to get her jacket after I took over. It was the last shift, eleven to midnight. We stopped charging at midnight."

"Wasn't the contest over by eleven?"

"The prelims were. But there were five women who were going to run through one more time to get the final winner. We were having a break, you know, so that we could stretch things out and people would stay longer and spend more money."

"But wasn't she one of the finalists?"

"Yeah, that's one reason I remember her. But there was another reason, too. See the earrings she's wearing?" She pointed to the photo. "They were really hot. You don't see a butch who can get away with dangly earrings very often. But the hook on one had slipped while she was dancing or something. She was about to lose it. I fixed it for her, and I told her how hot I thought they were. One of the stars was about to fall off, and she handed it to me like a token." A faint little smile appeared on her lips, and Alison wondered if she had also told Tamara how hot she thought she was.

An idea. "You didn't by any chance go out with Tamara, did you? A little quickie in the parking lot or the basement?"

"I wish," Carla responded wistfully. In spite of her own close call it seemed not to have sunk in to her that the woman about whom they were speaking was dead, for she did not hold back. Her voice did not contain any of the reverence that people tend to have when speaking about those who have passed over. In a way it was repelling to hear her openly lusting over the dead woman, but Alison knew all the same that Carla would be a good witness. She would not censor anything she had heard or seen out of respect for the woman who had been killed.

"But I had to work the stupid door. Margie would have skinned me alive if I had left. I did once, an offer was just too good to turn down, and she said she'd fire me if it happened again." Carla pouted, obviously feeling her employer should have been more understanding about losing revenue while she was tricking. "But even if I hadn't been working I wouldn't have stood a chance with her. Maybe on another night. But she had just been in the contest and she was so hot."

"Good stage presence, huh?" suggested Alison.

"I'll say! She just...." For a moment Carla's admiration put her at a loss for words. "When she was up there it was like she was flirting just with you, like she was the only one in the world who knew just what you wanted, and that she could give it to you. I'll bet she could have gone home with any woman in the place—even old Margie, and she's been married for years!"

Unexpectedly, Alison felt a rush of tears. She had never seen Tamara when she was decked out, flirting, in her long, dangling earrings, but only as a corpse in a drawer with a sheet pulled up to her chin. There was something she was missing, teasing her mind, but she was distracted by the sadness, and then it was gone.

She blinked back the tears, trying to get into the hard-core cop mode again. "But she wasn't with anyone when she went out?"

"No, but I'll bet she was meeting someone." Carla smiled, a faraway smile Alison recognized, and she knew that she must be fantasizing about Tamara trysting in a car.

"Why do you think that?"

"Huh?"

That, Alison said to herself, as she watched Carla struggle for composure, is how silly you've been looking, too. You've got to start being more cool. "Why did you think she was going to meet someone outside?"

"She didn't take her sweater or her purse with her, for one thing. I tried to give them to her—if you're working the door you're working the coat check, too—but she didn't want them. That's why I was so surprised when she didn't come back."

"But you didn't think about checking on her?"

"Why should I? There were a bunch of women in the parking lot smoking dope...oh, no, I shouldn't have said that, should I?" She put her hand over her mouth, looking dismayed. "Is that going to get us in trouble?"

"Forget it."

"Oh, good, Margie would kill me. Anyway, there were women out there smoking dope and looking at each other's bikes and getting away from the cigarette smoke and cooling off and making out and just plain coming and going. We have a real social parking lot. I never thought that anything was wrong. What I thought was that she got carried away with somebody who was just as hot as she was and they had decided to take it on home while it was still good."

"Without her purse?"

Carla spread her hands in a 'Who knows?' gesture. "Look, for all I knew she could have been a little high, she could have been a little drunk, she could have just been fucked till she saw stars and was planning on coming back as soon as she could walk. How was I supposed to know there was something wrong? We'd never had trouble before."

It was true. And how could Alison blame Carla for her lack of intuition when she herself, fully aware of the danger, had let her walk into the arms of a killer?

"Do you think this woman could have been the one she was meeting?" She pointed again to the photo of Dominique.

"Oh, of course! I'll bet you're right. Boy, that just goes to show you that buying it really doesn't have anything to do with being attractive, doesn't it? Yeah, I was kind of watching to see who else went out after her—you know, you make the job as interesting as you can—and I noticed Dominique because she was real loaded."

"Oh? How could you tell?"

"I couldn't have except I'd been the one serving her, and I'd already gotten over five dollars in tips off her just for bringing her beer. You figure it out. But, hey, don't get down on me!" She spread her hands again. "I'd seen her friend take her car keys a lot earlier—we're real careful about sending out drunk drivers. We have 'Designated Drivers' buttons and everything." She smiled proudly and for a moment Alison imagined her, shaved head and all, doing a spot with Nancy Reagan where she said earnestly, "Dykes, just say 'No!'"

"So was she staggering or what? I mean, why would Tamara do anything with her if she was that obviously drunk?"

"No, no, you don't get it. You have to know Dominique. Her eyes were like this," she made her own round and staring, "and they were real intense. And she was like I told you before, ready to start a fight. One minute she was really friendly with me, like 'Hey, cute thing, why don't you come outside with me sometime soon,' and the next she was all pissed off because I told her I couldn't."

"Would you have otherwise?" Alison asked just out of curiosity.

"I might have," Carla replied honestly. "Would have been a story, anyway. Except, you know what, I think Dominique must have hurt herself

106

when she went out."

"Why do you say that?"

"Because later on, when she came back in, she went right to the bathroom. And when I went in after, there was blood in the sink."

* * *

The ride home was uphill, and Alison pumped furiously, as if this would somehow help her sort out the tangle Carla had given her to think about. The young woman had told her so innocently without prompting: there was blood in the sink. Had it been blood from Dominique's own hands or nose—had she fallen, drunk, in the lot—or had it been the blood of Tamara Garrity? Dominique and Tamara had left the bar at almost the same time, and only one of them had returned, much later. Dominique had also been at the Blue Ryder that night at the same time Melanie Donahue was murdered. Had she been in the crowd which surged out into the parking lot when Carla was attacked? Alison had not seen her, and little would have been proved even if she had. She could have easily stashed a disguise in her own car and rejoined the group in the confusion afterwards. No one was looking for a woman.

Except, if Dominique was the murderer, why had she attacked Carla? It didn't fit with the rejection theory that Alison had formulated for the first two killings. According to Carla she had nothing to do with Dominique outside the bar, and Alison saw no reason for her to lie. Unless it was pride? Had Carla perhaps 'had to pay for it' after all and was now embarrassed to admit it? Perhaps. Or had Dominique become so sensitive that Carla's refusal to leave the door had been seen a sufficient reason for revenge? Either seemed like a long shot. Was she getting to the point where she was trying to twist the facts to fit the theory?

Alison had only asked one more question after Carla had dropped her bombshell. Carla was not like Dominique, who was reluctant, or like Krista, whom you wanted to question while she was still dull with grief. It was not essential that everything be covered Right Now lest there never be another opportunity. Carla she would be able to go back to again and again and she would enjoy the attention.

"Do you know this woman?" she had asked, showing the xeroxed copy of the morgue photo of Melanie Donahue. She hadn't expected a positive answer, asking it more in the manner of someone who is wrapping things up. She had four photos, she would show four photos. She didn't even take her fingers off the paper—Carla would say 'no' and she would stuff it back in the envelope and that would be that.

But Carla had surprised her. "Yeah," she'd said in a thoughtful voice. She slipped the paper out from beneath Alison's fingers and brought it up close, then set it back down. "Yeah," she said again and then as an aside, "Those other guys had a better picture than this."

"I'll bet they did. Where do you know Melanie from?"

"So, these other guys are like your set-up, right? I mean, they set me up with the general questions and talk to you and then you come in with more specifics."

"Well, they wouldn't appreciate being described like that." Obviously it was time to come clean. She wanted to guard her ass just in case this private investigation came up down at the station, and that meant she didn't want anybody to be able to say they had been duped into cooperation. "To tell the truth, Carla, this is kind of a private project that I'm working on. I'm not assigned to the case—in fact, I'm on vacation right now."

"Huh. That's funny."

"What?"

"Well, I was sure that they were working with you."

"Why?"

"Because they asked if you had already been here, and what you had been doing at the bar."

Wonderful, thought Alison. She was bound to hear shit about this one way or another. "What did you tell them?"

"I told them we were doing a hot fuck scene in the basement." She caught sight of Alison's aghast face and said hastily, "No, no, I was just kidding. I told them the truth, that we had talked inside and I asked you to go down to the basement with me because Margie told us not to go out alone. That's okay, isn't it? I mean, leaving out the sex part?"

"Fine with me," Alison assured her. "I don't think you should lie if they ask you directly—you'll get caught. But I don't see how what we were doing has any bearing at all on what happened." Somehow, until that very moment, it had not occurred to her anyone would want to know about the storeroom, and the thought of explaining to either detective made her blanch. And her dad was worried about her coming out! She had been so upset by that picture that she had entirely forgotten the original question and might have left without an answer had it not been for Carla's tenacity.

"Well, I'll tell you the same thing that I told them," Carla had said. "I do know her. I don't know from where, but I'm sure I know her. Knew," she amended.

"Casually?" Alison queried. "From a bar? A party? Softball team?" Where else did dykes get together? "A camp out? A rally? Did you work on a project together? Date her roommate?"

Carla shook her head. "Nah, nothing like that. I know I've seen her more than once, and I know I've talked to her. I'm sure of that. I just can't remember where."

Since that had seemed to be that Alison had given her a card and told her to call if she remembered.

She was getting crabby—low blood sugar again—by the time she arrived home and grabbed a bottle of orange juice out of the fridge before rewinding her answering machine.

"Officer Kaine," began the first message, "I would like you to call me at the station as soon as possible. This is Sergeant Obrachta." Shit. She bet that one had to do with butting into cases to which she was not assigned. Well, it was after five, and she was supposed to be on vacation. She could sit on that one.

"Alison, why didn't you call me back? Are you coming to the soccer game?" That was Stacy sounding annoyed. She must have been the faraway voice that had woken her. Alison glanced at the clock. The game was starting about now—she could catch most of it if she hopped in the car right away. The thought of watching Stacy handling the ball again was appealing. The message went on, "If you miss it we're going to Peony's afterwards."

Another message. She had been a popular girl tonight. She didn't recognize the voice, which sounded slightly hysterical. "We need to talk to you right away. Please call us right away!" The caller hung up without leaving a name. Well, that was helpful. Oh, another message by the same person. "That was Beth and Denise at 377-8976. Call us as soon as you get in." Alison reached for the phone, but there was one more message on the tape.

"Alison? This is Carla. I've remembered where I know that woman from."

* * *

The soccer players, at three tables pushed together in the back of Peony's, were talking quietly so they would not disturb the Scrabble and card players.

Carla stalled at the door, and Alison was forced to take her by the arm and practically shove her through. "You look fine," she said, though in truth, despite a scarf wrapped around her head, she looked just as ghastly as she had earlier. Carla was not at all reassured.

"Remember, it's this or being home alone," Alison warned. That was the threat with which she had gotten Carla out of the house to begin with. When Alison had returned all of Carla's roommates were still gone, and Carla was so nervous she was having trouble talking coherently. Earlier, perhaps, her near brush with death had not sunk in, and locking the door had seemed caution enough. Darkness, however, had brought her fear back full force and when Alison had suggested she come with her to the coffeehouse, it had overcome her vanity.

Conversation did not quite stop as they entered, but there were a lot of sideways stares and an excited buzz was left in their wake, though Alison suspected it was not so much about Carla herself as it was about the murders. On both the bulletin board and the front window were posters put out by the WAVAW group, urging dykes to watch out for themselves and one another. There was a table of gay men playing Pictionary near the entrance, and Alison noticed whenever any single woman left they offered to escort her.

She saw Stacy's dark hair at one of the end tables and steered Carla that way. Four of the soccer players were playing Boggle, but the others were merely sitting, exchanging a single sentence now and then. They looked, Alison thought, exhausted, as if all they wanted was to be lying in a hot tub at home, but were simply too tired to make the effort to get going. Liz, who was facing the door, saw them approach, and poked Stacy, who had her head almost down on the table.

"So why didn't you call me back?" Stacy demanded in a cross voice as soon as Alison was close enough to hear. "I would have appreciated knowing if you were okay." She eyed Carla in an unpleasant way and asked nastily, "Bring your own date?"

Carla did not help matters by pointing and saying, "Hey, that's her!" in a loud and pleased voice, like a child trying to perform her best. When Alison, foolishly hoping that ignoring her would make her shut up, did not respond, she nudged her and tried again. "Hey, that's the woman in...."

"I know, I know," Alison muttered hastily through her teeth. "Now shut up!" The other soccer players watched with interest as Stacy's eyes narrowed to ill-humored pinpoints.

Luckily at this moment Carla spotted a friend at the other end of the table. She started around the table, but Alison pulled her back and, giving her arm a good pinch, hissed into her ear, "Remember what I told you!" Despite the heartfelt reassurances Carla had given her in the car, she had some misgivings about her ability to keep their talk confidential if that had been an example of her idea of discretion.

"So?" Stacy asked again.

"Don't pay any attention to her," Liz said, shaking the cubes. "She's an absolute bitch. We got stomped and she's mad at everybody. We thought feeding her would make her better, but it hasn't worked so far." Alison sat down cautiously. "There was a reason I didn't call," she said. She told the whole story of the dream and the voice. Stacy was the only woman at the table from whom she did not either draw a smile or cluck of sympathy. Alison felt her anger rising. She had come by out of courtesy; she didn't need to be treated this way. She needed someone to whom she could talk about the disturbing information given to her by Beth, and who would wait patiently while she heard Carla out. Obviously she had been wrong in thinking Stacy might be that person. Well, Michelle and Janka would be home. She tried to catch Stacy's eye—one last chance—but she looked away with a little sneer.

Fine. Fuck that. She didn't need it in her life, not even for the hottest woman in the world. She was past the stage in her life where she actively courted unhappiness, calling it excitement or romance.

She stood abruptly.

"Nice seeing you," she said to the team in general. "Sorry about your game—better luck next time."

As she bent to pick up her sweatshirt Liz said under her breath, "Good for you! Don't let her give you that shit!" She did not look at Stacy again.

Carla was at the far end of the table, obviously telling the story of the incident, for she was smashing her head back into an invisible assailant energetically. Alison hoped it was the only part of the last night's activities she felt compelled to mime. She stood a few feet away to let her finish. She deserved at least that much for coming out into the dreaded public eye.

A woman sitting near the middle of the long table caught her eye and nodded. She leaned across and asked, "Did you get your poster? I stuck it in your purse, but I thought maybe in all the confusion...." Oh, okay, she was the whistle woman from the Rubyfruit.

"Yeah, I did. Do you need any help distributing those?"

"Let me take your number." She rummaged in her pack and then passed a pencil and the stub of a sales receipt to her. "We've really been working hard to get these fliers out to every lesbian organization that we've been able to think of, plus leafletting certain target areas and women we know individually. I think we probably have things covered. But if something comes up, can we call you?"

"Wait a minute." Another voice interrupted them. Alison had not really paid attention to the woman sitting next to the first. It was none other than Trudy, the team captain, who had been turned away talking to the waitress, but who had by now turned swiftly to face Alison. "We don't want her help," Trudy said, speaking to the woman next to her rather than Alison herself. "We don't want her politics muddying ours—S/M"

Alison leaned so far across the table that her face practically grazed Trudy's dessert plate. "Do you see that woman over there?" she asked in a voice of barely suppressed rage, flicking her chin in Carla's direction. "That woman

111

is alive because of me."

The whistle woman looked a little chagrined but Trudy tightened her lips contemptuously. "For what?" she asked. "So you can beat her black and blue later? Well, I'm certainly impressed."

Alison was so angry that for a moment she said nothing. When she finally spoke her words were short and jerky. "Talk about woman hating! I have never hurt and I don't ever anticipate hurting anybody to the degree that you are trying to hurt me right now!"

"Nonconsensually, incidently," put in one of the forwards who was sitting two chairs down, but following avidly.

"And you are totally getting off on it," Alison jerked out. "At least I'm honest about what I do."

She had no idea what might have happened next, for Carla, in a rare burst of sensitivity, practically jumped the table to take her arm and steer her towards the door.

Ten

Alison was glad to see there were still lights on in Michelle and Janka's apartment. It was not just that she wanted to share Carla's interesting information. She needed a sounding board, and who better than the two women already involved in her investigations of the Crusaders? She fumbled just a little with her key. She had been so angry after leaving the coffeehouse that she had raged five minutes in the car. Then Carla had pulled out a joint and persuaded her to take two hits, which had been enough to put things back into perspective, or at least dull the pain a little. Fuck Trudy, and fuck Stacy, too. She had more important things to do.

She knocked on the adjoining door Michelle style, not waiting for an answer. Carla followed her upstairs. Michelle and Janka were both reading at the table. Tammyfaye was sitting in Janka's lap and glared at them resentfully when they entered.

"Tell them what you told me in the car," Alison demanded, too excited for amenities like greetings.

"Hi, I'm Carla," Carla said coyly. She wanted to make sure that her moment in the limelight lasted as long as possible.

"Tell them," Alison urged impatiently.

"Well, Alison showed me the picture..." began Carla.

"Carla is the woman who was attacked last night," Alison interrupted.

"Alison showed me the picture," Carla repeated in a louder voice, determined to hold onto the reins, "and I knew I had seen that woman somewhere..."

"Melanie Donahue," inserted Alison.

"...and I even got the idea I had talked to her, or had at least listened to her talk. So I thought and thought about it, but I couldn't remember where I'd been. Then my mom called and she was all upset because she had read about the attack in the paper and she was saying," here Carla's voice became high pitched and almost sing-song, "'Oh, no, I told you what would happen if you hung out with those people, Reverend Malcolm was right, no good can come from this, it's a sin against God and this was his way of warning you that you still have time to repent. Satan must have blinded my eyes for me to

113

ever think that I could accept this'," Carla took a deep breath, "'you've got to go back to The Group and we'll help you fight this!' So, of course I said, 'No. I don't want you to call me if you're going to say this kind of crap, and if you have anybody from that place call me I'm going to get another restraining order.' She said, 'Oh, this is killing your father, and won't you reconsider and I'm praying for you,' and right in the middle of the whole mess I got this flashback!" Janka and Michelle were sitting side by side, watching Carla as intensely as if they were attending a Broadway first. The girl had missed her calling as an actress. "I remembered that was where I had met her! At the support group." She sat back, beaming.

The two women looked at each other. Michelle said tentatively, "Ah, did we miss something? Like, what the hell are you talking about?"

"The Crusaders," Alison prompted impatiently. "Remember our undercover operation? Remember what they told Janka about 'support groups' and how they would come to her house if they needed to? Well, Carla was in one of those groups! And so was Melanie Donahue!"

There was a moment of silence while everyone digested this information.

"So what are you doing working in a dyke bar, then?" Michelle asked bluntly. "Change your mind?"

"Hey," Carla defended herself, "I wasn't at those meetings because I wanted to be. Hardly anybody was. I was only seventeen. I was still in high school, and I had this kind of unspoken deal with my mom and dad that if I went over to the storefront once a week and listened to other people talk about how bad it was to be queer they wouldn't have me thrown in the loony bin again. Okay?"

"And Melanie was in this group?" Janka asked. Carla nodded.

"So you're how old now?"

"Just turned twenty-one," Carla said proudly. Alison's insides twisted in embarrassment.

"Which makes this about four years ago. But didn't you say," she pointed at Michelle, "that Melanie had met this Krista and gotten together with her some time ago? Longer than that?"

"At least six years ago," Michelle confirmed. "Maybe more like eight."

"Well, then what was she doing there? Did she break up with Krista and try to go straight and then give it up and go back to her?" Janka looked confused.

"No, no!" Alison was excited again. "Listen to this."

"Her girlfriend was with her," said Carla. "If I remember right the story went like this. I mean, I might not have all the details, because I've suppressed a lot of this, but I think it was like this. Melanie and Krista had been

114

together for a couple of years. Krista had always been uptight about being a dyke. Melanie was her first lover. I don't know if she was raised in some kind of church that was against it, or she was born again, or what the deal was, but she had been kind of pacifying herself for a long time saying that she wasn't really a lesbian, and their love was pure...."

"Which meant she put out as little as possible," said Alison. Carla, who had been saving that for a climax, gave her a dirty look. "Sorry."

"Anyway, they bought a house and they started a business together, and Krista had a baby. Now, I don't remember this part really well, but the little girl got sick or was in an accident or something like that and Krista got all freaked out and promised God that if he just saved her she would never fuck another woman again." Actually, Alison had been somewhat amazed and a little suspicious of how Carla had gone from total blankness to such a complete memory. However, when she had questioned her in the car the young woman had told her it was something that had happened to her before, and had to do with the abusive way her parents had reacted to her lesbianism. She had deliberately blanked out large parts of her adolescence, but could recall incidents in great detail when reminded of them.

"So the baby lived, and Krista kept her promise. Now, apparently Melanie wasn't really jacked about this..."

"I guess not," Michelle said.

"...but Krista got her to come to the group with her a couple of times to hear about pure love and all that."

"And she bought it?" Michelle asked incredulously. "Boy, not the Melanie I knew."

"She didn't," Carla told her eagerly. "See, right about then I graduated from high school and moved out of my folks' house, and of course the first thing I did was stop going to that awful place. Really, what I wanted to do was go back one more time to tell them I was too a dyke and I loved it. But I was afraid to. I didn't even let my mom know where I was for a whole year. But I ran into Melanie in the women's bookstore one day. At first I was totally freaked out—I thought somehow that they were on my tail, right? But we talked a little and she told me that she wasn't involved with the Crusaders anymore; she just hadn't been able to stomach it. But she was still with Krista. See, she really loved her, and she had decided it was worth it to stay with her even though they couldn't commit any 'homosexual acts' anymore. Isn't that gross? Like the only time you're queer is when you're fucking, and painting the house or going to the store isn't a homosexual act, too. But she had decided to go along with it, because she loved Krista and they had this business and the house and the whole bit. Also, she just adored the little girl and I guess Krista had basically said, 'Play it my way or you don't see her anymore.'"

There was a long silence.

"That's sad," said Janka finally. "That is the most pitiful story I have heard in a long time."

"No kidding." Michelle sat as if she had been shell-shocked.

Alison had been so excited about the connection she had hardly thought of the story as involving human characters. Now, like her two friends, she felt sad, and also a great rush of anger at the society that forced girls like Carla to black out whole years of their young lives in order to forget the suffering they had undergone because they were lesbians.

The feeling, however, was quickly overridden by her excitement. At last she felt as if the case were going somewhere, and not just in awkward fits and starts the way her theory had against Dominique. Thinking of Dominique reminded her of the hysterical message on her answering machine. She had deliberately gone to see Carla first, shelving Beth until morning. Perhaps it was heartless, but she simply was not up to anything trying—not Dominique's rudeness or Beth's anguish. She was, after all, not these people's therapist. She would call them in the morning. She would have to about the blood in the sink, although it was probably something totally innocent. This new theory about the Crusaders' being involved seemed to render Dominique incapable of murder.

Janka and Michelle were sipping their raspberry tea and did not seem to catch the implication.

"Don't you see?" Alison asked impatiently. "This is the connection that we've been looking for. The murders couldn't have been just random. The killer went to too much trouble for that. Melanie was a big, tough looking woman—only a fool would have chosen her if any dyke would do. Tamara and Carla were both attacked in a crowded parking lot—again, why put yourself in a vulnerable position like that if it doesn't matter which dyke you get?"

"Why put yourself to that kind of trouble at all if you can just hang around their homes?" asked Michelle. Alison felt crabby for a moment, as if Michelle were poking holes in her theory out of perversity. But she had to look at every angle. It had to be airtight before she dared present it to Jones and Jorgensen.

"I don't know why," she said slowly.

"Maybe some kind of sexual thrill?" suggested Janka. "You know, being in danger and all that? Or maybe the feeling that God is on your side and will let you walk right into the den of the wicked to do his work?"

116

"Hmm. Carla," Michelle said suddenly, "you said that you were afraid to go back to the group, that you kept your whereabouts hidden. Do you think that anyone involved with them could be a killer?"

"They scare me," Carla said simply. "It was so..." she shuddered, "...awful being there. So...just horrible. The praying and the shouting. They told us over and over that we were evil, that we were possessed by the devil. They'd get in like these crazy frenzies and I'd just think 'Okay, okay, I'll say whatever you want. Just shut up and leave me alone!'"

"But did they ever do anything physical, Carla? Try to remember," Alison urged.

Carla was silent for a moment, and suddenly Alison wanted to apologize for making her look back into the dark time that she had hidden from herself, wanted to tell her that no more recollection was necessary, but she couldn't. Another woman's life might depend on her memory

"They made people come in," she said finally, slowly. "I know that. Like I told you my mom and dad did, like blackmail. But sometimes somebody would fight. And their parents or whoever would just drag them in while they were kicking and screaming. Ugh, it was so gross. We were supposed to stand around and pray for them, but inside I was wishing that I had enough nerve to fight. And I think they did some of that reprogramming stuff. Because a couple of times these people came in to testify, like these guys that used to be drag queens and they were married now and living in Littleton. They talked about being restrained, like it was something that was done for their own good, you know, so they could finally see the light of God and cast out the demons. This one time I had this big fight with my mom and I told her that I was going to leave home and go live with this friend. And she told me that no matter where I went the Crusaders would find me and bring me back. I was so scared I couldn't even sleep at night. I read this story in a magazine about this woman whose parents had hired her kidnappers because she was a dyke. So these people that were supposed to reprogram her—one of the things they did was rape her. Like that was going to change her mind. There were these guys in the group...I could imagine them doing that and thinking it was for God. I didn't even think about leaving again. Not until I had saved up to buy a plane ticket for someplace far away."

The story was too pitiful for comment. The kindest thing to do seemed to be to treat it just as information being given, rather than anything personal.

"Anything else?"

"Well, sometimes some of the supporters were violent. That's what they called your folks or whoever was making you come in—supporters. Like,

117

Brother Malcolm never said that you should kill queers or anything," she gave a shudder, and Alison could see that she was remembering only because she was forcing herself to remember, "but sometimes someone would come in all beat up. Like there was this guy who did that to his son all the time. And nobody thought that was wrong or told him to stop. They thought it was the kid who was being an asshole to make his dad act that way. And my mom said that his dad must love him a lot if he was willing to do that instead of letting him burn in hell."

The three of them said nothing. Michelle gave Alison a quick look, no more than a glance, but it was enough to tell her that, for at least a moment, she resented her bringing this girl to their apartment, that she resented her interrupting the cozy life they had built in the gay ghetto with reminders that somewhere, and not even in other countries or continents, lesbians were being beaten and raped for daring to name what they were.

"Do you know Sharon Aldrich?" asked Michelle suddenly.

Carla nodded. "Real big singer, shouter. 'I used to be a dyke but now I'm saved and if the Lord can do that for me he can do that for you.'"

"Did you know that she used to have a mohawk?"

Carla brightened a little. "I'd have loved to see that."

"You know," said Michelle, "I think maybe I have a photo of her." She stood up, happy for a chance to break the depression that was creeping over all four of them.

* * *

Just then they all heard the cat door slam downstairs in Alison's apartment; immediately afterwards the doorbell rang. Alison looked at Janka and shrugged. Who could it be at this time of night? She stood up, and as she did she automatically reached back and touched the gun in the holster beneath her vest.

At the bottom of the stairs she called out, "Who is it?" and a woman's muffled voice answered. She cranked back the bolt and cracked the door cautiously. Just in case the killer was neither Dominique nor one of the Crusaders, in case the pattern really was random and she was the next dyke to come up in the lottery. She had not put up her poster, but Michelle and Janka's was in their front window and for the first time she wondered if that was really wise, if besides identifying dykes to one another it was also identifying them as dykes to someone who wanted to know for an entirely different reason.

Stacy was standing on the porch, holding the big woven hemp bag she used for a duffel. "Hi."

"Hi," Alison said back politely. She opened the door wider, but she did

118

not invite the other woman in. Stacy had put her lavender sweats on over her soccer uniform, and Alison was reminded of the two times that she had seen her play, and of the excitement she had felt when the game had gotten hard, centered around the goal, and Stacy had emerged with the ball time and time again. She did not feel excited now. She felt angry.

"I got my butt chewed after you left." Stacy said.

"Oh?"

"Yeah. Kind of a free-for-all lecture, you know—you've met a nice woman, she might even be kinky, don't be an asshole. You know, lecture 141. Lead by Liz and Jackie, but everybody got to put in their two cents. You know dykes." She put her bag down. Alison noticed that in her right hand she held her keys with the points laced through her fingers and that the brass whistle attached to the ring was clutched between her palm and her thumb.

"Oh."

"So I decided that being tired and cranky and jealous of jailbait was a pretty poor excuse, and I came over to apologize." She smiled uncertainly, perhaps realizing that the apology was not going as smoothly as she could have hoped. "Can I come in?"

"Why?"

"Well…." Stacy was beginning to look as if she was sorry that she had come. Alison realized that no matter how pissed off she was, it was foolish for both of them to be standing on the porch with the door wide open. Grudgingly she stepped back. KP twined himself through Stacy's legs lovingly, almost tripping her.

"Alison?" Michelle yelled down the stairs. "You okay?"

"Fine," she yelled back, but she could hear that Michelle, not assured by her answer, was coming down to take her own look. Paranoia was starting to run rampant. She could almost hear what Michelle was thinking. What if it had been the killer at the door? What if he had disarmed her and was forcing her to answer with the gun to her head? Without turning, she listened to Michelle cautiously cross the kitchen and then retreat without a word.

"Does your friend always carry a softball bat?" asked Stacy. "Boy, you must have told her that you were really pissed at me!"

Alison had to laugh at this, thinking of Michelle, fiercely loyal, chasing off any suitor she thought was bad for her. Well, she had never quite done that, but she had made herself very unpleasant to women of whom she did not approve. Alison had wanted to strangle her more than once, at the time, but her judgment had almost always proved sound in the end. About Stacy, however, she did not know. It was the first time Michelle had disapproved for political reasons.

"Look, Stacy," she said. It was the new, tough voice she had been practicing ever since she had split with Lydia, the one she had not yet had a chance to use on anyone but KP. "I don't know why you're here, or what that was all about. I told you why I didn't call you, and I think that I have the right to expect you to understand that I've been under a little extra pressure lately. But I don't need someone in my life who's going to treat me shitty. I used to, I used to positively look for it. But I don't anymore, and if that means that I'm alone for a while—hell, for the rest of my life—then that's just the way it's going to be." There, she thought, I guess I showed her that I'm the kind of woman who goes to therapy and reads *Women Who Love Too Much*. Part of her, though, was cowering, wanting to apologize quickly. A part that knew she wasn't ready to be alone at forty or fifty or sixty, that knew she was willing to put up with any amount of shit, willing even to support someone, as she had Lydia, to avoid that fate worse than death. She quelled it sternly.

Stacy lifted her hands as if she were going to gesture, but instead she ran them through her hair. The curls were stiff with dried sweat.

"What can I say? My feelings were hurt, I was a shit, I'm sorry. You know, I've been under a little pressure myself lately."

"What?"

"Come on, get real! Do you think that just because you haven't hauled me into the station house that I haven't known that I'm a suspect in this case? Did she do it or not? Is that why she likes to play kinky games, did she get carried away? Come on, admit it, you've been thinking those things, haven't you? And who knows how long before the guys on the case connect it and start thinking the same thing, maybe decide to pay me a visit? 'Where were you on the night of the murders, Ms. Pervert?' 'Well, twice I was right there on the scene of the crime, and once I was home all evening by myself reading *Newsweek*. No, no alibi, no neighbors popped in or anything like that.' Or, maybe if I didn't do it myself, maybe it was the sex that inspired it, huh? Maybe old Stacy didn't go bonkers, but maybe there was somebody watching, somebody that knew what kind of scenes she did and just thought they'd take it all the way, huh? Thought that a woman who liked to be tied down and have a crop used on her probably wouldn't mind going further, would probably think that death was like the ultimate orgasm. Come on, don't tell me you haven't been thinking those things!" She was close to tears now, close to hysteria that was probably as much from being exhausted as anything else. Alison could not think of anything to say to comfort her, because she had thought of those things. Had thought of every one of them, and more.

"I didn't think of you being stressed," Alison said finally, because that much at least was true. Somehow she had thought that Stacy must be oblivious to all the signs that were pointing at her. Right, Alison, the woman was not a fool. "Hey, why don't I run a hot bath for you?" She pulled her along to the bathroom without waiting for an answer. Her cure-all, Lydia had called it, saying that she was much more willing to stick someone, anyone, in the tub, day or night, than to talk about what the problem was. As she turned on the hot water it occurred to her that if she told Stacy about the information Carla had given them it might comfort her. But there was a part of her, the good cop part, which would not allow her to take the pressure off a possible suspect just as she was about to crack.

"Incidently, Carla is here—upstairs," she said, and started to explain that it was business only. Then she stopped herself. She wasn't engaged to marry Stacy, for crying out loud.

"Umm." Stacy did not reply until she had lowered herself into the tub. She turned the water on much hotter than Alison had dared. "I don't know her, you know," she said as she sunk down to her chin. The water lifted her breasts.

"Not at all?" Alison knelt by the tub and picked up the soap.

"Well, to talk to at the bar. But I didn't connect the name with the face until you came in tonight. We've chatted, she's tried to persuade me to come down and have a quick fuck in the basement."

Alison dropped the orange-scented soap onto the floor with a loud clunk. She could feel the flush climbing up her chest, onto her neck and face.

"Oh?" She tried to say in a cosmopolitan tone, but it came out a squeak, a sound effect for an old cartoon.

Stacy glanced up at her and started to laugh.

"Well, uh, I didn't want her to go out by herself...." Her voice still seemed to be stuck at the level of a cartoon cat's.

"Yeah, and I'll bet she didn't want to go down by herself, either." Still laughing Stacy reached up to pull Alison's head down. "That's what I get for throwing you out when you're all hot, isn't it?"

"I guess so." She was barely able to gulp the words out before Stacy covered her mouth in a sweet soft kiss. The kind of kiss where tongues are not involved, where it is easy to imagine that you could just eat your lover up, that you could nibble on her as if she were a bon bon or a delicate pastry. She felt Stacy's lips brush across her chin and the bridge of her nose, then over each closed eye. Alison lifted one hand to stroke her curls, the same kind of tentative touch she had used when she was a teenager, when desire could barely overcome her fear of rejection. Softly, as she kissed the corner of her mouth, Stacy touched her throat with her wet fingers. Alison could feel the warm trails of water that she left behind. She reached down for the bar of soap that she had dropped and then dipped it in the water. Gently she ran in over Stacy's breasts, working up a lather. She let the bar slide beneath the water, down to the bottom of the tub and used her hand to continue soaping. Rubbing it over both mounds as she gently nibbled Stacy's lower lip, as Stacy moved her head so that she could delicately trace the shape of her ear with her tongue. Soaping her shoulders and her neck and the top of her arms she then returned to those sweet, small breasts. Circling the nipples as they kissed again, Alison's mouth slightly open so that she could enfold the soft lips. Circling, gliding, back and forth and the nipples were getting hard now beneath the tips of her fingers....

"Alison?" There was a rap on the bathroom door. "Sorry to be a drag, but we want to go to bed pretty soon." Janka sounded apologetic but firm. "What should we do with your little friend?"

Alison lifted her lips to suggest, "Run her home?" because after all, Michelle was her oldest and dearest friend, and Janka had become the second. From whom else could you ask a slightly sleazy, slightly outrageous favor? Stacy was unbuttoning Alison's blouse even as she spoke, and all she wanted to do was crawl into the tub herself, overflowing water onto the floor as she slid her wet body along the length of Stacy's.

"There's a problem with that." Janka's voice said it was something that she'd better come and see about herself.

"Umm." She could not answer for a moment, for Stacy had pulled her face to hers again. Their mouths were under the warm water and it was as if Stacy's lips had expanded, were engulfing the whole lower part of Alison's face. She had to break away.

"Okay," she said to the closed door, "I'll be right there. Do you want to spend the night?" she asked Stacy in a whisper. Stacy nodded. "I'm going to have to run this kid home, but I'll be back soon." She stood for a moment at the door, just looking at her, and at that moment there was no fantasy that could possibly be more exciting than remembering that first gentle kiss.

Upstairs there was laughter.

"Hey, you've got to check these out," Michelle said when she saw her, holding up a handful of photos. Her eyes skimmed quickly over Alison's unbuttoned shirt, covered with water marks, but made no comment.

"The archivist," observed Janka. "She saves it all and she knows right where it is." She pointed to the cardboard box at Michelle's feet. It was filled with plastic ziplock sandwich bags containing photographs. Each was marked with a piece of masking tape that told the year, and sometimes the title of an event.

122

"Look," said Michelle, sorting rapidly through the stack on her lap. "There you are." Alison took the picture. There she was, indeed, with her hair long, and back in a braid, wearing a skirt made out of an Indian bedspread, a string of shells and nothing else. She was squatting by a firepit.

"My back-to-the-earth phase," she said. "Weren't we both ready to quit the city and raise goats and bees? Where is this?"

"Oh, I hit the jackpot." Michelle lifted the bag to show her the date, almost ten years before. The label said, 'Summer Solstice'. "Remember this? It was like the event of the year. Every dyke in the area went. I did so many drugs that I was high for days." She passed a picture to illustrate the point, herself sitting on a log holding a joint, a shit-eating grin on her face. She was wearing black gym shorts and had a bandana tied around her head. Her breasts were sunburnt.

"Who's this?" Alison pointed to the woman, looking equally stoned, who was sitting beside her.

"Don't you remember her? She was a brief infatuation. She was my first 'older woman'. She was like, wow, twenty four." She doubled up laughing and Alison joined her, remembering the feel of that summer. It was one of the first after they had come out, and certainly the first time that they ever got to go around half naked in front of a hundred dykes. She mourned it for a moment, for it was like your first kiss—it could never happen again.

"But we hit the jackpot," Michelle repeated proudly. "My mom had given me a camera for my birthday, and I was so into dykes and how beautiful they were that I took a shitload of pictures." She passed another one across. "Sharon Aldrich," she said, tapping it.

Alison took a long, hard look. It was before the days of mohawk haircuts, but still she could not reconcile the woman she had seen outside the office of the Crusaders with the woman in this photo. A young woman, topless, like everyone else, with a short, short, ultradyke haircut and twin tattoos twined up her arms.

Carla took the picture out of her hands and stared at it with something like awe. "I always wondered why she never wore short sleeves."

"That's not her," Alison protested. "You've forgotten, you've got this mixed up with somebody else." Silently Michelle flipped the photo over, pointed to the neat printing that told them this was Sharon Aldrich at the Summer Solstice festival.

"It gets better," she said. "Look at the woman she's hugging."

Alison looked. It was hard, for the second woman was quite a bit taller than the first and part of her had been cut out of the picture.

"I give up," she said, flipping the picture over. 'Melanie Donahue' it said

123

on the back. "No."

"Yeah. I had forgotten that I knew the two of them at the same time." She handed Alison another photo, obviously taken right after the first. Now Melanie and Sharon were facing the camera rather than each other, and little Michelle was standing between them. They had their arms around each other. On the back of this one it said, 'We worked on the newspaper together.' Alison turned the photo back over and stared. She had been there, too. She had undoubtedly talked to both of the women. Hell, she might have even taken the picture. Just more of Michelle's hoards of friends. The newspaper had folded long ago and she had turned her Indian skirt into a pillow that had been KP's bed for years before she had thrown it out. She didn't remember the last time that Michelle had even smoked dope. Sharon Aldrich was straight. And Melanie Donahue was dead.

Unexpectedly tears filled her eyes, and she held her head very still, not wanting them to fall, not wanting to explain that she was crying for the young dykes they had been that summer.

She would have liked to have taken a quick look through the rest of the photos from the camp out. But Michelle was stacking them up. Alison caught brief glimpses of herself, trees, a campfire, faces and breasts that looked familiar. Michelle rapped the stack once against her hand before dropping it back into the plastic bag, a signal, Alison knew, that it was time for bed. Well, Michelle and Janka had to get up in the morning, while she was hoping to spend it in bed.

"Well," she said, looking at Carla, "time for you to go home." Uh oh, something wrong. Carla's lip was trembling, and she was looking down at her lap. Alison glanced at Janka and Michelle, who looked at one another. No help there.

"What's the problem?"

"I don't want to be home alone." Carla barely whispered the words.

"What?"

"I'm afraid to be home alone. No one is there and they might not be home for hours. Starflower is out of town and Ramona had to work a graveyard shift. I'm afraid. What if it is the Crusaders? I'm in the phone book now. They must know where I live." Her voice was shaking. She was changing into a little girl, and it was with difficulty that Alison, thinking of Stacy waiting for her in the room below, kept from asking where the dildo-packing dyke about town, seducer of older women had gone. But that would have been mean, and, softly heard through her pounding waves of anticipation, a little voice pointed out that maybe Carla had a point, maybe home alone wouldn't be the best place for an attempted murder victim, especially when

124

the killer was still on the loose. After all, the best night with Stacy was not worth Carla's life.

"Okay," she said, trying not to sound grudging, "you can stay."

She swiveled to cast an appealing glance at Michelle and Janka, but Janka anticipated her and said, "Jan and Vickie borrowed our sleeping bags to take to Zion last week, and they haven't returned them." They sat happily hand in hand, smiling at her, secure in the knowledge that there was no place in their small apartment where a guest could possibly sleep without getting a bicycle spoke up her nose. Michelle in particular looked pleased. Anything to keep Alison away from the Evil One.

It seemed cold to put someone who had just gotten eighty stitches in her head on the floor, especially when she had a waterbed that would sleep three. She knew because Michelle and Janka had come down to cuddle a couple of times when she had been depressed. But maybe if she gave Carla the big pillow and ran over to borrow some blankets from the boys next door...? After all, Carla was young and resilient.

She went downstairs to check the tub; Stacy had finished. Alison opened the door to the bedroom to confer with her, then stopped. The light was still on, but Stacy was sound asleep in the middle of the bed, flat on her back, snoring just a little. Sleeping the sleep of the exhausted, the sleep from which you wake up eight hours later in the same position. What the hell. "You can sleep in here," she said to Carla.

Eleven

Alison woke and looked at the clock. It was two a.m. She had been having an intense erotic dream. It took her a moment to realize that waking seemed to be an extension of the dream. Her thighs and arms were being stroked from behind. In spite of already being wet and wanting she was irritated. That damn Carla!

"Death to the twenty-one year olds," she thought crossly. They had too much energy.

But just as she lifted her hand to push the young woman away the back of her neck was brushed in a kiss. A jolt went through her like a shot of electricity. Instinctively she knew this was not Carla. She tried to turn to face Stacy quietly because, after all, Carla was asleep not more than a few feet away, but Stacy held her back to belly. She could not really reach around to touch her so she simply sunk into the pleasure of the long slow strokes, of the way Stacy's hands felt as they caressed her thighs, her arms, her ass, her belly. She stifled a moan, again all too aware of Carla. Stacy was kissing her neck, her shoulders, kissing her hair and ears and Alison was writhing soundlessly against her. Stacy's voice from earlier in the evening sounded in her mind—"...if she likes to be tied up and have a crop used on her...." She imagined light blows falling on her thighs and ass, no longer wondering if it was something she would enjoy.

Now Stacy was whispering in her ear. Things she had hardly had the nerve to imagine before, and just hearing them was making her gush. As if she were a third person she saw them from above, spooned together, saw even as she felt Stacy spread her legs so that she could reach between them to stroke her. Saw them together as if bathed in a golden light; saw the way that she stiffened against Stacy's fingers almost immediately, heard the little bird-like cries she was not able to hold back.

She came back to her own body and laid her head back on Stacy's shoulder, content for a long moment. She almost drifted back to sleep, but there had been too many times that they had almost talked, and she had questions that she wanted to ask now. "Let's go into the kitchen," she whispered.

Alison was glad that she had snagged her robe off its hook on the way out of the bedroom, for there was something very different about being naked as she put together a snack, as opposed to lying in bed in the dark. Stacy too disappeared into the bathroom and came back out with her sweats on.

"This is the only time that I wish I still smoked," said Alison. "It's the perfect thing to do after sex. Tea seems so candy-assed in comparison."

"I used to smoke." Stacy opened the refrigerator hungrily.

"Who didn't? We were all tough young dykes." Too late Alison remembered that this wasn't true, that Stacy was married when she and Michelle were experimenting with tattoos and cigarettes and running around with their shirts off.

"So, are you ever going to let me touch you?" Way to go, Alison, just blurt it right out there. No sense letting this woman think you know anything about tact and then be disappointed later.

Stacy looked up at her and smiled. "Oh, yes," she said, "and touch me, and touch me...."

"Oh, good! I was afraid, I mean I thought...." Images gleaned from sleazy dyke novels drifted through Alison's mind; big tough butches in leather jackets they never took off, who only came when their sex slaves sucked their dildos. "I didn't know if...."

"Look," said Stacy, "I make my living with do-me queens, I want to get a little good stuff myself on my own time." She shifted her legs as she spoke and Alison imagined herself kneeling on the floor between them; imagined the taste lingering on her lips, on her tongue, as she raised herself to Stacy's mouth for a kiss. The temptation was great, but there were more questions she wanted to ask. She was tired of feeling like the new kid at school.

"I didn't know you could do it that way." Why change the old foot-in-the-mouth style now, when it seemed to be working so charmingly?

"What way?" teased Stacy. "With my hands? In bed? Without waking someone else up?"

"No, but you're into s/m, right? I mean...."

"Oh, that's the great thing about being kinky. It's like a little chocolate sauce for the dessert. You can be as vanilla as you want for as long as you want, and then when you're in the mood for something else..." she lowered her eyelids flirtatiously "...you can play." Alison felt her stomach knot up with excitement, but there was relief also. Oh, thank goodness she wasn't going to be expected to be a sex goddess all the time. There were still going to be the good old 'Why-don't-we-do-it-real-low-key-before-we-go-to-sleep?' scenes.

"Mmm, you know those razor cuts that Dominique was doing with Tamara?" She let her voice trail off, but Stacy did not come to her rescue and

127

fill in the sentence for her. She tried again. "I don't want to do that."

"It's not something that I usually do, even for money. To tell the truth, I'm pretty vanilla as dominatrixes—dominatri?—go. I don't like to draw blood or anything like that. Just my own personal thing. Women who stay with me like the drama. I'm good at that." She lowered her eyes again and Alison caught her breath. She flashed back to the leather skirt and studded blouse Stacy had been wearing the night they had first kissed, and imagined her talking dirty, making her beg. Her face felt hot.

"Yep, toys, bondage and drama," said Stacy, biting into a bagel. She spoke as if she were talking about any job, as if she were saying, "Yep, I put the cans in the bottom of the bag and the bread and eggs on top."

"How do you know what women want?" Alison asked curiously.

Stacy chuckled. "Just a minute. Where did I put my bag?"

Tell me what you like said the form she pulled from her date book. Alison read the list of suggestions silently. Half way through it, she began squirming. She glanced up at Stacy who was spreading cream cheese on the bagel. "I, um, mmm...." She didn't know quite what to say, except that some were making her wet just to read about them. She pointed to one line. "Mmm...."

"Oh, yeah, baby," Stacy said seductively. She reached over to run her hand down Alison's leg but Alison squirmed away. Not yet.

"So you just hand everybody a little business form, huh? Very professional."

"No, I'll talk, too. But a lot of women would prefer to make a few check marks. It's not embarrassing and it makes things feel more spontaneous, less like you wrote a script and brought it in. You know—okay, now you say 'You've been a very naughty girl' and I say, 'Oh, no, no, please' and you say, 'You're going to have to be punished'...I'm actually pretty good at following a basic suggestion or theme."

"I'll bet you are." Part of Alison could not believe that she was having this conversation. Not she, who had always been such a good little dyke, who had only been able to attend the s/m workshop at the festival by sitting in the back and pretending that she was really one of the softball players who just happened to be taking a break right there; who couldn't even buy a copy of *On Our Backs* at the women's bookstore unless she bought something else to hide it beneath.

"So, do you update these frequently?" she asked.

"You mean, can you say, I changed my mind, I don't like being spanked, or I saw a toy in the sex shop that I think I would like, or let's try a different scenario, 'cause this one is boring the shit out of me? Sure! You have that rule, too, don't you?" Stacy looked at Alison, her face drawn up anxiously, though her eyes were twinkling. "If I don't want you to go down on me tonight, it doesn't mean that I've lost my chance forever, does it?"

"No," said Alison. Suddenly she had lost her desire to discuss the topic anymore. She crossed the room, pulled her robe up around her thighs and sat down on Stacy's lap, straddling her. "But I hope," was the last thing she said, as Stacy began undoing the robe, "that you do want me to tonight."

* * *

Alison had no idea what time it was, only that it was much earlier than she had planned on waking. There was someone knocking on the front door and not just the paper boy or a Jehovah's Witness, either. The evenly spaced banging was too loud and persistent for that.

Wonderful. She swung her feet over the side of the bed. Carla and Stacy were still dead to the world.

"All right, all right, I'm coming," she called crossly. She stuffed her arms into the sleeves of her robe and then stomped to the door and snapped open the lock. Only after she had jerked it open did she realize that she should have looked first—they all needed to be extra careful—and only a second after that did she realize that her robe was on inside out.

"Oh," she said, an acknowledgement not a greeting. "Dad."

"Oh, yourself," he answered, sweeping past her as if he had been invited.

"Have I got a date with you?" She followed him into the living room, as confused by his presence as she was by the buttons on the inside of her robe. She clutched it over her chest. "Did I forget to write it down?"

"No, you don't have a date with me. How could you, when you were supposed to be out of town and I didn't even know you had changed your plans until I heard it through the grapevine?" That one was going to be a sore topic for a while. "But I know trusting you to answer anything on that machine of yours is like whistling into the wind."

Oh. He was not of the era of answering machines, but she hadn't realized that he knew she used hers to screen calls.

Her father caught her look. "Do you think I'm stupid?" he asked in a scathing voice. "Do you think they just keep me around because I cut such a fine figure in a uniform? Guess again. I thought I'd better get over here and talk to you before you got yourself in some real trouble."

She resisted the impulse to regress to fourth grade and whine. "Now, Dad," she began calmly.

"Get dressed, I'll take you out to breakfast and we can talk about this."

"Dad I..." she began, searching her mind frantically for a tactful way to say there were two naked women in her bed, and after she had dumped one,

129

she was planning on spending the morning fucking the brains out of the other. Maybe lunch?

She was saved from this tactical dilemma, however, by Stacy's timely appearance at the door of the bedroom. Fortunately, she was in a state of semi-dress—a T-shirt of Alison's that she must have picked up off the floor. When her eyes hit Frank Kaine in uniform, they flew open wide and she gave Alison a very readable, very reproachful look, accusing her of calling the cops after all, and after everything that had happened the night before, too!

"No," Alison protested, "Stacy, this...."

"Uh." Carla staggered in next, rubbing her face with both hands. She was still stark naked except for the scarf wound around her head. Her eyes were tightly shut. Stacy took her by the arm and tried to steer her back into the bedroom, but she resisted, saying loudly, "I've got to piss like a racehorse." Alison winced and felt her father do the same. Stacy opened one of Carla's eyes forcibly with two fingers and pointed her face into the living room. "Oh, shit," said Carla, "don't you guys ever give up? I told her every damn thing I know about everybody in the whole world. I feel like my goddamn brain is empty." She jerked away from Stacy and marched into the bathroom.

"Stacy..." Alison was feeling a bit frantic. Her father's eyes were wide. Great, how was she going to explain to him that she had not been up all night in an orgy? He was probably expecting a couple more naked women to pop out of the bedroom. On the other hand, who had invited him to come over without calling first anyway? Let him think what he wanted. Again she tried the introduction. "Stacy, this is...."

There was a knock on the connecting door and Michelle came in carrying a measuring cup. "Hey, Alison," she began, and then stopped and gave a squeal of delight. "Mr. Kaine!"

He opened his arms wide and she ran over for a hug. "Mikey!" Alison looked on sourly. Michelle got the hug while *she* was going to get bawled out. If they started talking football she was going to slap them both.

* * *

In the end Alison's father insisted on taking all five of them out to breakfast. There had been no turning him down. During the meal he paid attention to everyone in turn, insisting that Michelle and Janka tell about their latest commissioned pieces, that Stacy give a small lecture on quilt making, and that Carla, oblivious to Michelle's elbow in the ribs and Alison's discrete signals across the table, be oooed and ahhed over as she described her attack. Although he had seated Alison at his elbow he ignored her, except for a sad look in her direction during Carla's story. He had never called her to task in

130

front of her friends when she was a child, either. Oh, well, she supposed she should be grateful that Carla had remembered, under his charm, to delete the sex scene.

In fact, Alison was beginning to hope that she was going to escape a lecture altogether when Stacy clued into her father's hums and long looks and suggested brightly, "Why don't we all go get a donut and let Alison have a few minutes alone with her dad?" Thanks, traitor.

"Now listen here, my girl," he began immediately after they left. "I don't know what you've been doing, but you've caused a big stir at your station house, and your chief's not too happy with you. You tell me the detectives aren't doing their job, and what I'm really finding is that they're angry, and rightly so, because you've been trying to do it for them. And puttin' yourself in danger doing it as well!"

"No, Daddy." Christ, there she went right away. She took a deep breath. "I saved that woman's life!" She said in an angry whisper. "Did you see her head? That was her throat he was trying to do that to. Are you going to blame me for that? What should I have done? Held up my hands and said 'Sorry, I'm not assigned here and I don't want to step on anybody's toes?'"

"No, you did the right thing, and you did save her. But what I'm asking is, what were you doing there to begin with? And on a week night, too," he added, as if the next issue they were going to tackle was her study habits.

"I'm a lesbian, I was on—"

"Ah, don't try to feed me that line of crap! Maybe you can shock those two jerks, but I don't buy it. You were snooping, is what you were doing. You've always been a snoop, ever since you were a little kid. You never could keep your nose out of anyone else's business. If anybody in the neighborhood got in trouble you were always the first one to know and the first one to tell."

"Yeah, well you always told me that was what was going to make me such a good detective."

"If you ever get recommended for a promotion…which is never going to happen if you keep this up!"

"Anybody can ask questions. I didn't get a word out of anyone by telling them that I was a cop!"

"Right, anybody can ask questions, but only if she's discreet about it, and can give up what she finds in a tactful way. Not if the detectives find out that she's been interviewing all their witnesses before them. Not if they find her directing traffic at the scene of the crime and telling them what to do."

"I didn't do anything wrong!" said Alison in frustration. "If it had been anyone else they would have thanked me. But those men don't like lesbians. Read my lips. They think we are the scum of the earth, and they are not bust-

131

ing their butts to solve this case. What they resented was that I had every-thing set up so that they had to follow through. Come on, you called them jerks yourself—you must know there's a problem."

He pursed up his lips and turned his head, caught, but not about to admit a thing.

"They're not even admitting that these attacks are related, are they?" she pressed.

"There's no evidence that they were. There was nothing found at the scene of the crimes that indicates one attacker. They have to go by what evidence they find."

"Look, Dad," she said, "what would you do if you ever found out that I was taking bribes?"

His face blanched, and for a moment she thought he was going to faint. Hastily she assured him. "No, no, I'm not, it was just an example. It was just to say that you wouldn't be able to deal with it if I were. Because you taught me not to be a bad cop. Dad, if I know that something is happening in a murder and it is not being brought to light because of someone else's incom-petence or bigotry, and I don't do something about it, then I'm still being a bad cop. And if I don't do anything, if I say, okay, I'll give it up so I can get a promotion, isn't that promotion a kind of bribe?"

"If you really think that the officers involved aren't doing their best because they're prejudiced, you should go in and talk to Sergeant Obrachta."

"And he's going to listen to what I think, based on interviews while I was in a highly emotional situation that took half my face off, and put them over the word of two men who have been on the force for twenty years?"

"He's a fair man."

"I know that. But let's get real. You were concerned when you heard that I had come out to Jorgenson, because you knew that it amounted to coming out to the whole department, and you were afraid that I would be discrimi-nated against. The official policy, the goddamn law is non-discrimination, but you were still afraid that it was going to happen. Now if you can think that, without a minute's hesitation, about people that you can call fair and good, then why the hell can't you believe it about a couple of guys that even you call jerks?"

He was silent and she felt that for once she had scored her point.

* * *

All the women unloaded noisily from Mr. Kaine's large sedan at Alison's house. Alison gave her father a hug.

"Well, at least," he said, returning it in the style of the old Irish cop who treated all farewells between family members as if one of them were emigrating, "at least if you find out something, tell me or Rob so that we can leak it with some tact. You never were a tactful child."

"A promise." She waved as he drove off.

"I can walk home," Carla announced. It was the first thing Carla had said all morning that Alison was actually glad to hear. If Carla left immediately maybe she would still have time to jump Stacy's bones. She shivered deliciously with anticipation, a feeling heightened by a long sensual look that Stacy shot at her.

Alison was so excited, in fact, that she almost had her hand on her front door before she noticed that anything was wrong. Then she acted automatically.

"Get back!" she barked, accompanying the command with a sweeping motion of her right arm that caught Stacy in the chest with a thud. There was some confusion, but Carla who had already been attacked once, dropped not only immediately down, but tumbled off the side of the porch, pulling Janka with her. Stacy and Michelle followed a moment later. Alison's gun was already in her hand. Cautiously she flattened herself against the side of the house and then reached sideways to push the front door open—the door that had been locked with a deadbolt when she left for breakfast. A million questions ran through her head: Was it the Crusaders on Carla's tail? Were they armed? Was it related at all, or just your normal Capital Hill rapist or burglar? But these were like background noise, like the chattering of a crowd to which she paid no attention. She was thinking in slow, careful steps. Pushing the door open and drawing no fire, she could hear the intruder now; it sounded as if he were in the kitchen. More than one? She thought she heard voices. Cautiously she entered the room and crossed it, still against the wall. Now, as she approached the kitchen, she realized that she should have sent someone to phone for backup. Procedure had gone out of her head in the heat of anger at having her own home violated. It would be all right. The intruders were either idiots or novices, for they were chattering to one another as if they were making coffee in their own home. In fact, she thought she could hear dishes clanking. She took a deep breath and leapt into the doorway, the gun extended in both hands. "Freeze!" she shouted.

It took a moment to process what she was seeing. The woman who turned from the cupboards, one hand still reaching up to take down the sugar, looked as incredulous and frightened as if Alison had burst in on her in her very own kitchen. She was tall and had long, dark blonde hair which she was wearing in two braids. The ends were tied with beaded leather thongs and a feather was stuck into one. Had they met elsewhere, Alison would have immediately classified her as either a goddess-worshipping dyke or an old hippie. So what was she doing pilfering her cupboards?

The other woman was squatted down on the floor sorting through her pans. From the back her appearance with purple drawstring pants and tie-dyed rainbow top, agreed with that of her companion. There was, however, something strangely familar about her multicolored spikey hair....

Alison dropped the gun. "Hello, Lydia," she said.

Lydia straightened and turned around. "Hi!" she said in cheerful voice that told Alison she not only missed the fact that Alison had drawn her gun, but also had not noticed her friend leaning against the counter clutching her throat. "Lavender. My name is Lavender now. I thought you were probably at work."

"No, I'm on vacation." Alison was surprised at how calm her voice sounded.

"Great! Perfect! You're just in time for breakfast. Pull up a chair." Lydia had the habit of falling immediately into the hostess role wherever she happened to be crashing. "This is Seven Yellow Moons." Without looking she gesture towards the tall woman who, still terrified, managed to give Alison a nod. Lydia had probably not, thought Alison, informed her either of her vocation or that they were unexpected.

"Excuse me for a moment," Alison said politely, backing out of the room while she put away her gun. She hoped that Lydia's friend would rake her over the coals for letting them into a cop's house without advance warning.

As she strode back through the living room she saw the sleeping bags and packs piled up behind the couch. Great, a long stay. She stuck her head out the front door.

"It's okay," she said. "False alarm."

"What are you talking about, 'false alarm'?" Stacy was the first one in, talking in the loud, querulous voice that Alison had by now come to recognize as representing any excitement or upset. "I saw you lock that door when we left! You going to tell me that the cat did that?"

"No." Alison turned her head to address everyone so that she would not have to say it again. Carla and Janka were coming back up the steps, Carla's eyes bright with interest. She probably thinks she's walked into a TV show, thought Alison sourly. We're never going to get her to leave. Janka was holding her left arm with her right hand.

"Michelle!" Her friend appeared from around the corner of the house, brandishing a rake. Good old Michelle, guarding the back escape.

"What is going on?!" Stacy demanded. Michelle exchanged a look with Janka that said plainly, 'Oh, bad temper as well as being kinky. Definitely

134

not the girl for our Alison.' For a moment Alison wished that she were a friendless orphan.

"It's a misunderstanding. An old—" she almost tried to get away with 'friend'. But, hell, Stacy was going to have to learn about the embarrassments of her past eventually, "—lover dropped by to visit. Come on in." She gestured, but only Carla, eager to see the next installment, sprang up to the door.

"Who?" asked Michelle.

"How did she get in?" asked Stacy at the same time.

"Lydia. And I presume she kept a key when she left." Actually, the amazing part was not that she had kept her key, but that she had been able to locate it on her jailer's key ring. Lydia could let herself into crash pads all over the U.S.

"Oh." said Michelle. She did not put the rake down, and Alison got the distinct impression that she was rather sorry that Lydia had not tried to escape out the back door so that she could have hit her over the head.

"No killers?" asked Stacy, calmer. Alison took her by the hand and pulled her inside. Carla was already in the kitchen, from where came once again the sounds of water running, dishes clattering and eggs being broken. Alison closed her eyes. Lydia was an excellent cook, but she regarded cleaning up as someone else's job. Behind them Alison thought she heard Janka say, "I think I've broken my arm," but she chose to believe that she had misunderstood.

Carla was standing by the door with a huge smile on her face, staring at Lydia's hair. Alison, who had not really had time to appreciate it fully before, gave it a look herself. It was cut off no longer than an inch long all over her head, except for a tag in the back, and had been bleached and then rainbowed in the same brilliant colors as Lydia's wide-sleeved shirt.

"Carla, Stacy, this is Lydia. And this is Lydia's friend." She wasn't even going to attempt the other woman's name; she was sure she would get the combinations of numbers, planets and colors wrong. The woman still looked as if she were going to jump out of her skin. Out of pity, since Lydia had obviously not explained a thing, Alison said to her, "My name is Alison. I live here. I'm a cop. I thought someone had broken in. I didn't have any idea that I was expecting company."

"Oh." The woman breathed out a long sigh and relaxed visibly. She was wearing a pair of drawstring pants the same style as Lydia's—cotton, gathered at the ankles—only hers were red. Over a matching turtleneck that had seen better days, she had on a short vest that looked as if it had been hand-woven. Maybe she would enjoy talking to Janka.

"Lavender," said Lydia to Carla and Stacy. "Seven Yellow Moons." She

135

pointed to the other woman. Stacy glanced quickly at Alison as if asking what the woman was called for short?

"I did contact you, Alison. Is that still your name?" She turned from ransacking the refrigerator to peer at Alison hopefully.

"Yeah. I think I'm going to keep it for a while."

Behind their conversation Alison heard Seven Yellow Moons say to Stacy, "Boy, you look just like someone I used to know."

"Oh. I had hoped since renaming usually signifies change...." Lydia turned back to contemplate the refrigerator. "Three days ago our family had a circle and sent you an image of our arrival. I know we reached you while you were sleeping. I felt your presence leap up to greet mine, and sleep is the only time that you relax enough to allow it that freedom. But you probably decided it was just a dream, right?" She spoke wearily, as if reminding Alison for the thousandth time that she had to look into her mailbox if she expected to get postcards. "Did you know that you have a flat tire?"

"No doubt," Alison replied to the first question. As far as Lydia was concerned the explanation was over and done with, and if she hadn't gotten the message it was Alison's fault for being such a tightass. There was no use arguing. "Did you tell me why you were here and how long you're planning on staying, too?... What?" Only now did the second question sink in.

"I noticed that, too," Carla volunteered, happy to be given a speaking role at last. "When we came in. Right front. I was about to tell you when you pulled your gun. Alison almost shot me in the foot the other night," she told Lydia and Seven Yellow Moons proudly, making it sound as if Alison frequently rode into Dodge and shot things up.

Lydia raised her eyebrows, but before she could comment on the politics of violence, Michelle stepped into the kitchen with Janka in tow. "Janka thinks she's broken her arm," she announced with a dark look at Lydia. "Hello, Lydia."

"Lavender," Lydia corrected. "Do you know what kind of disharmony you were feeling in order for you to need to hurt yourself?" she asked Janka.

"She fell off the porch because Alison thought the dyke-killer had broken into her house!" said Michelle heatedly. She looked back over her shoulder as if wondering where she had left the rake.

"Well, we all make our choices, don't we?" Lydia replied somewhat mysteriously.

Seven Yellow Moons asked, "May I look at it?"

Michelle looked as if she would rather receive the assistance of anyone else, even one of the dreaded leatherdykes—she did, in fact, glance at Stacy for a moment as if hoping to form an alliance—but Janka quelled her with a

136

glance. Lydia turned back to her eggs; presumably if Janka chose to be injured it was her own problem, but not before she said, "Seven Yellow Moons is a healer. She does wonderful things with crystals."

Alison thought it was very inopportune for the phone to ring at that moment, for she wanted to be there to catch Michelle's expression if Seven Yellow Moons decided to whip out a crystal and slap it on Janka's arm. She even debated, for a moment, letting the answering machine pick it up, but before she could commit herself, Stacy leaned back into the living room and snagged the extension off her desk.

"It's for you," she told Alison. The receiver still pressed to her chest she asked, "Am I hallucinating, or is this place turning into a nuthouse?"

"Different strokes," answered Alison. "But do try to keep Carla from cornering Lydia for a quickie unless you want to hear a very long lecture about the importance of pure sex for spiritual power.... Hello?"

She heard the words with a feeling of déjà vu. "We need to talk to you right away!" said a woman without identifying herself. "Why didn't you call us?"

Oh, shit. Beth. She had totally forgotten her. "Oh, the machine must not be working," she lied. "What's happening?"

"We need to talk to you! The police have been here! We think they may be coming back!" Obviously this was as close to coherency she was going to get over the phone.

"Look, I'll be right there, okay? Just stay put."

"You have a flat tire," Lydia sang out from the other room. "And I'll bet your spare is flat, too."

It was an accurate guess, one that Alison would have preferred not to have confirmed in front of Michelle. Okay, all right, she could handle the fact that she wasn't Wonder Woman, that car maintenance happened to be down low on her list of priorities and skills. "There may be a slight problem," she told Beth, trying to calculate rapidly how many buses would be involved in the trip and what the estimated time would be.

"I can give you a ride," said Stacy who, like the rest of the household, seemed to have decided to take time off from the personal drama in order to give full attention to the phone call.

At the same moment Seven Yellow Moons announced, "She's going to need an X-ray."

And Michelle said, "Oh, Alison," in the sad, sad voice of a disappointed teacher who can't believe her student's very best has not been enough.

137

Twelve

"This is it." Alison pointed to the well-kept little house, opening the car door even before they were at a full stop. "You can't come in." She was too on edge to try for tact, even if it had been a strong point. It had taken forever to decide that while Stacy was delivering her to Beth and Denise's, Seven Yellow Moons would take Janka to a Med Express Clinic in her van, Carla would stay with Lydia, and Michelle would change the spare tire. This last task was insisted upon by Janka. Alison, who had once herself suffered from Michelle's protective belligerence in an emergency room, totally approved. Janka and Seven Yellow Moons had been chatting about weaving as they went out the door, an ice pack on Janka's splinted arm. Alison had been so amazed to see this instead of a crystal bracelet or a healing circle that she had let it show on her face. Seven Yellow Moons had said to her in a voice that managed to be serene and withering at the same time, "I practice cross-disciplines. I'm a nurse practitioner as well as working with physic healing." She had lost the serenity altogether when she put her hand on her hip and said, "And who hasn't taken a multi-media first aid course these days?"

"You can just drop me off. I can catch a bus back."

"No way," said Stacy, and though it could have just meant that she didn't want her new squeeze to be subjected to that kind of inconvenience, heart sinking, Alison felt it was more in line with the enraptured expression Carla had had upon discovering Lydia and Seven Yellow Moon's arrival. This theory of living soap opera was confirmed by Stacy saying, in a rather coy voice, "Carla told me some interesting things when we were eating our donuts."

Alison tried to brush her off. "Carla is an interesting girl." She started to get out of the car but Stacy shot a hand across, and laid it on her wrist.

"These things were about a new theory you might have in the murders." Alison was silent. "Were you going to tell me about this? Considering the fact that I was so worried that you might think it was me?"

"Oh, yes," Alison lied, since Carla had spilled the beans already. They needed to put a gag on that girl. "But it didn't really come together until after you had passed out last night. There hasn't really been a chance since." She knew that it was not good to start a relationship with lies, but she couldn't see how it would be helpful to tell Stacy the truth. "Well, no, I wasn't going to tell you because there's still a possibility that you're fairly deeply involved in a murder case, in fact, possibly the killer herself, and though that possibility is so small that I'm willing to ignore it in order to become your lover, I would just like to kind of cover my ass by not telling you everything that I know." Right. It would go over real big.

Stacy appeared somewhat mollified by this explanation. She fished a library copy of *Everything That's Yours Is Mine* out of the bag she had flung at Alison's feet on the passenger's side, and settled in with it.

The front door was pulled open before Alison could knock. Beth nodded to her. Again she was wearing a tasteful, office outfit, and her features were composed. But Alison could see that the composure did not go far beneath the surface.

"The police have been here," she announced again. "They asked Denise to come into the station for questioning."

"Did she go?"

"Certainly not," Beth said coldly, as if Alison had somehow insulted them just by asking. "When I asked if it were a request or a legal order they had to admit that they had nothing, no reason at all to compel her."

Alison entered and glanced around the room. Denise was sitting on the sofa, sprawled back as if she had been thrown. Alison walked over to her.

"What haven't you told me?" she asked her, resisting the impulse to take her chin in her hand and tilt her face up. For a moment she thought that the question had not registered.

Then Denise spoke, "I just didn't think...I didn't see how...it didn't seem...."

You didn't see how? Alison wanted to shout. They're not fools. By now, of course, they know that you were at the bar that night. They know that Tamara left her things in the coat room like she was planning to come back. How are they not going to ask questions about that? But she spoke carefully, recognizing that Denise was almost paralyzed with fear and would have to be coaxed.

"You didn't think that they would find out that you tricked with Tamara in the parking lot that night, did you?"

"Oh, god," muttered Denise, passing her free hand over her face. Beth began to chirp comfortingly. It was obvious to Alison that no matter how well intended Beth's fussing was, she would have more luck with Denise if she could talk to her by herself. She tried to think of a way to get rid of the other woman. That particular job was usually handled by Robert, who had a talent for phrasing commands like polite requests.

139

"But they *will* find out about it," Alison said, "if they haven't already. And of course they're going to want to hear about it, because you might have been the last one, besides the killer, to have seen Tamara alive." Or, you might have been the killer, she added silently. Denise certainly seemed shaken enough.

"I went outside with Tamara," Dominique began heavily. "I remember that. Just little bits. Her asking me. Talking to the girl at the door. But not all...."

"Oh, it's the drinking, it's the drinking, it wasn't like she was herself, surely they can't blame...." Beth interrupted. Tears were rolling down her cheeks. Alison sensed what she must be going through since Beth had been with Denise for years and obviously cared a great deal for her, but they were never going to get anywhere if she didn't put a sock in it.

"Beth," Alison said, "I'm going to have to ask you to keep quiet so that Dominique—Denise—and I can talk. You know how important it is."

"Yes, yes, I'm sorry." Beth nodded her head in agreement, but Alison doubted Beth would be able to keep quiet.

"Go ahead," she said to Denise.

"I remember talking to the girl at the door," Denise repeated in a whisper.

"Oh, God," moaned Beth.

Alison stood up. "Let's walk," she said to Denise. "Just you and me," she added, just in case it wasn't quite clear.

Denise seemed to have become one with the couch, so Alison grasped her by the elbow and wrestled her up. Denise was so depressed that she made no protest as Alison hustled her down the steps and out the gate, though Beth stood at the door and watched them anxiously. Alison started them off briskly. In a few minutes, when she thought perhaps Denise had been stirred out of her lethargy, she slowed to a pace at which talking was possible.

"Tell me what happened. You're going to have to sooner or later."

"That's just it." Denise slammed her fist into a tall board fence, making Alison jump. She had gone suddenly from comatose to hyped-up with no stops in between. "I don't *know* what happened. Damn it all, I just don't remember."

"You had a blackout," Alison guessed. Denise nodded. "Then tell me everything you *can* remember, and we'll try to put it together."

"I was at the bar the night of the contest," Denise began, "with some friends of mine. I was drinking a lot. I had thought maybe I would pick up a couple of quick...jobs." She looked sideways at Alison to see how she was going to react to this. Alison nodded encouragingly. "I remember Tamara asking me to go outside. She was excited from all the energy and she wanted to do a quick scene. She was willing to forgive me because I knew what she liked, and I wouldn't bother her asking for a date later. I remember going outside. The church people were there, and some of the bikers were standing around. We met at my van. And then...."

"Yes?" coached Alison. They had come to a complete stop.

"I don't remember," said Denise hopelessly. She began to walk again, her hands in her pockets. "The next thing that I remember is waking up in the van alone. Tamara was gone. I was cold. I thought, okay, I passed out, and she went into the bar by herself for the rest of the contest. I was kind of pissed off. I opened the door and got out. But then I stumbled and fell down on the pavement with my hands out. When I lifted them...." She stopped for a moment, looking over Alison's shoulder as if she saw something.

"What?"

"There was blood on them." She spoke as if in a dream. Suddenly—she did not know if it were a psychic experience, or just her own imagination—Alison saw the whole scene Denise had described. She saw the brown van parked behind the bar where the lights didn't reach very well. She saw Denise coming to and climbing over the front seat to open the door. Dressed all in black with her hair slicked back, falling as she tried to alight, falling and putting her hands out to stop herself....

"There was blood on my hands," Denise repeated, her eyes still unfocused. "I thought it was oil at first, and I was really angry, wondering if I'd gotten it on my clothes, and why the stupid bitches couldn't keep their cars fixed so they didn't leak. But when I put them up by my face I could smell that it was blood, and then the moon came out...." She raised her hands now and looked at them wonderingly.

"What happened then?" Alison whispered.

"I froze. I was so frightened that I couldn't move. I didn't look around. I didn't want to look around. I was afraid of what I might see. It seemed like I stayed there forever. I could hear the bikers laughing and talking...I was that close to them...but I couldn't make a sound. I was so scared that I thought I was going to be sick. Then really carefully, I started to get up."

"Why were you so frightened?" asked Alison. "Why did you think that there was something wrong, instead of just assuming that there'd been a fight or an accident?"

"There was too much of it," said Denise simply. "There was too much blood there. Nobody could lose that much blood and live."

"So what did you do?"

"I started to get up. But when I moved my knee back I felt something underneath it, something sharp. I reached back and picked it up." She stopped again. Her face was drawn and white.

"What was it?"

"It was a knife. It was all sticky with blood too."

"You picked it up?" Alison pushed, remembering the police report mentioning a knife too smeared for fingerprints.

"Yes."

"And then what?"

"I dropped it. I threw it down. It went beneath a car."

"Then?"

"I stood up and I walked away. I must have tried to start the van earlier, because I knew that I didn't have my keys, that it wouldn't do any good to get back into it. I just walked away really slowly, and I didn't look back."

Alison was silent a moment, not sure what to ask next. But Denise continued without prompting.

"When I threw the knife..." she said.

"What?"

"It never clattered."

"What?"

"It landed on something soft."

Thirteen

"Lunch," said Stacy firmly. Fine. Breakfast seemed an eternity ago. Alison was certain that if it had not been for Stacy's fine touch(she knew Beth slightly and had invited herself in while Alison and Dominique were walking), she would still be back in the little house with the women and the cats, unable to give them any better advice than that they get a lawyer and then go immediately to the police with the evidence. Not, she knew, what they had wanted to hear. They had been hoping she could just say she understood, she knew it couldn't be Dominique and that would be the end of it. She had wished, looking at their drawn, frightened faces, that she could have. Yet what if Dominique's convenient blackout had erased the memory of something even more gruesome than what she had told Alison?

"That was nice of you to help them with the lawyer," said Alison.

"Beth's a real nice woman. Made me coffee and showed me their place. Liz will do a good job with them." Stacy did not look at her as she spoke.

"Did she tell you the whole scoop about Dominique?"

"Yeah, pretty much. God, I feel sorry for that woman."

"She might be a killer."

Stacy shook her head decidedly. "No, not her. I can't see it in her. She likes a lot of power when she's playing, but she's not a strong woman. Not strong enough to carry out something like that."

"She woke up on the scene of the crime," Alison protested. "She was right there. She touched the weapon. She went back into the bar with blood on her hands and the knees of her pants."

"No, not her," Stacy repeated stubbornly. "Maybe if it was only Tamara. Maybe. I guess she could have freaked out. But not all three. I can't see her planning the other two. She would have broken under it. She's the kind that will get really mad and slap you or throw her drink in your face, but I can't see her sitting down and planning something like that, twice."

Alison did not reply, for truthfully her assessment of Dominique was much the same. After a moment she asked, "If you were going to cut someone, how would you do it?"

"You mean as part of a scene?"

143

"Yeah."

"What I've mostly seen used is some kind of razor, although I did see a woman who was working with flints. She'd mounted the heads onto some old wood that was all decorated with feathers and bells and the tail of a weasel her cat had brought her. They were beautiful."

Alison skipped that sideline, tempting as it was. "But mostly razors?"

"Yeah, they're good for that kind of work because they're so little and sharp. You can be delicate with them."

"What kind of razors? Blades from a package for your razor, to shave?"

"Sometimes. But that's not really very convenient for whoever's topping. It's too easy for her to slip and cut her own fingers. Something with a handle would be better. Like a straight razor, or..."

"Or what?"

"One of those little knives that you use for cutting cardboard. An exacto knife."

"Oh." They were at the restaurant now, and neither of them spoke, aside from telling the waitress their orders, until they had downed an entire basket of chips.

"Suppose," said Stacy, as their burritos arrived on hot plates, "that this isn't one killer?"

"What do you mean?"

"Well, like you say, if you get right down to the bare facts, Dominique looks like the perfect candidate for the first murder. God, I feel so sorry for that woman."

"Better feel sorry for Tamara Garrity instead."

"But the fact is that she's dead. It's all over for her now. And Dominique is probably going to have to face an investigation and all kinds of publicity even if she's totally innocent. A hell of a time to try and give up the bottle. At any rate, let's say she did it. What if somebody else picked up on that? You know, they had a couple of dykes that they wanted to get rid of and they decided to do them just the same way, kind of slide them in and hope that nobody else was looking."

"Hmm. Who?"

"Well, you're the one with the Crusader theory."

"Yes," Alison agreed slowly, "and Melanie and Carla were involved with the Crusaders. But the question is, would those people go as far as killing?"

"I've been thinking about that ever since Carla talked to me this morning. And at first I thought no. I mean, they're nuts all right, but functioning nuts. I can't see most of them, Malcolm for example, with a knife. If for no other reason than the fact that they would believe they were sending the soul of an unsaved person straight to hell. You know, that's the reason they can be so ruthless in their whole program. It's not just that they're grossed out by the idea of two guys sucking each other off. They *really believe* God is going to throw queers right in the eternal trash can, and under those circumstances it seems like any step is valid in order to save them from that, particularly if it's your kid or your wife. To be fair to Malcolm I have to say he really believed what he was doing was right and for my best interests."

"Oh, let's be sure and be fair to Malcolm. Come on, Stacy, Hitler believed that what he was doing was right, too."

"Well, yeah. But to go on about whether I think that the Crusaders could have been involved. No, not as a group project. There are too many of them who are too close to being sane, and they'd blow the whistle for sure. And, on the other end, there are too many of them who are too close to being really wacko, and they'd spill the beans, too. It would be too hard to keep the fact that you were one of God's chosen avengers to yourself. But maybe..."

"What?"

"...well, maybe if it was only one of them, or at the most two. Did you ever think of that? Carla said that she was afraid of some of those guys, and I knew right away what she meant. They were the ones who could think of themselves as being God's sword to cut down the wicked."

"More like God's machine gun."

"Either way. But I had another thought, because I still couldn't reconcile that part about the unsaved souls. Suppose they had given up on Carla and Melanie, decided that they were going right to hell in a handcart and that was just the way it was going to be. No hope for them. My suspicion is that they'd just let them stew in their own juice. You know. The mill of God grinds slow, but it grinds exceedingly fine. We'll see you in hell."

"It sounds like you're talking yourself out of this again."

"Except what if the Avenger, he or they, decided that these women were corrupting souls that *could* be saved?"

"What do you mean?"

"Take Melanie for example. Okay, she refuses to listen to the Word of God, she's garbage, to hell with her. But what if she were also tempting Krista back down the path of the wicked, and Krista confessed that to the group? Wouldn't the Sword of God be tempted to get Melanie, who's going to hell anyway, out of the picture so that Krista could be saved? You can even stretch the point and include the little girl. I'm sure the general feeling was that a child raised by perverts would have a good chance of being one herself. So by getting rid of one woman who is already going to hell, he could save two other souls, one of them belonging to an innocent child."

"Wow." Alison sat back in her chair. She felt a little ill. "But what about Carla? Who was she corrupting?"

"Who the hell knows? Carla's a hot kid on a roll—she's had a bunch of different lovers, and any one of them could be connected with the Crusaders. Hell, her roommates could be. We don't even know their names. And it wouldn't have to be a very concrete connection, either. These people are ready to grab at straws."

"Hmm." It was something to think about. "I'm going to go call home and find out about Janka."

Michelle answered. She sounded crabby.

"Is Janka okay?"

"Sure, if you call an arm in a cast and a sixty dollar X-ray bill okay. She's not even going to be able to finish warping that special order. Why do you get involved with such flakes?"

"Hi, Alison." Janka took the phone from her. "Don't pay any attention to Michelle. She's the Queen of Crabs because she's feeling left out. I'm fine, it was only a fracture and the cast is small. It wasn't your fault."

"Why is Michelle feeling left out?"

"Just because I had a good time with Seven Yellow Moons when she thought I should have been moaning and crying. Seven is a weaver, too. She's going to help me finish that big warp. She showed me some beautiful pieces that she did on a backstrap loom. She's really envious of my setup. She can't do anything like it because she lives out of her van. That's part of the reason that they're here."

"To help you? Did they foresee the accident?" She might have to start giving Lydia a little more credit.

"No, to sell their stuff. You remember, at the lesbian artist's market. This Saturday? Before the Harvest Ball? Michelle and I have a table there, too."

"Oh, yeah." Dimly Alison remembered discussions about table space and what they were going to wear to the formal. She hadn't paid much attention because she had planned on being out of town at the time. "What does Lydia have to sell, or is she just along for the ride?"

Janka laughed. "You've got to see for yourself. I have to agree with Michelle. I don't see how you ever got hooked up with that woman."

"It was on the rebound. It wouldn't have lasted if she hadn't moved in."

"And it never would have ended if she hadn't moved out. We're going to send you to an assertiveness training seminar for your birthday."

"Never mind. I just wanted to see how you were. Incidently, how would you feel about doing some more undercover work if we decide it's warranted?"

146

"Get a chance to play Norma again? I'd love it. I'm sure I can work the arm in. Maybe my sister's lover is violent."

"Well, plan on it and we'll talk later."

"So how is she?" Stacy asked as she and Alison left the restaurant. Alison reported the news about Janka, Seven Yellow Moons, and Lydia. "Did she mention Carla?"

"No. I'm sure she went home to blab everything to her roommates. I'll bet she goes back to work tonight just so she can share with strangers."

"Do you think she should? Don't you think that the killer might still be waiting for her?"

"Surely not. It would be stupid, the way everyone is alerted. The Rubyfruit will be the most secure place to go now. I'm sure there're going to be extra patrols swinging by all night."

"She was fucking a cop and it didn't stop him." At that, Alison opened her mouth to protest, though she was not sure exactly what to say, but Stacy did not give her the chance. "Did you like it, baby?" she asked teasingly, pulling Alison close to her, whispering in her ear. "I know she packs a big dildo—did she use it in your cunt? Would you like me to do that, fuck you nice and slow?"

For a moment Alison forgot that they were standing on a public sidewalk, so hot was her quick rush of desire. She strained her pelvis up towards Stacy as if the woman was already inside her, thrusting with slow strokes. Daydreaming, she recreated the scene with Carla using new players—herself in the role of the lusty top, Stacy in the role of the naive bottom. Her fingers crept up to stroke and then pull Stacy's hair.

"Excuse me. Coming through." A young man with a cartload of laundry jostled past them and Alison was bumped out of her fantasy.

"Not here," she said to Stacy, who had slid her hand around her waist, beneath her T-shirt. "We're right in the middle of town."

"What we're right in the middle of is the gay ghetto. Who's going to care? Look at some of these poor women—watching us is probably the most exciting thing that's happened to them in years. We're saving their sex lives by giving them something to fantasize about while they dry hump."

"No," said Alison firmly, pushing her away.

"You'll be sorry later," Stacy teased. "I'll make you beg."

"You'll do that anyway." For a moment they locked eyes, again oblivious to their surroundings. Slowly, Alison ran the tip of her tongue over her lips.

Stacy looked away first. "Baby, oh, baby," she murmured. "Don't expect me to behave if you're going to keep on being such a hot woman."

"Think of me as Nancy Drew. Clean-cut. You can be my boyish friend

George." Happily she tucked her hand through Stacy's arm.

"Thanks, Nancy. Since we're right here, why don't we walk over to Womynbooks? They back-ordered something for me a couple of weeks ago and I want to see if it's come in yet."

While Stacy checked with the staffer Alison wandered to the back of the store and studied the bulletin board. There were handwritten signs from women looking for roommates, kittens, support groups and soccer teams, leaflets advertising concerts, poetry readings and this year's Gay Rodeo. Alison took one that told about the lesbian artists' sale and Harvest Ball. She noticed a stack of the WAVAW fliers next to them.

Stacy joined her. Alison tipped the book in her hands up so that she could read the title.

"George, I didn't know you were an aspiring carpenter."

"Ah, Nancy, there are many things about me you have yet to discover." Stacy was in a teasing mood now that they had eaten. "That's part of the fun of a new relationship."

"Oh, are we a relationship now?" The thought rather scared Alison. Much as she liked Stacy, couldn't they just be fuck buddies for a while?

"Mmm, I guess you're right. Joanne Loulan says that lesbians tend to get married on the first date—"

"Which we haven't even really had," broke in Alison.

"What about the quilt show? What about soccer?"

"They don't count. I mean a real date where you get dressed up and you're really nervous beforehand and you have firm plans...."

"And you can bring each other flowers? Let's do it." Stacy scanned the leaflets. "Look, here's the perfect event. The Lesbian Chorus is sponsoring another Harvest Ball. Did you go last year?"

"No. I was working."

"Oh, it was great. Everybody dressed to the teeth. I'm talking tuxedos and formals and heels, the whole bit. The prom you never got to go to." She made a face. "Or a chance to forget the prom that you did go to."

"Do we have to go butch/femme?" It wasn't the question Alison wanted to ask. What she really wanted to know was what would happen if she appeared in public, in real public, with Stacy. Would she immediately become categorized or even ostracized? She had already tasted it and wasn't sure she could deal with it.

"Yeah, they won't let us in at the door otherwise. You know how strict those chorus women are about role playing. No, of course not. Everybody just wore what they had the most fun with. I had this great purple formal that I ran up, sequins on the top and velvet on the bottom, and evening gloves." She indicated a place on her upper arm, showing how high they had come. "I even got my hair done up in a French twist and glittered."

"I don't know. That might be too much for me." Alison meant that she had nothing that fancy in her wardrobe, but in a way she also meant that she was not at all sure that she was ready for this second coming out.

"Oh, I got a little carried away. There were lots of women there in their regular clothes, or little numbers that they'd picked up at the Salvation Army. I just like to dress up."

"So I've heard," Alison remarked dryly. A little spark, the same heat that had overcome them on the sidewalk passed between them, and it seemed to Alison for a moment that they were not really making plans for a public dance, but arrangements that were much, much more intimate.

"So, do you want to go? On a real date?"

"But we won't get married?"

"Hell, no, we'll defy lesbian tradition. We not only won't get married, we won't even go into therapy together right away. We'll just date. How's that for unconventional?"

"Okay."

Stacy took one of the dance fliers and a WAVAW leaflet. "Do you want to go home now?"

"To tell the absolute truth, no. I'm not in the mood to deal with company, especially if it's Lydia reading the Taro."

"Lavender. I don't get it. If you didn't invite her and you don't want her there why don't you just tell her to leave?" Stacy put her book down on the counter and the staffer slowly began writing out a receipt.

"You're right, you don't get it. To get Lydia out of that house I would actually have to move her things out bodily and change the locks on the door. It's not that she would refuse, she just wouldn't get around to doing it. She stretched a week-long stay between apartments into a four month odyssey that way. It will take less energy to just wait her out." Alison stopped talking to look at a case of jewelry that was mounted next to the door. "Look at these," she said, pointing to pair of dangling earrings. "They look just like the ones Tamara was wearing in that photo."

"Oh, yeah, I remember those. They're made by somebody local. I've seen a couple of women with them." Stacy was more interested in analyzing her than the earrings. "I don't understand. I would think that you had to be fairly assertive, if not actually pushy, in your line of work."

"Well, sometimes it just doesn't carry over to the old private life. It's like strict teachers who raise really bratty kids. I suppose you always satisfy your lovers completely and never get bored with one another, huh?"

"Now that you put it that way. I have clothes that need mending, too. How about coming over and working on your quilt? I really have to work, though. You have to go home if you're going to be bad." Stacy unlocked the driver's door, got in and leaned across to the passenger's side. Alison opened the door and slipped in.

"I will be Nancy Drew practicing local crafts," she promised. "She used to do that, you know. If she was solving a mystery in Scotland she'd be out dancing the Highland fling in a kilt sooner or later." There was a book sitting in the middle of the seat. She was sure it hadn't been there before, because it was lying right on top of her seatbelt. "Where did this come from?"

Stacy glanced down. "Oh, my photos!" She took a manila envelope that was sticking out from between the pages. "Mark must have left it while we were in the bookstore. I've been wanting to see these. Look, it's my flier." She showed Alison the slick paper printed in blues and greys. There were two photos of quilts alone and two of Stacy working, interspersed with text and the name of the gallery.

"What does the guy do, follow you around?"

"Oh, no, he must have just seen my car. He knew how much I was looking forward to seeing these."

"Has he got a crush on you or what?" Alison really didn't want to talk about Mark, felt a distinct crabbiness at the mere mention of his name.

Stacy laughed. "Hardly. I've know him since he was a kid. Or, rather, I knew him when he was a kid, and then I met him again when he was older, when he came back from living with his mother. I only met her a couple of times, and I don't remember her well, but according to Pam...."

"Who is?"

"My upstairs neighbor. Haven't you met her? I'll have to introduce you. She's nice. She was one of Mark's co-mothers. His real mom basically gave him away for several years while she was trying to get her own stuff together, and Pam and three other woman took care of him. But according to Pam, I'm a dead ringer for his real mother. So, I think that if he has a crush it's not the kind that you mean, more like he sees me as a mother figure."

"But you're what, ten years older than he is?"

"More like fifteen, and you know how that is at that age. He probably isn't sure if they had cars when I was a kid. Apparently things didn't work out well with his birth mom. She wasn't real nurturing. I really haven't got the whole story...Pam is kind of sensitive about it. But I would guess that there was a lot of unsettled stuff between them when she died, and I think that he's kind of trying to reshape their reality with me. You know, kind of act out what he wished their life was like so that he doesn't have all these bad

150

memories to deal with. I think that's why the leather stuff freaked him out so bad last year—that wasn't the way he wanted Mama to be."

"It sounds to me as if he'd be better off getting some therapy and dealing with the old shit," objected Alison.

"Well, I think so, too and I've even suggested it. But you can't make somebody go to therapy."

"Not unless you're one of the Crusaders."

"Eech, don't remind me." Stacy shivered as she pulled away from the curb. "Look where that gets them. Carla was lucky that she got away. I'll bet that group is full of people who are right on the edge of freaking out because their hearts are telling them one thing and they're having the opposite screamed at them. But who am I to tell somebody to get into therapy? I've got some pretty dismal scenes from my own childhood that could stand working out and I haven't gone yet myself. It's hard enough to find a dyke you can afford, but I've also got to find one who doesn't think being in the scene is sick."

"Mmm," said Alison, and because she really didn't want to waste any more time talking about Mark, and didn't even want to *touch* the topic of whether *she* should be in therapy, she asked, "When's your next soccer game?"

* * *

Alison pushed her front door open gingerly. Of course it was unlocked. She was going to have to impress upon her uninvited house guests that a crisis existed and security measures would have to be stepped up. She was relieved to see no sign of Lydia though it was apparent that she had cooked another meal, leaving the second mess on top of the first. Well, Alison could think while she washed the dishes.

Suppose Stacy's theory about the copycat murders was correct? Suppose Dominique was indeed the first killer, and the other two were unrelated, chances seized by the as yet faceless person to whom Stacy referred as the Sword of God? The title was good, it gave Alison a kind of image of the kind of person it might be. Someone like the man who walked sternly through Cheeseman Park on sunny days when every faggot in town was working on his tan, carrying a homemade sign that said, 'Homosexuality is a sin.' Or maybe more like the kids who cruised around in the car that proclaimed in white paint, 'Jesus didn't smoke, why should you?' on one side and 'God didn't create Adam and Steve,' on the other. She saw them sometimes at King's Soopers, or when she was getting a salad at the Pizza Hut. She avoided them, even though she was quite sure that 'Dyke' was not painted on her forehead in luminescent letters. There was something too creepy about them.

151

Had Malcolm, perhaps, had that same look when, with a nod, he had ordered her hands pinned behind her back? Stacy had said that he had beaten her, tried to imprison her. He had struck back at her by marrying her lover, and, out of his obsession, had formed the Crusaders operation. Was he still striking back at her through other women? Was he in fact…. She stood still, her hands in the soapy water. Was he striking back by killing Stacy's clients, hoping to set her up to take the rap? She thought long and hard, her brow furrowed as she automatically scrubbed a handful of silverware. She hadn't thought of that angle before, and she liked it because it cleared Dominique. She still preferred that the killer be a completely loathsome man, rather than another dyke. Then she shook her head. Dominique might not be guilty, might only be an unfortunate woman with a drinking problem and the knack for being in the wrong place at the wrong time, but she could not make the story fit. If Malcolm or his buddies had killed the women to frame Stacy where did Carla fit in? For a moment she wondered if that attack had been a mistake. No, that was stretching it, wasn't it? And, additionally, wouldn't he have planted some evidence, leaked something to the police? As far as she knew Stacy had not even been questioned, and there were certainly no grounds at all to arrest her. No, if any of the killings were the work of the Crusaders, Stacy's theory made more sense—that they were removing certain women to save others.

So what could she do to advance either of the theories, to get them to the point where Jones and Jorgenson, via her father, might pay some attention? She could talk to Krista and see if Melanie had indeed been trying to convince her to leave the straight and narrow. She could try to establish the whereabouts of the Crusaders on the night that Carla was attacked. She already knew that they were on the scene the night that Melanie was killed. That reminded her of an idea she'd had earlier in the day. She wanted to call the gay paper and see if they had taken any more photos at the Ms. Leather contest than the ones printed. Perhaps she could arrange to look at them uncropped.

The light was blinking on her answering machine. For a moment she hesitated, imagining that it was more reprimands from her father or another call from Sergeant Obrachta demanding that she get her ass into the station and explain herself. But, though she had barely gotten home, the message might be from Stacy. One of the nice things about a new relationship—dating, Alison corrected herself—was that you could get away with phoning ten times a day, ten minutes apart if you wanted to.

The first voice confirmed her worst fears. "This is Sergeant Obrachta. I know you are not out of town. You had better be in here by ten o'clock tomorrow to tell me why I shouldn't recommend a suspension." The phone was slammed down.

Oh. She guessed she wouldn't plan anything for the morning. The second message began. No identification.

"Denise is in jail." Beth's voice was toneless, completely washed of color. Alison winced. Damn it, she supposed something else must have been found at the scene of the crime to tie her in. She'd have to see if Robert could find out for her. What a case the DA could make of a dominatrix gone berserk, cutting just a bit harder than she was used to. She shuddered. She would call Beth a little later to see if she was all right and had a friend who could stay with her.

She was sorry now that she had ever turned on the damn machine. At least the third message was Stacy's sweet voice. She waited for some teasing, a mushy comment about how she had enjoyed their day. Instead, what Stacy said was, "Alison? There's something really strange about this leaflet."

* * *

Sitting in the front of Seven Yellow Moons' van, Alison sighed. On her own she would have not chosen to go out tonight. But Lydia and Seven Yellow Moons, who had not been in a city for months, were determined, and she could not let them go alone in good conscience. She really did believe there was safety in numbers, especially if one of those numbers was toting a gun. Lydia might irritate the shit out of her, but she would still feel terrible if she were the next victim. So she had agreed to go with them to the Blue Ryder which had reopened under tight security by WAVAW as well as frequent patrol by the city police. The latter fact she knew she had to thank her father for. She had also arranged to have Stacy meet them there with the leaflet.

Somehow she had gotten the prize front seat, and she could hear Michelle and Lydia sniping at each other from where they sat on the floor of the back. Michelle was feeling jealous, and when Michelle was unhappy, everyone was unhappy. "What is it?" she snapped when Seven Yellow Moons pulled to a stop.

At the entrance to the parking lot of the Blue Ryder stood three women holding flashlights. They were wearing plastic orange safety vests, trimmed with white reflective tape, over their jackets. Behind them, and off to the side, were another half dozen women similarly dressed, clustered around a Coleman lantern. The middle woman, whom Alison was sure she had seen before, but could not place, waved the van to a stop. Seven Yellow Moons rolled down her window.

Michelle seemed to find the sudden silence something that needed to be filled. "You know," she said, "I just don't know how you didn't know your tire was going flat, Alison. You must have driven on the rim for at least a couple of blocks to destroy it like that."

"I don't know either, Michelle," she answered patiently. "Ask me a couple hundred more times and maybe I'll be able to come up with something." A second woman was approaching her window. This one Alison recognized as Trudy's friend from WAVAW. She cranked her window down.

"Hi," said the woman, giving no sign at all of recognizing her. "Do you guys know about the lesbian killings? Know that it might be dangerous to be out?"

"Yeah." Alison answered without explanation. Something about the first woman's voice sparked a memory in her and she half-turned to look at her across Seven Yellow Moons. She was one of the leather dykes from the Rubyfruit, the one whom Michelle had pointed out in the paper as an ex-lover of Melanie's. Behind her Alison could see one of the halfbacks from Stacy's soccer team, and beyond that, one of the staffers from Womynbooks. It looked as if everyone had agreed to forget their personal differences in order to provide protection tonight.

"You'll get an escort from your car to the bar, and one when you leave." The woman was speaking with some difficulty because she was holding a silver policeman's whistle in one corner of her mouth. Alison noticed that she was carrying a can of mace in her free hand. Alison glanced at the group beyond her, whom she assumed was the escort and saw that most of them were carrying similar cans, though a few had baseball bats instead. "There's a roped off area in front of the bar where you can go if you need to get some air, but otherwise you'll only be allowed to go back and forth when you arrive and leave. Please, everybody," she said earnestly, "this isn't a night for making out in the car. Do it at home behind locked doors."

There was a dollar cover. "Oh, it's country/western night," Alison said, hearing the strains of *Sweethearts of the Rodeo.*

Michelle looked sour and Lydia appeared positively aghast. For a moment it seemed as if she might ask for her four quarters back, but Alison jostled her gently past the table, intent on finding Stacy.

At first she couldn't believe how many women were there. It was like Saturday night, like Halloween, like New Year's. She would have thought that any dyke with a choice would have stayed safe at home. But, then, maybe that was why they were here. Maybe they needed to celebrate being alive, maybe they wanted to show that they could not be terrorized off the streets.

Alison remembered a snatch of a Holly Near song, something about fear turning to rage and fighting back. She turned before she entered, to ask if they could use her on a later shift in the parking lot, but their four-woman escort had faded back into the night.

She lost her friends almost immediately. Fine, she wanted to find Stacy and see what she meant about the fliers. Beneath her own arm she was clutching an envelope of photos. Michelle, who had connections everywhere, had gotten them for her from a friend on the gay rag. They had stopped to pick them up on the way. If she could find a place to do it she would like to take a look through them. Perhaps it would help in planning her strategy for the next day. As she weaved her way through the bar she was struck, first, by the wild party spit-in-their-face mood and secondly, by the number of women she knew. As in the parking lot, the bar seemed a wonderful mixture of groups she had never seen mingle before. There were leatherdykes doing the two-step with women from the newspaper. The lesbian mothers' group was mingling and overflowing into a huge group of soccer players, who were in turn mixed with women she had seen before only on stage, performing with the women's chorus. She wondered suddenly if Stacy's upstairs neighbor, Pam, was there. For some reason which she couldn't put her finger on, she thought that it would be a good thing for her to talk to Pam. But she forgot the whim in the next moment when she spotted Stacy on the sunken dance floor. She was one of the many women who had not forgotten it was country western night and who had come dressed for the occasion. She was wearing an emerald green shirt, silky, that had a long white fringe around the western yoke and down both sleeves, and she was dancing a very credible two-step with, of all people, Carla. Carla also had on a western shirt and—this surprised Alison—a denim skirt that stopped about three inches above the tops of her cowboy boots. She had a red bandana tied around her neck and a matching one around her head. Alison leaned over the railing to watch.

The singers mourned, for the last time, being midnight girls in a sunset town. As the dancers were leaving the floor Alison managed to catch Stacy's eye and waved. Both of the floor exits seemed hopelessly clogged and so Stacy, trailing Carla, jostled her way over to the railing.

"Have you ever seen anything like this?" Stacy practically had to shout over the music.

"Never." Now that they were up close, Alison could appreciate the details on their outfits. Carla's boots really caught her attention. Obviously second hand, they must have belonged to some rodeo queen in better days. They were dyed red and the top stitching had been done in multicolored thread.

"Hot boots, Carla," she yelled admiringly, wishing for a moment that she were decked out too. Carla preened happily.

"Have you got the night off?"

Carla stood on tiptoe to yell back. "No, the bar's closed tonight! Because of the murders!" She sounded just as pleased as if she'd unexpectedly gotten an extra snow day. It probably hadn't occurred to her the financial beating Margie would take because of it. It did, however, partly explain why there was such a crowd.

"Hey, you haven't been telling anybody about the stuff we talked about, have you? About the case?"

Carla looked hurt. "Me?" she said, touching her chest as if she simply couldn't believe the accusation. Stacy caught Alison's eye and they nodded. She had told every detail to everyone she'd met.

"Come on up," Alison urged Stacy. "I want to find a place where we..." She almost said ...can look at the papers, but, catching Carla's eager, 'what's-going-to-happen-next?' look changed it to, "...can talk."

Stacy glanced over at the exit which was still clogged. It looked as if a fight between a woman in a confederate army shirt and another in a gingham dress was going to break out on the steps at any moment. Stacy reached up and grabbed the brass railing and hauled herself over the bars, very nearly knocking over a pitcher of beer on a nearby table with her boots in the process. Carla, not the least upset about being left without a partner, danced happily away from the rail. Alison wondered for a moment if packing etiquette permitted carrying a dildo beneath a skirt. But fascinating as the information might be, it was not the time to pursue it. Alison reminded herself of this reluctantly, admiring the way that the fringe on Stacy's shirt swung as she walked. This was time for business, not for thinking of how the green satin would slide beneath her fingers, her mouth; how the pearl snaps down the front would all burst open with one good tug....

"Come on," yelled Stacy, "I want to see what you think of this." Stacy took Alison's hand to lead her through the crowd. Alison was painfully aware of more than one set of eyebrows raised in their direction. Stacy shoved through the hoards of women in front of the bar to an unlit corner. She pushed open a door Alison had never seen before.

They found themselves in a tiny office. "Well, are we one of the elite?" Alison asked with a lifted eyebrow.

"Oh, I've had a drink here with Jenny a time or two."

Which means exactly what? And am I going to do this every time she says anything, wonder if she means what the words say or something else? Am I going to be jealous of tricks? Alison opened her mouth and then closed it again. This was not the time for heartfelt confessions, particularly since they had decided that they were only dating. On the other hand, why not start out the way she intended to continue?

"So," she said briskly to Stacy, as if they were at a cocktail party with several hours to kill on chitchat, "are you monogamous?"

Stacy, who had taken a folded leaflet from her pocket, looked startled. "Aren't we playing detective right now?" she asked.

"Well, yes, but we want to show the audience that we're people, too. Kind of the Cagney and Lacey approach—you know, where Mary Beth talks about her son joining the Marines and Christine talks about her drinking problem."

"Are you sure that our audience wouldn't prefer to hear about my new kitten and the trouble he's having hitting the kitty box?"

"Positive. We're playing after eight to an adult audience. It's dying to know if we're compatible at all, just for dating, of course, or if I should go back to my lonely existence as third wheel to Michelle and Janka."

"Well, if you mean do I date more than one woman at a time, yes I do. Not that I am now, but I fiercely reserve the option. If you mean do I have more than one relationship—a relationship being when you've decided it's true love and it's going to last forever, not like all those false alarms with those other sluts, and people invite you places together and you've made at least one joint purchase—at a time no, I don't. I don't have fuck buddies, either. I find that I can't maintain emotionally. However, I don't count my work as anything but work, so if you're asking, am I going to forsake my job and become a saved woman the minute I fall in love and start thinking of joint mortgages, no, I'm not. Incidently, I don't date or see any of my customers socially or take on anybody in those categories. So, hypothetically speaking, my main squeeze would not need to eye the soccer team or my neighbors questioningly."

"Oh. So what's with the leaflet?"

"We end like this?"

"The audience is tired of our personal problems. It wants to move on with the plot."

Stacy shook her head. "Fine, but it may have to sit through a long boring personal scene later in which the dyke detectives bicker over the fact that one is supposed to spill her guts while the other puts out nothing."

"Oh, that's scheduled much, much later in the season. Now the scene is the exciting clue of the leaflet."

"Okay. Did you bring yours? You are going to be so amazed when you see what a good job of detecting I did on my own."

Alison laid her own leaflet on the desk.

"Okay, the difference is that this second flier has different contact numbers on it. See? Now I thought, maybe it's no big deal...."

Alison felt rather let down. "You're right, maybe it's no big deal."

"But then I thought, well, it *is* funny, at any rate. Look at this." Stacy held her leaflet up to the light. "See here? Look at the numbers really close. You can see where they've been changed. Somebody typed the new numbers on a piece of paper and then cut the little piece out and glued it over the old ones. Then they copied the whole thing. But you can see the shadow where they did it right here at the edge."

"Yeah, I've done that myself on term papers. So what's the excitement? They decided to add optional numbers on the later leaflets so the first two phones wouldn't be overloaded."

"It just seemed funny to me," Stacy repeated. "See, the reason that I even noticed was that, when I glanced at the leaflet at your house, I recognized both of the phone numbers. The first one is Trudy's, and I recognized it because it's on our soccer phone tree and it's real easy to remember. See, the last digits are 1234. The second one is the Gay Community Center's line. I worked there last year."

"Well, I think that was very Delafield-like, but I still don't see the point."

"There's no reason to change either of those numbers. They both have call forwarding. If Trudy, say, wanted to go out to a bar she could have her phone forwarded there, or she could have it forwarded to someone else's number and that person could take the calls. Same with the GCC. It's not like these calls are going to one person, anyway, because if they were, and she left to give a ride or something, then there'd be no one home for the next caller. They're going to somebody who's acting like a dispatcher. I'll bet that tonight anybody calling from that first flier is being bounced right to this bar."

"So you think someone put out a set of bogus fliers with different numbers," Alison said slowly. "What's the point in that?"

"Well, what if there was another reason that you wanted to get dykes in your car? What if, instead of helping, you wanted to do something else? Like maybe rough them up a little or...."

Alison's mouth dropped open. "No," she whispered.

"Yeah. Here would be this woman all trusting and ready to chat. Hell, she might even ask you to come in while she checked her house out."

"But surely no one would get in a car with a strange man," Alison protested.

"If he said he was from the Gay Community Center? That the Men's Chorus or the study group was helping their sisters out? Or it wouldn't even

158

have to be a man. What if you were a woman, an ex-dyke maybe even, who really believed that your sisters were going to hell and that the best thing for them would be a little reprogramming, even if it had to be forced? You'd be willing to run your station wagon into enemy territory to make a pickup and then join the guys later, wouldn't you?"

"The Crusaders," Alison breathed.

"And this number just happens to have the same prefix as their hotline."

"Did you call it?"

Stacy shuddered. "No. I know it's stupid, I know they don't know where I am and where I live, but I just couldn't bring myself to call. It was like—I don't know, inviting a vampire in your window. You know, they can be out there flapping against it, but you're safe as long as you don't ask them in. I felt like if I connected with them over the wire this voice would come on saying, "Ha, ha, ha, you slut, we've got you now!" She shrugged apologetically. "What can I say? I guess the audience gets a glimpse at my paranoia."

"Hey, I don't blame you. You've been through enough with those people. But do me a favor. Is your little lawyer friend here tonight?"

"She was earlier."

"See if you can get her in here."

Stacy saluted. "I take it your rank is higher than mine?"

"Always. Everytime you get a promotion I get a better one."

As the door opened a wave of music swelled into the small room, shaking Alison as if by a heavy wind. She put both hands on the desk to brace herself and shouted, "And grab Trudy!" Hell, everybody in the world was out there. She didn't see why Trudy wouldn't be. She had little hope, though, that Stacy heard her. She would have to send her out again, for they needed to make sure that the WAVAW women hadn't changed the number themselves as she had first supposed. Stacy might be gone as long as ten or fifteen minutes fighting her way through the crowd. That gave her enough time to look at the photos.

There were two sheets, covered with strips of photos no bigger than the negatives, but less than half were of the Rubyfruit the night of the Ms. Leather contest. The others were of other current events: The Lesbian Follies and what appeared to be a square dancing group. They were tempting, but she focused resolutely on the former. Not that it did much good. They were so small that she could see what was happening only generally; she could not pick out faces and detail. There was another, bigger shot of the bikers, with the Crusaders in the background. That must have tickled the fancy of the photographer, because the next shot showed six women dressed in leather right in front of the protesters. There were a couple of shots of the contestants inside the bar. One looked as if the flash had misfired.

And there was a shot of Tamara Garrity, easy to recognize because it was a close-up. She was pouting, posing and the light flashed off the dangling earrings that Carla had described. Alison put the sheet down, feeling sick. She would have to get the photos blown up if she wanted to see anything. It probably wouldn't be worth it.

Liz, for all that she'd had several drinks and was wearing two curled paper streamers in her hair, was quick to catch on.

"Can the leafletting be stopped legally?" Alison asked anxiously.

"Sure. Tomorrow. Just like I told Trudy."

"What?" Had she heard right?

"Oh, yeah, I forgot to tell you." Stacy was still looking pleased with herself. "I checked with Trudy when I saw her earlier. She said that the new phone numbers were definitely not theirs."

"You told her this theory?"

"Oh, yeah, she was real pissed."

"And she hauled me off the dance floor," said Liz. "All of a sudden I'm not leatherslime, I'm free legal aid. I'm trying to come on to some hot young thing and I keep ending up outside or in a corner."

"What did she say to you?" Alison asked. "Is she still here?"

"Nah, I saw her get her coat a while ago."

"What did she say before she left?"

"Well, she said, 'what can you do', and I said, 'nothing until tomorrow,' and she said, 'we may be talking about women's lives here,' and I said, 'that might be what you think and it might be what I think, but all we're talking about legally is fraudulent use of the phone system,' and she said, 'isn't that enough?' and I said, 'not to get a judge out of bed and get a warrant at night,' and she said 'don't you care what's happening', and I said 'I don't make the laws'. And then I said, 'why don't you you call the detectives on the case and talk to them?'" Liz stopped to take a deep breath.

"You've got a good memory," complimented Alison.

"I'm a lawyer," Liz said. "Having a good memory is what being a lawyer is all about. Anyway, she said, 'somebody else could get killed tonight and the police don't care. They don't care about women, and they especially don't care about dykes. That number has to be closed tonight, and if anything gets done it's going to get done by the women, not the cops.'"

Stacy and Alison looked at one another.

"If someone knew where that phone was located," said Stacy slowly, "couldn't they cut the wires to the house? Isn't that fairly easy? I see it all the time on TV."

"J.J. used to install phones, and I saw her head out with Trudy. But how could they get the address just from having the phone number? The phone company won't give that kind of information out."

"You could call it. You could have them come to pick up a rider. And then you could follow them home."

Alison was dismayed. "Do you think they did that?"

Liz interrupted, "Have I not painted a clear enough picture here? Do the two of you realize that back on the dance floor there is a woman waiting to fall into my arms? Is free legal aid over for tonight?"

Alison nodded absently, too engrossed in her own thoughts to thank her. "Do you think that's what they did?"

"It would be like Trudy. She's real into civil disobedience and doing whatever she thinks needs to be done, whether it's legal or not. She's been in court a couple of times for vandalizing porn joints. Hey, you want to know something funny? It's Carla that Liz is trying to pick up."

Alison hardly heard the gossip. "But that could be dangerous. Suppose they're the killers? Did she even think of that?"

"Well, we didn't talk about that," admitted Stacy. "Just that the group has hassled dykes before and possibly done some 'deprogramming'. Actually," Stacy looked a little sheepish, "I kind of ran at the mouth. I mean, this is the first time that Trudy has treated me like anything but shit for a long time."

Alison was too engrossed to be sympathetic. "Great. So what if they pop off the decoy as soon as they get her out of the parking lot? It's not going to do her much good if the back-up team is in a car behind."

"But they'd surely send in a woman. Trudy wouldn't get in a car with a man after she was warned. So there'd be one woman, maybe two at the most. Suppose they had one woman call but three got into the car? 'Hi, our car won't start. We all live at the same place.' There's no way, in that situation, that they could knife anybody. Just lean over the seat and say, 'Excuse me' politely? They'd have to stop for help, and once they stopped, the tailing car would be right on them. Plus there's the fact that the killer, even if it is somebody from the Crusaders, seems to be choosing specific women, like we talked about. I'll bet this is nothing more than a little nonconsensual evangelism, a case of seizing the opportunity. Which is a drag, but not deadly. And Trudy's not a fool. Did you see the organization in the parking lot? She wouldn't go in alone."

"And what if they lost the tail? What if they are the killers and they prefer using knives but happen to have a gun besides?"

"What if a woman calls that number tonight and is found dead tomorrow? They didn't need your permission, Alison. Not to be insulting, but I think that Trudy was right about this case moving really slow, and I think she's right about protecting ourselves. They had to decide what to do for themselves."

Alison bit at her fingernail. "Shit. Now what do I do?"

"Why do anything?"

"Because vigilantism happens to be illegal. Because we might already...."

"*We* as in the rest of the boys and girls in blue?"

"Technically the jerks in the three piece suits. They might already have the Crusaders staked and this would fuck up a legitimate operation. What if somebody gets killed? What if they kill somebody?"

"Forget it," advised Stacy. "You don't have a corner on controlling what people do. You don't even know what they're going to do. You don't know that they did anything. For all we know Trudy is back out on the dance floor or at home with a good book."

"Right. I just know she's mixing it up with those people. People think that they can just go into situations like this totally untrained and everything will just work out fine. Doesn't it occur to them that there's a reason we have to go to school?"

"Alison," Stacy said firmly, "you are obsessing on this."

Alison could not believe that she had heard correctly. She opened her mouth, but Stacy cut her off. "No, don't tell me that of course you are and it's a worthy thing to obsess about. I know that. I know you are a caring, concerned woman. But obsessing is obsessing, and it is obsession when you're driving yourself crazy about something you can't do anything about. Suppose you decide that it is best for everybody if you call up the dicks and get them out of bed. What are you going to tell them? 'We think that maybe this one group was misrepresenting themselves over the phone to maybe do something bad and maybe these other women called them and now maybe they're the ones who are doing something they shouldn't? They're somewhere right now. Maybe.' It isn't going to fly, Alison. What has been these guys' attitude when you had something solid to say? Wasn't it a variation of 'go away, little girl'? I'll bet you money that if you call those men and *if* they believe you and think that it's important to do something now and not wait till tomorrow, it will not be the Crusaders who are arrested. It will be Trudy and her gang. And where is the fucking justice in that?"

Alison closed her eyes. Her head was swimming, and suddenly she felt tired. Much too tired to make even simple choices, let alone have life and death decisions resting on her shoulders. She leaned against the shelves.

"Why don't you come home with me tonight?" Stacy asked gently.

"Yes," Alison said, so softly that she could barely hear the answer herself.

162

Fourteen

"I'd like a quick shower," said Stacy as they stepped through the door. Alison nodded. Her mouth was dry. She went into the living end of the work room, thinking that she would read a magazine. But she found it impossible. All she could think about was Stacy in the shower, soaping herself. There were three candles on the mantle of the fireplace and she lit them. Then she turned out the light and just sat. Finally she heard the water cut off. Then Stacy stepped through the door.

Her robe was the same emerald green as her shirt. It was cut full and the material, though Alison knew it was probably really a polyblend, draped and fell like silk. She was still wearing her long earrings. They caught the candlelight as she stood for a moment by the door, just looking at Alison. Alison said nothing, but she was aware that her heart had speeded up, that it was pounding in her chest.

Still without speaking Stacy crossed over to the stereo. She didn't have to search for the tape that she wanted. It was already in. In anticipation of me, wondered Alison, or left over from someone else? Stop that, this isn't going to work if you get obsessed. 'Obsessed.' Stacy's word. Was she really obsessed with the murders? Now wasn't the time to analyze, now was the time to keep her eyes on Stacy as the music filled the room. Please, not Bolero, she thought, and stifled a nervous giggle. But it was something entirely different, something light and inviting that her country/western background had not prepared her to name.

Stacy stepped into the room and took a slow twirl, the skirt of the robe flying out around her. Visions of ballroom scenes, shots from old movies, flew through Alison's mind and then out again, leaving room only for watching Stacy cross over to her. Watching, as if she were a third person, Stacy pull the other woman—herself—to her feet, hold her close and sway with her for a moment. Part of her was feeling the cool touch of the fabric beneath her fingers, bunching it in one hand near the small of Stacy's back, but another part was watching. This part was creating the lesbian scene that had never been shown in all the old classics late at night. This part approved of the candlelight and the music and the flowing robe, and wished that Alison were

dressed in something a little more romantic, perhaps full tails, a cummer-
bund that matched Stacy's green, or maybe a robe of her own, full and swirl-
ing around behind her as the music changed and Stacy began to waltz.

Alison followed smoothly; she had been to enough family weddings. But
never had she gotten this feeling of heady excitement or abandon from the
nice young men her relatives pushed her way. She tilted her head back so that
she could gaze into Stacy's dark eyes, and the watching director approved,
loved the way that the candlelight caught in their depths, just as it had on the
jewelry that she wore in her ears and around her neck.

Stacy brought her hand slowly up Alison's back to her shoulder, her neck,
her head. Still dancing, she drew Alison's face to hers and pressed one soft
kiss on her lips. Then she was kissing her neck, her eyes, her ears, while Alison's mouth grew even more dry with desire and the hidden director nodded
yes, take your time, make her want it, make us all want it. Alison's hand was
on Stacy's shoulder and without being aware that she willed it, found it suddenly in Stacy's dark hair, found herself clutching a handful of the curls close
to the scalp. Slowly, but relentlessly, she pulled back, pulling Stacy's face
away from hers and then forcing her out of her arms, down on her knees. She
was thrilled by the little gasp of excitement that escaped Stacy, followed by a
moan low in her throat. She was frightened, too, that she was behaving awk-
wardly, making a fool of herself, that at any moment Stacy would shake her
off and leap to her feet, saying briskly, well, that's enough of that. But the
passion overcame the fear, and she pulled Stacy's face hard into the crotch of
her loose pants, reassured by how eagerly the other woman pressed her
mouth against the thin fabric.

For a moment she stood still, memories, fantasies, flowing through her
mind, overlapping and weaving into what was happening now, the feel of
Stacy's mouth against her. The moment she had first touched another girl's
breast and miraculously the nipple had hardened beneath her hand. Standing
with her back to the door of the playroom, her hand slid beneath Stacy's
robe.

Alison pushed Stacy away from her, keeping her on her knees. Slowly she
began to pull her own shirt off over her head. Normally, she was not this dramatic. She wasn't that overjoyed with her body, particularly her breasts,
which were large and pendulous, too large, she thought, for the rest of her
body. But she felt beautiful tonight, a woman in a movie, a real woman at
whom the hidden director nodded approval, stretch marks, large breasts,
thirty-three year old stomach and all. None of those plastic Hollywood
model types for her dyke love scenes. Alison stood for a moment with her
arms upraised, teasing Stacy as she had been teased, and then she tossed the

164

shirt on the floor. She bent just a very little from the shoulders. Stacy was tall enough that, on her knees, she could take Alison's nipples in her mouth, and she did so, eagerly, greedily. Sucking and licking and switching from one to another like a child who cannot decide between two luscious treats, and then finally pushing them together with her hands so that she could take both at once. Alison stood motionless, her hands resting lightly on Stacy's head, her own head thrown back, her mind empty of all but the rush of sensation. She hardly knew when Stacy tipped her backwards onto the couch. Only when she stopped did her head clear for a moment. She looked down in confusion.

Stacy was kneeling between her spread legs, her elbows on Alison's knees. She was grinning wickedly, a woman sure of conquest.

"Do you want to play?" she asked softly, and went on in a tone so soft and sexy that she could have been mouthing meaningless monosyllables and still Alison's blood would have risen. "You know what I'd like to do with you?" she asked, a question not meant to be answered. "I know you like to be fucked, I know you really got off on having that big dildo of Carla's in your cunt. I'd love to lay you on your back and fuck you. Maybe with your hands tied, just a little vanilla bondage. But first I'd really like to fuck your ass. I know you'd like it, and it would make you so hot for that dildo."

Alison felt her pupils constrict to pinpoints, so that for a moment she could see nothing in the dim light. Her throat did the same, shrinking tighter even than when she'd had strep last winter and had first feared, then prayed she would die. Her breath was coming in hard pants. Speaking was not possible. But she did not draw back when Stacy took her by the hand and pulled her to her feet. Not once did she feel the floor as she was led to the bedroom. At that door the hidden director vanished; she filmed only romantic interludes.

"Give me a safe word in case—" Stacy stopped, all business just for a moment.

Alison gulped back her anticipation and managed a whisper. Stacy repeated the word to make it clear she understood.

As Stacy pushed her down onto the bed Alison was aware of many candles already lit, and that Stacy was being cautious, allowing her plenty of time to back out, and though part of her was grateful, another part wanted to scream, wanted to tell her not to hold back. She held it in check, sure that if she got what it asked for, that within a few minutes she would be retreating. Stacy ran her hands gloating down her torso. When Alison raised her own hand to touch her face, she flung it back down on the bed.

"My game, now," she said, in a voice that sounded delightfully wicked. Alison remembered what she had said, that the women who came to her came for drama. It was easy to see why, for Stacy had become a villainess, and herself the innocent at her mercy. She felt as if she were in one of her mother's Harlequin novels, only this one was beginning where the others left off. Only if she wanted it to, she reminded herself when a flash of panic rose. Only if she wanted it to.

"In fact, if you're going to try that...." Stacy bent across her, but suddenly Alison knew that it was not Stacy any longer, but Anastasia the wicked sex goddess for whose favors women paid, Anastasia who sat up and trailed a long silk scarf across her breasts, Anastasia who pulled her hands above her head and wound the scarf loosely around her wrists.

I can get out of this any time. Alison had not thought it possible for her heart to beat faster, but now she was feeling the pulse pound in her temples, her throat, the pit of her stomach as it did when she ran. I've got a safe word, it will work like magic. Only what the hell was it? For a moment her mind went blank and she could not remember her own name, let alone the word she had whispered to Stacy. She almost rose up on the bed in panic, fighting blindly. Then she remembered to breathe and with the rush of breath everything returned—her name, the word, the feeling of excitement. Now that she remembered it she didn't need to use it.

Anastasia paused in the middle of tightening the scarf to glance at her face, and Alison knew that she had felt that bolt of panic, was checking to see if she was all right or paralyzed, freaked out. Alison departed from her role of terrified governess (unknowingly her mind had provided her a whole plot and background) to smile reassuringly. Anastasia winked, then so fast that it might have been imagined, her face returned to its beautiful but cruel set.

There was a terrible cry from the back of the apartment, and both women were jerked out of character as, simultaneously, they turned their heads towards it. An awful thought began to form in Alison's mind, but before it could even be completed another cry followed the first, and this one had enough of a yowl in it to make it clear that it was the kitten, not a human.

"Damn it all." Stacy had returned. The sexy and wicked Anastasia had disappeared without a trace, it not being her job to deal with earthly things like kittens. She turned to Alison apologetically. "I know just what he's done. He's crawled through a hole in the back of the kitchen cupboard, and now he can't find his way out. He's going to keep that up until I come and get him."

"It's okay," Alison reassured her, and though she could scarcely get the words out, so dry was her mouth, it was true. The excitement was too strong to be broken. Even if Stacy were called away for an hour it would only prolong things. She would still be wet when she returned. She could actually use a break now to calm her heart.

"Thanks." Stacy pulled the scarf loose before she stood up. "I don't want my widdle baby kitten to think I don't wove him." Over her shoulder she added, "Help yourself to the soda there."

Good planning. That was the professional at work, remembering every detail. Gratefully Alison picked up the can, still cool, from the headboard, popped it open and took a long swallow.

In the kitchen she heard Stacy say, "Come on, you little shithead!" There was a crash of pans. The kitten continued to yowl.

A very old desire crept up on Alison. It had been over eight years since Michelle had nagged her into giving up smoking, but she had never lost that odd craving for a cigarette during sex. She sighed and turned to set the soda down. As she replaced it she noticed that Stacy's clutch bag was also sitting on the shelf. She remembered how, at the bar, it had spilled open and Stacy's 'prop pack'—a term she had not understood at the time—had fallen onto the floor with her wallet. She was sure that Stacy would not mind if she smoked one. Of course, she wiggled her toes in anticipation, Anastasia might, and she might be angry. Alison reached out to pull the bag to her, but the zipper was turned away and she did not realize that it was open until she had spilled the contents over the pillows.

Cursing, she began to retrieve them, stopping long enough to light a cigarette off one of the candles. A pocket flashlight slid down by the frame to nest beside a bottle of Advil; a pen hid beneath a pillow. About the same kind of things that Alison carried in her own purse, though Stacy must not have used this one recently, for it contained neither her wallet, her checkbook nor her keys. Alison did that too—switched back and forth from her purse to her daypack to her briefcase. Come to think of it, she had not seen Stacy with this one since that first time at the bar, after the soccer game.

She thought that she had everything now, and she replaced the bag on the shelf. No, behind the second pillow was a crumpled sheet of paper. She picked it up and smoothed it out. Actually, it was two pieces of paper stuck together. The second looked like a check. Carefully, because there was nothing else to do while she waited, she pulled the two apart. Neither tore. Apparently the brown substance that dotted them was sticky when wet but did not bond as it dried.

"So."

Alison dropped the paper on the bed, and it was with great difficulty that she refrained from doing the same with the cigarette. For the wicked Anastasia, mistress of the isolated house on Storm's Head, had returned. She was bound to be angered by such a show of indulgence by the poor helpless governess. (Poor relation/companion, corrected Alison's mind. She didn't want

167

to have to worry about the kids waking up during a bondage scene.)

"So," repeated Anastasia. She walked slowly towards the bed, her hands on her hips. She had taken the time to change while she was out of the room. She was wearing a pair of leather pants, tapered at the cuffs over short black boots, and the same purple tuxedo shirt Alison had seen the night that she had dressed in the kitchen. Over her shoulders was draped a short cape made of some rich, black material that flowed down her back and ended at her waist. She looked like a Hell's Angel biker chick dressed for the opera. Alison's heart, so carefully calmed, shot right back into fourth gear.

"This is what you do when I leave you alone for a minute?" Anastasia reached over and took the now dead cigarette from between Alison's trembling fingers. On her hands were a pair of sleek black leather gloves with the tips of the fingers and thumbs cut off. She tossed the butt over her shoulder, but not, Alison noticed, before she pinched it to make sure it was out. Anastasia might not deal with earthly things, but enough of Stacy seeped through to make sure no one burned the house down.

"I am definitely going to have to punish you," she said in a tone of mock regret, underlaced with glee. Before Alison could reply she found herself turned onto her stomach. Her hands were bound swiftly behind her back, but even though it took only a few seconds, she was aware that there had been a quick flexing and measuring to make sure her arms were long enough for this contortion. Anastasia pulled the pillow from beneath her head and slipped it under her hips, and again Alison was aware of that quick scan, the check to see that everything was away from her face.

"What a bad girl." Anastasia was peeling her pants down her legs, though in her mind Alison had given herself a full-skirted gown of dull gold. A hand-me-down from the mistress, far too expensive for a poor relation to afford. She trembled as it was pulled up and her poor undergarments, totally inadequate for what was to follow, were exposed. (In her mind Alison ran a quick reality check, trying to remember if she had put on one of her three decent pairs of panties. Dammit, she distinctly recalled putting on a cotton pair that was not only stained, but ripped. Well, Mistress Anastasia was just going to have to remember that she only gave a pittance for an allowance.)

There was a ripping sound and Alison turned her head to see what was left of her underwear following the cigarette butt. Oh. She felt the leather of Anastasia's gloves caressing her bare ass and flinched away from it just a little.

"Very bad," said Anastasia, and then suddenly, unexpectedly, Alison felt an open palm, the smack of leather hit her ass. A gasp of air was jerked out of her chest, and again she located her safe word, not to use yet, but just so that she knew it was there. Anastasia slapped her again, and she let out a little moan because, after all, her character—who she suddenly knew was named Prudence—was not expected to be very brave. In fact, that was one of the things that the Mistress of Storm's Head liked about her, how easily she squirmed and moaned. Again Alison felt as if she were existing on several planes. There was the part of her that was just Alison, Vanilla Sex Queen, clutching her safe word like a talisman, and with a tendency to analyze every feeling. Then there was the part who had become Prudence the sex-slave, helplessly yielding before the punishment that was making her wet, knowing that far worse was to come. The hidden director, too, had reappeared, deciding that after all, it was the nineties and she could film bedroom scenes. Alison could see the slaps that the director was picking up on her soundtrack, and the red hand marks which she contemplated with a nod.

Suddenly the spanking stopped, and again Alison strained to see. Anastasia pushed her head forward firmly. With nothing to look at but the headboard Alison noticed that the flier and the check had both drifted down and gotten lodged between the mattress and the frame of the bed. She felt a sudden cool sensation as her ass was spread, and involuntarily she tightened.

"Oh, that's not a good idea," crooned Anastasia, as she spread the lube over the tight outside of Alison's asshole. Her fantasy made it into chilled butter; the wicked Mistress had decided to punish the poor, unfortunate Prudence right at the dinner table. Possibly with the rest of the staff watching? At least the beautiful cook and the scullery maid, who would probably suffer at the hands of the wicked Mistress themselves later.

"I mean, you can tighten that sweet little asshole all you want, but I'm going to fuck it anyway, and it will just make it go harder on you." She inserted just the tip of one finger inside as she spoke. It was not the first time Alison had been buttfucked, and almost against her will she opened up in pleasant anticipation. Old memories of Sandy kneeling behind her came flooding back, superimposed over a close shot of her ass spread and being explored. The director experimented with a soundtrack of intense classical, then slipped back into something a little more building.

"Ah!" Prudence, who in her sheltered upbringing had never experienced such violation, was not able to suppress a sound as the Mistress, who must have slipped off her glove, shoved in one well lubed finger all the way.

"You like that, don't you?" asked Anastasia triumphantly, and she didn't know what to answer, for yes, they all liked it. Alison on the bed, Prudence bent over the dining room chair with her skirts up over her back, the director, Alison in memory with Sandy's hand slapping against her as she pumped, all of them liked it, loved having their ass fucked and loved it even more when Anastasia slipped in a second well-trimmed finger, beginning to move it in and out in earnest. Already, too soon, unwanted, Alison could feel an orgasmic tension building inside her, and she tried to think of something else, tried to ignore the full length picture being presented by the director; herself bound, face down while a beautiful woman in leather fucked her butt-hole unmercifully.

Frantically she cast around for something on which to fix her attention, but before she could start in on the multiplication tables the pumping suddenly stopped. The fingers were withdrawn, though she clung lovingly.

"Oh, you've had your ass fucked before, haven't you?" Alison dared look back again, and this time Anastasia did not stop her. She was carefully peeling off a thin latex glove, which also went back on the floor for Stacy or Lawrence to deal with later. Alison realized she wanted her to watch as she picked up a slender object off the bed. In the candle light she saw a silhouette more than anything else, a shape like a short sword in that it had a hilt and a handle, but far too fat and round. Back at Storm's Head the maid presented the Mistress with a silver tray full of sex toys, some of them smooth silver themselves, and she picked through them carefully before finally choosing one and, just as Anastasia was doing to Alison, lubing it slowly in front of Prudence's unbelieving eyes. The director pulled back for a moment, wondering if she had gotten in over her head. But it was far too late to be squeamish, and so boldly she showed a close-up of the ass plug slipping through Anastasia lubed fist, and then slowly followed it as she lowered it and parted Alison's ass once again.

"Ah!" Alison felt a flash of pain that was really more Prudence's than her own. The cook and the maid likewise were not able to keep from gasping as they watched the butt plug being shoved into the virgin asshole. Then the scene faded back to Alison, and the feeling was overwhelmingly intense. Her ass was fuller than it had ever been, being fucked harder than it ever had before, and it was intense and exciting and, every four or five strokes when Anastasia plunged deeper, it was just a little bit painful, just enough so that Alison couldn't relax and become complacent in the rhythm. She was crying out with sounds that she would not have recognized as her own, and the camera pulled back from its close up of the dildo being shoved up her asshole to show Anastasia's face, her eyes glittering with excitement.

Again Alison felt the orgasm building up far too soon. As if she had read her mind Anastasia said, "Don't you dare come yet! I love to fuck girls like you in the ass, and I want to do it for a long time. You're not to come until you've got this big dildo in your cunt." Alison couldn't see the toy that she indicated, but Prudence's eyes widened as the huge instrument was indicated on the tray, and she both despaired of taking it and craved it.

170

Alison struggled to obey. She came easily, but she was not multiorgasmic. Once she came she knew that she would want to use the safe word and be held, too sensitive to be touched further. She didn't want to come now, she wanted to prolong it further, wait till it was a block buster, until she had a dildo both in her ass and cunt, until she was being fucked so hard that she simply could no longer stand it. She tried to fix her mind on something else: Presidents' names, the chart of elements. The papers which had fallen from Stacy's bag caught her eye, and gratefully she latched onto them. The leaflet was for an autumn festival. Alison read the details, cost, and as she did so Prudence tried to figure out the weaving pattern to the cook's dress, both of them being fucked so hard from behind that it was making them gasp. The cost was forty dollars overnight, and it included meals. Oh, god, she couldn't stand it much longer, she was going to have to come soon.

"Fuck my cunt," Alison begged, and Anastasia gave a triumphant laugh. Prudence, who did not have the words for what she craved, had to content herself with moaning, "Oh, please," and the camera cut down to focus on the hot juices pouring out from between her spread legs. The handle of the silver butt plug still protruded from her ass as her Mistress beckoned once again for the silver tray.

Anastasia was not so merciful asking, "Do you think you're in charge here?" The fucking became a bit less relentless, enough so that Alison was no longer teetering on the verge of orgasm, but it did not stop. "I'll put a dildo in your cunt when I'm good and ready," she teased, running the tips of two fingers along the opening. Alison tried to slow her breathing, tried not to think of the feeling that was building inside her. It did not help that back at Storm's Head a fat, smooth, golden dildo, its handle decorated with the same rubies that encircled the neck of the wicked mistress, had been selected and was now being slowly and needlessly lubed in front of the moaning Prudence's eyes.

"I love to fuck hot women," said Anastasia, "and you are the hottest I've met in a long time. Maybe you should just get ready for a marathon, baby, because I might not get to your sweet pussy for hours."

An annoying little part of Alison's mind that had managed to stay separate from both fantasy and screenplay, wondered to whom exactly she was being compared, and tried to wonder if it was just a line that Anastasia fed to all of her girls when they were helpless. But it was shoved out by an extra deep thrust into her ass, and once again Alison found herself fighting coming. Desperately, she tried to fix once more on the papers five inches from her face. The check had a picture on it—a sailboat with a bright striped sail that was tilting sharply into the wind. At Storm's Head the golden dildo had been thrust, all at once, up to the hilt into the wet cunt of the trembling Prudence. She cried out, though this opening was not as innocent as the first. Though she would never have admitted to such a shameful act, Prudence had experimented more than once with the ivory handles of her Mistress' hairbrushes. The dark eyes of the Mistress of Storm's Head shone with wicked excitement as she withdrew and thrust again deep into the innocent girl. Anastasia was crooning, but Alison was not listening, trying to concentrate on the written words before her face. The account was for either Melanie Donahue or Krista Jo Day. It was dated for the fourth of the month.

Anastasia had reached beneath Alison and pulled her up so that she was no longer lying flat, but on her knees with her shoulders down. The director ordered a close-up of her breasts hanging down to the bed, of Anastasia's long fingers rolling and pulling the nipples. The amount of the check was filled in, but the long line in the middle was blank. It was not made out to any name. At Storm's Head the Mistress had withdrawn both the dildo and the butt plug and beckoned to the servants. While the cook washed the instruments lovingly in a basin of warm water, the maid brought out a harness of supple brown leather, trimmed on the sides and back with jewels. Carefully she helped the Mistress fasten it securely over her long emerald gown. (There was some little problem as to the actual mechanics of this, but Alison did not ponder over it. It was a fantasy, and anything she wanted could happen. Of one thing she was sure, and that was that the Mistress of Storm's Head did not lift her skirt to fuck anyone.) The line on the check that was labeled 'memo' was also blank, but it had been signed by Melanie Donahue. Anastasia was dipping the tip of the big dildo in her cunt, just the tip, while she continued to fuck her open ass. The director showed a shot of Alison's straining, panting face next to the apprehensive face of Prudence as she waited, anxious, afraid to turn around and look. The fourth was the day that Alison's vacation had started. It was the day that she should have awakened at Colleen and Nancy's, but instead had gone over to Stacy's studio. The cook fastened the two toys, the smaller above the larger, into the padded rings on the front of the Mistress' harness. The candlelight glinted off them as she snapped her fingers commandingly. Obediently each servant took one in her hands as the Mistress knelt gracefully behind the passive body of Prudence.

Without warning, Anastasia pushed the dildo deep into Alison's pussy, and Alison could not hold back a cry. The director daringly showed a close up of the move, of her wet lips stretching to take its girth, the handle of the butt plug jerking as she tightened with excitement. Not once, but several times, so that Anastasia's hand thrust it in again, and again, and again. Alison could come now if she desired, both holes being fucked with abandon, just as

172

she had craved. But something, one little thing, was occupying a corner of her mind, stopping her from giving it over. The fourth was the first day of her vacation. The fourth was the day she had gone to the bar with Stacy after the soccer game. The fourth was the day that Melanie Donahue had died.

The servants had guided the dildos into Prudence's tight ass, into her open cunt, ignoring her pleas for mercy. Now the Mistress was beginning to thrust against her, pulling almost all the way out and then slamming back in. She opened her mouth and the cook, ready for the signal, began to spoon into it bites of chocolate eclair, filled with a rich custard.

Alison was totally filled. The director had fixated on one image, the two dildos being thrust in and out in tandem. But though there was really no reason to wait longer Alison still held back. She needed to think. Stacy had a check from Melanie Donahue dated the day she died, but she had never mentioned seeing the woman before the moment that she had pushed out into the alley. She had spent the day with Alison; Alison had followed her to the soccer game. That left the early morning or... Suddenly Alison remembered how she had waited at the bar for almost half an hour before Stacy showed, long after the other players arrived. Alison could feel herself peaking, it was the matter of a minute at most. Krista had said that Melanie had arranged for this extra meeting with her counselor only on the morning of the appointment. Melanie had been found not far from the bar where she was not a patron. There was no reason for her to have been there unless the 'counselor' had arranged for an emergency session, for something quick, say, in the back seat of a car. Melanie always paid cash for her sessions. But if she had been short wouldn't she have just left the check blank, and trusted Stacy to have it cashed somewhere she was known? She could have filled in the name of Womynbooks, for example, or the little grocery store across the street.

Almost by surprise, orgasm overtook her and her mind was emptied of all thoughts, concentrating on the feeling that, from childhood, had always been represented by a burst of color, an exploding star. She could hear her own voice mingling with Prudence's in a kind of wail that was so high that the kitten, locked in the bathroom, joined in. Her whole body was convulsing and Stacy, who had thankfully reappeared, was holding and caressing her, murmuring wordless comfort into her ear. Alison felt tears on her cheeks.

"You," she managed to whisper after a moment, and never had she been so grateful as when Stacy whispered back.

"No. Later. In the morning. You go to sleep now." Obediently Alison curled fetally, letting Stacy cover her gently, spoon her from behind. At Storm's Head the Mistress was beckoning imperiously to the cook, motioning her to kneel beside Prudence, who had fainted in ecstasy. Well, they were just going to have to play that scene themselves. Already, Alison was drifting.

But, after Stacy had blown out the candles, Alison roused herself for just one more moment. Just long enough to reach up and, with the tips of her fingers, tuck the check down securely so that it was hidden between the mattress and the frame.

* * *

Alison's preference would have been a lazy morning in bed, but she knew before she opened her eyes that Stacy was already up working. The room looked as if a tornado had hit it, tossing clothing and sex toys from end to end. She wasn't even going to think about picking it up before at least two cups of coffee. She was glad she had brought over coffee and filters the night she had cooked.

She borrowed Stacy's robe and shuffled into the kitchen. The swish of the cloth brought back the fantasy of the night before, and she felt herself growing wet, remembering. Then, hard on the heels of the pleasure she remembered the check. Shit, what did it mean? At the least Stacy had been withholding the information that she had probably been the last one to see Melanie Donahue alive. And at the most.... Alison could not think of it without coffee.

Her mind was just starting to clear after one cup when a man spoke directly behind her.

"How are you this morning?"

She jumped so that the dregs of the coffee hit the ceiling. "Dammit!"

Lawrence, in his pink apron, was standing in the door of the playroom holding a rag and a spray bottle of cleaner, looking not unpleased at her reaction. "Fingerprints," he said, waving his rag back in the direction of the room, "and cum all over. Or does it have a different name for women? I don't know, pussy juice just sounds to me like somebody put their poor little kitty in the blender. At any rate, it's so clean in there now that the next girl who gets beaten in there is going to think that she's the very first one."

Alison could think of no witty reply. She poured herself a second cup of coffee.

"Oh, Stacy told me that you weren't any good in the morning till you'd had coffee. Well, I'm just going to run off and clean the bedroom until you're fit for a little gossip." He marched out of the room. In the work room Alison could hear Stacy conversing.

Suddenly she wondered if cleaning the bedroom meant changing the bed. She arrived just in time, as Lawrence was ripping the bottom sheet off, dramatically, as if it were part of some kind of play he had running in his mind to beat the boredom of housecleaning. The check came with the sheet

174

and Alison caught it in midair. She looked over her shoulder to see if he had noticed, but he was looking at the floor.

"My," he said, picking up the rubber glove, "we *did* have a good time last night, didn't we?"

It occurred to Alison to blush, but instead she said, "Well, I figure if it turns you on to get tied up and fucked in the ass you should just say so."

Lawrence laughed. "Good girl! So tell me, is it true that they have that bitch Dominique behind bars?"

"Oh, don't say it like that."

"I know, I know, it's ugly. I just can't forgive her for trying to read me out in front of my customers. But you're right, I can't see her knifing anybody. Maybe hitting them over the head with a lamp or throwing them through a window, but not anything that took planning. But I had heard she was with that poor girl right before she was killed, and drunk, too?"

Alison smiled and spread her hands to indicate she knew nothing. The old grapevine was sure performing at high speed.

Lawrence pouted. "Well, if that's the way you want to be. You'll be sorry the next time I have something good to tell. And I'm going to tell everybody that you sleep with your gun on too." He picked the holster up off the night table and dangled it by one finger. "Of course, that might bring tons of those little submissives just running."

Carefully Alison took it from him.

"Who's in there with Stacy?"

Lawrence made a little face to let her know that he was still pouting. "Oh, that nasty Mark. You'd think he lived here. I don't think he's nearly the dutiful son he pretends to be to Pam. I think he just comes by to see Stacy. She's just too good to send him away."

"Stacy said she knew him when he was a kid." Alison was fairly sure that Lawrence would not be able to resist the bait, even if he were miffed at her.

"Maybe. But I don't think that they were buddy-buddy or anything. I mean, maybe she had him in Sunday school or something a couple of times, but I think that's about the extent of it."

"He went to her church?" Alison was confused. "With Pam?"

"Oh, no, honey, we're talking about before that. No, I think she knew the kid's folks when he was real little."

"But the mother became a lesbian?"

"Oh, off and on. She was a crazy lady and being mixed up with those Jesus people did *not* help. You know, she was the kind who would be convinced she was a dyke and fall in love and get some poor girl all entangled with her, and then as soon as something went wrong she would suddenly become repentant—she'd sinned and she was a horrible, weak person and she'd go right into therapy to try to straighten herself out—literally."

"Did she go back to the church program?"

"Off and on. I think they were a little crazy even for her. I'll tell you what I think the truth is. I think the woman just liked drama. Now, I like drama myself. That comes from being an adult child of an alcoholic, did you know that? They say that you try to recreate all the turmoil of your childhood by causing little scenes to happen around you. Now, I've figured out if I do that in my sex life I don't have to do it in my real life. I don't have to pick fights with Dave or the lady in the grocery store. I think what this woman Candy needed, was a good kinky sex life with lots of dramatics, and then she wouldn't have had to be going to church or jerking Pam and her friends around."

"It must have been hard on Mark."

"Oh, I'm sure. Now, Pam isn't a real talker, and I wasn't around when this was all happening." Lawrence looked decidedly regretful. "But, from what I have picked up, Candy just dumped that little boy on those four women, just said that she couldn't handle him *at all*. And she had all kinds of money coming in from the father's insurance and Aid to Dependent Children and the whole thing, and they never got a cent of it the six years that they had him. But she was going to Mexico and Hawaii and just dropping by long enough to stick them a little. You know, Pam tried to get custody, she tried to get Candy to allow her to adopt him legally, but it was strictly no go. Candy wanted to make sure that she had the power in the end."

"So what happened?" Alison felt as if she were watching a soap opera on fast forward.

"Well, what I heard is that one day Candy came storming in from out of the blue and pulled Mark. Said that she'd realized how wrong she had been, and what a bad mother she was to have let him live with these lesbians for all this time, because, of course, she was going through a straight period. Said she needed her boy and she was going to make a home for him herself. Well, of course he didn't want to go—you don't have to be grown up to tell if your mother is looney-tunes and Pam, at least, doted on him. So Candy caused a *big* stink with Pam and accused her of turning him against her, and hauled him off screaming and crying and wouldn't even allow them to visit. But—"

Stacy stuck her head into the room. "I thought I heard you." She smiled at Alison and again Alison found herself immediately excited. "I don't want to nag, but I've got some buyers coming over later, and I'd like everything to look nice by then."

"Oh, sure," said Lawrence. He scooped up a handful of sex toys and began to march out. At the door he stopped. "Dishwasher safe," he said, waving them at Alison.

"Sorry I had to leave," said Stacy, "but I had someone coming in."

"That's okay." Alison was uncomfortably aware of the check in the pocket of the robe. Her mind picked up precisely where it had left off the night before. She had told Stacy about Dominique, and Dominique had been arrested later that same day, when suddenly the police had firm evidence. Carla had told Stacy about her connection with the Crusaders, and Stacy had taken the theory and smoothed it out and shaped the parts that didn't fit. She had been the only one who had noticed a different number on the flier, and she had not told Alison about it until it was too late to prevent the vigilante committee from acting. Alison tried to stop; she didn't want to think these things. Stacy had not come forward with the check because she had known it would cast suspicion on her, and that would be awkward, considering the business she was in. That was the only reason. She hadn't decided to go that extra step further with Melanie and try the ultimate thrill of killing.

"Penny?"

"Huh?"

"For your thoughts. Didn't you say something last night about a meeting with your boss this morning?"

"Oh, shit yes! I totally forgot."

"Well, it's getting about that time. Incidently, here's your shirt." She tossed it to Alison. It looked as if it had been used to wipe up after an orgy. "Remember, we have a date tonight."

Alison nodded, too preoccupied to answer.

* * *

"So, Officer Kaine." Sergeant Obrachta was a small, dapper man whose hands were always busy. Now those famous hands, thin and long-fingered, were making a steeple.

Alison resisted the urge to squirm. She wished that she'd had time to shower and wash her hair.

Now the fingers were drumming, each against its mate. She stared at them with a stupid kind of fascination, as if their movement was somehow going to tell her what the Sergeant was going to say, and how in the world she was going to answer it. "So, Officer Kaine," he repeated, "have you been enjoying your vacation?"

"Yes, sir," she answered, and then snapped her mouth shut. Say as little as possible.

"I thought you were going to be going out of town." Obviously he already knew what had happened, but she explained about her change of plans anyway, as if they were just friends with time to kill. She left out the specifics about the herpes. No need to perpetuate stereotypes.

"That must have been disappointing."

She acknowledged it. Now he had a Swiss army knife out and was using the scissors attachment to trim an already smooth cuticle, just as Stacy had used hers the evening she had cooked her dinner. His nails were much better cared for than Alison's.

"But you've found some things to amuse yourself."

"Yes," she said, and almost blurted out the fact that she'd found a new lover, just on the off chance that it would startle him enough to save her from the lecture—and she just hoped that was all it was going to be—that he was going to deliver. But he was no Jorgenson. He would just lift a polite eyebrow to inquire why she was telling him her personal life.

"And what do you think about these two murders and one assault we've had?" He was fencing with her, another trait for which he was famous. He liked to get an offender off balance, or overconfident, thinking that he was on the wrong track, and then go in for the kill. In fact, he liked to question his staff much the same way that she liked to question her witnesses.

She answered honestly, knowing that he already knew. "I was at the scene of the second murder by chance, and then at the scene of the attempted murder two nights later at the Rubyfruit."

He ruffled through a stack of papers on his desk and pulled out a report. "So," he said, looking at it as if for the first time, although she knew he could recite every detail, "you think the three crimes were related?"

"Yes, I do." She was ready for his next question, ready to tell him why, but he surprised her.

"What were you doing at the bar the night of the assault?"

"Because of...." A few words slipped out before she realized that he was asking for something different. "I'm a lesbian, Sergeant."

He made an impatient gesture, as if she were telling him something obvious. "That doesn't explain, Officer. There are hundreds of lesbians in this city, and only fifty of them were at that bar at that time. There are several lesbian officers on the force, and you were the only one who was right on the scene of the crime. Now, I'm curious to know how that happened."

"It was coincidence."

He reached across his desk. There was a collection of small toys and games sitting near Alison's side. Thoughtfully he wound up a small pool full of plastic fish. It began to rotate, the fish opening and closing their mouths.

"So it just happened?" He did not look at her. He picked up a plastic fishing rod with a magnet on the end and attempted to snare the fish while their mouths were open. He was very good.

"Yeah." she answered dreamily, mesmerized.

"You weren't there because you were investigating the crimes on your own?"

Oh, yeah, that too, she *almost* said as she watched him land one brightly colored fish after another, but he must have had pity on her, or more likely decided that she was too easy.

"Before you answer that, I would like to remind you of our policy concerning officers performing their own private investigations. Do you remember what that is?"

"Umm, we don't like it?" Alison guessed, her mind a blank.

The fish had all been landed. He looked at her with an exasperated expression.

"I suppose that's one way of paraphrasing it. How about more like the detectives on this case have been foaming at the mouth, and have called me three times to complain about unauthorized interference?"

"I haven't interfered with anything," Alison protested.

"Oh? How about just plain butted in? It doesn't matter what they call it, I don't like to be nagged over the phone about one of my officers."

"Sergeant, those men have a real attitude problem with this case. How could I have butted in? I happened to be there and turned everything over when they arrived."

"Officer, you have been asking questions. Those men are the ones assigned. You are not. I am not their boss. I am your boss. I am ordering you to cease interference with this case. I'd like to be able to keep this between you and me, rather than something that has to go in your file."

Well, there it was, plain between them. Stop snooping or start worrying about your job. She should have known better than to try to criticize a superior. She felt angry, yet at the same time there was just a touch of relief, because now she had absolutely no obligation at all to do anything about Stacy's check.

"Do you understand?"

"Yes, sir."

"Then do me a favor. Go make sure that the rest of your vacation really is a vacation." He motioned that she was dismissed, but then stopped her at the door. "Do you know anything that you think you should tell to Detective Jones or Jorgenson?"

"No," she answered without the slightest compulsion. "No, sir, nothing at all."

179

Fifteen

Lydia met her at the door of her apartment. "Come look at my display." Alison followed curiously. Lydia had dabbled with a variety of crafts while living with her, tiring of most before they were finished.

"There!" Lydia made a little flourish towards the living room, where she had pulled several of the kitchen chairs up behind the coffee table to arrange a display space. They were draped with a number of scarves and a few shawls.

"Really nice, Lydia," Alison said, lifting the edge of one long scarf to stroke the fringe. They were actually much better than she had expected.

"Lavender. That's not mine, it's Seven's. I did the pottery."

The pottery was drab lumps arranged lovingly atop the textiles. Alison picked a piece up and turned it over, trying to figure what it was so that she could make a suitable comment.

"Cunts," announced Lydia proudly.

"What?"

"I wanted to make artwork that would celebrate my womanhood. So I decided to make a whole cunt series."

"Oh." Alison could not think of anything to say. She could see that the ridged objects might be portraying cunts, if one squinted and imagined that they had been made by a Neanderthal child with little talent.

"Guess which one is yours," Lydia said coyly.

"I couldn't." Alison hoped she did not sound as horrified as she felt, and quickly scanned the exhibit for name cards. She'd never get another date in her life if one of these things was labeled with her name. Luckily Lydia had not thought of it.

"Well, most women can't," Lydia admitted. "It's such a shame. We're taught that it's not okay to know, to really know our cunts when they're such a power source. I mean, like, you'd recognize a model of your hands, wouldn't you?" She picked up one of the pieces and handed it to Alison. "I have this fantasy where every lesbian has this beautiful earthware model of her own cunt that she can keep out where she can look at it and stroke it every day just to reaffirm its power and beauty."

"On her desk at work," said Alison absently. Tentatively she tried to stroke one of the straight ridges that was probably supposed to represent folds

180

of flesh. A jagged piece poked her finger. God, if she really looked like this it was a miracle she had ever gotten anyone to go down on her.

"And I also really wanted women to be able to use them in their everyday lives, so I got this wonderful idea, like, to curve them in," she made a lotus shape with her hands that had no resemblance to the gouged out squareness of the clay, "so they could be used for, like, bowls. Like, can't you just imagine serving an oyster stew with, like, a thick white sauce out of this?"

Alison could, and she was repulsed.

"And then I made this big piece that could be, like, used for serving, like for a ritual or a family dinner." She picked up a piece as big as a casserole dish. The ridge that represented the clit was so sharp and extended that it could have been used as a weapon.

Luckily Alison was saved from answering by Janka's appearance at the door. She took the opportunity to escape.

"Gotta go, thanks for showing me, Lydia." She almost sprinted towards the back stairs, snagging the brown envelope of photos off the kitchen table where she had foolishly dumped it. Foolishly, because Lydia had piled up her breakfast mess around it with disregard and it was distinctly sticky.

"So did you get to see the cunt of the Earth Mother?" asked Janka.

"Yes, I'm afraid it might set the body-worship movement back a bit."

"How was your hot night with the sex goddess?"

Alison kissed the tips of her fingers. "Great." Her cunt contracted with the memory. "Kinky. Michelle would shit."

"Look, promise me you won't tell her right now, will you? That's all I need, to have her more stirred up. Do you want to join me in doing something really self-indulgent and bad for your body?" She didn't wait for an answer, but went to the refrigerator and brought out a big china bowl. It was filled with chocolate chip cookie dough. She got two spoons out of the dish rack and handed one to Alison. "Dig in," she said.

For a moment there was silence as they both began eating out of the bowl. Alison knew that she would regret making this her first meal of the day, but cookie dough was a personal weakness. "Did you see this?" Janka spoke with some difficulty. Her tongue seemed to be stuck to the roof of her mouth. She pointed to a pile of newspaper.

"What?" Alison picked the paper up. "I think I've had enough."

"There." Janka hit a photo with her spoon. "Do you feel sick?"

"No."

"Then you haven't had enough."

Obediently Alison scooped out another spoonful of dough, her eyes on the article beneath the photo. *Anti-gay group attacked* read the headline. *Preacher found nude* said the subtitle.

181

"Trudy!" she said, without looking up.

"I'd guess. Go ahead and read it. It's great." Janka was intent on empty-ing the bowl.

"'Police blah-blah-blah Reverend Malcolm Eisenburg, well known in the city for his anti-gay crusade and his assistant, Jerry Armstrong...' They painted them orange and blue?" She was delighted.

"All over. And I have it from an inside source that it wasn't poster paint, either." Janka, finally looking sick herself, leaned back in her chair. "I don't know why I do this to myself."

Alison was still scanning the story. "'Found nude in front of the office of the *Rocky Mountain News*...bound together with their heads shaved and also painted... Eisenburg refuses to comment except to say that their assailants wore Ronald Reagan masks, but a statement fastened around his neck, a copy of which was delivered to the newspaper office, claims that the action was in retaliation for the fact that Eisenburg tapped into a lesbian hotline, and that he and other church members were picking up women who were expecting safe rides home from work and bars and forcing them to listen to an anti-gay lecture by Sharon Ringer, who admits that she was in a lesbian relationship before she 'saw the light'.'"

"From what Michelle says it was more like she was into every relationship in town."

"Well, there's no saint like a reformed sinner, is there? 'Ringer, and Eisen-burg's wife, Nina, were also found at the site, clothed and unshaven. The statement said that it held them to be pawns of the men and that, because of the long history of abuse and exploitation of women's bodies, stripping and shaving them would not make the same statement of powerlessness as it had the men. Blah-blah-blah, blah-blah-blah'. The statement said that the shaved heads and paint would help to warn to other gays and lesbians, and also added that blue and orange had been used because they were the colors of the Denver Broncos and 'we like to support our team.'"

Alison looked at Janka. "Too much," she said. She noticed her queasy expression for the first time. "So why *do* you do that to yourself?"

"Because I'm totally pissed at Michelle, and like any well-trained woman, I turn my anger back on myself instead of just smacking the shit out of her."

"Smack her," advised Alison with the assurance of one who would never take her own advice. "What's her problem?"

"She's jealous of Seven Yellow Moons because we had such a good time talking and weaving and she felt left out. So now she's decided that I'm going to leave her and go live in a yurt, and, by god, if I'm going to do that then I deserved to be treated shitty."

"There is something to be said for force," said Alison thoughtfully. "I know that it's PI, and how can we obtain world peace if we can't even settle our own problems without force, but Michelle really does get her head up her ass from time to time. We used to have fist fights regularly until my dad told me I was too old."

"Hmm." Janka sat without speaking, her hands folded over her stomach. "Do you have a magnifying glass I can borrow?"

"Yeah." Janka rummaged in one of the baskets. "Here. Hey, I don't mean to be rude, but I've got to get back to work."

"No problem. Do you mind if I sit up here to do this? I don't want to view the petrified cunt show again."

"Be my guest."

Alison pulled the proofs from the envelope and scanned the sheet of photos again. This time she looked at all of them. She might as well; it had turned into an amusement rather than a clue search. Obrachta had called her firmly off the case, making sure she understood that her job was on the line. After she was through she had better call her Dad. No, she'd call the boys on the case herself and tell them everything that she knew. They could do their job, and on Monday she'd go back to patrolling a beat.

She moved the glass off the photo of a banner that, magnified, read 'Lesbians for Lesbians,' and over to the picture of the three dykes in front of the Crusaders. Several signs were visible now, the largest being one held by Malcolm that started 'God hates the sin…' Well, how did God feel about orange and blue, Malcolm and did you kill those women? Sighing, she moved the glass over the picture. She moved on to the next photo, and then stopped and moved it back. She sat for a moment, and then got up.

"Do you mind if I take this with me?" she called to Janka, already opening the door. "I have something I need to go do."

* * *

She was in luck. She hadn't been staked out more than fifteen minutes before she saw a woman who had to be Stacy's upstairs neighbor hurrying down the street, holding a newspaper over her head to keep off the rain. Quickly Alison slipped out of the doorway, timing herself so that she was turning away from the front door just as the woman was arriving.

"Oh, hi," she said.

The woman gave her a quick once over, assessing the situation and deciding it was harmless, just another dyke in a mostly dyke house, before answering. "Hello." But she didn't pull out her key.

"I just hate this," Alison said, trying to sound upset, but not as if she were the kind of person who would vent on a stranger. Or kill her. "Stacy *told* me she would be here at six and now she's not, and I'm all wet." She winced as she heard herself saying the last. *She can see you're all wet, asshole.* The woman smiled, but still hesitated, so Alison played out her next line.

"Well, I'm not going to stand around all day in the rain. But I *am* going to give her hell when I see her." She started to turn, and then looked back into the woman's face. "Haven't I met...no, I know where I've seen you. You sing with the Women's Chorus, right? I was at your winter concert, the one where you sang—oh what is it?" She sang a snatch of the song, "Foxglove woman, marigold child...."

The woman's face underwent a complete transformation, changing from cautious suspicion to a beaming smile. Obviously the chorus was to her as soccer was to Stacy, and Alison felt a stab of guilt for using it this way. She hadn't even been at the damn concert, Stacy had, and had been singing that tune while she quilted till Alison thought she'd go crazy. Well, dammit, she was trying to catch a killer, and sometimes the end did justify the means.

Now she had almost missed the woman's response with her moral fussing. Luckily it was something that didn't require much more than a nod—about how the chorus was going to go and sing at the National March on Washington. It might have been exciting any other time, but she didn't want to stand in the rain talking about it.

"That's so great," she said. "But I guess Stacy's not coming, and I can't stand here any longer waiting for her. I wonder if you... you see, she was supposed to leave me a package, and she knew I needed it. Could you just look outside her door and see if she left it in the hall? Just yell down if it's there?" *Let me in, lady,* she thought, her fingers crossed in her pockets. *Come on, we're about the same age, we probably worked on a flier together ten years ago.* A sneeze, not forced, escaped her.

"Oh, come on in and look for yourself. By the way, my name is Pam Farnsworth."

"Alison." She did not give her last name, just in case Pam had seen the story about Carla in the paper.

"So we're having our Harvest Ball fundraiser next Saturday...."

"Yeah, so I've heard. Do you have an extra flier?"

"Sure. It doesn't look like she left anything."

"Huh?" *Oh, yeah, they were on the second floor now, and she was supposed to be getting a nonexistent package.* She pretended to think, pulling at her lower lip. "Boy, this isn't like Stacy," she said, hoping that she was right in that. "I wonder if she got in a fender-bender or something." She hesitated half a second longer. "Well, I'm going to have to go. But can I run up and get that flier from you, first?"

As she had anticipated, it was only a short step from that to being invited in for a cup of tea. She looked around curiously when Pam excused herself to change. It was a nice, single dyke's apartment. She had been right in guessing that they had come out at about the same time—she could tell it by the posters on the wall that hadn't been available in years. The ripped corners told her they had been stuck up with masking tape at first. Pam had become more upwardly mobile and now they were matted and under glass. There were also several watercolors and a long, rectangular wall-hanging of blue and grey corduroy that was definitely Stacy's work. On one wall were three black and white photos of Pam and a second woman chopping wood. They looked like Mark's style.

The teakettle shrilled, and Alison called quickly, "I'll get it," glad of an excuse to case out the kitchen. She wasn't like those cops in the movies who could search a house while their hostess was in the bathroom, find exactly what they needed without disturbing anything else and then be back in their chairs before she emerged. She would get caught. And what she was really only looking for was a way to start the conversation she needed. She found it in the kitchen.

The photo was on the refrigerator. As she moved closer she wondered briefly why it was that two things, pictures and children's art, consistently showed up on people's refrigerators. Had it become a cultural norm? Pam's were in better shape than the ones on her own refrigerator, which had been taped up, and then taped again when they had curled and fallen down. These were in neat plastic covers with magnets on the back, so they couldn't be dated by wear and tear. But there was Pam herself in one of them, ten or twelve years younger. Alison had never thought she'd get so good at reading subtle lines around the eyes and neck until they'd started showing in her own mirror. There were three other women in the photo but it wasn't them whom she studied first. It was the little boy who was sitting at the picnic table with them. He was blond but she could not be sure it was Mark. He was about eight in the picture and Alison mentally adjusted Pam's age, giving her another five years over her own. The picture was unposed and only two of the women were looking straight into the camera. The third had been caught moving her head, so that her face was slightly blurry, and the fourth was looking at something the little boy was holding. From her expression Alison guessed that it was something not only startling, but possibly alive.

"Did you find what you needed?" Pam asked. She had changed out of her work clothes into a pair of overalls, another indication of her age. As near as Alison could tell young dykes didn't wear Osh Kosh overalls anymore.

"I did if you like Red Zinger tea."

"That's fine. That's the flier." She pointed to a lavender sheet of paper with the outline of a crowd of women across the top. It had been done by the same woman who had drawn the WAVAW poster.

"Can I have this one?" Alison took it from beneath the magnet when Pam nodded, thinking that now she'd probably have to be at the damn thing.

"Would you like an orange?"

"Please." She was going to lose the moment to ask naturally if she didn't get to it. "Is this your son?" Maybe not the most graceful lead-in, but she doubted Pam would catch it, especially since she had just noticed there was another, older photo of the boy alone on the other side of the refrigerator. In this one he was in his teens, holding an oboe.

"Yeah." There was that smile again. Almost. Maybe Alison wouldn't have noticed if she hadn't been looking, or maybe she was seeing things that weren't there. But wasn't there a little reserve to the smile this time, as if there was something in Pam's mind that wasn't quite right about the answer?

"Do you have any other kids?"

"No. Actually, Mark isn't my birth child. I helped co-parent him for a number of years. With these women." She pointed to the first photo.

"Really? Is this his biological mother?" Alison pointed randomly, though the woman did have roughly the same shade of hair.

"No." Pam answered shortly. Alison said nothing, and after a moment she added reluctantly, "His mother didn't live here. We took care of him our-selves." Her mouth was pursed up as though she was tasting something nasty, and Alison knew instinctively not to pursue that line, that any more ques-tions would simply close her up altogether.

"I've wondered about co-parenting," she said casually, "Did you like it?" It wasn't a hard lie to tell, because she *had* wondered. She listened intently to the answer, which was about what she expected, just about what other women had told her. Some parts of it—not having to devote your whole life—were good, and others, notably dealing with other adults who had dif-ferent ideas in child raising, were a pain in the ass. She broke in as soon as it seemed reasonable.

"Tell me, what did he think about having a different family when he got a little older? Like when he was in high school?" Again, it was something which she had genuinely wondered.

"He didn't live with us in high school. He went to live with his mother." Up until that point the atmosphere in kitchen had been warm and friendly. Suddenly, that changed, and Alison felt herself shiver. It wasn't one thing that she could put her finger on, like the look on Pam's face, or the tone of her voice. It was more an air she put off that told Alison that she didn't just dislike the unnamed mother, that she wasn't just angry with her for whatever she had done, but that she actually, actively hated her.

Pam stood up. Quickly, Alison squeezed in one last question.

"What's this woman's name?" Again she pointed randomly, this time to a woman with short curly hair who was sitting on the table behind Pam. Her arms were around her, and her chin was resting on her shoulder. "I think I've met her."

Pam shook her head. "Not unless it was a while back. She was killed in a car accident about three years ago. Teresa is dead, and Sue doesn't live here anymore." Her voice had taken on such a sadness that Alison knew that there was no way to get around that faux pas to inquire about the others. For a moment she forgot that she was investigating a horrible crime. She saw only another woman who had lost someone she loved. Gently she took Pam's elbow and led her into the other room.

They talked about the chorus, and the upcoming march and how close the vote on Amendement Two would be.

"Do you mind if I put the kettle on again?"

"Let me." Pam started to rise.

"No, you look beat. I didn't work today." Pam gave in without argument. She did look tired. If it had been an innocent visit Alison would have excused herself. Instead she went back into the kitchen and replaced the kettle. She stared again at the photo of the boy and the four women. There was something bothering her, something which she couldn't quite put her finger on. Something familar about it, as if she really had met one of the women before. But all she could see were four dykes and a child, one of the former mostly hidden by a long curtain of hair as she looked into the boy's hands.

Pam came in as she was pouring the hot water into her cup.

"You know," Alison said casually, not looking at her, "I think I've met your...son? Isn't he Stacy's friend? The photographer?"

Pam smiled. "Yes, that's Mark."

"He seems very nice." Alison lied without compulsion.

"He is."

"Does he live with you now?"

"No, he has his own place. But he comes and visits me a lot. We've always been very fond of one another." Pam turned. "I hate to rush you," she said apologetically, "but if I don't get to the store I'm not going to have anything for dinner."

Alison apologized for intruding. As she hurried down the stairs buttoning her jacket she thought that for all her prying, she didn't really know much more about Mark other than what Lawrence and Stacy had already told her. She should have plunged right in and asked questions about what he was doing now, rather than listening to stories about people who were long dead. Which reminded her, was Mark's mother dead? Everyone talked about her as if she were.

And she also wondered, as she let herself out the front door, why it had been so essential for Pam to get to the store when her refrigerator was crammed full.

* * *

"There," said Lydia, as she stepped back into the foyer of the MCC, where the dance was being held. "That's it!"

"Thank-fucking-god," Alison murmured beneath her breath. She gingerly climbed off the table and stood back to look at the display. It looked okay considering the merchandise. Still, how had she gotten herself in the position of pounder and go-fer? Janka was right; she had to take assertiveness training or something. Well, at least it had given her something to do besides fussing about the forbidden mystery. Although, even as Lydia had been confronting the organizer about their allotted space, Alison had managed to scribble a little chart on a piece of paper, something like a family tree where she tried to fit everyone in and show how they related to one another. It was busy with lines that went from Stacy to Dominique to Melanie to Malcolm, with a few—Mark and Candy and Pam—that wouldn't have been there that morning. But there was no way to hide the fact that Carla was still stuck out all by herself, connected to no one but Malcolm. If she was still trying to solve the case she would question Carla closely about her lovers and friends, try to see if one of them might fit the outline Stacy had suggested; the girl was still worth saving. But...she'd shrugged, and then penciled out Mark and all connections to him. There was nothing to connect him but the photograph from the Outfront, the one of him in the background with the Crusaders who were picketing the Rubyfruit, and when she'd looked at it a second time with the magnifying glass she was not nearly as certain that it was him in the crowd. It was just an excuse not to think about the check. She still had it, folded in her purse, so that she, too, was guilty of withholding evidence. She didn't know if she had just decided that Stacy was right, it was unimportant and would cause harassment, or if she was afraid of what she might find out if she pursued it.

"What do you think?" Lydia turned to Seven Yellow Moons.

"Beautiful." She was leaning against a wall eating cottage cheese out of a carton. Something had been bothering her all afternoon, and her conversation had been short and terse.

"I don't know," Lydia said critically, reluctant to let go of her role as boss.

"I've got to go home before they start letting people in, Lydia," said Alison. "I'd like to change clothes."

"Lavender!" said Lydia peevishly.

"Chill out," advised Seven Yellow Moons. "I've still got friends who call me by my other name, and I haven't gone by it for almost ten years." As Alison waved good-bye, Lydia looked as if she would rather die than chill out.

188

* * *

Alison could hear Janka and Michelle thumping around in their bedroom as she entered her apartment. Just the sounds told her that they were still on ill terms. Wonderful, and she was giving them a ride. Well, she had weathered their storms before. She slipped the black dress that she had picked up at the Vintage clothing store, over her head and eyed it critically. Even she had to admit that it looked wonderful, transforming her into a sultry, foreign spy type. But was it going to be too dressy? Fretting, she climbed the stairs.

As she had promised earlier, Janka had dug out a black lace shawl and an evening bag, (presents from a hopeful mother and never used before) from the back of her closet. Great accessories, especially the purse, because she wasn't about to leave her revolver at home, but even she had realized that a holster would spoil the line of her bodice. There was also a pair of black heels that she ignored completely. No way.

Several bags of Michelle's photos were sitting beside the shoes. She opened one bag with a smile, ignoring the slamming in the bedroom. There she was, squatting by the fire. There was Michelle with Melanie and Sharon Aldrich. Now she was beginning to see just a little of the young dyke in the stern woman who had become a Crusader. The sharp line of her nose more than anything. Alison stared at the picture with the strange feeling that she had seen something like it earlier, another photo of Sharon Aldrich, older than this, but still very much a dyke; it eluded her for a moment. Then, suddenly, she remembered the picture on Pam's refrigerator. Pam, Teresa, the woman who had died, the woman with the long hair, and the other woman who had been facing front, slightly blurred. Sharon Aldrich. She had been one of the mothers! That was why she'd had the feeling of déjà vu.

It was a startling piece of information, but after a moment, Alison shrugged. It explained why, if it had been him, Mark had been in the photo of the Crusaders at the bar. He had kept contact with one of the women, why not two? He had been there because of Sharon. But where did she go with it? Where did she go with any of it now that she had been bluntly told not to interfere, that even her information was not wanted?

Alison looked at her watch. She barely had time to get to the florist's to pick up the corsage she had ordered for Stacy. She tucked the bag under her arm and threw the shawl over her shoulder.

* * *

There was already a crowd of women when Alison, Janka and Michelle arrived at the Ball.

For a few minutes Alison was content just to stand by the door, watching the women stream in. As Stacy had told her, it was a sight not to be missed at

189

any cost. She had never seen such an array of finery. It was more than just the basic costumes she had grown to expect at every dyke event: the woman in the tux, the woman in the man's suit and, more increasingly, the woman in the short black leather skirt, who tonight was also wearing lacy little anklets with a pair of black pumps. The women entering the hall were seriously decked out in a much wider variety of chic fashions. Alison did not look at all out of place as she had feared. Even the black evening bag and shawl were not too much.

While she watched the women arriving, excited, laughing, Alison thought again of the dykes of her youth, who would never have turned out for an affair such as this. At their dances—women's music only—dressing up had been Frye boots and vests and jackets. No makeup, and if a woman did occasionally wear a skirt it was batiked and worn with Earthshoes bought at a rummage sale. Now those same women were here, some of them tottering on spikes that would be discarded within the next half hour, and she and Michelle were the only ones she knew who still didn't shave their legs. Well, there was topic for a dissertation if someone could pull it together.

She drew the black shawl tighter around her shoulders and wished for a cigarette. For the first time the nip in the air seemed to promise that, yes, winter really was coming. Summer had gone well into October—what more could anyone want? She would be chilled soon.

There was really no reason to wait for Stacy outside, since she didn't know when she was coming. Still pissed her off! They had planned the goddamn thing as a real date. Only, when she had arrived home from the florist's there had been a message on the machine changing plans. Stacy saying, in a rather distracted way, that something had come up and that she'd meet her at the hall.

At first Alison couldn't believe it. There she was, standing with an orchid in one hand, and here was this message that didn't even give a fucking explanation! In fact, she had been so astounded that she had rewound the tape and played it again, just in case she had missed something. That had pissed her off even more, because the second time, with the sound turned up, she had caught something that had slipped by her at first, though it was definitely not what she had been hoping to hear. After the message there were bumping and rustling sounds, and it had become obvious that the phone had not been hung up properly and was still recording. She'd heard Stacy's voice, pacifying, and then one that was male. Mark. He had sounded petulant, and it had not taken Alison more than a moment to jump to the conclusion that this was the reason their date had been rearranged. Mark was choosing to have a crisis and Stacy, acting out of guilt for a bad childhood at which she had not even been present, was going to sacrifice Alison's needs for his. She had tried to put it into a more reasonable perspective, after all, Stacy was going to meet up her at the dance, she wasn't cancelling, for god's sake, but Alison was consumed with a jealousy she did not know she possessed.

"What a crowd, huh?" Michelle leaned back across the rails beside her. She was wearing a long tailed suit that Janka had made. The fabric had been hand-painted in shades of lavender and blue with a great deal of white showing through. The transformation from Mikey the bicycle mechanic was amazing, and showed by the way women in the ticket line looked at her.

"Where's Janka?" Alison asked, not because she really wanted to know, but because Michelle obviously wanted to talk. If it had been anyone else she would have grunted rudely until they left her to think her crabby thoughts alone, but Michelle had rights that others did not.

"She's dancing. She said she was going to have a good time whether I was or not." Michelle ran a hand through her hair, which she had even consented to have moussed up in front. A silver earcuff dangled a blue stone from her ear. She sighed. "I can't stand myself when I get jealous."

"Neither can anyone else. Why are you being such a butthead? You know she's not going to run off with that woman. Even if she was going to leave you it wouldn't be to go live in someone's van or a collective house made out of cardboard. All she wants to do with Seven Yellow Moons is talk weaving."

"I know." Michelle sighed deeply again. A single woman entering gave her such a long look that, misinterpreting, she frowned and looked down, examining her shirt for a spot. "I really know that in my heart of hearts. But sometimes I feel like...I mean, don't you?...like there is this other woman who lives inside me, and sometimes she gets out and does all these horrid things while I'm standing politely in the background saying, 'Ah, excuse me. Pardon me, but do you think...?' However, she never stays around to deal with any of the fights she causes."

Alison laughed. "I know her. Her sister is visiting my house tonight."

"Have you seen Lydia's booth?"

"I built the damn thing."

"I can't believe Seven Yellow Moons displays with her."

"She's a tolerant woman. More tolerant than you or I."

"I guess. They were driving me crazy talking this afternoon."

"About what?"

"Well, that was part of it. I didn't know quite what they were talking about so I couldn't quite follow. I didn't want to ask because I knew it would be something weird. But Seven Yellow Moons would say, 'I'm really worried about him,' and then Lydia would say, 'Why do you suppose you want to feel worried?' and Seven Yellow Moons would say, 'She's not going out, or seeing anyone. It's just like it was when he was a kid,' and Lydia would say,

'Well, what was her aura like?' and Seven Yellow Moons would say, 'I know he feels like I deserted him when he was in the hospital, but I wasn't going to play into him acting like that,' just like Lydia was listening or saying something that made sense. It went on like that for hours, and Lydia never asked her one single question or indicated she was paying attention in any way, and Seven Yellow Moons never acknowledged it. It was like listening to two five year olds. You know, how they have two monologues that are interspersed but think they're having a conversation?"

Alison laughed again, this time at Michelle's interpretation of Lydia, played with big round eyes, staring up at the sky. "Who were they talking about?"

"Who the fuck knows? The only reason that I was even listening was because Janka invited you-know-who up to talk weaving on her break and Lydia followed. And then they just never fucking left. I guess that Seven Yellow Moons had spent the day visiting old friends, and of course each of them had their own little soap opera going and she was all concerned. This one was about a mother and kid, but I never did get the characters right."

"Hmm." Alison spent a long moment thinking how delightful it would be to have her house back. The first thing she was going to do was change the locks. "Well, we can stand out here all night and whine and get cold, or we can go inside and delight hundreds of women."

"Let's stand outside and whine," said Michelle. "I want to torment myself a little longer by thinking of Janka dancing with women more beautiful and interesting than me."

Alison nodded agreeably and they stood in companionable silence for several minutes watching the fashion show parading before them.

"Could we whine inside?" Alison asked finally. "I really am getting cold."

"Sure. I'm almost done, anyway. I think after a beer I may be ready to go apologize for acting like a jerk. Of course, if she's dancing with Seven Yellow Moons I may do something that will raise the state of being a jerk to heights that have remained unreached before this."

"Let's hope she's not. I don't want to ride in a car that full of hostility again. I'd rather have you making out in the back, nauseating as I usually find it." They climbed off the rail and were swept up into a crowd of older women, all of whom were wearing tuxes with glittering red cumberbunds.

"Do you want a beer? Hey, what did your boss have to say to you this morning?"

"No, but do they have anything to eat? He told me to mind my own business and hinted that there were going to be job hassles if I didn't." Again Alison felt that tinge of guilt about the check. Well, Obrachta had made it very clear that it wasn't her job anymore.

"So that's that?" The line for beer and food stretched past the merchant's booths. Lydia and Seven Yellow Moons were on the very end, closest to the concessions. "I think they're selling some kind of veggie plate."

"That's that." Alison rummaged in her purse, trying to get her wallet out without advertising to everyone around them that she was toting a piece.

"I didn't think you'd give up so easy."

"Goddammit, don't say that! Why is it my job to find this out, any more than it's yours or Janka's? You've got the same information I have. Don't make me responsible for these deaths!"

Michelle did not reply, but tightened her lips and looked out in the crowd. Alison knew that Michelle was still thinking that she had given up, and she could not blame her, because secretly, no matter how much she tried to justify it, she was thinking the same thing. But she had been ordered to keep out. It had nothing at all to do with not liking which way the information was pointing.

To distract herself she stared into the booth directly across from them which displayed vibrant silk screened T-shirts. A number of women who were holding them against tuxes or slipping them on over strapless gowns.

"Have you seen this show?" Michelle nudged her and pointed with her chin at a booth across the way.

"Not this year's. I love it." Alix Dobkin sang *If It Wasn't For The Women* as slides flashed onto the screen at the back of the booth. She did love the medley of local dyke photos and music. It was put together by a woman from Boulder and aired often. It combined an air of professionalism and home movies, showing marches, soccer games, concerts, the local bookstore. She saw events that she had attended herself and even thought she spotted her foot in a photo of a Memorial Day Picnic.

"Hey, look." Michelle jostled her arm. "There you are."

There she was, standing with her back to the camera, leaning against the bar at the Rubyfruit. Only there was something wrong.

"That's not me." She knew it couldn't be, though the photo certainly looked like her. But she didn't have a shirt like that and before this week, she hadn't been to the Rubyfruit for years.

"Oh, come on, you can tell me. I'll respect you even if you are a barfly."

"That's mighty big of you, but I still don't think it's me."

"Well, it looks just like...."

The carousel turned and the bar was replaced by a picture of three women sitting on the lawn with three huge dogs. They could not argue about the picture now that they could not see it. Both began to turn, then once again the projector clicked and they found themselves back at the bar. This photo was almost exactly the same as the first, except that the woman in the foreground, the one whom Michelle had mistaken for Alison, had turned so that she was facing the camera.

"Oh," said Alison. She felt as if she were rooted to the spot.

"Hey, are you guys in line or are you just standing there?"

As if in a daze she moved up and paid for a plate of vegetables and dip. Michelle was paying for a beer in the same distracted way, and she knew it was because they had shared the same flash of illumination.

There was nowhere to sit but Michelle took her hand and ducked beneath the rope that sectioned off Lydia and Seven Yellow Moon's booth. Lydia gave them a dirty look as they settled down on a box in the back, which jolted Alison out of her daze just long enough so that she was able to appreciate the moment of being an unwanted guest rather than a reluctant hostess. "That woman in the picture," said Michelle. She took a long pull on her beer bottle.

"Yes."

"It wasn't you."

"No." Alison stuffed a piece of broccoli in her mouth. She was eating automatically now, a growing horror eclipsing her hunger and crabbiness. Neither said a word as she chewed the vegetable and swallowed it as if it were a piece of pasteboard.

"That was Carla in that picture."

"Yes."

Michelle was talking as if to a first grader, and Alison was not impatient, for though her mind had already made the leap, it was as if it had arrived there alone, and all the steps on the way had been forgotten. Michelle was filling in those steps. "Carla looks just like you from behind."

"Yes." From behind, or in the dark, or particularly if they had changed clothes and she was wearing Alison's one-of-a-kind red sweater as she came up the stairs with a big box held in front of her. That could only mean that the killer had been quite aware of her going into the Rubyfruit, had already identified her.

And why had no one noticed the resemblance before? Because the very first night when she had brought Carla home and introduced her, Carla's head had been shaved like a demented punker.

"It wasn't Carla that killer wanted at all, was it?" Michelle had to spell it out as though a part of her brain also refused to believe.

"No."

"It was you."

Alison winced and did not reply, because if she said yes, she would have to go further. She would have to acknowledge that this was why Carla had never quite fit into the pattern, that now the pattern was complete and, like rays shooting out from a sun, every woman who had been attacked was now linked back to Stacy. Three. Too many to be coincidental.

"It was you. God, and you were with her last night. She could have killed you while...I knew that stuff was wrong! I knew it led to violence...."

"Shut up, Michelle," Alison said almost pleasantly. "Just shut the fuck up." She stuck a carrot into her mouth. The last thing she needed was Michelle saying I told you so when already her mind was pumping in questions far too fast for her to answer. Was it only Stacy's word that she didn't play really rough? and *did* she really like to hurt women? and *had* she liked it so much that she had decided to go for just a little bit more, for the ultimate thrill of a snuff scene? She tried to squeeze in another, to ask why, if this was true, Stacy hadn't just done away with her while she was tied down the night before, but the answer was so obvious that it did not reassure. Nobody shits in their own backyard. Just because Alison had not become a body in Stacy's apartment, where disposal would have been difficult, did not mean that it had not been attempted in the parking lot and would not be attempted again.

"What are you going to do?" Michelle asked.

"I'm going to eat," she replied, because she really could not think of doing anything more than stuffing the vegetables into her mouth as fast as she could chew and swallow them.

"Well, I have to go pee. It's an emergency. But I'll be right back and we'll talk about it." Alison watched her squirm through the crowd and disappear.

"...and then his Mom died, and it was really weird, you know, the police never came out and hauled him in or anything, but everybody knew that they wondered if putting the ashes in the can had really been a mistake. So how do you get back to being close to someone like that, when you're always wondering...."

"I think this would be really nice for dip." Lydia picked up a particularly angular cunt dish and fondly held it close. Christ, Lydia and Seven Yellow Moons were talking just as Michelle had described them, and apparently still on the same topics.

"I mean, it's true his mom was not what I'd call a good person. She didn't love him, dumped him and then took him back just to jerk us around, and kind of as an offering to God, to show him what a good person she was."

"A white, frothy dip," mused Lydia. "Cum dip. Maybe I should include some little books of recipes with them."

"So I don't know what kind of weirdness is going on now, but the kid has a history of violence, and it doesn't matter how much she loves him or how much she wishes it wasn't true, because it is true...."

No wonder Michelle had wanted to slap them both. Where was Michelle?

195

Sixteen

"Sue!" It was a familiar voice, someone with whom Alison had spoken not long ago. She lifted her head to see Pam approaching the booth, her hand outstretched to Seven Yellow Moons, who seemed almost reluctant to take it. "Oh, don't be that way. I'm really sorry I was so crabby with you. You know how I am about it, just a mother hen."

"You're doing the wrong thing, Pam." Seven Yellow Moons spoke in the tone of one who knows her advice will not be taken but must try nonetheless. "You're the only one with any influence on him at all. He thinks I'm one of the bad guys now. He needs some help...."

"Sue." Pam put her fingers against the other woman's mouth in a shushing motion. "Truce. Okay? At least for tonight."

Sue. Pam had used the name when she'd spoken to Alison in her apartment. Alison wracked her brain, knowing somehow that this was important. To whom had she referred as 'Sue'?

Suddenly it came to her, and as she remembered she saw the photograph on the refrigerator, the one of the little boy and the four women, the fourth turned to the side. Pam had pointed to the fourth woman and called her Sue. And the fourth woman, her hair now pulled back from her face in a long braid, was Seven Yellow Moons.

Alison peered at them both, trying to see what she already knew. As she did so, Pam leaned across the table a little further and her earrings swung forward, catching the light. They were long lines of tubular beads with stars and moons on the ends, just like the ones she had seen at the bookstore.

Except for one thing. One star on the right earring was missing. 'One star was coming off,' Carla had said, 'You don't see a butch who can get away with dangly earrings very often.' Dangling earrings, but the corpse, of course, had worn none, and they had not been listed in the possessions. That was what had been bothering her about that report.

"Where did you get your earrings, Pam?" She had moved to the front of the booth without being aware of it. She knew by their stares that she had interrupted, but she did not apologize.

"Mark gave them to me. Aren't they pretty?" Pam spoke as if she were trying to sound gay, but somehow there was a ring of falseness to it, and sud-

196

denly Alison realized that on some level she knew that there was something not quite right happening with Mark, but that she was blocking it from her mother's heart.

"There's a star missing."

"I didn't notice...I...." Pam stammered, confused.

"They're not new." Alison said flatly. She wondered if she should ask for the earrings and hope that the lab could lift just one print of Tamara Garrity's from beneath Mark and Pam's. No, no chance. But Carla could testify about the star, and she herself had the photo that showed Tamara wearing them earlier in the evening. For a moment she wondered why he had taken them. Some kind of token, prize? Did he have a similar one from Melanie? She remembered Krista choking off sobs, saying that all they had taken was her necklace, her goddamn necklace. Was it at home on the top of Mark's dresser?

"What happened to Mark's mother?" Alison asked. "His real mother?"

"Um, Alison, we're trying to wind up a private conversation here." Seven Yellow Moons attempted to interrupt, but Alison ignored her, turning directly to face Pam.

"He killed her, didn't her?"

"No! It was an accident! She started the fire herself, she put hot ashes from the stove into a trash can on the back porch. It had a wooden floor. What did she expect to happen? She was always spacy.... He burned his own hands trying to get her out." Pam's face was red, her voice outraged. Or rather, was it the voice of someone forcing outrage, indignation?

"But why? That's all I need to understand, the motive, and you can tell me. Why did he do it?"

"I don't have to listen to this crap," said Pam. "I knew there was something funny about you the other day." She turned to leave, but Seven Yellow Moons shot a hand across the table and grasped her by the arm, so hard that the skin around the fingers immediately began to turn red. For the second time Alison noticed how large and strong her hands were.

Alison turned to her, the woman who had once been called Sue and had been another of the boy's mothers. She said, "Do you remember my friend who you met the other morning? The one who reminded you of the woman you used to know?"

"Sure." Seven Yellow Moons was noticeably uneasy, not wanting to hear what was coming, not willing to turn away. "The woman who looked like Candy, Mark's mom."

"Mark is a friend of hers. Mark is very, very fond of her. She says that he looks on her as kind of a substitute mother." Though the noise of two hundred women still flowed around them it was as if they were surrounded by their own little bubble of silence.

"All of the women who were killed were her lovers." Alison did not bother to distinguish customers from lovers because she no longer thought what Stacy did for a living was relevant.

A gagging sound came out of Seven Yellow Moons' mouth. Alison lifted her hand as if to pat her on the back and then lowered it again. She was choking on the past and no amount of pounding could make it go away.

"You knew!" she growled at Pam, thrusting her other hand across to grasp her other arm. "You fucking knew, and you didn't tell me a thing!"

"There was nothing to tell! There's nothing to know! So what if they're friends?" Pam struggled to release herself but it was useless. She would go free when Seven Yellow Moons decided to let her and not a moment before. "The police said it was an accident!"

"Because they couldn't prove it! Because you and Teresa always had an excuse for him, because you wouldn't tell them that damn lazy woman never carried her own ashes out once in her whole life. That was his job, wasn't it? Such a good boy!"

"So what if it was? It was still an accident. Why should he have to suffer more than he already had? He burned his hands trying to pull her out of that fire. He suffered smoke inhalation himself. You know that!"

"I know that maybe he changed his mind at the last minute. Maybe he realized that it was for real this time, that it wasn't just some kind of weird fantasy in his head, something to make his mother love him the way he wanted her to. She was a shitty mother, Pam, but she didn't deserve to die because of it."

"She died because she was a shitty housekeeper! She died because she was too fucking dumb to even know how to clean her stove out! That's who we let that kid go live with, a woman who thought that fossils were just God's way of testing the faithful, a woman who told him that we were perverts even though we gave him the best life he'd ever had, a woman who was so stupid that she put hot ashes in a can on a wooden floor!" She was trying mightily to convince herself, and despite it all, Alison could see that she was not succeeding, that a hole had been made in the dam and doubt was pouring in.

"Explain it away, Pam. Then explain away the things he tried to do to her lovers. Only the women, Pam. Only the women. You can't. The police have it down, the hospital has it down. He cut that woman, Pam, he cut her face."

The police have it down. It was something that Alison could have gotten from the computer if only she had known the right name to feed in. He had tried to keep his mother's lovers away, tried to keep them from stealing the love she should have given to him, and when that hadn't worked he had made sure that she wouldn't love anyone at all.

"Is there a problem here?" One of the ticket sellers had pushed her way through the silent crowd that had formed in front of the booth to watch the drama. She was half the size of Seven Yellow Moons, but determined. There was going to be no trouble at her dance.

"No," said Alison. Because there was one thing more that she had to know from Pam, and she had to know it before Seven Yellow Moons released her, before she had time to pull herself together again, think protector.

"Where—"

But Seven Yellow Moons leaped in, almost shouting now. "He doesn't like women, Pam. He doesn't like lesbians. That fucking Sharon and his god-damn mother saw to that." Pam's lips moved, and though no sound came out, Alison knew that she was trying to deny it, trying to say he loved her. But there's always an exception for Mother, isn't there? For a moment Alison had a stab of sympathy for the child who had been told that the women who had mothered him were wicked and sinful, bound to burn in hell, that their caring had all been a joke voided because of their sexuality. What must it have cost for him to hang onto that love for Pam in the midst of it? Then she shook her head. The boy was a man now. Two women were dead, and it didn't matter whether he had killed in an attempt to save Stacy from herself, or merely to eliminate the competition.

Seven Yellow Moons was still ranting. "There's no other reason that he would want to be friends with that poor woman, not unless he was setting her up to be another Candy, a better mother. And god help her if...."

The bouncer, not at all convinced by Alison, attempted to thrust a shoulder between the two, no mean task because Seven Yellow Moons had dragged Pam half across the table, was holding her as tight as logistics would permit and was starting to shake her. She brushed the bouncer away like a fly and the smaller woman's lips tightened in anger. She gestured over the heads of the crowds. Alison put her own hand in, prepared to duck. But, whether she respected her right in some strange way, or whether she had simply come to the end of her spiel, Seven Yellow Moons did not strike out.

"Where is he, Pam?" Alison asked the question quietly, and then, when the woman simply stared, she asked again. "He wanted you to come out tonight, didn't he? He encouraged you to come, even though he usually wants you to stay home. Where is he tonight?" Her mind went back to the phone message, to the few petulant words she had heard before Stacy's phone had started to buzz. Had he spoken to his mother that way, giving her one last try, the night before the fire had started?

"Where is he?" she said again, almost shouting herself, and she could not, for a moment, understand the look of relief that crossed Pam's face before she answered.

"Glennwood Springs," she said. "He had to go down for a photo session."

If he was in Glennwood Springs he could not be here, could not be waiting for another woman, could not be with Stacy. Alison wanted to believe it, but her instincts told her differently. She barked a quick order to Seven Yellow Moons. "Look for him," she said. "He may be around here."

"What's the problem?" Reinforcements had arrived, and they were women who had been picked because of their size, women who looked as if they were positively dying to mix it up a little. The crowd tensed and suddenly Alison knew that she was about to be caught in the middle of a scene, caught by the crowd and held, because there wasn't a dyke in the whole world who could mind her own business and whatever Seven Yellow Moons did, even if it were merely releasing Pam gently and brushing her off, there was bound to be interference, protests from the bouncers and the audience in every possible combination and permutation. Already she could see that women from the main hall were flowing out to join in the commotion, and the front door was barely visible.

If she were stuck in the crowd she would not be able to check on Stacy. Fuck it that Pam had said he was out of town. She wanted to hear it with her own ears, wanted to hear Stacy's sweet voice telling her that of course she was okay, she was just a little late, and why was she asking? She had to get to Stacy, and quickly.

"Excuse me," she said, hoping that Seven Yellow Moons would understand why she was being abandoned. There was almost a solid mass of women in front of them, but the tables had kept them out of the booths, so she ducked beneath the rope that separated them from the photographer, and beneath the rope that defined the potter's space. Voices were being raised as she came to the T-shirt women, who stared at her as if she were an alien but made no move to stop her. She thought she might have heard the smack of a fist and hoped, if violence could not be avoided, that at least the dreadful cunts would be destroyed in the brawl.

* * *

"Yes, who is it?" It was almost a let down to hear Stacy's voice calling calmly from the window. Alison had to struggle for breath before she could answer. It had seemed to make more sense to run the block and a half rather than fighting to reach the phone. She had been grateful, her skirts hoisted up around her knees, that she had clung to the tennis shoes instead of the heels Janka had suggested. Her legs felt leaden, worse than they should have, and in the middle of her concern, an unrelated thought stood out like a jewel: she wasn't as fit as she needed to be for her job and she was going to have to make that appointment with the specialist her doctor had recommended after all.

"It's Alison," she finally panted. She moved out beneath the street light so that Stacy could see her.

The window flew up and Stacy leaned out, looking more beautiful than ever before, especially because she was safe. Her shoulders were bare, and her dark hair had been twisted up in a French knot and then glittered silver. She perched one hip, clothed in dark purple velvet, on the sill.

"Ooo-eee," she called out into the night, long and low and sexy, "I think I'm in love." She threw a kiss, and Alison's heart bounded. "I was just on my way over. Why don't you come on up? You're not too mad, are you?"

Alison had run over many possible scenarios on the wild dash, scenes that, to be truthful, she had seen more on TV than in the line of duty, and it had occurred to her that if Mark were in the apartment he might force Stacy to say that she was okay. But she could not for one moment believe that under those circumstances, Stacy would be flirting out a second story window.

Still, she had the revolver out when she reached the door of the apartment. She pushed Stacy brusquely to one side and made a quick scan. Stacy had been having a quick snack, as evidenced by a partial loaf of French bread and tub of margarine that were sitting on the windowsill. He was not there. He was not there. She had arrived in time. She wanted to cry and laugh at once, wanted to sweep Stacy off her feet in a joyous celebration of being alive.

"Uh, Alison." Stacy was eyeing the gun nervously. "That's a little too kinky even for me."

"No, that's not it." The broad smile splitting her face was keeping her from explaining as she tucked the piece back into Janka's bag. She dropped it on the table. "That's not it at all. I was so worried...I'm so glad...." She put her arms around the other woman, planning to hold her close, to hold her gently, but suddenly she was swept up in that wave of passion that always seemed to be lurking for her lately. She struggled for a minute and then rode the crest, for she could feel Stacy against her being similarly swept.

Stacy's gown was soft beneath her hands, and for a moment she felt that it was enough, that she could be happy forever running her hands over the yards and yards of thick velvet while she kissed Stacy hard on the mouth, and then drew back and nibbled lightly, teased with her tongue. It was hard to find the woman beneath all that velvet. She was surprised by sudden flashes of firmness beneath, by the thrust of Stacy's hard thigh between her own, by Stacy's hip pressing into her belly. Her breasts were more accessible, and as Alison eased them anxiously out of their casing of sequins she wondered how much dance finery would be similarly discarded later that night. She had a quick picture of the hall, of women dancing in sequins and velvet and lace, and overlaid a hundred smaller pictures of those same women coupling joyfully, discarding boas and shawls and high heels and cumberbunds. She was filled with a joy so intense that she almost removed her mouth from Stacy's to tell her, to shout that she loved dykes, that she loved being a lesbian. Then that general love shrank and spun within her, becoming a focused circle within a circle, and in that smaller orb were the women close to her—Michelle and Janka and her old friend Zori who lived in California and her friends out on the land—all the women she felt that were her family, for whom she would care forever, and this intense love was flowing out of her and onto Stacy, as if she were the cloth beneath a horn of plenty, as if she were the cup into which the everfilling pitcher in fairy tales poured. She wondered, burying her mouth in Stacy's hair, and then pulling at it with her lips, if this was how people felt before they spoke in tongues. She imagined herself capable of it, imagined that she might fall to the floor to shout unknown words of praise were she not able to express the feeling inside her by making love to a woman. For a moment she was sorry for everyone in the world who was not a lesbian. She was sorry for Nancy Reagan and Howard Hughes and Raquel Welch and her mother, and then that feeling was swept along because there was no room for it in the tidal wave that washed over her as she lowered her mouth to Stacy's breasts. She sucked gently at first, flicking her tongue teasingly over first one nipple and then the other. Then she was gulping greedily, pulling hard with just a hint of teeth, listening to Stacy's moans as if they were an aria from an opera, sound that told the audience that now the love scene was about to happen.

She lifted her head because the feeling was simply too intense for her to handle. She felt as if she were plummeting headfirst down a roller coaster and when the ride ended it was not going to pull tamely into the station at all, but would start all over again before she even had time to catch her breath. She looked into Stacy's face, but her eyes were glazed. She was at that place Alison had been the night before, where she had all but cried, "Take me, take me!" and given herself up to the other woman.

Alison's heart was pounding as she took Stacy by the shoulder and laid her back on the work table. There was part of her still functioning rationally, and it scanned quickly for pins and needles and scissors, and swept the sheathed cutter to one side, but she was not even aware of it. She was too busy tucking the great joyous feeling away, squeezing it down to a bundle that she could hold in her heart without being in danger of bursting into tears. She knew that crying was not the only danger, that if she continued in this matter she would certainly fall in love, that she would want to move in with Stacy and share everything with her, and she did not want to repeat that instant marriage again. Deliberately she slowed her heartbeat, moving her hands just enough over Stacy's breasts to keep her aroused, to reassure her that it was just a breather, not a crisis.

In her relief her fantasy kicked in, a new one, in which she was the one who held power.

Alison waited a little anxiously as she felt the familiar cameras beginning to roll, bending her head again to Stacy's breast, hoping that a sequel to last night was not in the wings. This time she wanted to top, and she couldn't imagine Prudence in that position, even if the Mistress of Storm's Head would allow such a thing.

But she was able to heave a sigh of relief only a few seconds later. She should have trusted her director, that gifted award-winner who was now focusing on their two skirts bunched up together. The camera panned over the rich purple velvet almost covered by the black satin, catching the shimmered threads of silver, until the viewer wanted to reach out and touch them, wanted to stroke the textures with the same intensity that Alison now wanted to stroke Stacy's velvet opening. She was not ready yet to touch her there, that must be savored, but she did take a long look. Stacy was wearing black stockings again, and the black and red garter belt that was by now looking familiar. Doesn't this women ever wear panty hose like a normal person? Alison wondered. She wasn't even sure where one bought garter belts. It was not, however, a puzzle that weighed long on her mind. Alison lifted Stacy by the thighs, pulling her up close so that she could feel that heat against her belly, through her satin skirt.

Then, much to her dismay, Alison felt a tiny voice that seemed to speak to her from an entirely different part of her brain than the part so occupied with the sensation of Stacy locking her ankles behind her back. The director shot Stacy's sleek black spike heels, strapped across the instep, then slid the camera up her leg and lingered for a moment on the gold-edged top of a stocking. She caught just the shadow of Alison's hand as, unable to resist any longer, she played two fingers across Stacy's swollen clit. The shot traveled up to Stacy's breast and the sequined bodice crumpled beneath them. Alison dropped to her knees on the floor, pulling Stacy's ass to the edge of the table, but even as she winced beneath Stacy's spikes on her shoulders, the little voice was continuing to drone in the background in a tone that was hard to ignore. It was saying, 'What about Mark?' and 'This isn't safe.', and 'How could he be in the Springs if you heard him on the phone earlier?' Alison wanted to ignore it. She had pulled Stacy's lips wide apart so she could admire every little fold, so the director could pan lovingly over the tight opening, the creamy wetness that sparkled under the lights. This was not a time for reason, this was a time to cover Stacy's clit with her entire mouth and suck it in....

Forget it, asshole! Desperately, the small voice had called in backups, and the backup was using a voice that sounded distressingly like Michelle's. A voice that in a minute would be saying, 'I told you this kinky shit would get you in trouble.', and 'You've been acting like a madwoman when you're around her.', and 'You don't even fucking recognize when you're in danger anymore....' Regretfully Alison drew her mouth away from temptation and got to her feet.

"Fist me," moaned Stacy, unaware of the struggle Alison had just lost to reason, and for a moment she just held her. "Fist me, now—"

How was she going to tell this luscious, dripping woman that whatever scene playing in her head was not in the cards tonight, more so, that someone Stacy regarded as a friend had murdered brutally—twice?

"I've got to talk to you," she said gently. Stacy's eyes flew open as if she had been slapped in the face. She gave Alison an incredulous look and slid her own hand down between her legs as if to perform a reality check—We were just getting ready to fuck, right, I didn't just imagine that?

"Really," insisted Alison, turning her head so she wouldn't be distracted by the sight of Stacy touching herself. She tried to take Stacy's hand to help her to her feet, but Stacy brushed it frostily aside and stood unaided. Major pissed, and Alison couldn't blame her. It wasn't a tease. It was like the lights had gone out in the middle of an erotic movie. No warning, no picture, no sound.

"I'm sorry," she said, as Stacy tried to push past her. She caught her shoulder. She had to make her hear. She had to fucking call Jorgenson. She really should have taken the earrings, she thought, insecurity beginning to creep in. Suppose Pam had decided to toss them? Maybe she hadn't handled things the right way, rushing off like that. But, playing the scene back in her mind she couldn't see a way to change it. She had been wrong; Stacy had been perfectly safe. But what if her premonition had been right? What if Mark had been here and she had stayed in the hall collecting statements?

"I've got to talk to you," she said. She wanted to slip her arm around Stacy's waist and pull her close, but Stacy was standing stiff as a board, adjusting her dress. Alison had to content herself with resting her hand on the small of her back.

"Look," she began. She was never to finish the sentence. Later she couldn't tell if there had been a sudden silence, if, remarkably, there had been no cars or jets outside just as the conversation lulled, or if it had just been some trick of acoustics that had made the sound as sharp and clear as a shot. Either way, it didn't matter. Alison stopped in midsentence when she heard it—the click of a key in a lock. And then, as drawn out as if it were lifted off the soundtrack from a horror flick, a slow creak, creak, creak as the front door of the apartment was pushed open. The sleigh bells shook slightly.

Alison did not know that she could react so quickly, not until after her hand was already clamped over Stacy's mouth, pulling her to her. She could see by Stacy's dark eyes that she thought at first it was a game that Alison wasn't playing particularly well. She wasn't even fucking worried, thought Alison in despair. Stacy was probably like dozens of dykes she knew who had passed out more keys than they could count. Shit, look at own her situation. Michelle and Janka both had keys, as did her dad, Robert, and, unfortunately, Lydia. But Alison knew that this wasn't just a neighbor or an old girlfriend. Knew even before the voice.

"Stacy?" A young man's voice, but a little boy's whine. "Stacy?" More demanding this time.

Damn, Alison swore to herself, how could she have been so complacent, have stayed here and let both of them become completely vulnerable just on his word to Pam? He had lied to Pam countless times before, and yet Alison had let relief and lust overcome common sense. How easy for him to take Pam's keys any time he wanted to get in. Another clue that she had seen far too late. Flipping the lock behind her had been as effective as leaving the door wide open.

Stacy raised her eyebrows and motioned with her head. Come on, we can't let him catch us half-naked in the kitchen. She was still more worried about embarrassment than anything else. Alison's mind was darting. Her heart felt as if it had stopped, and then started again only with reluctance. She again located her purse in her mind's eye. It was on the coffee table two rooms away, dammit, on the coffee table and no amount of wishing could change that. She had no choice but to confront him unarmed. She tried not to think of how one-sided it might be, tried to hope that he had returned only for comfort, and not to kill. At the very least she must alert Stacy so that she would stay out of the way, not slow her with 'What are you doing, Alison?' and, 'Mark's my friend'.

She put her hand over Stacy's mouth, and then brought her lips to Stacy's ear, so close that they brushed it as she spoke in her softest tone, "Mark gave Pam Tamara's earrings." It was not the sentence she would have chosen, had she been sitting safely at her own table attempting to condense the evidence. Now, under pressure, unrelated words and phrases flew through her head as she struggled to make Stacy understand in the space of seconds, before he became suspicious, entered the kitchen and any advantage was lost. His mother...fire...jealous...police record...knifing...mental hospital...all came to her in a flash, complete with pictures. She saw, as if a slide carousel had been shaken and dumped, and then put back together in any old order, the snapshot from Pam's fridge, the police photo of Melanie Donahue, the miniature picture of the Crusaders—Mark beside Sharon, the picture of Tamara Garrity at the bar, her head thrown back as she flirted. All in the space of a second, and all condensed to one sentence. "Mark is the killer."

Just as she had feared Stacy's eyes widened with disbelief, her mouth moved in protest beneath Alison's palm. Again the collage of phrases ran through her head—Seven Yellow Moons...Sue...the picture...the earrings...all the pieces that she knew fit neatly to form the puzzle. But she didn't have time to explain. Desperately she gave Stacy a shake, touching her much harder than she had in play.

"You have to believe me now," she whispered, a whisper that wanted to be a shout. "You have to stay out of my way. He might be armed. He might be dangerous. He tried to kill me, Stacy, me, not Carla." That was it. There was no more time for her to add to or edit the story. All she could do was hope that her feeling of helplessness, her knowledge of truth, had been carried across in those five lines.

She didn't know what it was. Maybe her absolute desperation. Or maybe unconsciously Stacy had been putting her own puzzle pieces together in the dark and it had just taken a flick of Alison's light for the picture to be illuminated. Either way, she could see suddenly from the horror in Stacy's eyes that she did believe. Alison dropped her hands. Four separate fingermarks were outlined in red along Stacy's cheek and jaw.

"Get back," she whispered, nodding towards the kitchen wall. There was a frying pan, dirty, of course, sitting on the stove, and Alison picked it up by the handle, trying to plot her moves. He would probably be surprised to see her. Unless, of course, he had been watching the house, a trap with Stacy as the bait. Unless he had come specifically for her.

"Stacy?" he said, closer, more petulant this time. Alison took a deep breath. One step forward. Another. Then suddenly Stacy grasped her arm. With one hand she jerked open the door to the playroom, and then propelled Alison backwards into it.

She caught Alison completely off guard, but still, they were much the same size and strength, and it might not have worked if she had struggled. She didn't simply because she thought, as she was flying backwards, that Stacy must have some plan she had overlooked. The back door! Of course, they could hightail it out the back without injury and send in someone armed to take him.

Not until too late did Alison realize this was not what Stacy had in mind. Not until she was tumbling back on her ass and she saw the wedge of light from the kitchen suddenly getting much smaller, did she remember the lock and the key that was hung by the front door and the mad rush through the house that had preceded her last back exit. She jumped up and reached out for the knob, nearly catching her fingers in the crack. But it was too late. Already she could hear the bolt on the outside of the door being sent home.

For a moment, as she stood there in the dark, Alison was totally unable to take in this new information. She couldn't have...she hadn't been wrong about Stacy. They were not in this together, Stacy and Mark. She would not believe it, not after the way she had held her and laughed not fifteen minutes before. And Ted Bundy was supposed to be a charming man, said a relentless little I-told-you-so voice. A small stream of light was funneling through the old fashioned keyhole, and Alison dropped to her knees in front of it. It was a straight shot through the kitchen and into the next room. What she saw strengthened her trust. It was not a woman consorting with a co-conspirator.

"What are you doing here, Mark?" Stacy was smoothing her dress around her. Could he hear the fear she was trying to hide in her voice, see her hands trembling? "I thought you were going out of town."

"I had to see you." His voice was still pouty, childlike, and Alison drew a breath in, then another, when she realized that the first had been an audible gasp, that she might have given herself away. What was he playing with in his hand, flicking back and forth?

"I'm glad you came back." Stacy's voice was no longer shaky. She was an actress, Alison remembered, and now she might be acting for her life. "Now we can go out for something to eat. I decided that I didn't want to go to that dance." She did not quite glance back over her shoulder at the closed door, she was too good for that, but she gave a little quarter turn, just a twitch, but enough so that Alison knew she had been right. Stacy had locked her in the playroom to protect her, in the hopes that she could lure Mark away. What had convinced her so quickly of Alison's danger? Had it been something Mark had said before she arrived?

"You said you were going with that woman," Mark said accusingly. "I don't like her at all." Now that his guard was down Alison found it hard to believe that she had ever looked anywhere else. But, then, he was a good actor, too. He'd had to be.

* * *

Where was the goddamn light switch? Alison ran her hand up and down the wall looking. There. The bulb was red and even in the midst of crisis, she regretted being in this room a second time without a chance to look at it closely. She had seen Lawrence emerge twice with a vacuum cleaner. She couldn't imagine that it sat out in the middle of a scene, which led her to believe that there was a supply closet. If that closet was anything like the one at her house it might have something in it which could be used to open the connecting door.

"I changed my mind." Much eerier than watching them was listening to their disembodied voices float through the keyhole. It took all her resolve not to run back and plaster her eye to the patch of light. Bingo. She'd hit pay dirt on the first door. The closet held the vacuum, a broom, a mop; Lawrence must have arranged the shelves, for everything was tidy and lined up in place.

"She's been here, hasn't she?" His voice sounded strange, as if it had been created by a synthesizer, by something without a soul. "You've been doing it again. Don't deny it. Your clothes are all over the floor. Doing it like pigs."

Alison had gone through string, tape, paper bags, everything one could hope to find in a well stocked pantry. Everything but a tool chest. She was almost sobbing with frustration. Okay, calm down, freaking out won't help anyone. She tried to take deep breaths, tried not to focus on the pictures that she could not keep from sliding through her head. Stacy, her chest stained with blood as Melanie Donahue's had been beneath her blouse; Mark quietly opening the door to the playroom, the red knife shining in his hand.

"Don't talk to me like that!" Stacy spoke assertively. Good girl, don't show him you're afraid. Alison had gone through everything in the closet. Maybe the next one.

"I asked you nicely," Mark was talking dreamily. "I asked you nicely to stop seeing those women. I told you that you would go straight to hell if you didn't. But you didn't listen, did you? I asked you and asked you, and as soon as I left, you had that bitch back in here. I know. I watched her come in."

The second closet was full of clothes. Stacy's costumes. Alison leaned her head against the doorframe, ready to weep. No, pull yourself together. Think, Alison, think.

"And I realized you were right." Stacy was trying to sound sincere, but her voice was starting to crack under the strain. Alison could only hope that the effect was better in person. "I realized that everything you said was right. That's why I sent her away. I knew I had to talk to you again so you could tell me the right thing to do."

Lawrence must have also arranged the clothes closet, for everything was hanging neatly, skirts with skirts, blouses with blouses, jackets with jackets. Alison recognized the zippers on the sleeve of one of the jackets. It was the one Stacy had worn the night she had grilled her, the night she had changed in front of her. Now, as she flashed back to that night, Alison realized that Stacy had been afraid that Krista had somehow told her about her appointment with Melanie right before her death. Now she couldn't even tell Stacy that she had found the check, couldn't parade that bit of detecting in front of her. But there was something about the jacket that was more important to remember. Alison strained for it, crossing the room again to the keyhole.

"You didn't send her away." They were standing now with the worktable between them, and Stacy was touching its surface as carelessly as if he were anyone, a customer, a friend dropped by to chat. But Alison knew that there was nothing on it that could be used for a weapon, not even a pin. Hadn't she swept it carefully before she had laid Stacy on it?

"She never came out. I would have seen her."

The knife. That night, as she had teased Alison, Stacy had taken a Swiss army knife out of the pocket of her jacket, trimmed a hangnail, and replaced it. Her pouch had contained exactly the things she had put in that night at the bar. Perhaps it was a habit not to empty her purse, her pockets. Swiftly Alison returned to the closet and began searching the jacket. It had so fucking many pockets, inside, outside, breast pockets, pockets within pockets. It seemed as if it was taking hours instead of less than a minute. There. Her hand closed on a familiar shape, but for a moment she did not pull it out, afraid that somehow she was wrong, that under her eyes it would turn into something useless.

"She's still here." Was that all the time it had taken, just the space between Mark's dreamy sentences? "I'll find her. I'll make sure she doesn't bother you again. I'll make sure she doesn't lead you into temptation."

Now Alison was scanning the blades. Scissors, awl, bottle opener. There was what she had been looking for. The screwdriver. Back she dashed, light-footed, to the door.

"Don't be stupid." Again Stacy was trying to be authoritative. "I'm too hungry to deal with this shit. I want to get dressed so that we can get something to eat. And didn't you say that your church had a meeting tonight? Could we go to that?" The lure flashed. For a moment Alison thought that he would have to bite it, and she heaved a sigh of relief as she attacked the first screw. If Stacy could get him out into public, surely she would be safe. She could excuse herself to go to the bathroom and call the police, she could...she was clever, she would think of something. The first screw on the bottom hinge, one of three, fell out onto the floor.

"No" Mark's voice was regretful, but firm. "It's too late. I gave you a chance. I begged you. I offered to pray with you. And you told me to get the fuck out. Everything is polluted. It's even flowing from your mouth."

"You were right, Mark. I've had time to think about it. Remember, it says in the Bible that if your brother sins against you and then asks for your forgiveness you must forgive him, even if it happens seven times seventy." Stacy's stint as a preacher's wife was serving her well.

"Fuck that!" Mark was no longer talking dreamily, reasonably, he was roaring, the voice of a little boy who has been offended time and time again, and suddenly finds that he has power beyond his years, power which can give his tantrums a whole new meaning. One of the few quotes Alison remembered from several half-hearted years at Sunday school was the one about fearing the wrath of the Lord. She thought now, frantically attacking the third screw, that they should also have warned her to fear the wrath of one who sees himself as the Sword of God, who revenges his own slights in the other's name. "I forgave you again and again. You told me, you promised when you took me away that it would be just the two of us, just you and me. But there was always someone else. You'd have her in your bed and then when she left you'd cry and pray and ask me to forgive you. Well, not any more!" Stacy was silent. What could she say?—He was listing the sins of a woman dead ten years. "I stopped it all once." His voice had changed, he sounded less like the mouthpiece of a harsh Lord, almost as if he were close to tears. "I stopped it all. I cleansed the place. Why did you have to come back, Mother? Why did you have to make me believe you loved me again?"

"Mark, that wasn't me." She had to try, even though it sounded to Alison as if he had gone off the deep end. "You can't blame me for something I didn't do!" Want to bet? Alison thought grimly, as she struggled with the fourth screw. It wouldn't budge, rusted maybe. In her quick once-over Alison had seen a bottle of massage oil. Back across the room, cursing the screw. She doused the whole hinge and tried to move the screw again.

"Souls are reborn again sometimes, Mother. Why is it always the evil ones?" He sounded genuinely sad and puzzled. "I suppose it's because our Lord wants to keep the good ones with him. Maybe next time help will arrive sooner for you, Mother, and you'll be saved. Think of it that way," he said pleadingly.

"If you think you're going to kill me, you've lost your mind." Stacy's voice was crisp, so assured that for a moment, Alison envisioned her brushing past him, just walking out in indignation. Which would leave him alone with her. She tried not to think of it, tried only to hope that it would work, that Stacy would escape safely.

There was a sudden scream followed by another in a lower voice, and she dropped the knife in her haste to get to the keyhole. They had moved beyond its limited theater, and she almost cursed aloud in her desperation. What had happened? Was Stacy all right? Then, suddenly an arm, dripping blood, was flung back angrily into her view and she bit her lip to keep from calling out.

"You cut me." Mark's voice was filled with disbelief. The sleeve of his shirt was split from cuff to shoulder and blood was dripping from the perfect cut beneath it. "You cut me." Then the disbelief changed to anger, changed to bull rage and he screamed, "You're going to die for that, bitch!"

He lunged and Stacy, dodging, pirouetted back into the picture. In a spilt second Alison took everything in. Stacy was holding the metal roller, the rotary cutter with which she could slice so effortlessly through five layers of material. He must not have recognized it as anything which could be used for a weapon when she picked it up.

But she was also bleeding. The bodice of her dress was stained and ugly, growing black.

Then Alison was on her feet, yelling as she pounded on the door. "I'm the one that you want, you bastard! Come for me!" She didn't know what she would use for a weapon if he complied, how she would defend herself, just knew that she could not bear to watch the shaft of the knife again sink into Stacy's flesh. Stacy gave the door one despairing glance, as if she had truly thought that Alison would remain silent and save herself.

He didn't even turn. Not even so that he could call the words over his shoulder. He spoke them, instead, as if he were speaking to Stacy. "Don't worry, I will." He sidled to the right, the table between them, and Stacy moved an equal distance the same way. Her face was white as if she were close to fainting. "She wanted to be with you. Now she will be. Forever."

Alison yelled again, words that might have been senseless or provoking, she had no idea. This time he didn't even bother to answer. He lunged suddenly towards Stacy and just as suddenly she used both hands to bring her chair up between them, hitting him in the chest. For a moment hope bloomed again within Alison. He was no longer between Stacy and the door. If she could keep him off those twenty yards....

She refused to think about the long hall and the stairs and the fact that no one else in the building was home. As Stacy pushed him again, holding the chair by its padded back, the two silver prongs which held it slid forward, just as they had when Alison had picked it up on Tuesday. The body of the chair crashed to the ground and before Stacy could recover, before she could even comprehend what had happened he was over it and had her again. Only by the foot, because he had caught his own in the works of the chair, but that was enough, because he was slashing with the blood-covered knife, trying to pull himself up on her body. Alison stayed long enough to see Stacy land one perfect goalie kick on the side of his head, and then she was back at the hinge with a frenzy and intensity she had never in her life thought would be associated with using a screwdriver. Because that was the only way that she could help, if she could get out of the damn room. He could not be distracted from where she was. He would kill Stacy, and then he would come for her.

The sixth, the last screw was yielding, and she tried not to worry about the bolt on the outside of the door. It was a cheap one, put on to prevent prying, not prowlers, surely its little screws would rip out the first time she hit the opposite edge of the door. Tears of frustration were pouring down her face. There was another outraged scream from him, and a smashing sound, like a ripe melon dropped on the sidewalk. She hoped Stacy had caught him

211

right in the face, in the belly.

The last screw dropped and she threw herself against the door, wishing she were as big as Robert, as Seven Yellow Moons, that she was like the cops in movies who could smash right through any locked door the first time they put shoulder to it. The door yielded just a little, and she prepared to hit it again.

Then there was another sound, one which brought her back to the key-hole. Voices.

She thought, she prayed, that perhaps it would be the cops, that someone had heard the disturbance and called them, even though her mind told her that it was unlikely. She was totally unprepared for what she actually saw— Michelle stepping into the room, followed by Seven Yellow Moons. For the first time Alison remembered that she had left Michelle at the dance without explanation.

Perhaps it was her astonishment that sent a rush of adrenaline rippling through her. At any rate, the next slam was the one that thrust the door for-ward. It was still hanging from the hinge of the bolt, but there was a space big enough for her to crawl out.

Alison caught her breath as she straightened. Across from her, the other two women were standing as still as statues, their eyes big and round. She wondered, as if it made a difference, how they had gotten into the building. It was just something to take her mind off Mark, not more than ten steps in front of her, of the sight of him clutching Stacy to him like a shield, his knife resting lightly on her neck. She had fainted, or perhaps she just knew that a dead weight was harder to handle. Either way, blood-stained, bleeding from at least one new slash in the chest, she lolled against him, her head to one side. She had only fainted, she was not…no, she had fainted. But she was los-ing blood at an alarming rate.

"Call the police," Alison shouted across to Michelle, "call an ambulance."

"Don't." One word, no threats, all the authority in the world. "Don't even think about it. Just step out of the way." He turned almost casually towards Alison. "Don't you think about it, either."

She stood without speaking. There was a table between them; she would never be able to reach him, disarm him, before he killed Stacy.

Seven Yellow Moons and Michelle had moved obediently away from the door, and she saw that the latter had her eyes fixed, not on the unfolding drama, but the coffee table. She turned her head a fraction of and inch towards Seven Yellow Moons and her lips moved soundlessly. The other woman began to speak.

"Mark, you—"

"Shut up! You never came to see me, not once after she took me! You never visited me in the hospital!" Now Alison realized what Michelle was looking at. Her bag, into which she had watched her place the gun earlier.

"You know your mother wouldn't let me. We've been over this a hundred times!" Seven Yellow Moons took two steps, not to the front, but to the side, drawing his attention away from Michelle who was slowly drawing the gun out of the purse.

"You said I was bad." His face clouded darkly at the memory. "You said that I couldn't come to your house."

"I didn't say you were bad. I said the things you were doing were bad. And they were. I wasn't going to let you act that way in my house. Not just for my sake, Mark, for your own good."

"Always for my own good. Drop it, bitch," he said almost conversationally, still looking at Seven Yellow Moons. Perhaps because of that Michelle was a bit slow to respond. Expressionless he lifted the knife from Stacy's throat and plunged it into her shoulder.

"Drop it," he said again, removing as if for another thrust, and immediately the gun went skittering across the floor. He went on as if there had been no interruption. "How can you call me bad when...."

There was another sound at the door, and all four of them turned to look, though Mark did not let his guard down for a minute. Alison did not know whom she had expected. Certainly not Pam.

Michelle and Seven Yellow Moons were horrified at the carnage, but, although something that might have been horror flitted quickly across Pam's face, it did not stay. Pam looked merely cross.

"Mark," she said, in a tone that reminded Alison of her own mother, "I'm surprised at you." As if, Alison thought, he had skipped school, or dipped into the cookie jar without asking. Then Pam's lips twitched just a little, allowing the mask to drop, and she realized that Pam, too, was playing a game, acting a part. Well, they had no choice but to let her, to hope that she was a better actress than any of the rest of them had been.

The man's mouth dropped open, and he seemed uncertain, saying weakly, "You were going dancing tonight."

"Not if you're here doing something that you shouldn't." Pam responded gently. "Not if you need me."

"No, I...." He licked his lips, suddenly uncertain. "Yes! I do! Get them out of here!" He indicated Michelle and Seven Yellow Moons with a flick of his knife, and blood went flying from it.

One drop struck Pam on the cheek and she lifted her hand to wipe it very slowly. "Put Stacy down first, Mark." She said it with authority.

"No! I have to...you know I do...."

"Put her down or you will no longer be welcome at my house." There was a half a minute of silence, then Pam spoke again. "Fine," she said, and turned, "don't come around again." She walked three steps towards the door and then turned again. "I don't want your presents anymore, Mark." Viciously, with shaking hands, she reached up to strip off her earrings. She threw one down on the floor and raised her hand with the other.

"No!" Stacy fell to the floor with a crash and he stepped over her without a second look. "No, Mama, don't...I...."

"That's my good boy," she said, and her face was wreathed with smiles, as if they were somewhere alone, as if he really was a little boy and there was no blood on his hands. She bent down to retrieve the earring, and that was when she also picked up the little revolver than lay at her feet. He lunged at her, his eyes disbelieving.

"My good boy," she repeated, just before she pulled the trigger, once, twice, four times. Alison could not comprehend, could not will herself to move until he fell to the floor groaning. By the time she had moved forward Seven Yellow Moons had Pam wrapped up in her arms, and Michelle was on the phone. The only thing left for her to do was kneel beside Stacy.

Seventeen

There was one more rally near the end of the game, one final rush when the other team gathered itself together and stormed the Blue Ryders' end zone. The ball was pushed in and then out, in and then out a number of times. Alison danced on her toes in the goal, clapping her gloved hands together, for warmth as well as in anticipation.

"Get it out of here," she shouted. "For god's sake, clear the goal, Trudy!" Though Stacy had been coaching her she was not quite sure if it was the appropriate instruction to be giving. Even if it wasn't, certainly her voice must be expressing the panic she felt whenever the ball got near the backfield. She considered it just this side of a miracle that only four balls had gotten by her in the two games in which she had played, and she had no desire to press the favor of the fates, which would certainly be what was happening if they kept hammering it into the goal area.

The referee's whistle sounded, long and shrill, and gratefully she ran out of the box. It was considered good manners for the players of both teams to mingle on the field for a few minutes after the game thanking one another and showing that they were good sports, but tonight, with a hint of snow in the air, this civilized procedure was taking place in fast motion. Everyone was much more interested in putting on their extra clothing.

Alison skipped the ritual altogether and jogged over to the side of the field where her father was standing, holding her coat up anxiously as if she were five years old again. She hoped he wouldn't try to zip it up and tie her hood. He turned to say something to Stacy standing beside him, and Alison supposed that he was trying to urge her to go sit in the car, as he had been at half time. She could have told him that he was wasting his breath. Stacy had missed one game while she was in the hospital, and nothing was about to keep her away from this last one, even though Alison could not stop imagining her stitches freezing and then snapping like straw in the cold. The best they had been able to do was to dress her in so many layers of clothing that she looked as if she were wearing a spacesuit, moving her arms and legs in that awkward, disassociated way that divers and astronauts have.

"Good game, honey," her father enthused as he wrapped her coat around her. Her face was too stiff for her to correct him, to tell him that the only damn thing she was doing was being a good sport, and that she wouldn't have done it at all unless the Blue Ryders had been absolutely desperate. She was not yet admitting to anyone the secret satisfaction she was getting, and the secret despair she felt when she wondered if she would be capable this time next year.

The team was breaking up without their usual hugs and hashing out of the play, and she supposed that most of them were heading for dinner at the Blue Ryder. Well, she would just have time for a shower and sandwich at home before heading to work. She looked around for Michelle and Janka, who had ridden over with them. Liz passed, arm in arm with Carla.

"I told you we'd get you!" Liz called, the first thing, as far as Alison knew, that she had said to anyone else in days. She was in love, and it was only relentless hounding from her team members that had gotten her out of bed even long enough for the games. Alison had heard that she had gotten a restraining order placed on the Crusaders, keeping them from coming within 100 feet of Carla, and that she was looking into a lawsuit on behalf of some of their victims.

"I've got to go now, Sister," said her father, and she gave him an absent-minded hug, still looking for Michelle over his shoulder. She noticed that he patted Stacy on the arm when he left, which was just one step away from hugging. She was sure that the questions about settling down with a nice girl were going to be increased dramatically the next time she went home for din-ner. Luckily, nothing about Stacy's nighttime activities had come out in the paper, though there had been a nice little blurb about her quiltmaking.

Finally she spotted Janka's red jacket down the field. "Look," she said, nudging Stacy in her well-padded side.

"Oh. Seven Yellow Moons must have gotten Pam to come out." They stood for a moment side by side without speaking, watching the four women standing together. It looked as if Janka and Seven Yellow Moons were doing all the talking. "That's good."

Alison took her arm, and they began walking towards the car. "How long is Seven Yellow Moons planning on staying?"

"Till after Pam's trial, I think. It worked out well for her. It's getting cold down on the women's land, and I think she was really glad to have a chance to take a break from Lydia. She's got a lot more room to work at Pam's place, too."

Alison did not reply, and after a moment Stacy resumed. "It's good for Pam. I think she would have totally isolated herself otherwise."

"I can't help thinking," said Alison slowly. "You know, they're going to ask us about it at the trial. They're going to ask us if she really had to shoot him, if it was a life threatening situation."

"I was bleeding to death," said Stacy shortly and Alison knew that she didn't want to talk about it. But it was something that she could not put out of her mind.

"But was that why she did it? She pulled the trigger four times—that's going to be a sticky point. I can't help...was it that, or was it a kind of atonement?"

"What do you mean?"

"She must have known. On some level she must have known, or at least suspected he had murdered Tamara and Melanie, as well as Candy. Was shooting him her way of making up for that?"

"She wanted to stop him!" Stacy said. "And I, for one, will never forget that."

"That makes two of us." Alison fell silent.

Stacy nodded down the field. The foursome had split up and Seven Yellow Moons was leading Pam away by the hand, gently, as if she had been sick. Alison remembered the photograph at Pam's house, the four women and the little boy caught in that magic moment on a picnic.

"Hi there, Tiger." Michelle jogged to catch them. "I hear you're going on to the Gay Games."

"And I hear you're going to the doctor finally," said Janka from the other side. "Do you want me to take you?" Alison wondered how much Seven Yellow Moons had told her after their long discussion on holistic healing the week before.

"No," she said, "Stacy's going to go." And then, "Yeah, I do. You too, Michelle." Because she was loving dating Stacy, but Janka and Michelle were her family.

"Me, too," said Michelle, pressing close to her.

She thought then that they would go into one of those long silences that had become so common since that night they had divided between the police station and the hospital. More than the blood splattered on the walls, on the bolts of muslin that had to be thrown away, the silences had come to represent her nightmares. Long periods of time when they stood without talking, each wondering, reproaching herself for clues they had not recognized, things they had not done.

Then Janka, linking her arm through Stacy's, began to sing one of the songs they had heard at Pam's concert the week before. "High on the mountain, my Lord spoke, out of his mouth came fire and smoke." Her high, clear voice drifted across the field and Alison could hear two other soccer players, who also sang in the chorus, answering with the alto part.

"You'll never guess who I saw in the bookstore." Michelle leaned across Alison to talk to Stacy.

"Dominique?" Stacy said. "Doing a booksigning! *Dominatrix in Prison.*"

"She does have an article in this month's *Out Front* ," said Alison, "but it's on cat adoption. She and Beth are going to open a kennel."

"Who then?" Stacy pressed Michelle.

"That woman whose husband they painted blue and orange."

"Sharon?"

"No, the other one. The one you were lovers with."

"Nina?"

"Yeah. Buying a copy of *Lesbian Connection.*"

"Huh."

"More harassment?" suggested Alison.

"Maybe. But we can always hope that it's something better."

From all over the field voices had joined in with Janka's, floating thin on the wind. Alison bent to unlock the door of the car.

Kate Allen grew up in Idaho and New Mexico, but had to escape to the big city when she realized she was a dyke. She currently lives in Denver with five cats all of whom were rescues or throwaways, and is supported by a loving and loyal lesbian extended family. When she is not vacuuming or writing, she makes quilts and goes two-stepping at the Country/Western bar. She is writing another book about Alison—Stacy and Michelle just got into a fight at a wake. Tomorrow they'll be going to the flea market to consult with the lesbian phone psychic.

At the time this book went to press, Colorado gays, lesbians and friends were involved in battling a hate law sponsored by a right wing group calling itself Colorado for Family Values. This amendment not only denies civil rights protection to gays and lesbians but also revokes local gay rights ordinances already passed in Denver, Boulder and Aspen, and prohibits the passing of any further local protective ordinances.

Right wing groups all over the U.S. have hailed this as a victory, and are looking at Amendment Two as a model for similar amendments in their own state. If it happened in Colorado it can happen in your state! This is a struggle we must all face together.

For information on ways to become involved in this struggle, call the Gay and Lesbian Community Center of Denver, 1-303-831-6268